KU-472-276

As most of you will know, Jacqueline and I have rather a lot of dogs! We are at seven at present, five having been rescued and adopted, and one rehomed. Since we came to the Fens, and started our precious dog collection with Max and Rowan, our first two Springer spaniels, and then our beloved Alfie and Woody, we have been with the same veterinary practice. So this book is for them, as they have seen us through some very happy and some devastatingly sad times. Big thanks to Allen Briggs and Turner of Kirton; to Stephen Elwood, now retired, to Maxine, Nigel, and especially Sue, who has valiantly taken on our tribe of mixed-up little rescue Bretons! In fact to all the staff, the vets, the nurses, and the client care team, thank you!

The Bag of Secrets is also dedicated to Linda and Rob Holmes for their generosity and friendship, that all began because of a mutual love of spaniels! Thank you to you both, and to Dash, for allowing us all to enjoy your lovely garden.

With love from Joy, Jacquie, Jasper, Rory, Scampi, Ju-Ju, Ellie, Darcey and Nina

CHAPTER ONE

'I think I might just have discovered a mystery of my own, darling.' Liz Haynes carefully placed the large bag she had been holding on the kitchen floor at Matt Ballard's feet.

Matt stared at it. It was a bit like an old carpet bag, with faded tapestry sides and faux leather plastic handles. It had seen better days but was still serviceable. 'I've seen one of these before,' he murmured.

'Yes, they are a giveaway. If you spend more than a certain amount of money at one of those online clothing sites, you get one for free. I think they're very nice, but few people use them and they finish up in charity shops,' Liz said, her eyes still on the bag.

'Okay,' said Matt patiently. 'So, where's the mystery? It's obviously really bothering you.'

Liz flopped down on to a kitchen chair. 'Yes, it is. Look, I know how busy we are at the moment, but . . .'

Seated opposite her, Matt could see how anxious she was. Her expression was almost beseeching. She was right about their workload. Their private detective agency was going through one of those periods when they had more work than they could cope with. Nevertheless, his interest had been piqued. 'Come on then, let's have it.'

'I called in at the library on my way to the bank. Chris Lamont was working there this morning. As soon as he saw me, he said there was something he wanted me to see. He was doing a bit of shelving before they opened and found this bag lying on the floor. At first, he was suspicious — unattended baggage and all that — he's a retired copper after all. Then he saw it was partially open, so he took a closer look and found it was stuffed full of papers. Clearly, it wasn't dangerous, so he delved deeper.' Liz picked up the bag, put it on the table and unzipped it.

Matt found himself looking at what appeared to be the contents of an office litter bin — papers of various sizes, envelopes, labels, memos, and larger A4 size sheets. 'What on earth is all that?'

Liz frowned, 'I'm not sure, Matt, but I think it's important. Do you remember old Molly?'

'The bag lady? The one who used to chat to Smokey Joe before he moved on?' It made a quaint picture — the two vagrants, side by side on a park bench, deep in conversation — that is, until you remembered how hard their lives must be.

'That's her. Well, she goes into the library regularly, especially when Chris is on duty. He sneaks her a cup of coffee and lets her sit and warm up with some of the older books. He once told me, ages ago now, that she's a very intelligent woman, but he can never get her to talk about her past life. If he asks her, she gets up and leaves, so now he limits his conversation to books.' Liz stood up and went to the sink to fill the kettle. 'I'm in need of coffee myself.'

'So, are you saying this bag belongs to her?' Matt asked.

Liz spooned coffee into two mugs and remained leaning against the counter, waiting for the water to boil. 'Let's just say that Molly was in the library just before it closed. The librarian on the desk remembered her having it with her when she arrived but didn't notice Molly leave and didn't see it anywhere near where she had been sitting, so she thought no more about it. Chris found it pushed behind one of the computer stations.'

'So, she deliberately left it behind?'

'Looks that way.' Liz brought the mugs back to the table. 'I think she purposely left it for Chris to find. The thing that's worrying me is as soon as he realised it belonged to her, he took his break and went to look for her. Molly has a regular routine, so he went to her usual haunts but she wasn't there. He asked around, and no one had seen her since she visited the library the day before.'

This was a street dweller, a vagrant . . . so why did Matt suddenly feel apprehensive? He stared at the bag. 'What is all that crap, Liz?'

For a moment she didn't reply. 'Chris and I pulled some of the papers out and had a look at them. After a while we wondered if the old girl might have been writing a book, using whatever scraps of paper she could find. I know that sounds weird, but she is well educated, and judging from what we read, we thought it might be either a biography or a crime novel.'

'Do I sense a "but" coming on?'

'You do. We began to come across papers with dates and times on them, so we then decided it could be some kind of journal. If it is, some of what's written there is very worrying.' She blew on her coffee and took a careful sip. 'I think she left it for Chris to find knowing he is a retired police officer and would not just disregard it. Plus, when I left the library, I asked some of the street people if they'd seen her but none of them had. I even went into a little café whose owner gives her a bit of breakfast, and Molly never turned up this morning.'

Matt scratched the back of his neck thoughtfully. 'Given what you said about how busy we are, what, may I ask, is going through that beautiful head of yours, Ms Haynes?'

'Ah, well, yes . . .' Liz looked at him from beneath her eyelashes. She reached across the table and squeezed his hand. 'I was wondering . . .'

He laughed. 'Don't look at me like that. You know very well I can deny you nothing.'

'Excellent, because I thought I'd ask young David if he'd like a week in the Fens again. He's not the luckiest of lads, as we know. Well, this time he was about to set off on a week's holiday with two of his friends and they've both gone down with flu. He didn't feel like going on his own so he's at a bit of a loose end.'

Matt smiled at her. 'Sounds like you've already got it all worked out. So, what are you going to ask the poor kid to do? Sort that lot out?' He pointed to the bagful of handwritten notes. 'Because he'll need a whole lot longer than a week.'

'I suppose he wouldn't need to read them all closely, just try and make some sense out of them. Or find some statement or name that we could verify? Oh, I don't know.' She sighed, all humour gone. 'I have to know what this means, Matt, I have a very uncomfortable feeling about it.'

'Then you'd better ring that nephew of yours, hadn't you?'

Liz jumped up and put her arms around his neck. 'I do love you, Matt Ballard. Thank you!'

While Liz was on the phone to David, Matt fished out a few odd sheets of paper from the bag. They were all in the same distinctive hand, and it wasn't hard to see that the writer took pride in her writing skills. He read through a scrap of paper that had started life as someone's shopping list. On one side was a list of groceries, on the other, someone, presumably Molly, had written:

> *On innumerable occasions I was troubled by a sense of unease, although there was no apparent cause. Some nights I lay awake, trying to unravel the twisted threads of supposition. What was wrong?*

Matt grunted. He was beginning to understand why Liz had found this bag and its contents so disturbing. He read through another quite lengthy note that seemed to be a description of a room somewhere, with only the words "Early March" scribbled at the bottom.

Now well and truly hooked, he delved once more into the bag. This time he pulled out a birthday card, probably expropriated from a waste bin. The greeting read, *Happy*

Birthday, Mick! Have a good one, mate! He turned it over and found an altogether more sinister message:

> *I fear for the woman! And not just for her. I fear for myself. Am I being paranoid? This place would make the strongest mind doubt itself, so who knows? But what to do? To do anything could prove dangerous for one or the other of us, so it seems that doing nothing is the only solution, and that does not sit well with me.*

Matt began to hope that David would say yes to Liz's "invitation", and that the two cases they were presently working could either be shelved or brought to a satisfactory conclusion. One of these cases concerned a habitual runaway teenager, while the other involved surveillance on a store that was experiencing a high rate of theft. The second should not be a priority, as the store had its own security guards, but the management thought they had been in place so long that the thieves had got wise to them. The store owner was an old friend of Matt, so he didn't want to let him down. He and Liz had been posing as shoppers, and already had a good idea who might be responsible. A few more days could see that one put to bed, but the runaway was proving a far more difficult case.

Matt glanced at his watch. Damn it! He needed to leave soon, as he had an appointment with someone who professed to have seen Liam, the missing boy, within the last few days.

Just as he stood up to leave, Liz hurried back in.

'David's leaving Thetford later this afternoon! He was delighted to hear of our offer. What's more, his rucksack is still packed for the holiday that never happened, so win, win!'

'I hope you told him we can't promise anything as dramatic as the last case he helped us on. Compared with that, this one could be mind-numbingly boring for him.' But was that strictly true? His copper's nose was itching like crazy. Already he was feeling as anxious as Liz about Molly the Bag Lady.

'He'd come here even if we had nothing for him to do, you know that,' said Liz happily. 'And he said it would give him a chance to call in at the police station and thank DCI Charley Anders for all the encouragement she gave him when, as he put it, "his life went all Pete Tong". He's back on track now and loving his new work. It's not what he had planned, but now he's out of the doldrums and is a happy bunny again.'

Matt recalled how despondent Liz's nephew had been when he failed the fitness test for the police force. Now, partly thanks to Charley Anders, the officer who took Matt's post as DCI when he retired from the force, David was at university and studying forensic computer analysis, and seemed to be doing very well.

He pulled on his jacket, and gave Liz a quick hug. 'I'm delighted . . . gotta dash. I'll be back later this afternoon, okay?'

'I'll get the guest room freshened up and take a swift stroll through the store before they close,' said Liz, kissing him lightly. 'See you later.'

As he left, Matt glanced back at the innocuous-looking bag on his kitchen floor and wondered where its strange contents would take them.

* * *

George Miles paced along the top of the sea bank, his wax coat flapping about his knees and the wind whipping his hair into his eyes. (George badly needed a haircut.) He was counting his steps. He didn't know why he did this, it was something he had always done whenever he walked alone. Not that he was entirely alone, because Alfie, his Springer spaniel, was his constant companion, although the daft dog wasn't at his side. Alfie spent his walks with his nose to the ground, racing up and down the steep slopes of the sea bank, sniffing out and chasing invisible prey on the marshy edge of the river that ran parallel with the high path.

6

George stared into the distance and saw what he always did, a grassy path that disappeared into the horizon, a huge, endless sky. Only the colours ever varied. Today was a grey day, like most at this time of the year, yet each one was subtly different. This grey was soft with a pinkish hue, like the downy feathers of a young collared dove, grading into a darker and more ominous hue closer to the horizon. The skies here were like nowhere else. Each single stretch of sky presented the watcher who cared to look with a different cloud formation. George knew that if he turned around and looked behind him, towards the little nature reserve where he had left his old Land Rover, he might well see blue skies and fluffy clouds. Or, he might see something more like Armageddon. He didn't turn around. He had 400 more steps to take before he did that.

If he ever wondered about it, which he rarely did, he supposed the counting stopped him thinking. Which, in George's case, was a good thing. Thoughts about today, about the landscape that he loved, the dog he adored, or what to have for dinner, were fine. He could cope with those. Thoughts about tomorrow were okay too, although he rarely bothered about the immediate future, which promised little in the way of excitement. It was the past that gave him a problem. An empty mind often wanders backwards, a place George did not want to go. Not ever.

So, he counted, his eyes on the dog, who was always in the present, until he reached his allotted number of steps.

When George finally did turn around, he was pleased to see no storm looming, no imminent end to the world. It was what he like to call a "busy" sky, full of small clouds scudding at different speeds depending on their height above the earth. Walking was easier too, now the wind was behind him. He would make good time getting back to his vehicle.

Alfie was still charging around, always on the hunt for likely smells, and something unpleasant to roll in if George didn't see it first and call him off.

They were halfway back, George counting quietly to himself, when he came to an abrupt halt. Alfie was down near the marshy river's edge, standing rooted to the spot, one front paw lifted, sniffing suspiciously and then jumping back. Then he growled. Alfie never growled.

'What have you found, lad?' asked George. 'Dead bird? Or some rubbish dumped off a boat? Whatever it is, come away!'

Alfie didn't respond. Instead, he lowered himself and edged forward. He seemed to be quivering.

'Leave it!' called out George sharply, and grunted in annoyance. He had no choice but to go down the bank and put a lead on the dog.

Halfway down, slipping slightly on the long damp grass, he saw something dark lying in a lagoon of brackish water at the edge of the river. If it was a refuse sack he wanted his dog well away from it. People dumped poisonous stuff sometimes and he didn't want Alfie sticking his nose in it.

George looped the slip lead around Alfie's neck and scolded the dog for ignoring his calls. Then, being slightly interested to see what was the cause of Alfie's uncharacteristic disobedience, he edged closer to the object that lay half in, half out of the water.

He gasped in horror. This was no discarded sack of rubbish. It was a human being, and it was dead. For a few seconds he couldn't move, as transfixed as his dog had been. Then he edged forward, as if some dreadful magnet were drawing him closer. He did not want to look, but he had to.

Then George turned tail and ran, dragging his dog with him.

The past he tried so hard not to think of now rushed back, overwhelming him, as if that dreadful sight had caused the floodgates to open. The memories rolled over him, relentless, one after the other. George found himself gasping for air, gulping back sobs.

Up on the sea bank, he fell to his knees, hugged his dog to him and finally found the courage to pull out his mobile and dial 999.

* * *

PC Debbie Hume, stared at the bedraggled body. 'Poor old soul,' she whispered to her colleague, PC Jack "Swifty" Fleet. 'I thought the guy who discovered her had made a mistake to start with. She looks like a tangle of discarded rags and old clothes thrown in the river.'

'You do know who it is, don't you?' asked Swifty.

Debbie frowned. 'Should I?'

'It's Old Molly,' he said quietly. 'A street dweller from Fenfleet town. She's been in this area about eighteen months now. You haven't come across her then?'

Debbie shook her head. 'I know a lot of the homeless people, but I can't say I know this poor lady.'

'Lady is right, Debs. I have no idea how she finished up on the streets, but she was a proper lady, I know that much. Spoke beautifully she did.' Jack sighed. 'I wonder what happened to her?'

'Probably it all got too much for her. Winters on the streets . . .' Debbie shivered. 'It's no way to live.'

Jack Fleet agreed with her. He had no idea how they survived, but each year there seemed to be more of them — in doorways, on benches, in bus shelters, under bridges, anywhere that provided some protection from the elements.

He looked down at the pathetic remains of Old Molly and felt unaccountably moved. It tugged on his heartstrings to see her, poor, lonely, abandoned, friendless soul. No woman — no, no one at all — should ever have to finish up on a riverbank like a bag of discarded rubbish.

He stared at her in silence, pondering the world's injustice, when he suddenly noticed something. He stiffened. If this was what he thought it was . . . Careful not to contaminate the scene, he moved a little closer.

'Swifty. What are you doing?' Debbie said.

He took a step back. 'I could be wrong, but I don't think she took her own life. I think she was killed.'

'What!' Debbie stared at the old woman in her shroud of sodden clothing. 'What on earth makes you say that?'

'Look at her mouth.' He pointed. A small piece of material was protruding from between her lips. 'That looks to me like cloth, possibly a handkerchief or something.'

Debbie stared at him. 'You mean she was asphyxiated? Material stuffed in her mouth so she couldn't breathe?'

That was exactly what Jack Swift meant. 'Okay, Debbie. Time to report this one to the skipper. We need forensics out here before nightfall.'

With yet another sigh, he took out his radio.

CHAPTER TWO

Arriving just in time for the evening meal, David was greeted with a warm embrace. 'We've missed you!' Liz exclaimed.

'And I've missed you and Matt,' said David. 'Things have been a bit flat since my last visit here — not that I'm hoping for more of the same, mind you.' He pulled a face.

'Don't worry. This one is just a simple investigation, not a murder mystery,' said Liz. 'Now, get your things up to your room. Matt is on his way home, and dinner will be ready in ten minutes. I think your visit calls for a bottle of wine, don't you?'

He grinned at her. 'I certainly do!' He dived into his rucksack and produced a bottle of Cabernet Sauvignon. 'Thanks for inviting me, Liz. I was so pissed off when my mates bailed on the holiday.'

She took the bottle from him. 'You didn't have to do that. After all, you'll be helping us out, so really we should be thanking you.'

Liz loved David to bits, he was like the son she'd never had. The investigation he had helped them with before had turned out to be harrowing in the extreme. During the investigation he had demonstrated a sensitivity that went far beyond his twenty-one years.

Liz checked the oven. The meal was ready, now all she needed was Matt. She took plates from the cupboard and put them in to warm, and right on cue, the front door opened.

'Bloody road works,' cursed Matt. 'The traffic lights spring up like weeds, and no one is ever doing anything that I can see. If it was down to me, I'd fine every one of them.'

'And hello to you too, Matt,' said David, stepping into the hall.

Matt broke into a smile and gave him a bear hug. 'Good to see you again, lad. Sorry for the outburst, but they really get to me. How are you? How's university?'

'All good. It's hard work but I enjoy it, and I'm learning a lot.' The two of them strolled into the kitchen, still talking. 'And I'm intrigued by what Auntie Liz told me about your carpet bag.'

Matt laughed. 'You might not be so enthusiastic when you see what's inside. I warn you, it's a pretty daunting task.'

'Well, maybe it won't look so bad after a couple of glasses of wine,' Liz said. 'Have a seat, I'm just dishing up.'

While they ate, Matt and Liz told David about their two current cases, and David expanded on his uni course. Then they turned to old Molly and her bag of notes.

'You don't know much nothing about the old lady then,' David said.

'Only what Chris the librarian told me, which is very little indeed.' Liz glanced at Matt. 'And you only knew her from seeing her with old Smokey Joe, didn't you?'

'Smokey Joe? What a name. Where does he come from?' David said.

Matt gave a short laugh. 'He was a real character. He had this old "sit up and beg" bicycle — it was ancient. He used to carry a bag of his "possessions" hanging on one of the handlebars, and on the other, he had an old, galvanised bucket. He used to either cadge or steal handfuls of coal and a bit of kindling and light a fire in the bucket. He'd ride around with it happily smouldering away. Talk about a hazard. No matter how many times he had his collar felt over it, he kept on lighting that fire.' Matt shook his head. 'Apparently, he would talk to no one but Molly. Many is the time I've seen them deep in conversation on a park bench, or huddled under a bridge over his famous bucket.'

'You said "was". Is he dead?' asked David.

'He disappeared,' Matt said. 'One day he rode off on his old bike and was never seen again. The other street people seemed to think he'd moved on. Before he met Molly, he did move about a lot. Sometimes he'd stay for a bit, other times just a couple of days. He's been gone for weeks now.'

They fell silent, each probably reflecting on the plight of the homeless and what two of them might have discussed in their long conversations in the meagre warmth from a bucket of glowing embers.

David broke the silence. 'Guys, I can't stand the suspense any longer. Please, can I see Molly's bag?'

Laughing, Liz stood up. 'I'm not sure if you've had enough wine yet, but okay, you asked for it.'

She hurried out of the room and returned with the bag, which she dumped on to David's lap.

'Bloody hell!' he exclaimed when he looked inside. 'You weren't exaggerating, were you? What *is* all this?'

Matt laughed. 'I said much the same when Liz showed me.'

'And you thought of me. Thanks a bunch.' David picked up his glass and took a long swallow.

Thus fortified, he tentatively reached in and lifted out one or two of the papers.

Liz watched his features express first puzzlement, then concern. 'We wouldn't have asked you to look at this if we hadn't believed there to be something very worrying, maybe even sinister, about what Molly has written.'

David nodded, his eyes still on the scraps of paper. 'Yeah, I'm beginning to see what you mean.' He smoothed out a crumpled sheet of paper that looked like an advertising flyer and began to read what Molly had written on the reverse. 'Here she's describing a change in someone she cares about, and it's a change for the bad. She's desperately worried for them.' He looked up at Liz. 'I reckon the lady that wrote this held a position of some respect. She's well educated, isn't she? So why is she on the streets?'

'Are you up to trying to find the answers to those questions?' asked Matt.

'I do believe I am.'

'We hoped you'd say that,' said Liz. 'Well, the answers must lie somewhere,' she pointed to the bag, 'in that.'

'Where can I work?'

'How about the incident room?' Matt said, referring to what had once been a dining room, and which they now used for their detective work. Just like a real incident room in a police station, it held computers, printers, filing cabinets and a whiteboard. The original dining table remained, now serving as a work-table or large desk. 'I've cleared the table for you. Everything we need for our misper case is up on the whiteboard or in the computer, so the table is all yours.'

'Right. I should work out a strategy, I guess.' David scratched his head. 'Maybe I'll sleep on it and start first thing tomorrow.' He looked at Liz, and then Matt. 'I feel the same as you, and I've only seen a page or two. Add that to the fact that the old lady is missing . . . need I say more?'

'Welcome back to Cannon Farm, lad,' said Matt. 'The team is back in action.'

* * *

They had sat up late, listening to David enthusing about his new life at university. Matt was not a little proud of the role he and Liz had played in getting his life back on track after the bitter disappointment of being turned down for the police force.

Now Matt lay in bed, snug in Liz's reassuring warmth but unable to sleep. He was frustrated at not being able to give his attention to the puzzle of Old Molly, who was beginning to haunt him. If only they didn't have these other cases running. Okay, the shoplifting case was nearing a conclusion,

Liz had told him earlier that after her visit to the store that day, she had become certain that she knew who the culprits were, and they weren't the lads they had first suspected. The thieves were two teenage sisters. The problem was, Liz knew the family quite well. She now had a decision to make, either to speak to the mother and father, who were honest, hard-working people, and get them to deal with their wayward daughters, or report her findings directly to the store owner who had hired them. Matt had offered another solution — why didn't he and Liz confront the girls themselves, and basically put the fear of God in them. Sometimes a short sharp shock did the trick, but occasionally it failed, and the teenagers simply continued their life of petty crime elsewhere. He suspected that Liz would opt for talking to the parents, then telling the store owner that they had dealt with the problem unofficially. She knew that it was store policy to prosecute all shoplifters, but she was certain that if no more thefts occurred, she and Matt could talk the store owner, an old friend of Matt's, into letting it go.

His investigation, however, was far from being concluded. His missing runaway was worrying him badly.

His eyes wide open in the dark, Matt recalled the first time he had been engaged by the Cooper family to find the recalcitrant Liam. Then it had taken him only three days to find the boy and take him back home. The second time had not been quite so straightforward but, even so, within six days, Liam was back with his anxious parents. On that occasion, as Matt left the house, Liam had yelled after him, "It won't be so easy next time, you'll see!"

Matt turned over, trying not to disturb the sleeping Liz. Little bastard. He'd been right. It was now day ten, and every lead had come to nothing. Liam wasn't in any of his usual haunts, nor was he following his normal pattern of behaviour. The parents were beside themselves, and Matt understood why. They were an ordinary, caring mum and dad, with two lovely, well-behaved daughters — and a son who seemed to have come from another planet. The police were fed up with their constant calls reporting him missing. Matt knew they would continue to watch out for him, but he was no longer a priority. A sixteen-year-old habitual runaway was of no great concern while they had serious cases running. Indeed, at sixteen, a child has the right to leave home, and the parents or carers cannot stop them. However, that was not the case with Liam. He had no intention of making a life elsewhere, he was just being a little sod. He enjoyed testing the system, and to hell with the anguish it caused his parents. Matt had his own ideas about how he'd treat the boy, but he'd probably end up in court if he carried them out.

Calling in Matt and Liz had been a last-ditch attempt on the part of Jim and Maisie Cooper to instil some sense into their son. The police obviously made no impression on the boy — in fact, their attention seemed to make him worse, so maybe someone like Matt, with a very different approach, and who wasn't governed by too many regulations, might be the answer.

Matt sighed. Liam had ignored his and Liz's warnings about what his irresponsible lifestyle would lead to. Now Matt feared that the boy saw them as a challenge, and his cat and mouse game would finish in a dangerous, downward spiral. Despite wanting to shake the lad until his teeth rattled, Matt was seriously concerned that this time, Liam seemed to have really disappeared. Before now there had always been evidence of his presence, they knew he was around, just one step ahead of them. This time, nothing. The kid was bright, even his teachers agreed — on the few occasions Liam bothered to participate in their efforts to educate him. But he wasn't so clever as to eradicate all trace of himself. Had something really happened to him this time?

Matt came to a decision. He must let Liz and David concentrate on Molly and her bag of tricks while he put all his efforts into finding Liam.

That decided, Matt fell asleep.

* * *

The night was cold for spring. Not bitter, not freezing, nevertheless the wind chill ate through whatever clothing you were wearing and made your blood feel like iced water. Clem and his dog, Gunner, huddled together in a shop doorway. It was a choice pitch, and he'd got there first, so the other street dwellers conceded it to him. He was, after all, Fenfleet's longest surviving rough sleeper.

Tonight, he had more reason than usual to feel cold and miserable. Yesterday, while he was cadging food for Gunner from a local pet shop owner, someone had taken his sleeping bag, the one thing that kept some of the night chills from him and his dog. This was even more upsetting because Molly had given it to him, and now Molly was missing. Molly had told him to keep it close. She'd told him there was something inside the lining, and that should anything happen to her, he was to give it to the first policeman he saw.

As he waited for the night hours to pass, he thought back to Molly's request.

'I need a favour, Clem.'

He laughed. 'Sure, but I don't have much to offer you, Mol, me old duck, especially if it's a loan. Don't tell me your Rolls has broken down again.'

But she wasn't laughing. 'Will you keep something safe for me?'

'Yes, Molly,' he said, serious now, 'as far as is possible on these streets.'

'That's all I can ask.' She handed him a tightly rolled up sleeping bag. It was a faded royal blue in colour, shabby, but usable.

He looked at her, perplexed. 'You need that yourself, girl. The nights are still cold.'

'I'll get something else. Just keep this close, Clem. It's a kind of insurance.'

This he really didn't understand. 'Against what?'

A fleeting look of anguish passed across her face. 'Against people not knowing the truth about something very important.' She looked at him, her expression stern. 'Will you take it or not?'

He took it. 'How can this old thing tell anyone anything?'

'It's what's inside it, Clem. There's a letter in the lining. Now listen, I'll only say this once: should anything happen to me, get it straight to the police. Understand?'

He stared at her. 'Molly! Whatever is wrong?'

This time she did smile, but very sadly, 'Everything. Just keep it safe, okay? And if you can, pray for me.'

He watched her walk away, the words, "pray for me" lingering in the night air.

Maybe he hadn't prayed hard enough. Clem hugged Gunner closer to him, sad that the inevitable must have happened and Molly had been right to be so concerned. Whatever she feared had come about, while he had lost the thing she had entrusted to him, something, he feared, that was desperately important.

Gunner shivered and nuzzled closer to him. Clem shivered too, but not entirely from the cold.

* * *

On the bank of the tidal river, two SOCOs stood in the darkness watching the lights dim on a familiar old Citroen Dolly, as its owner parked as close as he could to the sea bank.

'Why is the head honcho turning out in the middle of the night for a dead bag-lady?' asked one. 'Well, perhaps I should say *murdered* bag-lady. I guess there's a difference.'

'His technicians are tied up elsewhere, plus I was reliably told that the prof reckons this case is going to be a big one.' Ella Jarvis, the senior forensic photographer, grinned behind her mask. 'He said there's a bad moon rising, he can feel it in his water.'

Her colleague, Laurie, gave a laugh. 'And the prof's urine is an accepted method of divination, is it?'

'In Professor Rory Wilkinson's case, I'd say definitely,' said Ella, gathering up her equipment cases. 'At least the lights have arrived, though the natives are getting restless.' Ella had heard several uniformed officers complaining that they could have moved the body ages ago but for some reason, Professor Wilkinson wanted to see the deceased in situ.

'Ah, my patient children!' Rory Wilkinson gave Ella and Laurie a humble little bow. 'I'm sorry to have kept you waiting in this rather unpleasant and boggy stretch of our beloved Fens. But the Maestro is here now, so let us proceed.'

They trooped across to the oily looking waters of the river, and stared into the little marshy lagoon where Old Molly had finally been washed up.

'I need photos, Ella, from every angle, exactly as she is. I hope you have your wellies on?'

'Yes, Prof.' Ella grimaced. 'As soon as I heard the word river, I just knew I'd be getting my feet wet.'

When she'd finished, the professor beckoned to the waiting constables. 'Very gently, please, get her out and lay her on the tarpaulin.'

It was a pathetic sight. Ella felt unaccountably moved, almost tearful. It surprised her. She'd believed herself to be inured to death and all the horrific ways it could present itself.

Rory had been watching her. 'You feel it too.'

'Sorry, Prof. It's just, well . . .' She shrugged, not knowing exactly what to say.

'I know,' he said quietly. 'But you must never apologise for having feelings. We should treasure our humanity, and never forget that the deceased were human too. This woman's death was unjust and should never have occurred in a civilised world. She ought never to have been reduced to living on the streets, and she certainly didn't deserve to have someone kill her.' Rory patted her shoulder. 'So, let's do the best we can for this lady, shall we? And the first thing I need to do is see what that is.' He pointed to the piece of fabric protruding from the old woman's mouth. 'Photos all the way, please, Ella.'

He knelt down and very carefully probed the mouth. 'No good. Rigor mortis has set in, so I can't get to it. It appears to be a handkerchief blocking her airway, but I can't be certain. It'll have to wait until we get her back to the morgue and rigor mortis has worn off.'

Ella took photographs as he conducted a painstaking search of the rest of her body and clothing. When he'd finished, he got stiffly to his feet and looked down at the body. 'Well, my dear lady. I wish I could promise you a warm bed for the night, but at least you'll have shelter.' He turned to the uniforms. 'Let's get her off this marshy ground and take her home. Have you checked the site for evidence?'

'Yes, sir,' said one of the constables. 'The only footprints were those of the man who found her — and his dog. Guessing from the high tide, I reckon she went in nearer the town and was washed down here.'

'In that case, we can bring down the curtain on tonight. Thank you all. Ella, you can go home. I'll book her in and we'll deal with her tomorrow, her secrets will keep until then.'

'Who would kill a bag lady?' asked Ella, rummaging in her bag for her car keys. 'And will a busy police force have the time and money to devote to the murder of a street-dweller?'

'Good question,' said Rory dourly. 'I hope so. She's a human being after all, and she deserves the same consideration as the rest of us.'

'Will she get it though?' Ella was well aware of the budgetary constraints and the heavy workload the police were subject to.

Rory helped Ella with her bags of equipment. 'She might have ended her life on the streets but she didn't start like that. Who is she really? What kind of life did she lead before she ended up like this, I wonder. If only our bag lady could speak, I think she'd have a fascinating story to tell, and I hope I can do my part to find out what that is.'

Ella drove away, musing on the professor's words. Maybe she too could feel it in her water . . .

CHAPTER THREE

When Liz went down to make an early morning cup of tea, she heard the sound of rustling coming from the old dining room. She opened the door to find David in pyjama bottoms and T-shirt, surrounded by heaps of pieces of paper spread across the dining table.

He grinned at her. 'Not all uni students slob in bed till midday — well, not all the time. I woke up an hour ago and couldn't wait to get started.'

'Well, I'd better make you a cuppa then, hadn't I?' She moved closer and peered down at the various piles. 'Have you worked out a plan for dealing with this lot?'

'I had several during the night. First off, I thought the most recent bits of writing would probably be at the top and the oldest underneath, but that's not the case. I think she pushed the later ones down in the bag with the others. Since I can't put them in chronological order, I'm sorting them according to the different pieces of paper they're written on.'

'That does make sense,' Liz said. 'My friend at the library said she sometimes "stole" the odd sheet of paper from their printer tray. He knew she was doing it but turned a blind eye. Which means she probably used the same kind of paper until she ran out of it.'

'If that is the case, it could give us some continuity to the story. Whatever, it's going to be a mega task.' He smiled mischievously. 'But with a cup of tea inside me, I'll soldier on.'

She cuffed his shoulder lightly. 'In that case, I'd better put the kettle on.'

Smiling, Liz went into the kitchen. She liked having David around again. They had always got on, even when he was a small boy. The difference in their ages had never been a barrier to the strong bond the two of them had. Luckily, it hadn't faded as he grew older.

She took him a mug of tea and placed it on the table beside him.

'I wondered how she managed to use the same pen for all her writing,' said David, 'then I found these at the bottom of the bag.' He pointed to a collection of blue biros. 'They're the pens you find on the counter in banks, so that you can fill in forms. Looks like she half-inched quite a stash of them.'

'Resourceful lady,' remarked Liz. 'I'm just going to take Matt up a cup of tea, I can hear him in the shower already. Oh, and perhaps you'd like to do a little shopping later?'

'Shopping?'

'It's all right, we're not going to Tesco. I'm on the trail of a couple of teenage shoplifters. With any luck, I can sort them out today, then I can pitch in and help you — unless, of course, Matt needs me.'

'Perfecto! I'd welcome your help. I'm dying to unravel Molly's story. I've a feeling it's going to be one hell of a tale.' He sipped reflectively at his tea. 'Maybe it is just that, Auntie Liz. A story. What do you think? Could she have been writing a novel? An autobiography? Is what she wrote fiction, or fact? Maybe she was going to give all these notes to someone to write the book for her? You know, someone who's not on the streets and has a computer? What if—'

'Whoa! So many questions. We could spend hours speculating on what she may have intended and never come any closer to finding an answer. What we need to do first is get hold of some concrete facts, sort this lot, and see where it leads us.'

'Sorry, I get carried away sometimes.' He smiled rather sheepishly. 'You're right, of course. What I need is to find something concrete.' He fished into the bag and pulled out a scrap of paper. 'Hey! Look at this one.'

Liz cast her eyes over it. 'It reminds me of when people used to fold napkins into water lilies or swans.'

'Origami, isn't that what they call it?' David was looking at the strangely folded paper. 'When I was a kid my dad used to make me little boats and paper aeroplanes.'

It was shaped like a box, or a slightly flattened lotus. 'Why would she . . . ? Oh!' David exclaimed.

He had been trying to unfold it and something had fallen out, a ring. 'That's gold,' Liz said..

'And it's heavy, Auntie Liz. It's a wedding ring, isn't it?'

She took it from him. 'It is. What a beautiful one. It's old, too.' Years of wear had caused the edges to smoothen out and obscure parts of the pattern engraved on its surface. 'My goodness. How did this end up on the streets?'

'So, was it hers? Or did she steal it?' asked David quietly.

Liz didn't believe Molly had stolen it. Helping herself to the odd sheet of printer paper was one thing, but a valuable ring? No way. 'If she'd stolen it, she'd have turned it into money straightaway. You don't hang on to something like that on the streets. I think it's hers.' *But why hide it in a bag of papers?*

David gave her a quizzical look. 'So, is this one of your concrete facts?'

'Absolutely, though I haven't the slightest idea what it might mean. I'm going to see what Matt makes of this.'

* * *

Matt, Liz and David ate their breakfast in speculative silence, the eyes of each one of them drawn again and again to the gold band in the centre of the table.

As the time approached eight thirty, Matt made his now customary phone call to the Coopers, to ask if they had heard anything of their son and his whereabouts. As was also customary, they'd heard nothing.

Like Liam's parents, he was increasingly anxious about the boy. At the same time, he reminded himself of how the lad had crowed about his ability to disappear at will. If he was playing them all for fools, Matt might not be responsible for his actions when he finally had the little toe-rag in his clutches.

Then there was Molly, and the mysterious ring. Like David and Liz, his head was full of a hundred different possible explanations for how it came to be sitting next to a jar of marmalade on their kitchen table.

'I think Molly left it with the papers specifically for Chris Lamont to find,' stated Liz, waving a knife on which a wedge of butter was perilously close to landing on her lap. 'She knew he was a retired police officer and was banking on him finding the thing.'

David frowned. 'So why didn't she just tell him what it was all about instead of going through all this rigmarole? If she trusted him enough to leave her precious bag with him, why not just talk to the guy?'

'It's my guess that she was too scared, David,' said Liz. 'Fear can make you act in some very odd ways. In fact, I'd go so far as to say she was terrified and didn't dare open her mouth.'

'Meaning that whatever she knows, or is frightened of, is a very serious matter,' concluded Matt. 'Much as I'd like to join you, I'll have to leave this conundrum to you. I'm still nowhere near finding Liam Cooper.' He looked at Liz. 'And I'm afraid that if I continue to make no headway, I might need you working with me.'

'Of course. David understands where our priorities lie. He can press on with our Molly, and we'll see how things go.' She swallowed the last of her tea. 'Now, what's the itinerary for today, boss?'

'I'm going to give Swifty a bell and hopefully go and talk to him. Charley Anders knows I'm investigating the disappearance of this teenager, so I should let Swifty know where I am with it. She won't have a problem with him updating me on any recent developments. I suggest that after you make your proposed trip to the store, David presses on with Molly's papers, while you, my darling, take that ring into Cropper's, the jewellers. If anyone can tell you about that ring, it's Andy Cropper.'

'My thoughts precisely,' said Liz. She began clearing away the breakfast things. 'Keep in touch, Matt. I know that Liam is starting to get to you.'

David got to his feet. 'If it's all right with you, I'll go and get stuck in, shall I? Just shout when you want me to go shopping with you.'

Matt smiled at his enthusiasm, happy to have him on board again. He would never tell her so, but he was always concerned that Liz sometimes tried to do too much, and then she suffered for it. She hadn't fully recovered from the injuries she had sustained at the hands of a bunch of evil, twisted men. She had almost lost her life in the attack, which had ended her career in the force. She now functioned well, but easily became overtired, so David's arrival was a godsend.

He hugged her tight. 'Take care. I'll keep in touch, you too. Let me know if you get things sorted with those two thieving sisters.'

'If we can sew up the shoplifting, I'll be well happy.' Reluctantly, she pushed him away. 'Go. Let's make the most of our early start.'

He left the house, the words 'And I love you', still ringing in his ears.

* * *

By one p.m., Liz and David were sitting in the lounge of a modest Fenfleet house, facing two very anxious parents. Jennifer Steele had been a civilian working in the control room when Liz was still in the force, and she knew her well, so this was not an easy thing to say.

'We've come to you first, Jen, because the last thing you want is for the police to be knocking on your door. But I'm afraid I've seen them three times now, and today my nephew here caught them on his mobile phone. Stephie and Blythe have been shoplifting in the retail park, in their lunch-breaks and after school.'

Jen threw a look at her husband. 'I told you they were up to something, but would you listen? You would not. Now, what are we going to do?'

Bob shook his head. In his eyes, his daughters could do no wrong. 'Surely this can't be right. They're such good girls.'

'*Were* good girls,' Jen retorted. 'Ever since they got pally with that boy from the Academy they've been secretive, and now they don't listen to a thing I say.' Jen looked beseechingly at Liz. 'So, what happens now?'

Liz felt for her. The girls had always been nice kids, but she knew how easy it was at their age to fall under the influence of the wrong sort of friend. 'I suggest you have a long talk with them, both of you together, and you, Bob, read them the riot act. Threaten them with the police, make it sound as if you mean it.' She smiled at his forlorn expression. 'I know it's not easy, but you have to nip this in the bud, and fast. Luckily, the owner of the store is a friend of Matt's. I think I can get him to waive their policy of always prosecuting theft, but only as long as they never do anything like this again.'

'Tell them that something like this,' David indicated his mobile phone and the video clip he'd just shown them, 'could totally ruin their chances for the future. It might make them think twice if they're considering going on to university.'

Jen looked as if she were close to tears. 'They are my girls and I love them, but right now, I'm ashamed of them. How could they do a thing like that?'

'Come on, love, don't take on so,' said Bob. 'They'll come round. You're right, it's that boy's influence. Teenagers go through these awful phases, but they'll come good, you'll see.'

Jen didn't look convinced, so Liz added, 'It's true. I've always thought they were lovely girls, and a credit to you both. Bob's right, this is just a phase, I'm sure. You just need to administer a short and very sharp shock, and try to keep them away from whoever is egging them on.'

Bob was obviously persuaded by her words. 'Dead bloody right! Leave it to me.' He turned to his wife. 'I'm sorry I buried my head in the sand, but I'm with you now. We'll sort this.' He looked back at Liz. 'We are very grateful to you, Liz. If you can possibly get the store owner to understand, we'll make sure that this never happens again, and I'll also return anything they stole. Little idiots!'

If they haven't already sold it on at school, thought Liz, knowing how these things worked. 'Will you ring me and let me know how it goes?'

'Without fail,' said Jen firmly. 'The minute they walk through that door after school they won't know what's hit them — figuratively, of course.'

Thinking that she wouldn't want to be in the girls' shoes, Liz smiled and stood up. 'Well, we wish you luck. And don't forget, make sure they know just how close they are to getting nicked.'

As they drove away from the Steele house, David said, 'Poor parents. I felt really sorry for them, but at least we can now concentrate on Molly.'

'I've been thinking about that,' Liz said. 'I've got to go and see the jeweller about the ring. Come with me, and we'll try to speak to a few of the homeless people. We can ask if there's been any news of her, or if any of them knows something about her.'

'Good idea. Why don't we go there now?' said David eagerly.

Wisely, Liz knew her limitations. She needed a short rest before they took to the streets. 'We've had a very successful morning, haven't we? So, let's go home and get some lunch, touch base with Matt, and I'll tell you about some of the street people.'

David regarded her shrewdly. 'You okay, Auntie Liz?'

She laughed. 'I'm fine. It's just that since I got hurt I've learned to notice the little signs and not ignore them. Some food, a hot drink and a sit down for half an hour, and I'll be raring to go again.'

'Just tell me if I get too pushy, won't you?' said David seriously. 'I'm here to help, not to cause you problems.'

David knew the gist of what had happened to her, a trauma that had left her hanging between life and death. He was quite sensitive for someone so young, and she admired him for it. She smiled at him. 'You, believe it or not, are just the tonic I need. Don't worry, I'll tell you when I need to back off a bit.'

'Right. I'll make you a cup of tea and then I'll fix lunch while you put your feet up. How does that sound?'

'Music to my ears. Cannon Farm, here we come!'

* * *

Matt was also sitting with a couple of distraught parents, but his interview was proving far more difficult than Liz's had been.

'It's different this time,' said Maisie Cooper tearfully. 'We both just know that something is terribly wrong.'

'For once, I agree with Maisie,' added Jim gruffly. 'We're all aware of what a little bugger Liam can be, but it's more than that. I can feel it, right here in my heart.'

It wasn't like Jim to express his emotions, and Matt felt for him, felt for them both. They were right. It did feel different this time. On top of his worry about Liam, Matt had received a further shock. When he met up with his old mate, Swifty, he noticed that he looked a bit subdued. Swifty had grunted that finding murdered bodies by the riverside didn't do much for one's frame of mind, even if it was an old bag lady. When Matt learned that the old lady had been Molly, for some reason he neglected to mention the bag of letters, or the fact that they were looking for her. Now, no matter how badly he felt for the Coopers, he kept seeing images of Molly rising before his mind's eye.

He mentally shook himself. 'I've had a word with the police this morning, and told them that on this occasion Liam really is giving serious cause for concern.' He shrugged. 'I thought it might sound a bit more convincing coming from a former detective rather than a distraught parent, if you see what I mean. They've promised to do what they can.' He looked at each of them in turn. 'And there's no one else you can think of who might know where he is — no friends, people he mixes with? Anyone who might have seen him, no one he might have spoken to about his plans? I need to find someone who is close to him.'

Jim shook his head slowly, 'We've told you of everyone we know about, but he doesn't tell us much, I'm afraid.'

'What about his sisters? Does he ever confide in them?' Matt asked, guessing what the answer would be.

Maisie Cooper gave a humourless laugh, 'They barely even talk! The girls have tried their best with him, probably for my sake, because it upsets me so much, but he has no time for them.'

'Well, I have a few more people to talk to, although the last person was no use at all. I'll touch base with you again tomorrow, unless I hear anything in the meantime. I'd better get moving.' Matt got to his feet. 'I'm terribly sorry I've had no good news to give you yet, but we'll find him, Maisie.'

'Oh, I hope so, Mr Ballard. He's a bad-un all right, but he's still our son, and I always pray that one day he'll see sense, realise that he's loved, and he doesn't have to behave like this to get attention.'

That was what it was all about, of course. Matt had gathered that while he was the only child, Liam had been a model son. Then his two sisters appeared and stole the limelight, and he'd been angry and resentful ever since. 'I won't give up, Maisie, you can rely on that.'

Outside the house, he breathed a sigh of relief, thankful to be away from the atmosphere of distress and despondency.

And he wouldn't give up, it wasn't in his nature. Right now, he wanted to talk to Liz. He glanced at the time on his phone and then rang her, 'Where are you, sweetheart?'

'We've just got back home for lunch. How about you?'

'I'm on my way there too. I've got something to tell you, but it can wait till I see you.'

Molly's murder put a very different slant on things. They needed to talk, discuss how to proceed. Matt got into the car and sped away.

CHAPTER FOUR

Gunner at his side, Clem walked the streets of Fenfleet. He checked shop doorways, back alleys, wherever a homeless person might doss down for the night. He wanted that sleeping bag back. And especially, he wanted whatever was in the lining.

He had been trudging along for two hours now, and he was tired. His best bet was to give up, go to the drop-in centre and get a cup of tea, and then do the rounds after dark. He would recognise that sleeping bag anywhere, and if he saw someone huddled up in it, he'd damned well haul it off them. A few days before, he'd bought a cheap torch in Poundstretcher and nicked a handful of batteries from WH Smith. The homeless were used to having torches shone on them as they lay curled up in their chosen place of shelter. Do-gooders offering hot drinks, coppers checking they were not dead, and occasionally some faceless man or woman, searching hopelessly for a lost son or daughter. So, no one would take too much notice when he did the same.

With a grunt of irritation, and a word to Gunner, he turned and went in search of a hot drink, and maybe a biscuit for his best friend.

* * *

'Killed!' Liz exclaimed, her eyes wide in surprise.

'Swifty recognised her immediately. He was pretty cut up about it. He told me he'd had a few chats with her over the last few months, and was amazed that she had finished up homeless. He swore she was well educated,' he sighed, 'but as we well know, anyone can take to the streets, and some do it by choice.'

'But you didn't tell him we are interested in her?' Liz asked.

He shook his head. 'No. I wanted to talk to you first. We need to decide how to proceed, if indeed we do. Murder is a police matter, and it's not as if we were hired to look for her. It's complicated.'

Liz frowned. 'In essence, Molly hired us herself. She wanted that bag found, and I'm certain she left the ring as a starting point for an investigation.' She raised an eyebrow. 'Come on, Matt, with all Charley Anders has on her plate right now, do you honestly think the death of a bag lady will be high priority?'

'It's still murder, no matter how busy they are,' Matt said. 'So, if you want to go ahead with this, we must run it past Charley. And, please, Liz, don't be disappointed if she tells us to butt out. We could be muddying the waters when they embark on their investigation.'

'And she could fall at your feet, showering you with thanks,' she retorted. 'Molly is ours, and you know it, Matt Ballard. We have all the time in the world to piece together this jigsaw puzzle and find out what happened in her past. Charley Anders will be delighted, don't you worry.'

Matt knew there was no arguing with Liz Haynes when she had the bit between her teeth. He held up his hands in surrender. 'I'll ring her now, shall I?'

Liz gave him a smug smile. 'That's my Matt. No time like the present.'

As he'd expected, it wasn't as simple as Liz had contended. 'She wants to see us. Basically, we have a green light, but . . . there are stipulations, which is what she wants to talk to us about. Five o'clock at the station.'

'Excellent. We can go after we've visited the jewellers and spoken to the homeless people.'

'Can I come with you to the station?' chipped in David. 'I'd really like to see DCI Anders again.'

Liz smiled. 'A family outing, perfect. Now, young David, I seem to remember you promising us lunch.'

* * *

Jeweller's loupe to his eye, Andy Cropper gave a soft whistle. 'Lovely. Beautiful metalwork, even if it is rather worn.' He put the eyeglass down and looked at Liz. 'Family heirloom is it, Liz?'

'No, it's part of an investigation. In fact, it's the only clue we have to the identity of someone we're interested in.'

'Oh dear,' Andy said doubtfully. 'Well, I'm not sure how much help I can be — other than the initials, of course.'

'Initials?' asked Liz.

'Ah, they're quite faint, but there's definitely the letters MM on the inside of the band.'

'Molly?' David whispered.

'Maybe,' said Liz, 'but that ring is pretty old, isn't it, Andy?'

'It is, but people often buy antique rings, or it could be an heirloom. Good quality jewellery like this doesn't just hold its value, it appreciates over the years. I could run tests, but I'd say it's pure gold, not some amalgam.'

'It's quite valuable then.' Liz pictured Molly's bag, and the folded piece of paper the ring was in. How easily it could have been thrown away.

'Oh yes. Rings like this fetch between five hundred and a thousand pounds on the market. I could value it properly if you like,' Andy offered.

'Thanks, but not just yet, Andy. What can you tell us from the hallmarks?' Liz asked.

'There's an anchor, so that's the Birmingham assay office, and the year is 1921. It's twenty-two carats from the fineness mark, and there's a sponsor, or maker's mark, that I can easily check for you.' He looked up. 'Every jeweller has their own mark, and with antique gold it's more likely to be that of the actual maker than it is today, when importers, wholesalers and retailers can have their own mark. I'm guessing that could help you, couldn't it?'

Liz nodded. 'If it's not too much trouble.'

They left the shop knowing that the craftsman who had made the ring had been a Lincolnshire man and had sold a lot of his designs through a well-respected jeweller in Peterborough that still existed after over a hundred years of trading. 'I'll work on that info when we get home,' Liz told David. She glanced at her watch. 'We're due at the nick in five minutes, so we'd better get a move on.'

They arrived at the front door just as Matt came hurrying towards them from the opposite direction.

It still felt strange to Liz, being back at the place they had worked for so many years. Seeing DCI Charley Anders' name on what had been Matt's office door was even weirder. For a long time, Liz refused to set foot inside the station. It was just too painful. Her beloved job had been snatched from her by someone she had believed to be a friend, and who had turned out to be anything but. It was easier now, but still a bit unreal. She was no longer a part of it all, things were changing, new faces had appeared. It took a some minutes for her to remind herself how lucky she was. She still had a life, and it was a good one, albeit not the one she had planned.

'Come in and grab a chair,' said Charley. 'And hello, David. Nice to see you again. Back helping the family business to survive?'

They spent a few minutes discussing his university course, and David was able to thank her for her encouragement and support. They then turned to the matter of Molly and her murder.

'I can't lie to you, we are snowed under with cases,' said Charley, 'but murder always takes precedence, even if it is that of a homeless person.'

Matt raised an eyebrow. 'Do I sense a "but"?'

She sighed. 'You do. I am stretched to capacity on the budget and strapped for manpower. Much as I'd love to, I can't give Molly's death the priority I think it deserves, so . . .' She looked from Matt to Liz. 'Why don't you tell me the story. How come you're so interested in a bag lady?'

Liz described the finding of the bag, the mysterious writings. 'She was terrified of something, and now she's been killed. That says a lot, doesn't it? But it's complicated, and that's why we have David helping us. Just sifting through all those pieces of paper and trying to make sense of it is a mammoth task. I imagine it's not something you'd want to hand to one of your detectives, especially after what you've just told us about your lack of resources.' She raised an eyebrow at Charley. 'Whereas we have both the time to devote to it, and the interest.'

'Who is she,' asked Charley, 'I mean was?'

Matt answered, 'We know very little about her, other than that she was obviously an educated woman, maybe even to university level. Oh, and then there's the ring. Molly possessed a valuable wedding ring, which we found in that bag of hers.' He glanced Liz. 'It is valuable, isn't it?'

She nodded. 'Andy said it could be worth up to a grand. He gave us the name of the maker, which I can look up when I get home.'

Charley regarded them quizzically. 'Sounds like you guys have a whole strategy worked out.' She was silent for a few moments. 'Okay. You can run with it. But you must let us know exactly what you are doing and how far ahead you are at every stage. I'll delegate a detective to the case and a crew to assist them. That should cover me in the event of any queries from above. You do understand that there will come a point when you need to hand it over to us, don't you? If and when you have an indication of who killed that old lady, you must allow us to take over. If an arrest is to be made, it needs to be a copper doing it, not the Ballard and Haynes Detective Agency.'

Matt grinned. 'Haynes and Ballard. It was her idea. Seriously, Charley, I know our record isn't good for letting go, but we want whoever murdered Molly to pay for it, according to the law.'

'Okay. I'll ring you later and tell you who I've allocated to the case, and perhaps you'll fill them in with what you have to date. What have you got running at present, apart from this?'

'I've just tied up a small case this morning,' Liz said, 'so hopefully I'm now free.'

Matt shrugged. 'That leaves us with our missing runaway.'

'Ah, Liam Cooper. We've had the parents contacting us daily, but . . .' She scowled. 'Life is full of bloody buts at present!'

'We know where habitual runaways come on the priority list, Charley, don't worry,' said Matt. 'If you committed officers to every misper that was reported, you'd have no time for anything else. Having said that, my professional alarm bells are ringing where that lad's concerned. I have a horrible feeling that something really has happened to him this time. Anyway, I'm keeping uniform updated, as I know they are keeping their eyes and ears open for him.'

'Thanks. We appreciate that.' Charley sat back. 'So, we'll take it from there, shall we? Oh, and I guess you're aware that we can't officially share sensitive evidence like forensics with you? Much as I'd like to, my hands are tied over that one, as in disclosure of material to a third party.'

'I'd love to hear another "but" at this point,' said Matt hopefully.

Charley gazed up at the ceiling. 'I suppose when both parties, that is the police and the private investigator, are looking for the same outcome, there might be special circumstances? I mean, it's common knowledge that investigators cannot access medical records, but they can talk to acquaintances, family, and colleagues, and learn of medical history by word of mouth . . . Anyway, I really do need to get on, so I'm going to throw you all out now. I have a meeting in ten minutes, and I need to get you a detective lined up, so, vamoose!'

They trooped out.

It couldn't really have gone any better for them, Liz thought. It wasn't quite carte blanche, but it was close.

* * *

'I've never had anything to do with street people,' said David. 'You know what Dad's like. If I'm out with him and we pass some kid in a doorway, or a Big Issue seller, I only have to put my hand in my pocket and he goes ballistic. I'm funding drug habits, they only spend it on booze, yada yada.'

Liz laughed. 'Yeah, I remember his lectures on the subject. Sometimes he's right though, but not always.'

'So how do I approach them?'

'Just like everyone else,' replied Liz. 'Just be pleasant and respectful, and don't pry. If someone wants to talk, they will. Some of them might not have spoken to anyone all day and will welcome a bit of attention.'

'Right, and are we looking for anyone in particular?'

'I'd like to find an old guy called Clem. You can't miss him, he's got a dog with him. Clem used to be in the Royal Artillery, so his dog is called Gunner. He'll talk if I buy him a warm drink and a sandwich.'

David wondered if everyone on the streets had a story to tell. How did a soldier finish up homeless? Didn't the army take care of them?

'Oh, and if you see a little guy, kind of shifty and ratty looking, wearing black joggers and a dirty black fleece, steer clear. His name is Sid. Some of the uniforms who know him say it's short for Rancid.'

'Why? Is he dangerous?' asked David.

'He doesn't like anyone invading his space. Not that you'd want to get too close anyway, but cross his invisible boundary and he freaks out and can be quite violent. So, keep your distance.'

'Do you know why he's like that?' It seemed to David that he'd been right, and they all had some intriguing history.

'Look up something called limbic hijacking when you've got a moment, kiddo. If your personal space gets violated, it registers in your long-term memory where all your negative experiences are recorded. When that happens, it puts us into fight-or-flight mode. I have no idea what happened to Sid, for example, but he really does not want to go back there.'

'How do you know all this, Liz?' David said, impressed.

'The hard way.' Liz chuckled. 'Way back when I was a probationer, I took a pasting from a tramp, and I made it my business to find out why.'

They strolled through the town, down alleyways and pausing in shop doorways, speaking occasionally to people they saw, but no one knew anything about Molly. It wasn't until they reached the Outreach drop-in centre that they finally got word of Clem.

'He seemed to be bothered by something,' said a young volunteer who was dishing out hot drinks to a group of homeless people. 'Really rattled he was, and that's not like Clem.' She paused briefly, a Styrofoam cup in her hand. 'If I was you, I'd try St Benedict's churchyard. He meets up with a few others there some afternoons and lets Gunner have a run off the lead.'

Liz gave the girl a ten pound note for the donation pot, and they headed off to the churchyard. On the way, Liz stopped at a small convenience store, where she purchased a box of dog food pouches, some dog biscuits and a packet of bags for dog waste. David noted this latter buy with mild amusement.

'Oh, our Clem is fastidious about Gunner,' Liz assured him. 'The dog comes first in all things. Clem might struggle to eat but Gunner never misses a meal — and yes, Clem cleans up after him.' She waved the bags. 'He'll be chuffed with these.'

The Centrepoint volunteer had been right, and they found Clem hunkered down in the porch at the side of the church. David saw a big German Shepherd cross sniffing happily among the gravestones. He was obviously keeping a close eye on his master because when they stopped to talk to Clem, Gunner materialised out of nowhere to sit at his side.

'DS Haynes! Haven't seen you for quite a while.'

'Oh, I'm just Liz now, Clem. My days on the force are over. Matt and I have set up a private investigation agency, so I'm still happy to pay for information.' She placed the dog food and the small plastic package on the stone floor.

'Appreciate it, DS Hay — er, Liz.' He looked with satisfaction at the bags. 'Much more hygienic than using old MacDonalds bags.'

David suppressed a smile. The use of the word "hygiene" sounded a bit incongruous on the lips of this old rough sleeper.

'Hey, will you look at that!' Clem exclaimed. 'Gunner never goes to strangers, but he's taken to you, lad. That's a first, that is.'

David had been holding out his hand to the dog. Gunner's tail wagged, and he drew closer, nuzzling the proffered hand. 'He's beautiful,' said David, slightly in awe of the fierce animal's trust in him. 'How old is he?'

'Who knows? We found each other four years ago and we've never been apart since. I'm guessing he's seven or eight. But you didn't hunt me down to discuss my dog, did you? Who do you want me to dish the dirt on today?'

'Nothing like that this time,' said Liz. 'Clem, what can you tell us about Molly?'

Clem started, causing Gunner to growl and take up his post again at his master's side. 'Why do you want to know about Molly?'

Liz sat down on the stone seat at the side of the porch. 'Clem, I'm sorry to tell you, but Molly is dead.'

'Oh no.' Clem sank back against the cold stone of the porch wall. His hand sought out his dog and he ran his fingers through Gunner's thick coat.

'I'm so sorry, Clem,' said Liz softly. 'But the thing is, we believe that Molly was afraid of something. We want to know what that was.'

'How did she die?' Clem's voice shook slightly.

'We don't know yet, Clem, but we suspect foul play.'

The old man closed his eyes and started to rock backwards and forwards. Gunner whimpered. Then he cleared his throat. 'She was scared, I know that. And yes, she feared something bad was going to happen. Oh, Lord, I've let her down.'

'How so?' asked Liz.

Clem ran a bony hand through his hair. 'She gave me something, and then the other night some bastard stole it. I've been everywhere looking for it, but no luck.'

'What was it?' asked David. 'Maybe we could help you look for it?'

'It's a sleeping bag. But before you say anything, it's not the bag that matters, it's what she had hidden inside it.' Clem looked angry. 'If I get my hands on the stinking thief that nicked it, they'll regret going anywhere near that bag.'

David stiffened. What was this? First, a ring in a bag of papers, now something else inside a sleeping bag?

'Do you know what it was, Clem?' asked Liz. 'It could be important.'

'It's damned important, you don't need to tell me!' exclaimed Clem. 'That's why I've been traipsing the streets all day and will likely lose my spot for the night. It's a letter. Molly told me that if anything happened to her, I was to give it to the first copper I saw. Since you've asked me about it, I'll give it to you if I do find it.'

A letter could provide a multitude of answers. David looked at Liz.

Glancing back at him, she said, 'I'd appreciate that, Clem.'

'I'm going out later, after dark, and I'll search all night if I have to. I'd know that bag anywhere. It was royal blue, a bit faded, but it had a bright red lining that showed even when you zipped it up. It'd been a good 'un in its day, can't have been cheap.'

'I could go with you, sir,' David offered. 'Two pairs of eyes are better than one, as they say.'

Clem gave a chesty chuckle, which degenerated into a cough. 'Don't get me wrong, lad, I appreciate your offer, but you'd be a bit of a liability on the streets at night. You stay in your comfy bed. I know where to go and who to talk to. If I find that letter, I'll go directly to the Outreach centre and as soon as it opens, I'll ask the manager to ring you for me, then I'll stay there until you come, okay?'

Liz gave him her card and took another ten pound note from her purse. 'Get yourself a hot meal before you go out tonight, Clem. And be very careful. We have no idea if someone was after Molly, and whether they knew about that letter. You might not be the only one tramping the streets to look for it.'

'Mind, they'd have to get past Gunner,' Clem said, scratching the dog's ears affectionately. 'Which may not be a risk worth taking.'

Glad that Clem had this powerful bodyguard at his side, David was nevertheless becoming aware of the seriousness of this situation. It had gone far beyond the "little mystery" Liz and Matt had asked him to help them with. Molly was dead, murdered. What could she have known that was dangerous enough to lead someone to hunt her down and kill her?

David shivered, and it had nothing to do with the stone wall of the porch. 'Yes, look after yourself, sir. It's been nice to meet you, and you too, Gunner.'

They walked back to the car in silence. After a while, David said, 'Is that old man in danger, Auntie Liz?'

She exhaled. 'I hope not. Though . . .' They fell silent again.

CHAPTER FIVE

While Liz and David were talking to Clem, Matt was trying to get some sense out of someone far less willing to speak.

'Come on, Jax, you've been mates with Liam since you were nippers. He must have given you some idea of what hair-brained scheme he had in that head of his.'

Jaxon Briggs was a skinny teenager dressed in the ubiquitous style of the cool street kid. A hoodie that looked like it had had a can of paint thrown over it, vintage jeans that really were vintage, and high-top sneakers that appeared to be brand new.

'He never said nothing.' Jaxon scowled. 'I told you before, he's been dead cagey lately, didn't want to hang out, or talk, or anything.'

'And you haven't seen him for days?'

'I told yer all this already. A week, maybe longer. I dunno, I've given up on him. Sod the little prick, he can get stuffed. He's running with new mates, I guess. Must be. Good riddance to the fucker, that's what I say.' Jaxon plunged his hands deep into his pockets.

Matt knew he hadn't meant a word of it. Jaxon Briggs was smarting, hurt that he'd been left out of whatever Liam was up to. He decided to try a different tack. 'Listen, Jax. I'm going to tell you something, but keep it to yourself, all right?'

Jaxon shrugged. 'Please yourself.'

'Even you have to admit he's acting out of character.'

The teenager puffed out his cheeks. 'S'pose so. He's always been a prat, but he did used to tell me stuff, so yeah, I guess he is then.'

'Okay. Well, as you know, I've brought him home twice before, after he buggered off, but this time it feels different. I reckon something's happened to him. Now, if you know anything at all, even some small thing that might seem unimportant to you, I want to know about it. Look, Jaxon, I'm worried. Really worried. As you rightly say, he's a prat. I know he said I wouldn't find it so easy to trace him this time, but . . .' he shook his head slowly. 'This stinks. Something's wrong.'

Jaxon withdrew one hand from his pocket and gnawed on a fingernail. After a moment or two, he said, 'When you say something's happened to him, do you mean, like something really bad?' Jaxon was suddenly a lot less cocky. Finger in his mouth, he looked younger than his sixteen years.

'I honestly don't know, but my gut instinct is telling me your mate is in trouble.'

Jaxon stared at his trainers. 'I dunno if this is anything or not, but he kept going on about this place he called the Bunker. He never told me what it was, or where, except that it was close to the marsh. He just said it was zero cool.'

'But you have no idea what kind of place it is?'

'Nah. When he first said about it, I reckoned he was making it up. He did that sometimes. Invented stuff to make him look like the big man.' Jax sniffed. 'Then yesterday I heard some other kids talking, and it came up — Bunker — so I guess he didn't make it up after all.'

'Who were these kids, Jax? Do you know them?' Matt asked.

'I've seen them around; they act pretty hard. My dad says they're bad news and I'm to stay away from them. They hang out in the rec — you know, hogging the swings, drinking cans of lager they've nicked, and scaring the younger kids away. I think the main one's name is Kurt.'

'Did they say what kind of place this Bunker is? I mean, I suppose it's a place. It must be, mustn't it?' Matt would have to track this gang down and have a quiet word.

'I didn't hear no more, just that one word. Sorry.' Jaxon looked at Matt anxiously. 'You really think Liam's in trouble then?'

'I honestly don't know, Jax,' said Matt. 'But I know where to find you, so if I hear anything, I'll let you know. Here, take my card, and ring me if you hear anything about either Liam or this Bunker place.' He slipped a fiver behind the card. 'Keep your ear to the ground for me.'

The boy nodded. 'Yeah, all right. I, er, I hope you find him. He's a prat all right, but he is my mate. I don't want anything bad happening to him.'

Matt left him and walked to the recreation ground. He doubted the older boys would be there now but it was worth a try. He'd heard of the kid Jax had mentioned, a very unpleasant seventeen-year-old, already well on his way to the young offenders' institution. He also knew the kind of reply he'd get if he started asking questions. He'd need to be canny.

When he reached the area where the swings were, there was nobody around but a couple of mothers with youngsters, and no sign of the gang of young thugs. He was about to walk away when he realised he knew one of the young mothers.

'Penny? Penny Turner? It's me, Matt Ballard.'

She looked up, hostile, then a slow smile crept across her painfully thin face. 'DCI Ballard! Ain't seen you for a while.'

'That's because I'm not a copper anymore. I'm on civvy street now. May I?' He sat down on the bench from where she had been watching two little lads playing on a climbing frame. 'How have you been, Penny?'

She shrugged. 'So-so, I guess. In fact, life's pretty good. It's not been easy with Darren gone, and the kids can be a nightmare, but,' her face creased into a smile, 'we're getting there, thanks to you.'

'Get on with you, girl, I did nothing,' said Matt with a laugh. 'Take the credit you deserve. It was all down to you. I just pointed you in the right direction, that's all.'

'You were the only one to ever bother with us, and that's a fact. I hate to think where I'd be now if you hadn't helped me. Probably six feet under, and my two sons'd be in care.'

As a matter of fact, she was right. She'd lived in a tip with a bastard of a husband, terrified of his drunken rages, as well as having two little boys — identical twins — to care for. Then her idiot husband Darren had nicked a car and totalled it on the main road to Peterborough, totalling himself at the same time. He had never been good to Penny alive, and in death, he left her destitute. Her plight had got to Matt, enough to make him jump in and take on social services on her behalf. To his surprise, Penny had followed every one of his suggestions. She didn't know it but he had followed her progress from the sidelines, always hopeful that things would come good for her. He knew that she now had a little maisonette in a small estate on the edge of town, well away from the people her waster of a husband had associated with. She had a part-time job locally, and the kids were in school, and by the looks of them, were now thriving.

When they'd chatted for a while, she said, 'If I know you, you ain't here for the sake of your health. Who're you looking for?'

He chuckled. 'That transparent, am I? True, I'm no longer a policeman but I am still a detective, just a private one. I wondered if Kurt and his gang might be skulking around here somewhere.'

'That shite! If he was, I'd be well away, believe me. I wouldn't want him within half a mile of my boys. Poison, he is. He only comes here because there's a dealer out this way. Lives down Heron Crescent, number forty-two, if you're interested.' Even thinking about him appeared to be making

Penny angry. 'That why you're looking for him, is it, the drugs?'

Matt filed that tasty bit of information away in his mind, so he could pass it on to Swifty. 'No. He was heard talking about a place I'm interested in. I was hoping to get some info on it.'

'Where is this place? I might have heard of it.' She grinned at him. 'I keep myself well away from anything illegal these days but I still get to hear stuff.'

'Somewhere called the Bunker. The thing is, I'm looking for a missing boy, and he appears to have mentioned this place, wherever it is, several times. I've been told it's on the marsh, which doesn't tell me a lot — there's a whole lot of marsh in this county.'

Penny looked thoughtful. 'Some of my old mates used to go to raves at a venue called the Bunker — you know the thing, party till you drop, trance and house music. But that was somewhere in the Smoke, not here. Want me to sound out a few people for you?'

Matt shook his head. 'Not if it means you talking to some of the low-lives Darren used to mix with.'

'No way! But I can talk to a few people I trust. Now you mention it, I've heard that name somewhere, I just can't remember where.'

'Okay, Penny, then thank you. But only as long as no one starts asking you questions. I have no idea what this place is, or what goes on there, so promise me you'll keep it low key.'

She nodded. 'Gotcha. No problem. Give us your number then.' She produced her phone from her pocket and added him to her contacts. 'I'll do my best and give you a bell if I come up with anything.' She smiled at him. 'Now I'll have to love you and leave you. I need to get these two home and fed.' She called to the boys. 'Nice to see you again, Matt.'

She gathered up the lads and said goodbye. Matt watched her make her way to the park entrance. He didn't see too many people emerge relatively unscathed from a life of domestic abuse and violence, so Penny's transformation was heartwarming.

Matt roused himself from his musings and pulled out his phone. He ought to call Swifty and tell him of the existence of a drug dealer in Heron Crescent. He made the call, then asked Swifty if the name "Bunker" meant anything to him.

'Never heard of it,' said Swifty. 'But I'll ask some of the others. I'll be in touch if I strike lucky, and thanks for the heads-up on the dealer. Our Bryn will be delighted — poor bloke's on a mission to rid the entire town of dealers. Fat chance.'

Matt smiled. Bryn Owen had been his trusted DC. Having completed his sergeant's exams, he was obviously embracing his new post with gusto. Matt said goodbye, ended the call and noted the time. There were a few others who might know of this strange place. He would seek them out, and hopefully be back at Cannon Farm before it got dark.

Another day had gone by with no news of Liam Cooper, and the prospect of any resolution soon was starting to look bleak. It pained him to ask Liz to drop the Molly investigation, but he would shortly be needing her help if they were to stand any chance of finding the missing boy.

* * *

As soon as the supper things had been cleared away, David set about sorting and collating Molly's notes. He'd never considered himself to be a patient person, but he was going about the task methodically, painstakingly, and with a good deal of relish. He was determined to find some clues — it was fast becoming a mission. He'd already decided to stay on beyond the week they had originally agreed upon. He had three weeks until he needed to get back to uni, so why not make use of them?

David had found another name to enter into his notebook: Cedar Leigh. Was this a house? It sounded a bit like a retirement home. He turned to his laptop but found nothing of use on Google, other than a company located way beyond the area. Another name that had cropped up several times was "Benjamin", which could be that of an adult or a child, or possibly even a surname. References like *"Benjamin decided not to go with me"*, and *"Benjamin seemed rather preoccupied"* provided no clues.

He had been at it for two hours when Liz flopped down on a chair beside him and ruffled his hair. 'I think you should call it a day, don't you, our Davey? You'll end up cross-eyed if you carry on much longer.'

He stretched his arms above his head. 'You're right, I'm having trouble concentrating. I keep thinking about Clem and Gunner, out there in the night, on a quest for a sleeping bag, as if it were the Holy Grail.'

Liz sighed. 'I think it is the Holy Grail to him. He thinks he's let Molly down, so he won't be able to rest until he gets it back.'

'I just hope he's safe.'

'You needn't worry about him, David. He's been on the streets for years. He's a wily old fox, and he has Gunner with him. He's safer than most, you can be sure of that.'

'It depends on who else is out there though.' David ran a hand through his hair. 'I mean, Molly wasn't safe, was she?'

Beside him, Liz was silent.

* * *

The kitchen was warm, too warm really, but that was how she liked it. His wife sat opposite him at the table, staring moodily into her tea. The clink of spoon on china was the only sound in the room, as she stirred and stirred.

'For God's sake, woman, will you stop doing that. It's beginning to drive me crazy.'

She set down her spoon.

He regarded her miserable face. 'Look, I'm sorry, okay? It's just that we've been over this whole thing time after time, I thought you'd realise by now that you've nothing to get all het up about.' He walked around behind her and massaged her shoulders. 'They've never come here before, so why would they now?'

'Because of *her*.' She glared at him. '*She* knew, didn't she?'

'She guessed, that's all. She never knew the truth, did she, and now she's dead, so why get all anxious?'

'Molly knew everything, damn her!' She shrugged his hands away. 'Who knows how many people she told before she was got rid of. You mark my words, before this week is out, people will be here, asking questions.'

By now he was ready to scream at his wife. He reached out to pat her hand but she jerked it away. 'And what if they do? We know what to say. And even if they do find something, we know who to blame, so be reasonable.'

Her look told him he was wasting his breath. He marched out of the room, shaking his head. Meanwhile, she resumed the unending clink, clink, clink of her spoon.

He stepped outside and breathed in the cool air, relieved to be out of the stuffy kitchen. A hint of salty ozone wafted in from the marsh on the gentle breeze. He sighed. Molly had been dispatched, the handful of people she associated with were being carefully monitored. He had done everything he could to keep the secret. Anyway, who missed street people when they disappeared? The police were far too busy.

Meanwhile, his willing helper was out in the shadowy backstreets of Fenfleet, looking for the coveted item. At least his wife had no idea about the possible existence of a letter — she'd be beside herself if she knew.

In a way, his wife was right to be anxious. Molly had always been resourceful, and she might well have found a way to tell someone what she knew. One day, the police would arrive on their doorstep. Well, let them come. They were prepared, they had their scapegoats lined up. He almost wished they would turn up. This had gone on far too long. Time it was over.

* * *

Clem longed to get his head down somewhere. It was after two in the morning, on one of those nights when the chill and damp ate through to your very bones. His determination to find that letter kept him walking. He felt edgy, Gunner, too, was jittery. The dog's large ears were up and he turned his head this way and that, growling softly. There was something about the atmosphere that didn't feel right. Clem had been on the streets for years, and ordinarily the night held no fears for him. But tonight was different.

'Whazzup, Clem?'

The small figure was almost invisible, bundled up in an old bedcover and tucked away in a corner of a covered area meant for wheelie bins. 'Who's that?' Clem whispered.

'Only me. It's Lily, you old nitwit.' She yawned. 'Somethink wrong, is it?'

'I'm just looking for something, that's all. Someone stole my sleeping bag and I want it back. Sorry to disturb you, Lily. Go back to sleep now.'

'I wasn't asleep. Can't seem to settle tonight,' grumbled Lily. 'It don't feel right somehow. I even tried to get into the hostel on Pink Street but they were full. I dunno, Clem, I'm not happy at all.'

So, he wasn't the only one to have the creeps. That was interesting. 'I know what you mean, duck. Me and the dog feel the same. I'd feel better being somewhere else tonight.'

'You and me both,' muttered the woman. 'If you want, I'll shove one of these bins out of the way and you can settle yourself down here.'

'Thanks, Lily, but I've got to carry on looking.'

'What's so special about a sleeping bag anyway? Why can't you just get something from the Sally Bash tomorrow?'

'Sentimental value, Lily. You try to sleep, I'll see you around.'

Clem, with Gunner glued to his side, moved off, while with every step his unease grew stronger. He was not alone. Someone was following him.

It was time to cut and run. He bent and whispered a word to Gunner, and in seconds, man and dog had disappeared.

CHAPTER SIX

Having made an early start, Rory had almost completed Molly's post-mortem when senior technician Erin "Cardiff" Rees arrived to join him.

'Morning, Prof. I like the soundtrack. I didn't know you had such a lovely baritone. I'm rather fond of Irish ditties myself.'

'Must be your Celtic heritage, dear Cardiff. I'm pleased to hear that you appreciate my tribute to sweet Molly Malone.' He cast an eye over the sad remains on the mortuary table. 'Though, despite my choice of requiem, it's my belief that she is as English as you are Welsh.' He looked up to see a young man hesitating in the doorway. 'Can I help you?'

'I'm DC Darren Norton. I was assigned by DCI Anders of Fenfleet to the case of the bag lady found in the river.'

Rory looked at the late arrival with interest. A new play-mate, what fun. 'Come in, come in. Welcome to my humble abode, Detective Constable Norton. I see you are already correctly attired, so would you care to approach the table?' This was clearly the last thing this newbie wanted to do, he already looked a little green about the gills.

'Er, I'm fine, Professor. I'll not get in your way. I can easily make my notes from here.' DC Norton almost clung to the doorframe.

As this was their first meeting, Rory decided not to tease the fellow too much. Besides, having someone puke up in his spotlessly clean mortuary was not the best start to the day. 'Have it your way, dear boy, though you'll miss the more interesting bits — these fascinating stomach contents for one. Let us continue, Cardiff, and as we have a guest, I'll refrain from bursting into song.'

'What a pity,' said Cardiff with a broad grin.

'Heart-breaking, isn't it? Still, we'll make up for it later. I believe our next case is the retired owner of an old Victorian music hall. My rendition of "A Little Bit of What You Fancy Does You Good" is the stuff of legend.'

'I can hardly wait,' breathed Cardiff, smirking behind her mask.

By now, Darren Norton was looking so bemused that Rory felt sorry for him.

'You'll get used to it, Detective,' said Cardiff, with a long-suffering sigh. 'In a year or two.'

'So, back to business, and sweet Molly Malone.' Rory stood back from the table. 'Basically, DC Norton, we have a woman of around sixty to sixty-five years old — although the streets have not been kind to her. She is of average weight, although her diet was poor, again due to her lifestyle.'

'What you'd expect of some old drop-out, I imagine,' Norton said. 'I think I drew the short straw on this one.'

In an instant, Rory's tone changed. 'It doesn't do to judge someone when you know nothing of their circumstances. In the first place, this woman was well bred, probably more than you. Moreover, she was educated — again, to a higher level than you appear to be. This was a woman of exceptional talents. So, I should be careful with your choice of words, Detective, and look to your prejudices.'

Taken aback, the young man stuttered, 'I . . . I just assu—'

'You'd do well to look at the whole picture before you arrive at a conclusion about another person. You should know, also, that a good detective doesn't *assume* anything.'

Cardiff coughed discreetly. 'In what way was she talented, Prof?'

Rory lifted one of Molly's hands. 'Look at her hands. This woman was a pianist. Even after she was forced to abandon her former way of life, she looked after these hands. Her feet are calloused and in very bad condition, but her hands are immaculate. She still exercised them, as she would have done all her life. The muscles of her palm are particularly well-defined, which can only have come from a lifetime of playing. She would have had a strong grip and her fingernails are clipped short, as if in readiness to play her last piece.' He placed the hand carefully back down beside the body. 'Sometime in the past, she had expensive dental work done. She has most of her own teeth, and I suspect she still managed to take care of them. Find her belongings and you'll find a toothbrush among them, I guarantee it.'

Cardiff turned to the detective. 'That should be a great help as you try to identify her, shouldn't it? A missing pianist can't be too hard to find.'

'Uh, yeah. I suppose it's a starting point.'

By now, Rory was wishing they had assigned someone else to poor Molly. He had a strong urge to punch this young man on the nose. With this apathetic specimen on the case, Molly stood no chance of having her murder solved. 'Tell me, DC Norton, are you working this case alone?'

'Yeah, I am — unless you count having to pass everything I get on to some old private-eye bloke. They call it "liaising with a verified outside agency", I'm told.'

Rory felt a hint of relief. 'And does this old private-eye bloke as you put it have a name?'

'Matt Ballard. Used to be a DCI, apparently, before he chucked it all in.'

Thank God for that. Rory turned to the lifeless soul on the table. 'You're in good hands, my dear. We'll find the truth, never fear.' He turned back to Norton. 'You might as well go now. I'll send my report to the CID office as soon as possible. Good day.'

And the detective was gone.

'He didn't need telling twice, did he?' Cardiff said.

'Obnoxious little twat,' cursed Rory.

'So, Matt Ballard is investigating this, is he?' Cardiff said. 'I've seen him a few times, but never knew him when he was a DCI, it was a bit before my time. Is he a mate of yours? I saw you brighten up when his name was mentioned.'

Rory smiled. 'Matt Ballard and the lovely Liz Haynes, his partner in every sense of the word, are two tenacious and very astute ex-Fenfleet CID officers turned private detectives. I have no idea why they have an interest in our Molly, but I'll find that out as soon as I get a free moment. Right, shall we finish up and sort this dear lady out?'

Cardiff began the closure of the large Y-shaped incision accompanied by Rory, who really did have a very good baritone: "In Dublin's fair city, where the girls are so pretty, I first set my eyes on Sweet Molly Malone . . ."

* * *

Matt left immediately after breakfast, while Liz and David went into the incident room to discuss the strategy for the day.

'Matt didn't seem very happy with DCI Anders' choice of detective for the case, did he?' said David.

'He was hoping for someone who'd worked with us before and knew our ways. This kid is a rookie detective, whom Matt suspects of having delusions of grandeur.' Liz laughed. 'Matt was less than impressed with his attitude to the job until he remembered why the name Norton sounded so familiar. Darren Norton is the grandson of the chief superintendent.'

'Oh dear,' said David. 'Still, that won't affect Matt, will it?'

'It wouldn't anyway. Matt would still give him a tongue-lashing if he needed it, whoever's favourite grandchild he was. As it happens, Matt has no liking for Grandad

Edwin Norton either. He's always said it was family money and connections that got him so high up the ladder, not good policing. Still, at least this Darren will be able to pass on how far the police are with it. Speaking of that, I'd better ring him and introduce us, so he knows who we are.'

'And I'll push on with reading Molly's notes.' David gathered up some crumpled papers and carefully smoothed them out. 'At least I have a few sheets with quite a bit of content. Maybe I'll get lucky and come up with something concrete for us to work on.'

Liz made the call, and soon realised why Matt had seemed so rattled by the new detective. 'That young man needs a little bit of sage and friendly advice if he wants to make it on the force,' she grumbled to herself. 'And given that I'm an outsider, with more years' experience than he's likely to accrue if he goes on the way he is, I could be the one to deliver it.'

'Talking to yourself is not a good sign,' said David, looking up from his papers.

Liz grunted. 'It was just that young man's attitude. His indifference was coming down the line in waves. It's put my back right up. Our Molly deserves better.'

Before David could answer, the house phone rang.

'Haynes and Ballard Detective Agency. Can I help you?'

'Well, well, the inimitable DS Haynes. How delighted I am to speak to you again, dear heart. How are you, Liz?'

'Professor Wilkinson!' The bad taste left by Norton evaporated and a broad smile spread across her face. 'I'm good, thanks. How are you?'

'In the bloom of youth and as charismatic as ever — believe that, you'll believe anything. But no, I'm fine, thank you. Slaving away as always, up to my proverbials in muck and bullets.'

'So, Rory. Why the call?'

'Have you had the dubious pleasure of making the acquaintance of young DC Norton yet?'

'Not in person, but I've just been speaking to him on the phone.'

'Then no doubt you were as impressed as I was by the enthusiasm and fervour with which he is embracing a certain investigation. I, of course, had his corporeal being in my mortuary, and I can assure you he gives new meaning to the words apathy and lack of compassion.' Rory gave a snort of disgust. 'I all but threw him out, but not before favouring him with a short lecture on the attributes of a good detective.'

Liz laughed. 'Good for you, Rory. I was just planning a lecture of my own.'

'I'm sorry I won't be there to hear it, dear Liz. Now, to the reason for my call. I was wondering if you and the devilishly handsome Matt Ballard might care to meet with me for a drink soon? It's eons since we saw each other. What do you say?'

'We'd be delighted. When would suit you?'

'There being no time like the present, how about tonight? We could meet halfway between Fenfleet and Greenborough at that nice old thatched pub in Locksley Fen Village. They do great bar food too.'

'Can we bring my nephew, David? He's helping us with our most recent case.'

'If you are referring to that of our murdered Molly, then please do. Shall we say seven thirty?'

'Perfect. See you then.'

'Ciao, lovely lady!'

'Who on earth was that?' David had been listening in, an amused smile on his lips.

'One of the smartest men you could ever hope to meet, my boy. Also, one of the kindest and most compassionate. And given that he cuts up dead bodies for a living, that is quite an achievement. He's the area Home Office pathologist, David. He covers all the districts served by the Fenland Constabulary, so I had quite a lot to do with him when I was on the force.' She sat down next to David. 'And I could be wrong, but I think we may be getting unofficial access to the forensics on Molly's death.'

'Really? Awesome. Isn't he risking getting himself in trouble for divulging sensitive material though?'

'You heard the DCI. She clearly said that as we are all working to the same end, and people are willing to talk to us . . .'

'I'm not sure that she meant the Home Office pathologist, but hey! Who am I to quibble?'

'Exactly. You'll love Rory, he's quite a character.' She raised an eyebrow. 'He has his own distinctive brand of humour.'

'I'm looking forward to it,' chuckled David. 'But back to the notes. I think I'm beginning to work out a chronological sequence.'

Liz leaned closer. 'That's brilliant. Go on then. How does it go?'

'To start with, any papers that are dated are fairly recent, within the last eighteen months. The older sheets that are more detailed only say things like "early March" but they don't give a year. Take this one.' David picked it up and began to read. 'She recalls a time when she and this Benjamin — whoever he is — were discussing space exploration, specifically the attempts to reach the moon. Benjamin asked her when the first moon landing took place, and why there had been no subsequent excursions. She says she told him there had been six further voyages since the one in July 1969, and a total of twelve men had walked on the lunar surface. Following the Apollo 17 mission, the government considered the costs of space exploration just too great. This was still the Cold War era, the US had won the space race, so their aim had been achieved. Public interest and funding waned, and they cancelled all further missions.'

'How did Old Molly come to know all that, I wonder,' Liz said.

'*I* reckon she was a teacher,' said David excitedly. 'There are a few other things she's written which point in that direction. But, wait. This is where the timeline comes in. She says, *Forty-four years on and no one has ever returned.*' So, as it's now fifty-four years since the landing, this conversation took place exactly ten years ago.'

'I see. So all this,' she indicated to the notes, 'refers to events that took place in or around 2013. Well done, David!'

'Of course, we'll need more than that one isolated conversation to confirm it.' David glanced at the piles of papers. 'Oh, and there's one small detail that I found interesting, though it could mean nothing. She ends this note with the words, "*Then we returned to the Planets.*" The word "planets" has a capital letter, which, considering how well she usually wrote, seems odd to me.' He shrugged. 'But as I say, it's most likely nothing.'

Liz stood up. 'I think this calls for coffee, don't you?'

'I sure do.' David grinned at her. 'I think I'm becoming addicted.'

'I can see that from the glint in your eye,' returned Liz. 'So, what's your main objective at the moment?'

'To find a location, I guess.' David looked pensive. 'Apart from that one mention of Cedar Leigh, whatever that is, there is nowhere for us to use as a starting point for our enquiries.'

Leaving David to his work, Liz went into the kitchen to make the coffee. Maybe, she thought, she might be more usefully employed in talking to more people about Molly. She could start at the drop-in centre and have a word with some of the outreach volunteers, check the night shelters. Surely, Molly must have had other friends than Smokey Joe and Clem.

Clem! She hadn't heard from him, so he obviously hadn't found the missing sleeping bag, but was he all right? He might be safe with Gunner by his side in the normal way of things, but someone had murdered Molly. And they were still out there.

Having shared a quick cup of coffee with David, Liz drove into the town. Soon she was in the Outreach centre kitchen, speaking with one of the volunteers.

'No, I haven't seen him today,' he said, 'but he doesn't always come in. Try the pet shop just off the High Street, the people there often give him and his dog a drink and something to eat.'

Liz knew Billie and Andy Nettles, the owners of "Paws Awhile". They were good people, and she often dropped in for a chat when she was in Fenfleet. The trouble was that every time she visited their little side street shop, it made her long to get a dog of her own. Matt always argued that the demands of their job meant that they wouldn't be able to give a dog the attention it needed. Liz wasn't convinced. A dog would be company for her, especially when she had one of her episodes and had to back off for a while. Perhaps when this case was over, she would have another go at her partner.

And Clem was there, sitting with a mug in his hands that bore the inscription: "*I Like You, But I Like My DOG better*".

'DS Haynes. You checking up on me?'

He looked exhausted. 'I certainly am. I was worried about you. No luck, I suppose?'

He shook his head. 'No, but I gave up sooner than I meant to. There was a bad feeling out on the streets last night, and it wasn't just me. Everyone I spoke to felt the same.'

Liz knew what he meant. She'd experienced that feeling herself in the days when she'd been out on patrol. Her fellow constable had called it the "whim-whams".

'I'm not giving up though. I mean to check every damn rough sleeper in town.'

'Well, if you do find it, don't forget to ask the guys at the drop-in centre to give me a call.' She perched on a pile of sacks of birdseed. 'But, Clem, isn't there anything you can tell me about Molly that might help me find out what she was so frightened of?'

'You need to speak to Smokey Joe. She talked to him a lot.' He gazed at her thoughtfully. 'Know what? I reckon they knew each other before she was on the streets.'

'Really?' Now this was something new. 'What makes you think that?'

'Dunno. They just sort of understood each other, if you know what I mean. Almost like they were talking about old times.'

'Did you ever overhear them talking about anything specific?' she asked.

'Not really. They weren't like the rest of us, they always seemed a bit like outsiders. And Molly never talked about herself, not to us lot.'

Chris Lamont from the library had said the same thing. 'I don't suppose you know where Smokey Joe was heading, do you, Clem?'

'Nah. He was friendly enough but he was another one who never said much. And then we'd got so used to him coming and going that we never bothered to ask. Can't you ask your police friends to look out for him? You can't miss him, can you? There's not that many people riding around on a bike with a bucket of burning coals hanging from the handlebars.'

Liz laughed. Suddenly she missed being able to just get uniform to put out an attention drawn to someone of interest. Young DC Norton could, though, and she'd make bloody sure he did. As Molly's only real friend, Smokey Joe was indispensable to the inquiry.

'All I know is that he went off in the direction of Saltern-le-Fen,' Clem added. 'And by the way, everyone on the streets now knows that Molly was murdered, and they're pretty nervous, I can tell you. A lot of them reckon it's one of them weirdos that goes around bumping off homeless people. It's happened before.'

'That's understandable, Clem, but they shouldn't worry too much. We are certain this has to do with something from Molly's past. We suspect she knew something about someone from her old life that they didn't want made public, so they bumped her off.'

'Mmm. I suppose that's why she never talked to us about herself. Makes sense. Oh, damn it, I wish I could find that bloody letter!'

Liz wished so too, but it was pointless fretting over it. They'd need to find out about Molly by other means. She slid off her perch of birdseed, 'Before I go, are you absolutely sure there's nothing you can tell me about Molly? Even something that doesn't seem important.'

'Only that we'll never hear the Voice in the Night again.'

Liz stared at him. 'You mean Molly was the Night Singer?'

'Oh yes. I thought you'd have known that.' He shrugged. 'Then again, why should you? It was something only we homeless people probably knew about. Molly had the most amazing voice, sometimes she just couldn't stop herself from singing.'

'As a matter of fact, I did hear her once. Matt and I were at a wedding reception that was being held in a marquee in the grounds of a Fenfleet hotel. They even turned down the music because the singing was so beautiful. I even remember the song. It was "Because You Loved Me". We all fell silent, listening. It was a magical moment.' Liz was moved all over again, and amazed to realise that the owner of that marvellous voice was Old Molly.

Clem chuckled. 'That would have been our Molly all right. She hung around places that had music playing — pop or classical, didn't matter to her. She used to say all music spoke to your soul, or something like that.'

'Well, I'm damned! Thank you, Clem. That could be very helpful. Keep in touch, won't you, and stay safe.' She handed him another ten pound note. 'That's for hot food. If you're walking all night, you'll be needing fuel.'

He met her eyes. 'Find who did this, DS Haynes — Liz. She might not have said much but she was one of us, and we'll miss her. We'll miss her singing. It always brought a smile to our faces. There's not much to smile about now.'

CHAPTER SEVEN

Jack "Swifty" Fleet was on night duty, so Matt caught up with him at home.

Telling him the kettle was on, Swifty led Matt into his tiny kitchen, where they seated themselves at the table. 'Can't stop, Jack, I'm afraid. There's just a couple of things I need to know.'

'Fire away then.'

Matt was very fond of his old mate Swifty. He was an old-style beat bobby, sadly a dying breed nowadays. They had often worked together and he knew he could rely on Jack's assistance and his discretion. 'The DCI has given us the go-ahead to investigate Molly's death.'

'Good!' Jack looked delighted. 'I could see her case getting swept under the carpet.'

'By DC Darren Norton, by any chance?'

'Oh no. They haven't allocated it to him, have they? That makes your involvement even more important.' Jack shook his head. 'Norton won't like being given a bag lady's death to investigate, not one bit, he'll think it's beneath him. He reckons he should get the plum jobs.'

'That's why I'm here, mate. Can you keep an ear to the ground for us? Let me know if anything turns up, because I've a feeling Norton isn't going to be particularly communicative.'

'Of course. I'll ring you the minute I hear anything useful.'

'Ring Liz. She's handling it now, while I do my best to track down Liam Cooper, the little shit. Which brings me to my main reason for coming. Have you heard anything more about that Bunker place? I still have no idea what or where it is. Apparently, Liam was always talking to a mate of his about it, and I'm wondering if that's where he's hiding out.'

'Sorry, Matt, I've heard nothing. However, we've got a young officer working undercover on a drugs case at the moment. Bryn says he'll ask him if any of the characters he's investigating have mentioned it at all. That's the best I can do, though I have put out a number of feelers.'

'I appreciate it,' said Matt. 'Now I'll leave you to enjoy a few hours' peace and quiet before you have to get back into your uniform.'

Back in the car, his mobile rang.

'Hi, Liz. Everything all right?

'I've got some good news, Matt. Rory is meeting us this evening for a drink and a chat. He's very interested in Molly, and I think he might have something to tell us.'

'Brilliant!' he exclaimed. 'I was wondering if I dare contact him, or whether that was taking Charley's directive a step too far. Is he coming to us?'

'No,' said Liz. 'We'll be meeting him at that little thatched pub in Locksley Fen Village. And listen to this, Matt, our David found a date on one of the conversations Molly wrote about — ten years ago. He's looking for anything else dated from around that time, as well as where this event took place.'

Matt laughed. 'He's really got his teeth into it, hasn't he?'

'I'm glad to say. But he's having more luck than me. I've been into town, but . . .' Liz sighed. 'I do have one bit of news, but it can wait till tonight. Where are you now?'

'On my way to talk to one of my old snouts, on the off-chance that this Bunker place is the haunt of drug dealers and the like. I'm getting the feeling that Liam has wandered into something a lot deeper than he had expected.'

Liz ended the call, leaving Matt to wonder what it was about Molly's case that had caught Rory's attention. After all, they'd told him nothing about the carpet bag and its mysterious tale. He looked at the car clock. Midday. There were a good few hours to go before he could ask him.

He drove on, trying to focus his thoughts on Liam, but Old Molly kept getting in the way. Beneath the thrum of the engine, he could hear her, calling out to him. She was asking for his help, and he was determined not to fail her.

* * *

In a lonely spot, out on the field lanes, there was a small fen cottage, in which a man sat beside an open fire, his dog at his feet. It wasn't a cold evening but George Miles, chilled to the marrow, had needed the comforting warmth of its blaze.

'Why me, Alf?' he said to the dog. 'Why, of all the people in this massive county did I have to be the one who found her? It's not fair.'

For years, George had worked hard to put the past as far behind him as he was able. He had left his home and searched out this remote habitation, far from intrusive neighbours and anyone else who once had known him. He had taught himself how to free his mind of unwanted thoughts and memories. He had learned to forget names, faces, places, anything to do with the past. Then, gazing down upon the face of that washed-up body, it had all come flooding back.

'What now, old boy?' he asked of the dog, who opened an eye and shifted closer. 'Will this never end? Or is it just the beginning? They won't say who . . . just that it was a dog walker found her. The police won't give out my name, I've insisted on that.

'But I know things!' At the sound of his raised voice, Alfie opened the other eye, alert. 'Oh God! Now they've killed her. Will they come for me next?' George bent forward and covered his face with his hands. Alfie whined. He reached out and stroked him. 'All I want, little fella, is to hear her sing again. Now that will never happen.' And George Miles wept.

* * *

The quaint old pub in Locksley Fen, renowned for its local ales and excellent food, was a popular venue. Crammed at weekends, you could always get a table on a weekday evening.

They found Rory waiting for them in the car park.

David gazed in awe at the lime-green Citroen Dolly. He nudged Liz. 'He doesn't drive that thing, does he? It's a museum piece!'

'And his pride and joy,' she returned quickly. 'So be nice about it, lad.'

The four of them went inside and found an alcove table, far enough away from the busy bar to be able to hold a conversation without shouting. They ordered without lingering over the menu, and straight away got down to business.

Observing her dinner companions, Liz experienced a sense of unreality. Two retired police detectives, the Home Office pathologist no less, and a university student — all drawn together by the death of a nameless street dweller. It was as if Molly herself hovered above their table, pointing at the clues she had left for them and waiting impatiently for a solution.

Rory cleared his throat and took a sip of his tonic water. 'You know, every so often my immense brain gets side-tracked from the scientific problems it is engaged in and applies its genius to one that is more, well, esoteric. The moment it came to my notice that a body had been found, I had a premonition. Yes, a premonition. I knew this was going to be no ordinary case. I did not see that poor woman in the water as just another murder victim, I saw someone crying out for justice.'

Liz felt a shiver run down her spine. This was exactly the way she too had felt. She saw David and Matt both nodding eagerly.

'And, my dears, when I heard that nasty little boy detective referring to her as some old dropout — well, I felt positively homicidal.' Rory rolled his eyes. 'At that point I decided to liaise directly with your good selves, and protocol be hanged. By the way, Matt, I seem to recall that you were referred to as "some old private-eye bloke".'

Liz gave a snort of laughter.

They chatted about this and that until the food was served. As soon as the waitress disappeared, Rory asked, 'So, what do you know about Molly?'

Liz sighed. 'Not enough, although David is making headway. You see, Molly left us a present before she disappeared.' She looked at David. 'Tell Rory what your daunting task is all about.'

David explained about the bag and his attempts to make sense of its contents. 'All I know for sure is that somehow she found herself in danger, both she and someone else. I get the impression that she was a teacher. You can tell from the way she wrote that she was highly intelligent, which the few people she spoke to have confirmed.'

'We are not even sure when the events she wrote about took place, except that one short piece is dated ten years ago,' Liz said, sprinkling salt on her French fries. 'But something I haven't even told Matt about yet is that Molly was the Night Singer.'

Matt put down his fork and emitted a low whistle. Perplexed, Rory asked what she meant.

'During the last year or so, people in Fenfleet have been hearing someone singing, usually late at night. Matt and I heard it once, and it was so beautiful it stopped us in our tracks. It became a kind of local mystery, at one point even the papers took it up under the headline, "Who is the Night Singer?" No one ever found out — or so we thought. It turns out that everyone in the homeless community knew but no one ever thought to ask them, and they weren't volunteering the information. Molly was a very private woman, but she did tell another street person called Clem that she loved all music. He said she sometimes used to burst into song, quite spontaneously. He said she lifted their spirits and they would all miss her.'

Rory beamed at her. 'Ah, and I have another little soupcon of information to add to that. Molly was a pianist, my dears! The first thing I noticed about her were her beautiful hands. What with her love of music, and if you are correct in your assumption that she was a teacher, I suggest you are looking at a music teacher, possibly a private tutor.'

'Oh yes!' exclaimed David. 'That would take her into private houses. Maybe she discovered something untoward in one of them, something she wasn't supposed to see.'

'Exactly,' said Rory.

'In which case, it's even more important that we find where she used to live, or work,' murmured David. 'Oh dear. I'm not doing very well, am I?'

Liz reached across the table and patted his arm. 'You are doing a grand job, David. Believe me, it would have most people running for the hills. Keep going as you are and you'll find something, don't worry.'

Matt turned to Rory. 'As long as it doesn't put David here off his food, can you tell us what you know about how she died? I hope that's not an inappropriate question given our unofficial status.'

'I sometimes have an unfortunate tendency to talk to myself. If you should overhear me, that's nobody's fault, is it?' Rory gazed thoughtfully at his plate of scampi. 'Asphyxiated, using a men's handkerchief of Swiss lawn cotton, white, with a distinctive hand-rolled grey border. Expensive. Forty-eight centimetres square. Easily traceable to the manufacturer, although a stockist might be more of a challenge. It was not new, but the quality is beyond question, something a discerning gentleman would use.' He looked up at Matt. 'It's my belief that someone surprised her from behind, forced the material into her mouth and, going by the bruising, held her nose clamped tightly shut. She fought, but wouldn't have stood a chance.'

They all fell silent. It must have been a horrible death, fighting for breath against hopeless odds. Liz felt it viscerally. She took a large gulp of water.

Rory glanced at her. 'On a happier note, I've revised my opinion of her age. I don't think she was nearly as old as she seemed, and in her younger days she was probably quite a beauty. She had fine, shapely bone structure. Rough living no doubt aged her physically, though she must have been incredibly strong mentally to have survived as long as she did. I take my hat off to her. That woman deserves all our best efforts to redress the terrible injustice done to her.'

Matt lifted his glass. 'To Molly.'

'And to the Three Musketeers — not forgetting the Countess d'Artagnan, of course,' added Rory. 'An elite band, righting wrongs and fighting for justice.'

They turned their attention to their food, while Liz told Rory about the gold ring, the missing sleeping bag containing a letter from Molly, along with Clem's quest to get it back.

'That poor woman,' murmured Rory. 'Desperate to reveal the truth but too afraid to speak.'

David put down his knife and fork with a clatter. 'Of course!' The others stared at him. 'Sorry, folks. Something I'd been wondering about just fell into place. It was Molly's love of music. Liz, do you remember me telling you about what she wrote about the moon landing? I noticed that she spelled "planets" with a capital P. She was talking about The Planets Suite, wasn't she — you know, by Gustav Holst. When she said "they returned to the Planets", she and this Benjamin were listening to that piece of music. I reckon Rory's right — she was a private music teacher and Benjamin was her pupil.'

Rory looked at him over the top of his glasses. 'Dear boy, you have much to learn. Rory is *always* right. But well done. Oh, and before I forget — regarding Molly's age. I think she deliberately made herself look old. The clothes she wore and the way she did her hair were an attempt to disguise herself so that she'd be unrecognisable to anyone who came looking for her. I believe "Old Molly" wasn't old at all, in fact her age was more like fifty-five to sixty.'

'So, she was around forty-five to fifty when this terrible thing happened.' Liz nodded thoughtfully. 'Maybe I should speak to someone in the music or teaching world. Ten years isn't that long when you think about it. Someone might know of a woman who gave private music lessons, probably piano. Someone who suddenly stopped teaching.' Liz knew no one in that field but there was a college of music in Greenborough. She could start there.

'We could dredge up some old local newspapers and check the classified ads,' suggested David. 'Or Google piano teachers. Some of those listings aren't updated and they hang about for years.'

Liz smiled at him. 'At least we now have a specific area of interest to concentrate on. Meanwhile, this incident or discovery or whatever it was could have happened at the other end of the country for all we know, and Molly came here because no one in this area knew her. Then all our local research will have been pointless. We have to have a place.'

'Why not go back to Chris Lamont in the library?' suggested Matt. 'He might have picked up some indication of where she was from, like the trace of an accent, or her reading material. Maybe she liked to read about a certain place. And I'd get hold of Clem again and ask him if he thought she seemed to know her way about, or if she behaved like a stranger. He might know more about her than he realises.'

'Good idea,' Liz said. 'I'll start with Chris and then I'll hit the streets and look for Clem. If only we knew where Smokey Joe has gone. Clem had an idea they knew each other from before.'

'Forgive me for sounding like the Prophet of Doom, dear hearts,' said Rory. 'But you do know this doesn't bode well for this Smokey person? If they were indeed close, he might know what happened, which means he's either dead in a ditch or is being hunted by Molly's killer.'

'That's what we're afraid of, Rory. He could well be miles away from here by now, and then we'll know nothing about it. The death of a vagrant isn't going to make the headlines,' said Matt. 'Swifty Fleet is going to keep an ear to the ground for me but I can see Smokey slipping through the net. The one person who may know more than anyone, and he's nowhere to be found.'

'Well, as you know, yours truly covers the whole of the Fens,' said Rory. 'I can also ask some of my colleagues from the neighbouring counties to notify me of any homeless men that land on their tables.'

'That would help a lot,' said Matt, 'although we have to hope that we can get to him before that happens. He won't have much to say to us from a mortuary table. Our main problem right now is that we already had a case running before this happened, and it's got to take precedence. A missing teenager, Rory, a boy with a history of running away, but this time something bad really does seem to have happened to him.'

'Well, I hate to say this, but perhaps you should give me a description — you know, just in case. Dearie me, I am a right little pessimist, aren't I?'

'Nevertheless, you do have a point,' said Liz sombrely.

Matt dived into his inside jacket pocket and produced a photograph of Liam. 'It's fairly recent. He was last seen wearing denim jeans, a white T-shirt and a grey and black hoodie with a designer logo on the back. He had on black trainers — the parents weren't sure of the make but his sisters think they were Nike.' He paused. 'I suppose you've never heard of a place called the Bunker, have you, Rory? We have no idea if it's relevant or not, but apparently Liam kept going on about it, and so far we haven't been able to trace it.'

Rory shook his head. 'It doesn't sound like the sort of place a delicate soul like me would frequent. However, if anyone knows about it, Spike will. He patronises all the dens of iniquity. I shall ask him first thing in the morning.'

They turned to happier matters, mostly Rory's recent holiday. He had been cruising the Scottish islands, which he'd been wanting to do since he was a boy. Then it was time to haggle over the bill — Matt won. While he went to pay, Rory turned to Liz. 'Do your best for Molly, my dear. I'll assist wherever I can. She will be relying on us, I'm afraid. The police will definitely not be moving heaven and earth to find her killer.'

'Don't worry, Rory. We feel the same as you about Molly. And we appreciate your help.'

He coughed discreetly. 'I suggest we keep that last, er, activity a jealously guarded secret from officialdom, if that's all right with you?'

'Of course, and if your Spike comes up with any ideas about Matt's Bunker, he'll be eternally grateful. It's driving him mad.' Liz laughed.

They watched the lime-green Citroen disappear into the night, David smiling broadly. 'What a character! Is he really as clever as you say he is?'

'You better believe it, Davey-boy,' said Matt. 'That man is the sharpest pathologist I've ever come across, and I'm so pleased he's batting on our team.'

'Matt's right,' added Liz. 'Don't underestimate our Rory. We've never had access to forensic information before, and if it comes from Rory, it will be detailed and accurate. Rory's help could be key to finding who killed Molly — and why. We just need a bit more information from that bag of writings.'

David made a face. 'Then I'd better pull my finger out and find us a location, hadn't I?'

'That's the plan, lad,' said Matt gravely. 'Because if I have to ask Liz to help me with finding Liam, Molly will be relying solely on you.'

David rolled his eyes. 'Oh great! No pressure then?'

CHAPTER EIGHT

Una steadily made her way along the edge of the watercourse, the shovel of the Bobcat rising and falling as it scraped silt and mud and other detritus from the base of the ditch. Most people considered ditch-clearing to be mind-numbingly boring but she found it deeply satisfying. Watercourse maintenance was the responsibility of every landowner in the county, from massive farms to small plots, anywhere that had a ditch, a dyke, a culvert, or any other form of watercourse bordering their land. With the aim of assisting farmers to do this work, her grandfather had set up the small business with just a few pieces of basic machinery almost four decades ago. Now they were one of the most successful companies in the Fens, and granddaughter Una Johnson their most experienced engineer.

She had been working since first light, and was now in need of something to eat. Ten more minutes and she could take a break and have a late breakfast. The stretch she was working on wasn't that bad, mostly silt and a few minor blockages, nothing too arduous.

At the junction with the next field, she brought the Bobcat to a halt and reached for her lunchbox and flask. She poured a beaker of hot tea, took a large homemade sandwich from the box and gazed out across the vast expanse of fields.

Mornings on the Fens were the best time to be out. When the rumble and clatter of her Bobcat fell silent, peace descended upon the vast expanse of land. Beneath the huge canopy of sky, a breeze swayed the rushes. Somewhere a bird called. Una munched contentedly on her sandwich, at one with her surroundings.

She was pleased to be able to care for the land in this way. It was important work. They did their best to limit the impact on wildlife by doing the bulk of their work during the autumn and winter months. They also advised farmers not to clear entire ditch lengths in a single year but to work a rotation system that would allow local wildlife to recolonise the recently cleared ditches. That was what she was doing today. At the junction of the two watercourses that flanked the fields, she would leave the stretch to the left, and begin the one on the right, along the second field.

Una was about to start the Bobcat when something caught her eye. The next length of dyke was a bit more over-grown than the previous one, with patches of vegetation that had grown right down into the water. Most of these plants were no problem — the grabber would make short work of them — but it was important to make sure that it wasn't an invasive non-native species that if left unchecked, would choke out the native plants and reduce their value to wildlife.

It wasn't so much the vegetation that bothered her now. It was something else, an object protruding slightly from the foliage. She muttered a curse. Why people insisted on driving miles out into farmland to dump their rubbish while the local tip was closer at hand never ceased to amaze and irritate her. Just recently there had been an influx of rogue traders, offering to remove household waste for a small fee, then driving the rubbish on to the Fen and dumping it into the watercourses. It made Una's blood boil. It wasn't just the damage to the environment; the obstruction could cause the area to flood.

Una climbed out of the cab and lowered herself to the ground. Old Bob, her trusty excavator, would grab anything, but she liked to know what she was dealing with. As she walked across the overgrown edge to the ditch, she saw something totally unexpected.

'Smoke?' she whispered to herself. She slowed down and approached more cautiously. 'What the . . . ?'

Una found herself staring at an old bicycle, its front wheel buckled from its descent down the bank, and an ancient galvanised bucket. The smoke was issuing from the bucket. It had become wedged firmly into some of the vegetation that Una had been about to dredge up, and in it a handful of coals were still burning.

As she stood, wondering what on earth it was doing there, her phone rang. A cheerful voice asked where she was and if she'd had her break.

'Actually, I'm standing on the edge of a ditch trying to make sense of something I'm looking at,' she said.

'Oh, no. Not more fly-tipping?' asked Tom, her husband.

'No, not exactly. It's a bike that looks like it belonged to Methuselah, and would you believe—'

'Hang on!' interrupted Tom. 'It's not a bucket, is it?'

'Well, yes. How on earth did—?'

'Where are you, babe? I mean the exact spot.'

'In the fields on Raven's Lane, about a mile from Jim Campbell's farmhouse. But what's this all about, Tom?'

'I'll see you in around fifteen minutes. Just hang on there, would you, and do me a favour, don't touch anything, okay? Especially don't let Old Bob get his jaws around anything.'

After she'd ended the call, she went back to the Bobcat and poured herself another beaker of tea. What on earth did Tom want with a bike and a bucket? He was a police sergeant, for heaven's sake. He wasn't going to turn out for a bit of dumped rubbish, and anyway, it was the council's problem, not the police's. And how did he know about that bucket?

* * *

'The Bunker? What do you want to know about that for, Prof?' Spike asked.

'It's been mentioned in dispatches, petal. So I was wondering, dear Spike, since you frequent — how can I put it — a rather *different* sort of milieu to mine own, you may possibly have heard of it.'

'Mmm. I'm not sure if I can be of much help there, Prof. I don't even know if it really exists. I've always thought it must be one of those urban myths.' Spike placed a liver on the scales and called out the weight. 'What's the interest, Prof? Who is asking about it?'

'A friend of mine, and it's to do with a missing teenager. So, if you wish to escape the wrath of Wilkinson, tell me what you know about it.'

'Well, for a start, no one seems to know where it is, or even what it's about, but it's of great interest to teenage boys.'

'So, there could be a link between a missing sixteen-year-old and this mythical place?' asked Rory.

'Quite probably,' said Spike, and continued with his innards. 'Look, if it's important, I'll have a word with a bloke I know. He runs a local youth football club. If anyone's heard about it, Ewan will. The kids he coaches chatter, and he listens. I'll give it a try for you, if you like.'

'I should be eternally grateful, sweet Spike! And the sooner the better, if you wouldn't mind. My friend is extremely anxious about this missing youth — a lad called Liam Cooper by the way — and he fears for his safety.'

'Okay,' said Spike. 'I'll give Ewan a call at break, and try to check him at lunchtime. He's the manager of the sports shop in the High Street, so he's not far away.'

Passing Spike another internal organ, Rory said, 'Look, I can finish off here. Ring him now, and if he can see you, go straightaway.'

'It must be pretty important then,' said Spike. 'Okay, I'll see what I can do.'

Rory continued with the post-mortem. After a couple of minutes, he saw Spike wave from the doorway. 'I'm off there now, Prof. Won't be long.'

'Good. And if you pass the café on your way back, would you bring us some proper coffee and a Danish, and I'll reimburse you when you return. Good luck with your mission.'

* * *

On seeing Spike walk into his shop, Ewan Peart grinned. 'Have I finally convinced you that you'd make a great coach for the under-elevens?'

'Sadly, no. And as I have two left feet, it's probably for the best.'

'Ah well, can't say I didn't try.' Ewan glanced behind him. 'Michelle! Watch the till for me, please. I'll be in the back office if you need me.'

A wafer-thin girl in a black Reebok T-shirt acknowledged him with a wave and sauntered up to the till. 'Okay, Ewan. I'll finish the pricing later.'

In the office, Ewan flopped down at his desk and indicated the only other chair. 'So, if you're not offering to coach, why the visit? Everything all right, is it?'

Spike liked Ewan, he was one of life's decent people, someone who always had time for others. Plus, he was a brilliant sportsman and very happy to share his skill on the football field with anyone who wanted to learn, especially the young. 'I'm fine, mate. It's my boss. He's worried about a missing kid — a boy called Liam Cooper.'

'I know Liam, though not well. He's a bit of a handful. I once tried to get him to join the football team, because he's a strong kid, but he wasn't interested. Missing again, is he?'

'Again?'

'Must be the third or fourth time, I reckon.' Ewan shook his head. 'His poor parents. They even hired a private detective to go after him.'

So that's why Rory was interested, thought Spike, knowing who the private detective must be. 'Well, apparently the people that are looking for him think something bad may have happened to him this time.'

Ewan grunted. 'Crying wolf as they say. One thing I can tell you is that Liam isn't the street-wise kid he makes himself out to be. He's a cocky little bugger, a bit of a prat to be honest.' He sat back and clasped his hands behind his head. 'Sorry, but I can't help you there, I haven't seen him for months.'

'It's not Liam himself I wanted to ask you about actually. Apparently, just before he disappeared, he was going on about this place called the Bunker. It seems nobody knows anything about it.'

'Oh.' Ewan leaned forward, frowning.

'So, you know it then,' said Spike. 'Come on, tell me. It could be really important.'

'Listen, this is all word of mouth, and mainly from the kids, so don't take it as gospel,' said Ewan.

'Sure,' said Spike, 'and your name won't come into it if you're worried about losing the trust of your young 'uns.'

'I appreciate that. It's taken some of the boys and girls I'm working with a long time to come round to opening up to me. I can't risk losing that.' He put his elbows on the desk. 'The one thing I *don't* know is where this place is, which is a bit of a bummer, but as far as I can gather, it's a kind of adventure park. Like an assault course for kids — sort of a boot camp.'

'That doesn't sound too harmful,' said Spike. 'An adventure park?'

'If that was all it was, I'd take the kids there myself,' said Ewan. 'But there's more to it than meets the eye. There's this one lad I'm coaching who's been in the team a few months now. He's an ace player, fast and very skilled for a fourteen-year-old. I'm going to see if I can get a scout down to see him, because he deserves a place in a professional club.'

'And he's been to this Bunker place?' asked Spike.

'Yeah. He went a couple of times and never went again. He's very cagey about it, won't say what it was like or why he stopped going. It was almost like he was scared of something.' Ewan stood up abruptly. 'I'm going to grab a coffee. Want one?'

'Yes, please.' This was getting interesting.

Ewan made the coffee, handing Spike a mug with a football club logo on it. 'I'm not giving you my lad's name, let's just call him call him Toby. It's taken me forever to get anything out of him.' He glanced briefly at Spike, who nodded. 'The first thing you need to know is that there's a certain kind of kid that gets to hear about this place. They are all either tearaways, or from homes where the parents don't give a toss about what happens to them. Toby's dad is an alcoholic and his mum did a runner years ago.'

'That fits in with this Liam kid, doesn't it?' added Spike. 'He's got a good home but he's wild and prone to running away.'

'Exactly. Now, no one knows where the Bunker is because anyone who wants to go there is collected by car — well, a van actually. They are bundled in the back and told they are going on a mission to a secret location.' Ewan shook his head. 'They think it's the coolest thing ever.'

'How do they know where to meet this van?' asked Spike.

'Clearly someone does their homework on these kids. Only the type I've described are selected. The ones who've been chosen are approached by this friendly older guy who asks them if they'd like a free fun day out — no strings and no payment involved. If they say yes, they are given a date and a time to be picked up. The next time they go, they are sent a message.' He tapped the mobile phone on his desk. 'Time and place.'

'What is this place like? Did Toby describe it?'

'It's a mini assault course. You know the kind, Spike, where you swing, climb, crawl, jump, and sweat your way over obstacles, up nets, and through mud and water. There are instructors on hand, keeping an eye on them and giving out advice. Toby said that to start with it was brilliant.'

'And he went back?'

'Yeah, and it was more of the same, but this time Toby noticed that a couple of the kids from the van were taken off to a big barn, away from the others. When it was time to be taken home, these kids went back with them but he reckoned they looked kind of different.' Ewan shrugged. 'Don't ask me what he meant, he couldn't say more than that they seemed cagey, as if they knew some big secret and he wasn't included. He probably wouldn't have made too much of it, except that he overheard what the two kids were saying to each other on the way home, and he didn't like what he heard.'

This was beginning to sound sinister.

Ewan had obviously guessed where his thoughts were going. 'Don't get ahead of yourself, Spike. I don't think whoever is running this thing is a pervert, but there is definitely a dark side to it. I've been thinking about what Toby intimated, and I've come to the conclusion that someone is vetting these kids with a purpose in mind. From what Toby said, they pass through three stages. The first is the adventure course, probably to assess their fitness and determination. If they show sufficient aptitude, they are taken to the barn, and from what Toby overheard, they go before a selection committee. He heard one of the boys refer to it as a sort of "Who Dares Wins".'

Spike let out a low whistle. 'But what's the aim? You said there's a third stage.'

Ewan shrugged. 'I have no idea what that might be. Whatever it is, it has to be something heavy, or why all the secrecy?'

'And the kids don't talk about it openly? That's weird in itself,' said Spike.

'I'm certain they had the frighteners put on them,' said Ewan. 'That, or they were talked into believing that they were part of some really cool secret organisation. Hell, it made me so angry to think that Toby almost got caught up in it. He's got a great future ahead of him, and he might have blown the whole thing. I'm desperate to find out more about it but I daren't question my kids too closely and risk losing their trust. Right now, we make a pretty good team.'

'I get that,' Spike said. 'I'll tell my boss what you said but I won't mention any names. It sounds to me like Liam could well have got himself mixed up in it.'

Ewan glanced at his watch. 'Well, mate, I'd better get out on the shop floor, I've got a rep calling in a little while. Keep me updated, won't you. The thought that someone is taking vulnerable young people and messing with them . . . it makes my blood boil.'

Spike stood up. 'I'd better get back too. By the way, I suppose you haven't mentioned this to the police?'

Ewan shook his head. 'What could I say? No kid was ever going to come forward, so they'd just dismiss it as a waste of time.'

'Probably. Well, thanks for the coffee. I'll let you know what comes of it.'

Spike had just turned to go when Ewan said, 'If stage one is the playground, and stage two is the barn, stage three must be the Bunker.'

* * *

Liz found Clem in the churchyard giving Gunner a run, and inferred from his gloomy countenance that he still hadn't found the sleeping bag. She handed him a sandwich she had made before leaving Cannon Farm and sat down next to him on the stone seat. 'I'm here to pick your brains again, old friend,' she said softly.

'Not much left to pick these days, DS Haynes.'

It appeared that she would always remain DS Haynes to Clem.

'I've got some of the others looking out for that sleeping bag,' he said dejectedly, 'but we reckon it was a drifter took it, so it's goodbye to that letter, I'm afraid.' Clem stared into the middle distance where his dog played among the gravestones. 'And goodbye to the one thing that could have told you why she was murdered.'

'We'll find out anyway, Clem. With or without that letter, we won't let it drop until we get an answer,' said Liz, with more assurance than she felt. 'Now, can you tell me anything more about her, like do you think she was a local, or an incomer?'

He thought about this. 'I reckon local, although her education had knocked the accent off her. She sometimes used Fen expressions that anyone who wasn't born here wouldn't know. Now I think about it, she knew her way around the county too — you'd only have to mention a place and she'd know where you meant. Yes, she was definitely from these parts, she just never said where.'

That was something, Liz supposed. 'What about her music? Did she ever say where she learned to play?'

'She never even told us she *could* play, but we guessed.' He smiled for the first time since Liz's arrival. 'She sometimes used to sort of play tunes in the air, you know what I mean, like she was playing a piano.'

'The one time I heard the Night Singer, she was singing a popular song. Was that the sort of music she preferred?' Liz asked.

'Oh no. Like I said before, she loved all music, didn't matter what. I don't know about these modern songs, I just liked to hear her sing. She could have sung "Any Old Iron" and I'd have enjoyed it.' He grew despondent again. 'But that's all gone now.'

Liz decided he probably had little else to tell her. Saying goodbye to Clem, she went next to the library.

Chris Lamont was arranging a display of crime novels on a table when she arrived. 'Any news on our Molly?'

'You heard they found her, I suppose,' Liz said. The small-town grapevine was generally efficient.

He nodded. 'Everyone knows, and the rumours are flying thick and fast. As you can imagine, everyone has a theory about who did it.' He set down his pile of books. 'Do you guys know anything solid yet?'

'Oh, you know how it is, Chris. We're trying to gather as much information as we can about her, but when someone never talks about themselves it makes it bloody hard work. You probably know more about Molly than anyone.'

'And that's pretty well sod all,' he said. 'I've been racking my brains to try and remember anything she mentioned that could possibly be of help. I've even gone through some of the books she liked to read, just hunting for some clue, but — zilch.' He scratched his head. 'I suppose you haven't had any luck with tracing Smokey Joe?'

'Sadly, no,' said Liz. 'He's disappeared off the face of the earth. That's nothing new, I know, but I wish he hadn't chosen this particular time to go on one of his walkabouts. The police are keeping an eye open but he's not high on their list of priorities.'

'As will be the whole case,' said Chris wryly. 'Who's dealing with it? Do you know?'

'DCI Anders was pretty hard pushed to find anyone who wasn't up to their necks in other serious cases, so I'm afraid it's DC Darren Norton,' she said gloomily.

'Oh, shit. The chief super's darling grandson. I can't see golden boy Norton pulling out all the stops for a bag lady, I have to say.'

'All I'm going to say is that it's probably a good thing Matt and I have picked it up. Oh, and I have my nephew working with us. He's sifting through Molly's bag as we speak. David's no Darren Norton, he's well up for the challenge.'

'Thank heavens for that,' Chris said.

'Chris, you said you were looking at the books Molly read,' Liz added. 'What were they?'

'Come into the reference room and I'll show you.' Chris led the way into a small room lined with bookcases, with a reading table and a long casement window looking out over the gardens at the back of the library. 'This room isn't much used, so I'd pop Molly in here with a cuppa and let her read for as long as she liked. At first, I was a bit careful what she handled, giving her books that had seen better days, but I soon saw that in fact, she was far from dirty. I noticed, too, that she had these fine, graceful hands. She handled the books better than most of the other readers we get in here.'

'We believe she might have been a music tutor — a pianist, to be precise,' said Liz.

'Oh well, that answers a few questions,' said Chris, running his hand along one of the shelves. 'Ah, got it.' He took down a hefty volume and handed it to Liz.

The title read: *Fryderyk Chopin, a biography of his life and times.*

'She loved this book,' said Chris, pulling out two chairs. 'To the point where I offered to give it to her. I said I'd report it as damaged, and request a replacement copy. She declined, but thinking back on it now, she said something a bit odd.'

'Odd?'

'She said, "Thank you, I appreciate the offer but I can't accept it. Just remember that this book is important. This book is my favourite, and it's special." I didn't think much about it at the time, but looking back, wasn't that a slightly strange thing to say?'

Liz stared at the book in her hands. 'Molly seems to have been very fond of leaving clues for us, so maybe . . .' She flicked through the pages, half expecting something to fall out. 'Or maybe not.' She closed the book again. 'Perhaps it really was only a favourite book because she loved his work.'

'Chopin was a child prodigy,' said Chris. 'He was composing complex pieces at the age of six, and at one point in his short life he was a piano tutor. Perhaps there's a link there if she was a gifted musician herself?'

Liz didn't answer immediately. She was thinking of the ring, the letter hidden in a sleeping bag. This book had to be significant. 'Can I borrow it, Chris? Just in case it turns out to be relevant.'

'Of course. I won't stamp a return date on it, keep it as long as you like. It's hardly a popular volume.'

With the book under her arm, Liz left the library, returned to her car and rang David. 'Just touching base,' she said. 'If all is well with you, I'm going to head directly to the school of music in Greenborough. Someone there might know something about private tutors that were around a decade ago.'

He was fine, he said, but wasn't she overdoing it? He offered to go with her and drive if necessary. Touched by his concern, Liz nevertheless assured him that she was having a "good" day, and that Greenborough wasn't far. She would be back home by one p.m. unless she found any more leads to pursue.

As she drove out of town, she received a call from Matt. For once, he sounded upbeat about the case, having had a call from Rory with info on the Bunker.

'It exists all right, Liz. At last I know it's not a crock of shit and that I'm not wasting my time. I have a very strong feeling that Liam and the Bunker are connected. It's a step forward, even if I'm not sure in what direction.'

She told him of her plans, and they agreed to try to get home by two p.m. for a late lunch and a catch up. David would need a break from those papers, that was for sure.

'Poor kid,' said Matt. 'Rather him than me. Tell you what, Liz, let's treat him to a slap-up dinner at Bernie's place tonight. He really enjoyed his meal at the Pear Tree last time he stayed with us. What do you say?'

'Shall I book, or will you?' she returned immediately, pleased at the prospect of not having to cook. Although I suspect you have an ulterior motive. You reckon Bernie might have some inside info on the Bunker, do you?'

'Let's just call it two birds with one stone. I'll ring him directly. See you later, and don't forget that I love you.'

'As if I could. Love you too.' Smiling happily, Liz took the road to Greenborough.

CHAPTER NINE

Over at the other side of the CID room, DCI Charlotte Anders was holding an animated discussion with a couple of other detectives. As soon as he spotted her glance over at his workstation, DC Darren Norton put his head down and pretended to be deeply engrossed in a document on his desk. She left the two officers and made her way towards him. He could almost feel the temperature drop as she approached. It was obvious that she disliked him, and the feeling was mutual. Not that it mattered. With his connections, he was almost fireproof.

'Where are you with Molly's murder, DC Norton?' she asked curtly. 'Any progress?'

'I've spoken to the pathologist. I'm waiting on his post-mortem findings. I also had a call from the private detective agency. We will keep each other updated, ma'am, but there's nothing yet.'

'Any news on the ring, and where it came from?'

He frowned, puzzled. Ring? What ring?

'The bag of letters then.'

This meant nothing either. 'Sorry?'

'You said you'd spoken to the private detectives. Have you actually gone to see them? Are you aware of what they have to date?' Her voice rose. 'You do know the meaning of the word *liaise*, DC Norton, don't you?'

When he didn't answer, she said, 'They know a great deal more than you do, Detective, and why is that? Because they are committed to finding who killed that unfortunate woman, as you should be. As things stand, you are not convincing me that that is the case. I suggest you ring them right now and go and talk to them in person. You might think a street person isn't worth wasting your time over but, apart from the fact that every life taken has a right to be investigated properly, there is more to this case than meets the eye, and I want to know what that is.' She stared at him coldly. 'Do your job, Detective.'

He watched her leave the office, cursing under his breath. He should not be working crap like this. He should be with the team running the big drug smuggling investigation, not trying to find out who topped a vagrant. Who bloody cared? It was just one less to step over in the street. Even so, he did wonder what Anders meant by *more to it than meets the eye*. With a grunt of annoyance, he picked up the phone. He could do without another bollocking from that woman, especially not in the CID room. Luckily no one seemed to have noticed, and at least she'd kept her voice down. Better get genned up on this poxy ring and bag of letters, whatever they were about, then he wouldn't get caught out again.

If he'd disliked Anders before, he really hated her now. Maybe it was time for a few well-chosen words with Granddad.

The bloke answered. 'Hello, Matt Ballard here.'

Norton tried to muster a pleasant tone. 'Ah, yes. DC Norton here. I was wondering if it would be convenient for us to meet for a catch up — maybe later today?'

'I'm just on my way home, Darren. We could meet there if you like. Say three p.m.? Liz should be back by then. Do you know Tanner's Fen? Well, we're at Cannon Farm.'

'I'll find it,' Norton said, not having the slightest idea where Tanner's Fen was.

'Well, don't rely on your satnav or you'll probably end up in the Wash. We are a mile outside the village and close to the sea bank. See you then.'

'I can hardly wait,' muttered Norton when he'd put the phone down.

It seemed to him that there were two ways of dealing with this. One was to try and clear this poxy pseudo-investigation as fast as possible, and get on to something worth doing, or . . . let the private dicks do the work, and he could put his feet up. If they came up with anything useful, he would record it as a finding of his, but right now he had no option but to go out to Tanners Fen. He might as well see what they'd dug up, then decide how to play it.

Meanwhile, he had a good two hours before he needed to leave, so he slid out his iPad from beneath the papers on his desk and continued playing "Call of Duty".

* * *

Matt pulled up outside his front door and was about to lock the car when his phone rang again.

'Look,' said Charley Anders without preamble. 'I'm fully aware that my choice of officer to handle Molly's case wasn't exactly inspired and I'm sorry about that but, shit, Matt, everyone else is tied up tighter than Houdini.'

Matt laughed. 'I remember that feeling well, Charley, so don't apologise — even though I must admit to being less than enthused by young Norton's attitude.'

'I can imagine,' she said testily. 'But believe it or not, I do have method in my madness. For one thing, he thinks he's safe from scrutiny, but there have been several complaints about him and I don't intend to brush them under the carpet, chief super's grandson or not. If you don't mind, I'd like a report from you on how he discharges his duty. It needs to be acceptable at the very least.'

'Of course. I'll make sure we monitor his progress for you. I'll be sending you regular updates on our findings anyway, so I'll add a report on his performance.'

'I'd appreciate that, Matt,' said Charley. 'My other reason for using him is that if he could just lose these delusions of grandeur of his, I think there could be a bright young detective lurking somewhere beneath that arrogant exterior. I'm hoping that working with someone of your experience on an investigation of his own, he might just rise to the occasion.'

'I didn't have you down as an optimist, Charley,' said Matt, 'but leave it with me and Liz. We'll do all we can to drag the best out of Norton — if we can find it.'

Charley laughed. 'Best of luck with that. But, on a more serious note, this is make or break for that young man, even if he's not aware of it yet. I'll go higher than the chief superintendent if I have to.'

'Received and understood. Give us a few days to get the ball rolling, and I'll keep you updated. As a matter of fact, Norton phoned me a few minutes ago, he's coming here at three p.m. for a meeting.'

'Yeah, that's because I shoved a rocket up his arse,' she said. 'But let's take it from here. Oh, and thank you, Matt. I appreciate it. I'd hate to lose what might be a good officer, but on the other hand, I will not tolerate a bad apple in my team. So, let's see what a bit of the old Ballard-Haynes magic can produce.'

Deep in thought, Matt walked across to the house. Ballard-Haynes magic, eh? This could turn out to be a harder nut to crack than the very case itself.

* * *

Liz arrived at the old riverside building housing the School of Music and Performing Arts at around midday. The interior was something of a revelation — the old three-storey wharf had been completely renovated. She saw signs for recording studios, DJ suites, an auditorium and a bar. The twenty-first century had well and truly arrived in Greenborough.

'Hello, I'm Carrie. Can I help you?' The young woman, an identity badge on a lanyard around her neck, looked about twelve.

'Er, yes, but it's a bit of an odd request.' Liz glanced at the colourful posters advertising Debut Gigs and Open Mic Nights and her hopes sank. No one in this stylish building would possibly remember anything from before about 2022. 'The thing is, I'm trying to find a woman who taught piano in this area around ten years ago or thereabouts. We believe that she became a private tutor, and we are anxious to trace her.' She took out her card and handed it to the young woman.

'Private detective . . . Oh my!' exclaimed the girl. 'What's she done?'

Got herself murdered. 'Oh, nothing bad,' Liz said. 'We'd just like to find out about her history. Is there anyone here — perhaps someone who teaches piano — who might be able to tell me?'

'I think you need to talk to Georgia. She's one of the senior tutors and has been here for years. Shall I see if she's free to talk to you?'

'That would be great, thank you.'

About to return to the reception desk, Carrie paused. 'Failing that, there's Nathan Venner, a local musician who teaches keyboard. As far as I know, he's lived here all his life. He's a really cool guy. He's still in a band, which is awesome. He doesn't just play keyboard either, he's a classical pianist as well. He's in Recording Studio three now, if you want to talk to him.'

'Why not?' said Liz. 'Can you show me where to go?'

'I'll take you, no problem.'

It was quite a walk to the recording studios, which were on the other side of the campus. The light above the door of studio three showed green, so Carrie ushered Liz into a state-of-the-art recording studio, where a lone musician was busy adjusting the levers of a digital audio workstation.

'Nathan,' Carrie said. 'Have you got a couple of minutes to talk to this lady? She's a private detective.'

Nathan's eyes widened. 'I never did it! Honest, guv.'

From a distance, Liz had taken him for a rock musician, seeing his black hair and gypsy looks. Close to, the grey in his long curls and the creases around his eyes when he smiled told her he was probably in his fifties. He was an attractive man who seemed unaware of it. Liz took to him at once. She introduced herself. 'Carrie here tells me you've lived in Greenborough all your life, so I wondered if you might be able to help me. I'm looking for the answer to a couple of questions.'

He pointed to a stool beside him. 'Please, sit. I'm happy to help if I can. What do you want to know?'

His expression was open and friendly, so Liz had no compunction in telling him about the case. A woman had died, and they were trying to find her identity. From the little they knew of her, they believed her to have been a pianist and a singer. 'We think she might have been a private tutor somewhere in this area, so I'm keen to find anyone who knew her — or of her.'

Nathan sat back on his stool. 'Ten years ago, you say?'

'It appears she was teaching privately at around that time.' Liz looked at him more closely. 'I know you, don't I? Didn't you play at a police charity ball about three years ago?'

'That was a real piss up, that was.' Nathan grinned. 'Coppers can certainly drink when they put their minds to it. Yes, it was me and my band, Fen Myst. You were there too, a detective, weren't you? I remember you because you spoke to me afterwards about one of the songs.'

'You've got a good memory, Nathan. I was really impressed by your playing, quite blown away. And now you teach?'

'I've always taught, ever since I left the conservatoire.' He ran a hand through his hair. 'Yes, I'm classically trained, but my real love is modern music, so now I'm living the dream, teaching young people who want to give their lives to making music.' His eyes had a faraway look. 'Anyway. Former music teachers.'

He was silent for a while. 'Only one woman springs to mind, although I can't be certain whether she ever went into private tutoring. She taught, certainly, in several schools of music, and I know she was at the Guildhall School of Music and Drama in London in her younger days. She was both talented and gifted.' He raised an eyebrow. 'There is a difference, you know. You can be a talented musician, technically, but a gift is something innate that can't be taught. Well, twelve, maybe fifteen years ago, she left the area, at least I assume she did, because I never saw her again.'

'What was her name, Nathan?' Liz asked.

'Marika.' He smiled, reminiscently. 'Marika Molohan.'

Molohan? Molly? That could be right. Liz recalled the MM engraved on the ring. Had they finally discovered her real name? Liz thought for a moment. 'Did you ever hear the Night Singer?'

Nathan laughed. 'I certainly did, many times. I spent almost three weeks of my life about six months ago, just searching for her. I'd give my eye teeth to have a singer like that in my band. But, sadly, I never found her. Are you telling me that voice in the night belonged to Marika?'

'It belonged to the dead woman, we are sure of that. But you've heard both Marika and the Night Singer. Could they be one and the same?'

He thought again. 'Yes, now you tell me . . . I mean, I never thought of it before but, yes, it could be. And you say she's dead?' He heaved a sigh. 'What a god-awful waste!'

Liz saw his eyes grow moist.

'How did she die?' he asked. 'An accident?'

'I can't say much at this stage, Nathan, but I'm sorry to say she was murdered.'

Nathan Venner looked thunderstruck. 'Who the hell would . . . That woman was simply wonderful in every respect. Who would possibly want to deliberately kill her?'

'Well, someone did,' said Liz simply. 'So, you can see why I was so keen to find out who she was.'

He stared at her. 'How come you are investigating this? No disrespect, but I'd have thought it would be a police matter.'

'We were already looking for her before the police found her body, Nathan.' She looked at him seriously. 'I can't go into the circumstances under which she was found, but in light of them we have decided to continue our investigation. The police will no doubt be speaking to you as well, and we shall be informing them of our belief that the woman is Marika Molohan. I'd like to tell you more, but I'm afraid that's all I can say at the moment.'

He leaned forward and rested his chin on his hands. 'I suppose I could identify her, if it would help.'

'It would be down to the police to agree to that, but I think it would be a massive leap forward in the inquiry. I should warn you though, life has not treated her well. Apart from being dragged out of the river, she is . . . considerably aged. You see, it appears that in the last years of her life she was destitute.'

'Surely not. She was a genius, she could have found work anywhere she chose. What on earth happened to her?' Nathan looked astounded.

'That, Nathan, is exactly what we are going to find out,' she said firmly. 'With your help, I hope?'

'Yes, of course. I'll do whatever I can. This is just horrible.'

'I'm sorry this is so upsetting for you, but is there anything you can tell me about Marika? Where did she live? Was she married? What was she like as a person?'

'Do you have a few minutes?' Nathan asked. 'I don't have a tutorial for an hour, and I live close by. If you like, I can show you some pictures of Marika when she was younger. We did a great gig once, she joined me for a couple of numbers and brought the house down. I've still got the photos of that night.'

Liz agreed immediately. They left the campus and walked through the main street into a narrow, cobbled cul de sac.

'I'm the last place on the right, that big red brick building. It used to be a warehouse, but then it was turned into apartments and studio spaces.' Nathan took a bunch of keys from his pocket. 'It suits me perfectly. I've even got my own soundproof studio attached to my flat.'

The cavernous interior reminded Liz of a miniature version of the Tate Modern, not somewhere Liz would like to live, with its visible pipes and ducts and unplastered walls, but she could see how it would suit a musician.

'Over here.' He pointed to a high brick wall that was covered in photographs, all framed in grey aluminium.

'Wow! You've played with some big names, Nathan. Isn't that Eric Clapton?'

He laughed. 'Those were the days. Still, I don't regret them. I've never been happier than I am now, teaching kids. Now where . . . Ah, here we are.' He lifted one of the photographs from the wall and handed it to Liz. It featured a band on a brilliantly lit stage. Liz recognised Nathan on piano, with a woman singer at front of stage, holding a mike.

'That's Marika. She was so alive.' He shook his head. 'I can't believe she's dead.'

Could she really be looking at Molly the Bag Lady? Liz was overwhelmed by the injustice of life. This woman radiated energy, and she was very beautiful. Molly had been a frightened, weather-beaten derelict, washed up dead on a riverbank.

Nathan was staring at her. 'Are you okay? You've gone very pale. Can I get you a drink?'

Liz made her way to a chair and sank down. 'Oh, please, if it's not too much trouble.'

'Tea, coffee, or something stronger?' asked Nathan anxiously.

'Tea would be perfect. I'm so sorry, it's just . . .'

Nathan smiled at her kindly. 'Life can be a bugger, can't it?'

'You can say that again,' she murmured.

While he went to put the kettle on, she tried to get herself together. It hadn't just been seeing the stark evidence of the singer's dreadful transformation — Liz had seen her own. She had gone from an active and resourceful detective sergeant to a brain-damaged feeble shadow of the woman she used to be, within the space of a single day. She had

93

survived, fought her way back, but the old DS Haynes had gone forever.

When Nathan returned with two mugs of tea, Liz was herself again. 'I don't suppose you have a copy of this picture by any chance?'

'Oh yes. I have several on my computer.' He stood up and walked over to a desk made from a huge slab of wood laid on crossed scaffolding poles. After a while, she heard the whirr of a printer and he returned with three photographs. Two were taken at the same venue as the picture he'd shown her, and the other was a formal portrait of Marika seated at a grand piano.

This Marika had long, rich brown wavy hair. Her prominent cheekbones gave her an elegant, rather regal appearance, but the eyes twinkled, as if she were just about to break into a mischievous grin. This Marika didn't take herself too seriously.

'What can you tell me about her, Nathan?'

'You mean, apart from her skill, and her ability to switch between Chopin and Annie Lennox in the space of a bar?'

'Um, how about something more basic?' she said, noting the mention of Chopin. 'Did she work with you at the college?'

'No, I knew her when we were both on the professorial staff at Trinity Laban Conservatoire of Music and Dance. I only did a short stint there, but it was a magical time.'

'That's in London, isn't it? Forgive my ignorance, Nathan, but not many coppers, even retired ones, know too much about the music world.'

'Yes, in Greenwich. It was where I realised that I was heading down the wrong path with classical music. So I sidestepped from piano to keyboard. Marika stuck to the classics.' Nathan chuckled. 'But away from the concert grand, she easily rivalled the best women pop singers in the business. I was a little in love with her back then, if only from afar.'

'So, where did she come from?' asked Liz.

'Oh, right here in Lincolnshire, like me. I can't remember where exactly, if I ever knew. She came to the college several times as a guest performer, and she gave a masterclass once, but then she just vanished from the scene. She gave no performances, she just seemed to disappear. If you say she was a private tutor, then that must have been why, but,' he shrugged, puzzled, 'I can't think why she never kept in contact with the other performers. She was outgoing, and so talented that people flocked to hear her.'

'Was she ever married?' asked Liz.

'Not to my knowledge. Certainly not when I knew her.'

They finished their tea, then Nathan said he should get back to prepare for his tutorial.

'I really appreciate your help, and I cannot thank you enough for the photos. I know someone who will be able to tell us for sure whether or not our mystery woman is Marika,' she said, thinking of Rory. 'If you give me your number, I'll let you know. Maybe it'll save you from having to go and identify her, which I'm sure would be terribly upsetting for you.' She took a card from her bag. 'Ring me any time if anything comes to mind about Marika that could throw some light on to what happened to her. I want to find her killer.'

'I hope you do,' said Nathan vehemently. 'Whoever it was needs stringing up.' He went to his desk, rummaged around in it for a moment and held up a card of his own. 'This has all my contact details. I'll give it some thought, and talk to a couple of the other musicians who knew her.'

Liz left him at the campus and set off for home. Her visit to the music school had been a real breakthrough and she had made a diamond of a find in Nathan Venner. At last, they had a real name for their bag lady.

CHAPTER TEN

Matt, Liz, and David were having a quick snack lunch.

'So, we are to expect the charming DC Norton at three, are we?' said Liz, aiming a banana skin at the waste bin.

Matt rolled his eyes. 'Charley seems to think there is something deep down in that young man that is worth saving. She wants us to try to inspire him by example. According to her, it's "make or break" for his career, and she meant it.'

'I see,' Liz said doubtfully. 'We can do our best, I suppose, but the last thing we need is another project. We're stretched to the limit as it is, with two cases on the go.'

'We'll just keep an eye on him and note any causes for concern.' Matt cleared the plates and put them in the dishwasher. 'We do need some link with the police, so I suppose he's better than none. Right now we desperately need him to get a shout out to uniform to watch out for Smokey Joe. Swifty has unofficially notified his colleagues at Fenfleet, but by now Smokey could have got a fair way on that old bike of his if he'd a mind to. I'd like to think that all the stations in the area have a heads up to watch out for him.'

'Shall we take this into the other room?' suggested Liz. 'I've got quite a bit to tell you, and I want hear more about this Bunker of yours, Matt.'

They installed themselves in the investigation room. Matt began by rearranging their whiteboard. Moving the Liam Cooper information to one side, he drew a vertical line down the centre and wrote the name "Molly" at the head of the empty column.

'I'll just scan the photos Nathan gave me,' said Liz, 'and email them to Rory. By the time Norton gets here, we should have a proper name for her. That's a big step forward. Hopefully, it'll demonstrate to Norton that this is a serious investigation and should be treated as such.'

While they waited for Rory to get back to them, they added the rest of the information they'd gathered on Molly to the board. Posted like this, it was apparent how hard they had been working.

'I didn't realise we'd gathered such a lot. I'd certainly be impressed if I was him,' said David. 'I'm looking forward to meeting this detective of yours so I can see for myself what he's like.'

Matt looked at his watch. 'Well, you only have twenty minutes to wait, just enough time for me to tell you what Spike's friend said about the Bunker.'

'And for me to add *this* to the mysterious clues left by our Molly.' Liz laid a book on the table.

Matt read the title: *Fryderyk Chopin*. 'This was Molly's?'

'Her favourite library book, to be precise,' said Liz. 'She made quite a thing about it to Chris Lamont, and I can't help thinking that there was a reason for that.'

'There's nothing inside, is there?' asked David eagerly.

'I flipped through quickly,' said Liz, 'and didn't come across anything, but it needs a thorough inspection. I'm certain she wouldn't have placed such emphasis on it if it weren't important in some way. I'll get to grips with that the moment our reluctant detective leaves.' She grinned. 'Especially as I don't have to prepare dinner tonight.'

David looked at her askance. Matt explained that they had a table booked at the Pear Tree. 'Now, before our visitor arrives, let me tell you about the Bunker.'

Listening to the story, David wondered what was behind it. 'I get the idea in theory, I mean, on the surface what could be wrong with an adventure camp for tearaways — you know, keeps them off the streets, teaches them values and all that. But why all the secrecy?'

'That's the big question, David,' said Matt. 'And the more you think about it the more sinister it gets.'

'Pity I'm not a bit younger,' said David. 'I'd volunteer to go myself. Hey! I don't suppose you know any kids who might be up for a bit of undercover work? Getting someone on the inside may be the only way you'll find out what's really going on.'

'Even if I did, I wouldn't put them at risk like that. We have no idea what really goes on in that place.' Matt shook his head. 'Suppose something went wrong, there'd be no back-up for them. It's far too dangerous.'

'I guess,' said David. 'Though I know I'd have been well up for it when I was a kid. I bet you'd find plenty of others who would be too. I mean, no harm would come to them if they just went once. You could even follow the van that picked them up. They'd have a bloody good time for a few hours, and you'd have the Bunker's location.'

Matt smiled. 'You make it sound so simple.'

'It *is* simple,' David retorted. 'The boy from the football club went twice and he's fine. Why don't we find someone to go, Matt? It could help you find Liam.'

'Or cut out the risk altogether and persuade one of the kids who has already been there to tell us more about it?' suggested Liz.

Before Matt could answer, they heard the crunch of wheels on the gravel drive.

'That must be your detective.' David rose eagerly from his chair.

'Just listen and observe, lad. We're not hauling him over the coals,' said Matt. 'Yet.'

Matt could see nothing of the grandfather in the man strolling casually in through the door. The chief super was a

98

big man, in all senses of the word. Despite his evident fondness for the bottle — evident in the veins on his face and his paunch — he was still an imposing man. Darren Norton, on the other hand, was thin, with a sly, ratty look about him. He looked a little uneasy, as if unsure of his welcome.

Matt stuck out a hand. 'Matt Ballard. Pleased to meet you, Darren. Come in and meet Liz and David.'

Liz smiled at the young detective. 'I was just going to make some drinks. What will you have — tea or coffee?'

'Coffee, please. Black, one sugar.'

'Come into our centre of operations, Darren,' Matt said, a hand on his shoulder. 'We call it our incident room, though it's not quite so grand.'

Norton ran his eyes over the whiteboard, the computer equipment. He didn't quite curl his lip in disdain.

He thinks we are playing detective, thought Matt. *So, it will be down to actions and results.*

As he invited Norton to sit down, the phone rang. Matt swore to himself. Rory had chosen just the wrong moment to call. 'Liz! Pick that up, will you?' he called out, hoping she would understand that he wasn't keen for their visitor to know about their association with the Home Office pathologist.

The ringing stopped, and he sat down opposite Norton. 'Shall we begin? David, would you tell Detective Norton about the contents of Molly's bag and the work you are doing on them, please?'

David did as requested. 'We do know that she took to the streets to get away from something or someone that terrified her. Whatever this was seems to have taken place around ten years ago.'

Norton cast his eyes over the papers amassed in heaps and piles across the table. 'You are actually reading all that crap?'

'Every word, mate,' said David, grinning. 'And I'm building up a pretty interesting picture of our Molly.'

Norton merely raised an eyebrow.

Clearly, Darren Norton would have consigned the whole lot to the incinerator by now. 'Painstaking work, Darren, which is what it takes if you are going to conduct a proper investigation. We intend to catch Molly's killer. We have DCI Anders' full support, and we need your input from an official point of view. I assume we have your full cooperation?'

'Of course,' Norton said unenthusiastically.

At that moment, Liz came in carrying a tray of mugs. As she set Matt's coffee down, she gave him a very slight nod. So, it had been Rory, and he must have confirmed that Marika and Molly were one and the same woman.

'Okay,' Matt began. 'What do you have to tell us, Darren?'

Norton shrugged, 'Very little as yet. Until I get the reports from forensics, it's a bit of a waiting game really. The pathologist did say that she used to play the piano — as if that would be any help.'

'On the contrary, Darren,' said Liz, rather coldly. 'It would help a lot. In fact, if you'd pursued it, that simple observation might have given you Molly's real name.'

There was a slight pause. 'Why don't you introduce our detective friend to the real Molly, Liz?' Matt said.

Liz went over to the printer and picked up the portrait of Marika seated at the grand piano. She placed it on the table beside their guest. 'Darren, meet Marika Molohan, aka Molly — classical pianist, trained at one of the most prestigious conservatoires in the world, held a professorial position at Trinity Laban Conservatoire of Music and Dance, and who also happened to be a remarkable singer.' She then handed him the photo of Marika performing on stage with Nathan Venner. 'That, DC Norton, is Molly. Oh, and you might have heard her sing yourself. Molly was the Night Singer.'

He took pains to conceal it, but Norton was obviously flabbergasted.

Matt gave a soft laugh. 'Not too shabby for a pair of private dicks, huh?'

'You found all this out in just a couple of days?'

'That, and more. Drink your coffee and listen up.'

Between them they explained about the ring, the missing letter, and the fact that Marika had been a local but, wishing to keep her true identity secret, she had never revealed anything about herself.

'We think that after she took up private tutoring,' added David, 'she chanced upon something that terrified her.' He read out a couple of snippets from the papers in her bag.

'Phew,' breathed Norton. 'She was frightened, wasn't she?'

'And as it turned out, she had every right to be, since someone killed her,' Matt added darkly. 'And this is where we need your assistance, Darren.' He leaned forward. 'Molly's sole friend and confidant has gone missing. We need you to put out an attention drawn to anyone who has had a recent sighting of an oldish man. He rode an even older bicycle and always carried a bag on one handlebar and a bucket of hot coals on the other. He goes by the name of Smokey Joe.'

An odd look passed across Norton's face. 'Smokey Joe you said? Ah, well, in that case, can you ring PC Jack Fleet? I thought he was having me on, so I wasn't going to mention it, but I saw him as I was on my way out to come and see you, and he said he'd got something for you about a Smokey Joe.'

Matt pulled his phone from his pocket, pretty sure that if he hadn't brought it up, Swifty's message would been totally forgotten or ignored. This kid had a lot to learn.

Moments later he was speaking to his old friend.

'I had a call from an old mate of mine, Matt. His name is Sergeant Tom Johnson from Fenchester division.'

Matt recognised the name, and even had a vague picture in his mind of a somewhat rugged, weather-beaten face and a ready smile.

'He rang me earlier today about an unrelated matter, and I let him know that we were anxious to pick up Smokey Joe. He rang back later . . . and I'm afraid it could be bad news, Matt.'

'He's dead?' asked Matt, dreading the answer.

'Missing. His bike and bucket have been found in a ditch on farmland outside Fenchester, but there was no sign of Smokey.'

Matt sighed. Whatever, it wasn't good news.

'There's a chance he was knocked off the bike somewhere nearby. That particular fen lane twists and turns and cars using it as a short cut drive far too fast,' said Jack. 'I'm up to my neck at present, which is why I passed on the message to DC Norton, or I'd have rung round the hospitals for you.'

'We'll get on to it, Jack, thanks. I appreciate your help. Oh, and where is the bike now? Do you know?'

'At Fenchester nick, I believe,' said Jack. 'If it helps, I'll text you Tom's mobile number and you can talk to him direct. Now, I really must go.'

'Thanks again, mate. I owe you one.' Matt ended the call and, on cue, the message came through. Soon he was talking to Sergeant Tom Johnson. After a few preliminary salutations, Matt asked Tom if, along with the bike, they'd found a bag containing Smokey's belongings.'

'Yes, mate, and it's dead clatty. It's here with the bike, though I've left the still smouldering bucket for my wife to deal with.' Tom laughed.

'I hope you don't mind me asking, but why did you leave that bucket to your wife?' said Matt.

'It was her driving the Tomcat that was dredging the ditches, mate. She found it.'

Matt grinned. 'Ah, I see. Look, any chance of me coming over to Fenchester and taking a look at that bag? We are investigating a case involving a murdered woman, and we know she and Smokey were close. There's a chance she may have given him something, which could easily have been overlooked, but if she did, it could help us.'

'Be my guest, Matt. Rather you than me, just don't forget to bring some rubber gloves.' Amid gales of Tom's laughter, Matt ended the call.

Matt knew he should be concentrating on Liam but he couldn't leave everything to Liz, and this was something they really needed to follow up. He'd go the moment their visitor had left. He told Liz what Tom had said. 'I've got this, you concentrate on Chopin.'

If Norton was confused, which he should be, he asked no questions.

Matt turned to him. 'I have another question for you. We have another case running,' he indicated the whiteboard, 'a missing teenager called Liam Cooper.'

'A misper? I doubt I'll be much help there,' said Norton. 'They rarely attract the attention of CID.'

'This one will if he turns up dead,' Matt said between clenched teeth. 'And you'll find that in his case, there is cause for concern. Uniform have already received instructions to keep a close lookout for him. But anyway, will you please make enquiries for me about a place called the Bunker, as it seems to be connected with the disappearance of this boy.'

Norton actually took out his digital notebook and wrote down the names. 'Okay. It's not something I've ever heard of, but I'll make enquiries.'

Well, it's a start, thought Matt. And was that a hint of interest in the detective's expression when the Bunker was mentioned? 'It will be quite a sizeable place, probably, since it's supposed to be a kind of adventure park, with barns attached. We also believe that it's somewhere close to the marsh. We need a location.'

Norton made a note of it. 'Got it. I'll see what I can find out. Is there anything else you need to know about this Marika Molohan?'

So, Matt thought, Norton had shown no interest in a dead bag lady but a murdered concert pianist was something else. The kid was a snob. 'I want to know where that lady went after she disappeared from the spotlight. Start with a musician called Nathan Venner, a tutor at Greenborough School of Music and Performing Arts, and see if you can find where she taught, okay?'

Darren drained his mug and stood up. 'Yes, Mr Ballard, I'll do what I can.' He turned to Liz. 'Thank you for the coffee. I'll be in touch.'

After he had gone, they sat in silence for a while, no one wanting to be the first to comment on their visitor. Finally, Liz said, 'Oh dear, I think we've got our work cut out with that one.'

'To be fair,' said David, 'he was way out of his depth. I almost felt sorry for him once or twice. I think you two shocked the pants off him.'

'Well, I'm not sure that'll be enough to awaken the sleeping master sleuth within,' said Liz dubiously.

'Whatever, it had an effect on him,' said David. 'I was watching him while you spoke. I'm still not sure what to make of him, but he left here fully aware that you mean business. He'll also realise that unless he pulls his finger out and makes a contribution, he'll find himself having to answer a whole lot of awkward questions as to why you can achieve so much while his end of the investigation is at a standstill.'

Despite David's words, Matt still had serious reservations about Darren Norton. 'There was one thing I noticed — did either of you see his reaction when I mentioned the Bunker?'

'Yes,' Liz said thoughtfully, 'for one moment I thought he recognised the name. Though he said he didn't. Maybe it was the word "bunker". It does sound rather sinister, doesn't it?'

'Yeah,' David said, 'it makes me think of old military installations, or secret underground facilities established by the government. And Hitler's bunker, of course.'

Matt almost gasped. Something David had said struck a chord.

'What's the matter, Matt?' Liz said.

He closed his eyes for a second or two while he tried to get his thoughts in order. 'Know what? I think I've been looking at this all wrong. I've been imagining this adventure park to be attached to some kind of farm, you know, spread out over a field, with barns and the like. But what if that's not the case at all. What if it's on one of the old airbases? What if the Bunker is just that — a Second World War, or even a Cold War bunker?'

'Are there many of those around here?' asked David.

'More than you'd think,' said Matt, 'and there's some on private land too.'

'I didn't think they'd have been able to build underground facilities in the Fens because it's so low-lying and marshy,' said David.

'Get on that laptop of yours and check out Underground Wisbech, lad. You'll be surprised. There's a whole world beneath your feet in that Fenland town. Plus, there are quite a few Royal Observer Corps military bunkers in the Fens, a couple are even open to the public.' Matt started to pace the room. 'This is where I should be looking. Actual bunkers.'

'Hey, that makes sense.' David was already reaching for his computer.

'But back to Molly,' Matt said, taking a breath. 'Right now, I'm going to head off to Fenchester and take a look at Smokey's belongings. Now I have a direction to follow with Liam's bunker, I feel a lot happier, so I'll get this out of the way and then I can decide how to proceed.'

'If you want to do that now, Matt, I can go to Fenchester,' offered Liz.

'No, you're are already looking tired, sweetheart. This won't take long, and Tom is expecting me. Hold the fort here and read about Chopin. Maybe you should ring your friend Nathan Venner and warn him to expect a visit from one of Fenfleet's finest. It would be nice to hear how our reluctant detective deals with the public.' He paused in the doorway. 'I'll be back before you know it.'

Liz held up her hands in surrender. 'Okay, okay. Just take care. There are some rubber gloves under the sink, and remembering the state of Smokey Joe, don't bother bringing them back.'

CHAPTER ELEVEN

David was glad that Matt had refused Liz's offer to go to Fenchester. He could see she was tired, having been going full tilt for a couple of days. So, after Matt left, he insisted she go and rest for a while. Though she protested that she needed to do an internet search for Marika Molohan, she acquiesced without much of a struggle.

David did the search for her, but came up with little more than what Nathan Venner had said. He found old reviews of recitals, and a scanty profile, mostly listing the various conservatories she had attended.

Reluctant to return to his bag of papers, he idly surfed for old airfields and underground facilities.

He soon found he'd been wrong about the Fens being unsuitable for such places. It all depended on whether a certain area had once been more elevated than it now was. Originally, before they were drained, the Fens had consisted of flat marshy areas surrounding islands of higher ground, where settlements had established themselves. He recalled that Ely was sometimes referred to as the Isle of Ely and found that in some of the modern-day fenland towns, tunnels had indeed been excavated.

Now thoroughly absorbed, David went back to the sites of military bases and discovered that some of the old, disused airfields had underground bunkers beneath them. In Wisbech, the town that Matt had mentioned, there were crypts, cellars, storage vaults, passageways and tunnels below the High Street.

His search took him to the Royal Observer Corps bunkers, and he discovered that the one at Holbeach was still in use as an underground monitoring post. Forgetting all about Molly, he began to immerse himself in the history of the ROC which, he found, went from spotting and identifying incoming enemy aircraft in World War Two, to their later task of measuring the scale of nuclear bomb blasts and the resultant fallout.

His screen told him that forty-five minutes had passed. He stood up and stretched, thinking that maybe Liz would like a cup of tea.

He made the tea and took it up to her room. He knocked gently, in case she was sleeping, but she called out at once.

'Perfect timing, David. I think I've got something!'

He found an excited Liz sitting propped up on her pillows, Chopin in one hand and a notebook in the other. 'I was right. It took a while for me to see it but that clever woman did leave a message.'

David sat down on the edge of the bed. 'How?'

'There are these very faint pencil lines under certain words and letters. I've only just spotted them as they don't appear on every page. I've no idea what she's trying to say, but it's here all right — a message. I just can't work out what it says.'

'Lord! We'll be needing a code-breaker next.'

Liz stared at him. 'David, you are a genius. That's exactly what we need.'

'Er, I was sort of joking, Auntie,' he said, somewhat taken aback by her reaction.

'But I'm not. And I know just the person — Hazel Webber. She'll love this.' Liz waved the Chopin book.

David shook his head. 'You've lost me.'

'Sorry. Let me explain.' Liz laid down the book and picked up her mug. 'Hazel is an old mate of mine from my early days in the police. She was already coming up for retirement when I joined, but before she left, she acted as my mentor, and we got on from the word go. The thing is, her grandmother was one of the code-breakers at Bletchley Park, and Hazel inherited her analytical brain. I'm telling you, David, Hazel is something else. Deciphering the message in this book will be kid's stuff for her, and she'd love to help.'

'Why not ring her now then? Give me her address and I'll take it to her.'

Liz put her mug down and reached for her phone. 'She lives on the outskirts of Fenfleet in a retirement complex called Fenfield Court in London Road. You can't miss it, it's on the road into town, a collection of swanky-looking yellow-brick flats and bungalows.'

'I know where you mean,' said David, having previously remarked the smart buildings and the immaculate gardens. 'Nice!'

'So is Hazel, but she's a bit of a, er, "character", so be warned.'

Liz made the call, and in less than ten minutes, David was driving away from Cannon Farm, the book on Chopin on the seat next to him. He was under strict instructions to stop at the flower shop on London Road and buy Hazel a plant.

If he thought this an odd request, he soon discovered the reasoning behind it. Hazel Webber's lounge was a veritable jungle of houseplants — giant broad-leafed plants towered over miniature ones, strange and exotic species and more common flowery ones all vied for space, and seemed to flourish.

'A little hobby of mine,' said Hazel, beaming at him.

An obsession, more like, thought David, gazing at the sea of foliage.

Hazel certainly didn't look like a retired police officer. In fact, he wasn't sure quite what she did look like, in her camouflage cargo trousers and sweatshirt, and her very short cropped hair. She must have been in her late seventies but could have been any age. He would have dismissed her as a bit of a nutter had it not been for the startling blue eyes that regarded him shrewdly.

He held out the plant he had purchased. 'From my Auntie Liz, with love.'

Her eyes lit on the plant and she gave a smile of recognition. 'Ah, *Spathiphyllum wallisii*, one of my favourites. The Peace Lily, you know — and we could all do with some of that.'

Somehow, the plant was allocated a space, and she turned her attention to the book.

'Liz told me about your dead woman, now let me take a look.'

David handed her the book. 'This is one of a number of cryptic messages that Molly left. It appears she was too scared to speak openly about what was troubling her so badly.'

'And someone murdered her,' said Hazel, 'so, what she knew was so serious it was worth killing her to keep hidden. Of course, in a perfect world, the police would be all over this like a rash but unfortunately, the world is far from being perfect.'

Hazel went across to a small antique desk and fished around beneath the spotty leaves of a plant that seemed to have colonised most of its surface, finally producing a pair of spectacles.

She leafed through the book for a few minutes before looking up. 'No problem. Leave it with me and I'll ring Liz tomorrow.'

'You can decipher it?' David asked.

She regarded him like an adult with a child who needs things spelled out for them. 'Of course, David. You see, the person who devised this code wasn't a trained mathematician but someone in fear for her life. And amateurs always make the same mistake — they think they are scattering their keywords at random when in fact they follow a perfectly predictable pattern.'

'Shows what I know,' said David with a grin. He was starting to warm to this eccentric woman. 'I suppose there still are code-breakers these days?'

She smiled. 'Oh yes. GCHQ have a whole new breed of them, people of your age studying cybernetics. A new science but the same principles.'

'True,' said David. 'I'm studying forensic computer analysis at university, so I know what you mean. I can't help wondering, sometimes, about technology. We younger people are always thought to have an advantage over the previous generation, because we are so adept at it, but have we missed out on something? I hear Matt and Liz talk about the way policing was when they started in the force, and I guess you must have seen an even bigger change.'

'Don't get me started, young man! I could give you an entire oral history of the life and times of a beat bobby several decades ago. No, I'm serious. Bring a bottle and be prepared to listen.'

'I'll take you up on that, Hazel.'

'And don't forget that bottle now. Anything alcoholic will do. Anyway, I'll be in touch about the book.'

David made his way back through the forest of plants, thinking that he would be quite happy to spend some hours listening to Hazel talk.

* * *

Matt stared at the filthy mud-splattered bag, but rather than disgust, he felt nothing but anxiety for its owner. What had happened to Smokey Joe?

'Here you go, mate,' said a young PC, handing him a large plastic sheet. 'Skipper tells me you want to have a look through this bag of old crap.'

'That's right,' said Matt, smiling at the constable's bemused expression.

'I can think of nicer ways to earn a crust,' the latter said.

'Me too, but a man has to do what a man has to do.' With a sigh, Matt pulled on the rubber gloves, undid the top of the bag and peered inside. To make matters worse, the ditchwater had seeped in and a coating of duckweed and slime clung to the objects inside.

'Lawk! That stinks like a midding!'

Smiling at the Lincolnshire term for a dung-heap, Matt was forced to agree. 'Well, here goes. Better get this over with before we both throw up.'

What appeared to be a bundle of rags turned out to be Joe's wardrobe. Beneath the clothes, Matt found a plastic tray with half a mouldy sandwich stuck to it, and an assortment of objects stuffed in an old sock. These did interest Matt. He removed each one carefully and laid them out on the plastic sheet.

'What's a tramp doing with that?' The young PC pointed to a pocket watch that might have been silver.

'Ah, but he wasn't always a tramp,' Matt said. 'Smokey Joe was ex-army, so they say, and what you are looking at there is a Second World War British army GSTP pocket watch. Okay, he's not that old, but I'll lay odds that it belonged to his father or someone else very close to him.'

'GTSP?'

Matt turned the watch over. Beneath the grime, the lettering was still visible — the initials GTSP with a broad arrow above and a single letter T and five numbers beneath. 'General Service Time Piece,' said Matt. 'Probably manufactured between 1940 and 1949.'

'Well, I must say you know your stuff,' the officer said.

'Not really. There was one of those watches at home when I was young.' He looked at the PC, who appeared to be even younger than David. 'What's your name, Constable?'

'DC Billy Norman, sir.' He grinned at Matt. 'It's not really Billy, but Norman sounds a bit like No-mates, so the others call me Billy No-mates.'

Matt knew exactly what coppers were like for dishing out nicknames. He smiled. 'Could be worse, son.'

He returned his attention to the rest of the contents. There was a plastic bag, tied tightly, that held a small handful of disposable lighters. No doubt Smokey used them to keep that famous bucket alight after a night on the streets. A cheap Swiss knife and a waterproof wallet, which Matt opened, to reveal several sheets of hay-fever tablets, a small amount of cash, mainly coins, and, surprisingly, a bank card.

PC No-mates stared at this last item suspiciously. 'Wonder who he nicked that off?'

The name on the card was Johan de Vries. It sounded Dutch. Could this be Smokey Joe's real name? Matt had the feeling that it was. He knew of some banks that made accounts available to the homeless, and there was always the possibility that Joe had money of his own and had chosen this way of life. 'Billy, I'd like a word with your skipper. Would you be kind enough to ask him if he has a moment, please? I want to take this back with me and make some enquiries about its missing owner.'

While Billy was away, Matt laid out each piece of clothing on the plastic sheet, and carefully ran a gloved hand across pockets and down seams. He knew of old that people concealed things in the most unlikely places.

He was almost through when he felt something hard inside the cuff of an old raincoat. On further investigation, he discovered a slit in the stitching and was able to gently ease the item out. Matt found himself staring at a key.

What on earth would a man without a home need a key for? Matt slipped off one of the gloves and reached into his pocket. He removed a sealable freezer bag, slipped the key inside it and popped the bag into his pocket. He had no idea why he had done this, but for some reason he wanted to keep his find to himself.

He pulled the glove back on and resumed his investigation of the stinking clothing.

'And there was I thinking you private investigators spent your days watching adulterous couples. I take it all back. You seem to be positively relishing wading through that little lot.' Sergeant Tom Johnson stood above him, laughing uproariously.

'Hello, Tom. I get the choice jobs in this agency.'

'So I see. And not only that, Billy here tells me you like this stuff so much that you want to take it home with you.' Tom gave another guffaw. 'You're welcome to it, I must say, but why the interest in old Smokey? Do you think someone has done something to him?'

'A woman was found murdered on the sea bank, Tom, and Smokey is our only connection to her. Given what happened to her, I really am afraid for Smokey's life. Could you get your lads and lasses to keep an eye open for him, and if there's a sighting, let Swifty Fleet know?'

Tom nodded. 'Absolutely. Consider it done, Matt. My Una is dredging ditches in that area, and I've told her to keep her eyes peeled as well.'

'I hope it doesn't come down to that, but thanks, mate, I appreciate it.' Matt glanced across to the old bike. 'And could you get that into storage somewhere? Just until we find out what's happened to Smokey. It could be evidence.'

'Sure. What about this lot? Do you want to take that too?' He pointed to the bag and its contents.

'If you don't mind. It could give us a starting point. If we can find out who he was before he took to the roads, it might lead us to discovering more about our dead woman.'

'We have no crime committed other than fly-tipping, and should anything else rear its ugly head, we know where to find you, so be my guest,' said Tom, wrinkling his nose. 'And I suggest packing it in a sealed refuse sack for the journey home.'

'There's a roll in my car,' said Matt, 'and I'll keep the windows open.'

He took his leave after a brief catch-up.

'Keep me updated, Matt, or ask Swifty to. I've always had a bit of a soft spot for that old rogue. He's part of the landscape, isn't he? I just hope some nasty bastard hasn't topped him.'

Matt hoped so too, but he couldn't help thinking that the discovery of the bike and the discarded possessions signified doom for Smokey Joe.

* * *

The transformation of the vivacious and attractive Marika into a destitute street dweller weighed heavily on Nathan Venner. It pained him to think that this talented musician had gone for ever, in fact it had affected him so badly that it was hard to concentrate on his teaching. He took a few days' leave and shut himself in his studio, where he sat at his piano and played some of the pieces Marika had performed when he knew her. Despite his own virtuosity, his attempts to match hers were like that of a novice. Meanwhile, he had a missed call from the police and left their messages unanswered. He just didn't feel up to it right now.

With a final discordant clash of keys, Nathan abandoned his piano and wandered through to the kitchen. Having eaten nothing all day, he made himself a sandwich and took it into his living area.

He had moved the photograph of Marika at his gig to a more prominent position. Gazing at it now, it struck him that he was still in love with her. Though he hadn't seen her for years, she had been *somewhere*, and might one day come back. This hope was now gone. Nathan was grieving.

He ate his sandwich, which tasted of nothing, and wondered if he should ring this detective who'd been trying to get in touch with him, someone called Norton. He really ought to, but his offer of help had been made to Liz, not some flatfoot with not an ounce of sensitivity in him.

The phone rang again. He sighed. If it was this Norton, he might as well get it over with.

'Hi, Nathan. It's Liz Haynes. I just rang to say that you might get a call from a detective called Darren Norton. He's not the most dynamic of police officers, but he's the one they've assigned to Marika's case.' She laughed. 'And we're trying to ignite a bit of a spark in him.'

Nathan perked up. 'Thank you for the warning. In fact I did get a message asking me to ring him but I haven't yet built up the courage.' He cleared his throat. 'To be honest, I'm pretty devastated by what you told me, and I've been trying to come to terms with it. Oh, Liz, you should have heard her play! She was — oh, just spectacular. It's such a tragic waste, aside from the fact that she was a wonderful human being.'

'I really am sorry for your loss, Nathan. I do understand how much she meant to you,' said Liz softly.

'And now I feel guilty for never having tried to find her. Why didn't I think? Why did I not question her sudden disappearance from the scene? I must have been so wrapped up in my own stupid life that I just let it go. I did think about her — a lot — but I never did anything about it. What an idiot!' He suddenly realised what he must sound like to her. 'Forgive the outburst. It's just that I've been going over and over it ever since you left.'

'In which case, helping us find what happened to Marika might make you feel better. You, more than anyone — you move in those circles, know the kind of people she mixed with. I'd go so far as to say there is no one else that we know of who'd be able to help us like you could. How about channelling your grief into something positive?'

She was right. He owed it to Marika.

'Make some enquiries for us, would you, Nathan, please? Talk to people. Someone in your community must know something. If she gave regular performances, she must have had quite a high profile, so at the very least there must have been rumours circulating, or gossip about her sudden disappearance.'

Even as she spoke, Nathan was thinking of people he might try. 'You're right, Liz. It's doing me no good sitting around moping. I've taken a few days off so I can start right away. I know of people I can contact, and now I think about it, one man in particular who might know something. He's an old gossip, camp as a row of tents, and he thrives on scandal, so if there was anything odd about her disappearance, he would know about it.'

He pictured the pudgy face and darting, piggy eyes of little Pinky Sherbourne. He'd never liked him but if you wanted to know anything about what was going on in the music world, you asked Pinky.

'There. You have a starting point already,' said Liz. 'Help us find out who murdered Marika, Nathan. It will help you, too, in the long run.'

'And what about your policeman?'

'Oh, just make contact. Tell him whatever he needs to know, then go ahead and make your own enquiries. You have my number, so if you find out anything, no matter how small, ring me. Sad as it is, you'll get a whole lot more response from Matt or me than you will from the police.'

Nathan heard the sincerity in her voice, and the strength of her motivation. When the call had ended, Nathan felt some of that same determination.

Without further ado, he rang the detective.

* * *

As twilight stole across the marsh and stars began to appear between the scudding clouds, a scream was heard. This time it was not the blood-curdling howl of a vixen. Neither was it a barn owl. This time the scream that rang out was the cry of a terrified teenager, suddenly aware that he has made the most terrible mistake of his life.

CHAPTER TWELVE

The Pear Tree was a popular venue, and all the tables were full. The owner, Bernie, was one of Matt's more longstanding sources of information, and he had been hoping to speak to him tonight. Bernie was understandably busy, so while they waited for him to snatch a few moments to chat with them, they discussed where they were with the case.

'We need to sit back and sort out a definite plan of action for both the cases,' Matt said, while adding a generous helping of vegetables to his steak and ale pie.

'Shall we start with Liam?' suggested Liz. 'Given the amount of fresh information coming in, Molly's case will probably take longer.'

'Well,' began Matt, 'in Liam's case it seems to be all down to hunting for the Bunker. There have been no sightings of the boy himself, and in that context I have received a call from his best mate, Jaxon Briggs, who is now extremely anxious. He said Liam has never behaved like this before, and, in his words, he reckons Liam is "brown bread".'

At this, David laid down his knife and fork. 'Look, I know you're not happy about having a kid infiltrate that place, but I've had an idea of someone who really could do it.'

About to protest, Matt relented. It wouldn't hurt to hear what the lad had to say. 'Go on.'

'Well, you know you said about this boy who is training to be a footballer who went there twice and never went back. Well, what if someone else coached him for a while? It would have to be a bloody good footballer, better than the coach he's got. Then this new coach could kind of befriend the kid, and get him to open up about what he saw there.'

Liz raised her eyebrows. 'Uh huh. And would I be right in thinking you know the very bloke for this job?'

David grinned. 'How did you guess? It's my bestie from school. He'd be well up for it, I'm sure. The thing about Jeff is that he looks about sixteen. He's been turned out of that many pubs it's unbelievable.'

'And he's a footballer? He has to be a very good one for your idea to work,' Matt said dubiously.

'He could go professional if he chose to, but he doesn't like the way football is going these days — you know, all the money. He's very idealistic. If he thought he'd be helping to find a missing kid, and maybe keep others from harm, he'd do it in the blink of an eye.'

Matt said nothing for a few seconds. He didn't like it. He didn't like it at all. The thought of involving an outsider, and one so young, in something that could be dangerous was anathema to him. On the other hand, David was so sure that his friend could help, and if it were only a case of chatting to the kid and playing football, there was little to fear from that, surely? 'Okay. Since we haven't come up with anything better, we can try that. No one will be harmed at least. Give him a call tomorrow and I'll get in touch with Spike's friend, Ewan. If he's willing to bring in a stranger for a few sessions with his protégé, we'll go for it. My only concern is the time this will take. If Liam really is in danger—'

'I'll text him now, and put him on stand-by,' said David. 'He's on vacation from uni, so the moment you make contact with the coach, he can set off.' He paused, glancing at Liz. 'Oh. I, er, guess he'll need somewhere to stay . . .'

Liz shrugged. 'The more the merrier. I can easily make up the small guest room for him.'

David whisked out his phone, and Matt watched in awe as his thumbs raced across the screen. He sent the message and, in seconds, the response came back. 'He's in! He'll be here in the morning as long as everything is sorted this end.'

In that case, Matt thought he'd better ring Rory. It was a bit late, but he was sure Rory wouldn't mind. As luck would have it, both he and Spike were still at the mortuary.

'I'm sure he won't object, sir,' said Spike, when Matt had explained the plan to him. 'I'll get in touch with him and get back to you with what he says. He's also worried about what this Bunker place is all about.'

Matt sat back in his seat. 'That's done then. We just need the thumbs up from Ewan.'

'What's even better is that Jeff does the same kind of thing with the kids back where we live,' David added. 'You know, coaches them and encourages them to play fair and all that. We can say that Jeff's here on holiday and heard about the work Ewan's doing. They'll have that in common, and Jeff can take it from there.'

Matt eyed him shrewdly. 'Come on, now, David, be honest. You aren't just thinking of getting your mate to befriend that youngster, are you?'

David actually blushed. 'Wait till you see Jeff, Matt. You'll be surprised. He's my age but you'd take him for a teenager. He's as thin as a rake and would have no problem posing as someone a whole lot younger. If this other youngster could tell him what he did to get selected, Jeff could infiltrate this place like that.' He snapped his fingers.

'It's too risky, lad. I wouldn't send you into the unknown, and I can't send this friend of yours in either. Until we know more about the place, we daren't send anyone in alone, whatever their age. And that's final. So, no going in undercover.'

But David obviously couldn't resist making one last try. 'All right, Matt. Though . . . well, there is more to Jeff than meets the eye. He's someone who's well able to look after himself.'

'Not if he goes in blind,' said Liz. 'We know nothing about the place or the people and what they might be capable of. It's far too dangerous.'

'We'll see what you think when you've met him. Are we having a dessert, by the way?'

The slight atmosphere of tension dissolved in laughter. They ordered dessert and turned their attention to Molly.

'Over to you, Liz,' said Matt.

'First, and our most important success to date, is that we now have a name for Molly and, second, that Nathan Venner is helping us determine what happened to her after she disappeared from the scene. He has contacts in the music world, so at present, he's our best chance of finding that out. David has looked on Google but there's little there that we didn't already know, so it's going to be down to leg-work and talking to people.' She looked at David. 'Unless your papers tell us that, of course?'

'I'm ever hopeful,' said David. 'She's got to mention the name of a place at some point. Oh, and I haven't had time to tell you this before, but I've begun to notice something about the paper she was writing on. Everything she writes about her safety, hers and that of someone else, is part of a diary. It's the same type of paper, and there are tear marks down one side of each sheet.'

'So, she tore the pages out and kept them?' asked Liz.

'That's right, and I think she probably hid them and took them with her when she got away from wherever she was living or being held. All the stuff scribbled on odd scraps of paper are recollections and recent thoughts that seem to have been written down within the last year. Some I reckon are real clues, if I could only get them in some kind of order.'

'I'm desperate to know what caused a talented, vivacious musician to take up private tuition, and from there, to hide herself on the streets.' Liz shook her head. 'The more I think about it, the more scared I become.'

'If she hadn't been murdered, I would have said she'd had a breakdown,' Matt added. 'She could have developed a persecution complex and believed someone was trying to kill her. Paranoid Personality Disorder is a recognised form of psychosis. People suffering from it are always on their guard, believing that others are trying to harm them. But—'

'She wasn't paranoid, someone really was out to get her,' said Liz grimly.

At that point their desserts arrived. Liz had chosen Eton Mess, which was new to David. Matt had just embarked on a disquisition on the origins of the name when Bernie arrived.

He flopped down in a spare chair. 'Food to your liking, my friends?'

'As always,' said Matt.

'And — as always — you are not here just for the food.' Bernie grinned. 'So, what troubles you tonight?'

'A place called the Bunker, Bernie,' Matt said. 'Ever heard of it?'

An odd look stole across Bernie's face. 'What's your interest in that place?'

'A missing teenager,' Matt said.

'Ah.' Bernie looked pensive. 'In that case . . . I've heard talk, not much, I'm afraid, and it doesn't refer to a place as such, but more of a . . . well, an organisation, if I can put it like that.'

Matt frowned. 'Organisation? What kind of organisation, Bernie?'

Bernie shrugged. 'I've never asked. To tell you the truth, I didn't want to know. Maybe I'm getting older and that way of life no longer has the same appeal. I don't know. I do know that there's a new breed of criminal around these days, and they scare even me.'

He looked weary, even sad, nothing like the smart, ex-racketeer turned restaurateur that Matt had always known.

'These people have no morals, they're utterly ruthless. The only thing they care about is money. It may sound disingenuous coming from a crook like me, but there's no — well, honour. The good days are gone, Matt. Planning a clever scam, the thrill of pulling off a big job and getting away with it. It was sort of like a game of chess, using different strategies to avoid getting caught, especially with an opponent like you. Sometimes people got hurt, but it was never the intention, and believe it or not, we were always pig sick when something bad happened to someone. We always tried to play a clean game.'

Matt had never heard Bernie speak with such passion. He knew just what he meant though. 'Times have changed for all of us, Bernie, but why are you so troubled by this Bunker outfit?'

'Matt, I don't even know who they are. They're only ever spoken about in whispers. The only thing I've gathered is that the Bunker is an enterprise of some kind, run by a consortium. Rumour has it that a number of criminal groups have got together to form this Bunker thing. A guy I know — who shall remain nameless — suspects it's a kind of academy, a training school for criminals.' He flung up his hands. 'And that's it. That's all I know.'

'Shit,' muttered Liz.

A silence followed Bernie's words. It fitted, Matt thought. This group were vetting youngsters for their suitability for a life of crime, organised crime. 'I know you want nothing to do with this, Bernie,' he said, 'but if you do, by any chance, happen to hear anything, even a hint, of where this group operates from, would you let me know immediately?'

Bernie nodded. 'Of course. But I'm not sticking my neck out to make enquiries for you, Matt, not this time. Sorry, but I like my life here, and I'm not risking losing it for anyone, even a missing kid. Even you, my friend.' Abruptly, Bernie stood up and left the table.

After he had gone, there was another silence, an even longer one this time. Finally, David cleared his throat. 'Um, I was wondering, well, what does this criminal academy or whatever you want to call it, do with the kids that don't make the grade?'

Neither Liz nor Matt had an answer.

'Kids like Liam Cooper, for instance,' David went on.

'I don't know, David, but I can guess,' said Matt, feeling uncomfortable. David had just put into words what he himself had been thinking.

'Then you really do need to talk to Jeff. Unless you want vulnerable kids to continue to go missing. Just talk to him, Matt, please?'

There could be no harm in just talking, at least it might keep David quiet. 'Fine, I'll speak to Jeff. Now, let's have some coffee and get home, shall we?'

* * *

Liz lay awake long into the night. If she hadn't known about the disappearance of a real live boy, who might be in mortal danger, she would have found the idea of an academy for criminals risible, like a spoof on "Police Academy". The reality, however, was far from being funny.

She gazed up into the dark and saw herself as a child, watching *Oliver* with her dad. She could hear him now, pretending to be Fagin and singing along with, "You've Got to Pick-a-Pocket or Two". But Liam wasn't being taught how to be a pickpocket. These faceless men had to be teaching the urchins of the Fens far more sinister skills.

Seeking comfort, Liz snuggled up to Matt.

'Can't you sleep?'

'I'm sorry, darling, I didn't mean to wake you. It's just that my mind is racing.'

'No wonder.' He sighed. 'I've been over and over what Bernie said. The most frightening thing about it was what he wouldn't say. He's never clammed up on me like that before, never. He's given us some of the best info we've ever had. He's even helped us close cases, and to hear him say that he wouldn't help us, even to save a missing boy, well, that really hit home.'

Liz felt the same way. Bernie had his feet firmly in two camps. He had been a rogue, and had friends who still were. But he had gone straight, turned his back on all that to run a successful restaurant. Bernie had been close to Matt's friend, Adie Clarkson, who had died saving the lives of both Matt and Liz. The death of Adie had created a lasting bond between Matt and Bernie. Now, for the first time, Bernie had refused him his help, and in so doing, had loosened the ties that bound them. Liz felt for him. It must hurt like hell.

'Do you really think such a thing could exist, Matt?' she asked. 'A training school for prospective young villains?'

'You know it could,' said Matt flatly. 'You can serve an apprenticeship in most trades, so why not crime? I think what Bernie heard about a consortium, a group of criminal gangs who have joined together to turn out a new generation of crooks is true.' He turned his face towards her in the darkness. 'And those "instructors" the young footballer believed were advising them on how to increase their physical fitness weren't instructors at all, they were scouts, watching for the hard ones, the most focused, the really bad boys. If they passed the test, they moved on to the next stage.'

'I wonder what happens to the ones who aren't suitable. Are they just told they must drop out and allow other kids to have a go? Maybe they're told that as long as they keep it a secret, they may get another shot at it, or something like that.'

'Or they are scared into silence,' added Matt dourly. 'I wonder what age group they target? Liam is sixteen, and I think Ewan's little football wizard is fourteen. Impressionable ages, I guess, if you want to mould a tearaway into a criminal.'

After a while Matt went quiet, and his breathing began to slow. Liz was left watching the digits on her clock count out the hours, and trying to rid her mind of unwanted thoughts.

She wondered what was so special about David's friend, Jeff. David had made a big thing of how "special" he was. She vaguely recalled meeting the lad when he and David were small, but back then he had been just another kid. Those were good days, days of innocent fun. To the echo of childish laughter, Liz closed her eyes.

* * *

Yet again the farmhouse kitchen was too hot but he was unable to rouse himself from his torpor to go and do something about it. He sat with his elbows on the kitchen table, his head in his hands, wondering how everything had gone so wrong. Just a matter of days ago he had been so certain of their safety that he almost wished to see blue lights outside their window. Now he dreaded it.

If only they could find that bloody letter. They had searched everywhere for it and now there was nowhere left to look. He could only hope that it had been dumped in a litter bin and was now rotting in a council rubbish tip. But of course, he couldn't know that, and it was the not knowing that was eating away at him. That bitch Molly, even in death she was still causing him trouble.

He raised his head and put his palms down on the table. This wouldn't do. He couldn't even blame Molly for this latest catastrophe. That was entirely down to him. One stupid comment, and all the long years of being careful had been negated.

He stared down at his hands. They weren't shaking, were they? Christ. Telling himself to get a grip, he stood up and strode towards the door, barely glancing at his wife's prone body beside the Aga. Swift as it was, the glance had taken in the protruding tongue, the bulging eyes. He gave a shudder of distaste. She'd never been a beauty, but as she was now . . . well, strangulation never did make for a peaceful end.

He went upstairs to the landing and knocked on one of the doors. 'Wake up, Jamie.'

A groan came from within. 'Come on, boy, we have work to do.'

'Okay.'

He waited until he heard him moving around, and then went back down to the kitchen.

Sad that it should come to this, but he couldn't afford to dwell on it. He had been a fool, that's all, and his wife had paid the price. Her and her stupid annoying habits. Like the way she stirred her tea. This time it had been her pen. Click,

click, click, over and over. She had been sitting at the table writing a shopping list, clicking that bloody pen. Standing on the other side of the room, close to the door, he had muttered, 'If she does that one more time, I swear I'll throttle her!' He hadn't noticed Jamie behind him, didn't realise he'd heard. Didn't think.

Jamie lumbered into the kitchen, saw the body and smiled. 'I did good, didn't I?'

'Yes, boy, you did good.' The words stuck in his throat. 'You know what you have to do now, don't you?'

'What I always do?'

'That's right, Jamie. What you always do.'

The smile on the broad face widened. 'Leave it to Jamie.'

'Good boy. Off you go.'

The big figure started forward, then stopped. 'But who's going to cook my porridge now?'

'Don't you worry, lad, I'll cook your porridge for you.'

Satisfied, Jamie trundled over to the body. 'Leave it to Jamie. He'll do it good.'

The first part of the operation now underway, the rest was down to him. There would be questions asked, that was a given. He had to have his answers ready. Trusting his inventive brain to come up with something, he was back on track.

CHAPTER THIRTEEN

David and Liz were having breakfast when the text from Spike arrived.

Carrying his phone, Matt hurried into the kitchen and read it out to them: '*Ewan happy for Jeff to meet the kids. He has a session tonight. Bring him to the Fenfleet Community Centre at six thirty. I'll be there too. See you then, Spike.*'

David rang his friend and gave him the thumbs up, along with directions to Cannon Farm. 'He'll be here in a couple of hours,' he said, with a glance at Matt.

Though Liz would be a push-over, he was aware that Matt continued to have reservations regarding Jeff, and particularly the fact that what David really wanted from this visit was a green light for Jeff to infiltrate the Bunker and experience first-hand what it was all about.

'Earth calling David.'

Liz was staring at him, eyebrows raised. 'Sorry, I was wool-gathering.'

'I doubt that very much,' she said, handing Matt a mug of tea. 'More like plotting your next move.'

He had the good grace to look sheepish. 'Guilty as charged, Sarge.'

'Seriously, David, you are placing a great deal of faith in this friend of yours. You are not normally a risk-taker, so I'm wondering why you're so keen to send your best mate into what could turn out to be a death trap.'

'Since he'll be here soon, maybe it's best you make up your own minds, rather than me keep hammering on about how special he is.'

Liz laughed. 'At this stage, it wouldn't surprise me if he walked in wearing red underpants over his trousers and a cape fluttering behind him.'

'Maybe I do idolise him a bit,' David said. 'Jeff was my best buddy for years, but he was the complete opposite to me. He was everything I'd always wanted to be if my childhood illness hadn't got in the way. Like football. I just didn't have the stamina. I could barely get from one end of the pitch to the other.'

'Still, you never let it hold you back,' Liz said. 'I know I met Jeff but I have very few memories of him, other that he was a nice friendly kid.'

'Not even the car park incident?'

For a moment Liz looked blank, then it dawned on her. 'Oh, of course! It was *Jeff* who frightened the life out of me, wasn't it?'

'That was Jeff all right, and he was only around nine or ten.'

David could still see the look of horror on Liz's face. They had parked on the top floor of a multistorey carpark, some three floors up. They got out of the car when suddenly, without warning, Jeff dashed across the concrete parking bays, making straight for the perimeter wall. Balancing on the top of it, he proceeded to perform a handstand, remaining in that position for maybe twenty seconds, like a diver on the high board. Then he flung himself into a back flip, and landed, perfectly steadily, on his feet. Then he trotted back to the car. David explained to the astounded Liz that Jeff wanted to be a gymnast when he left school.

'Did he ever become a gymnast?' she asked.

'Not exactly.'

'David Haynes! You're doing it again, stop being all mysterious about him.'

'Come on, David,' Matt added. 'Tell us what the hell you are talking about and put us out of our misery for once and for all. I promise you it won't make a scrap of difference to any decision we make.'

The atmosphere was becoming tense again, so David decided he'd better show them. 'Hang on a minute, I'll get my laptop. It's best you see this on a bigger screen.'

He fetched his laptop and selected the video he wanted. 'Watch this. This is Jeff.'

They watched a young man in joggers and sweatshirt run full tilt across the flat roof of a building, spring into the air and somersault across what seemed to be wide abyss to land on the roof of the next building along. Without pausing, he went over the edge and dropped several floors — still at a rapid pace — from iron railings on balconies, to ledges, before landing on the ground and going into a roll. But it didn't end there. In seconds, he was up again and racing towards a blank wall with a railing along the top. Somehow, he ran several steps straight up the wall, grabbed the rail, paused briefly and hauled himself up and over. The camera caught up with him a few moments later, doing what had scared Liz in the car park all those years ago, a handstand on the edge of a roof. He then launched himself off the ledge, plummeting down to land, perfectly balanced, on the flat surface of a narrow wall before leaping from that, and sliding down the handrail of a steep flight of steps.

The video ended, leaving Matt and Liz speechless. Then Matt said, 'Is that what they call Parkour?'

'Well, Jeff's version of it. He's what they call a *traceur*. But that's only part of what he's all about.' David looked at Liz. 'I don't know if you recall anything about his family, but his father travelled a lot for his work, and immediately after he finished school, Jeff went with him to Korea. While he was there, he studied various martial arts. That's why I say that Jeff can look after himself.'

For the first time, David saw a glimmer of interest in Matt's expression. Hopefully, when Matt met with Jeff and saw how sensible and reasonable he was, he might be persuaded that Jeff had the qualities that were needed. As far as he could see, getting someone on the inside was the only way they would find out what was going on. Only then could they save Liam, and countless others.

'Well,' said Liz. 'After seeing that video, I'm lost for words. I'm certainly looking forward to meeting him again.'

Matt merely said he had calls to make. He needed to visit Liam's parents, so he'd better get moving. 'I'll see your friend when I get back.'

'Meanwhile, I'll get on with Molly and her bag of tricks,' said David.

'And I am going to make the room ready for our guest.' She grinned mischievously at David. 'Shall I leave the window open in case he prefers to shin up the drainpipe instead of using the front door?'

'Very droll, Auntie Liz. The door will do fine, thank you.'

* * *

Matt decided to go first to the Coopers. As ever, he had nothing to report but he liked to reassure them that he was doing all he could, and that they hadn't been forgotten.

Each time he saw them, they appeared to have come a step closer to accepting that their son was never coming home. They even looked smaller than they had, weary and defeated.

Matt, who had dealt with this kind of thing more times than he cared to remember, found this a little unusual. Generally, at least one of the parents held on to the belief that their child would be found, would one day just walk in the door. That parent would make a big effort to buoy the other up, they remained positive, if only on the surface. But where the Coopers were concerned, neither seemed to have the strength for this. Liam had pushed them to the brink, and they had fallen over the edge.

Matt sat with his cup of tea, desperately searching his mind for something positive to tell them. After a while, he heard himself say, 'Don't give up on him just yet. It's a long shot, but we've recently come across kids discussing something among themselves that they're keeping secret from the grownups. We have someone coming in to assist us to check these rumours out. I'll keep you informed of any new developments in this line of enquiry. As I said, it could turn out to be nothing but kids' stories, but there seems to be some substance to them, so don't give up hope.'

Matt detected a glint, first in Maisie's eyes, then in those of her husband. Had he gone too far and given them false hope? He hadn't even been considering using Jeff, but he felt so sorry for them he'd found himself blurting it out. As he prepared to leave, he said, 'Please trust that we are doing our level best to find your son.'

'That's all we can ask of you,' said Jim, reaching out and gripping his arm tightly. 'And thank you for not giving up on our boy.'

As he drove away, Matt realised that he had come to a decision without his even knowing it. There had been something in that video that spoke to him. The young man, who did indeed appear to be around seventeen, had been so controlled. It wasn't his abilities so much as the calm with which he carried out his remarkable feats, there had been an almost spiritual quality in him. Now he just needed to meet this young man face to face. They had to do something for that poor couple, and if David was right about him, Jeff might be their only hope.

* * *

Nathan Venner awoke feeling unexpectedly positive. Determined to find some answers that would help get justice for Marika, he showered, dressed, and went to his desk.

There, after a few minutes' thought, he began to list the names of people who might be able to help him. First on the list was Pinky Sherbourne.

While he was running through all the musicians he knew, Liz called. 'I forgot to tell you something, Nathan. We have found a ring, it's gold with the initials MM engraved in it. Does that mean anything to you?'

'Yes, it does,' he said immediately. 'It was her mother's wedding ring. She was called Maeve Molohan. Where did you find it?' When Liz had explained, he said, 'I'm just about to make some calls, then I'll be off to see a few people who might know something about why she suddenly took up teaching. I'll try Pinky Sherbourne first, he's always in his lair, or in the bar at Kool Annie's Place listening out for the latest bit of gossip. The moment I hear anything of interest, I'll ring or text you.'

With three very different people on his list and determination in his stride, Nathan left his apartment and walked off in the direction of Pinky's house. If he wasn't at home, the bar was only five minutes away, and Pinky rarely strayed further than that.

Nathan had never liked Pinky, whose piggy little eyes always seemed to glint with malicious glee. He had often watched him take an unsuspecting victim and dig into their life until he found some dirt to crow over. He had applied this dubious talent to his career as a music critic, and was a regular contributor to a satirical magazine. Nathan had read one or two of his articles which, as far as he could see, served as an excuse for a vitriolic, queenly attack on some poor victim. If people got hurt in the process, so much the better.

Making his way along the High Street, Nathan recalled the time when Piggy had applied his paring knife to him. Unfortunately for Piggy, Nathan had no secrets. However many layers Piggy peeled away, he could never get to a rotten stratum beneath. Nathan didn't give a damn what Pinky said about him. He knew very well who he was, a brilliant musician and a flawed human being. He was doing something that he loved, and had no regrets. He and his band performed for the pleasure of it rather than for adulation or monetary gain. Most importantly, he had a fulfilling job, teaching enthusiastic youngsters to love music. He took his pleasures in moderation, never drinking to excess, and drugs were a dim, distant memory from a long-abandoned past life that Piggy had made a vain attempt to sensationalise before turning his attention to richer pickings.

Pinky's house was an end-of-terrace property in a back street not far from Greenborough town centre. Nathan hesitated outside the front door, suddenly daunted by the prospect of his forthcoming visit.

'Well, hello, dear boy! This is a surprise.' Pinky flapped his podgy hands in a gesture of welcome. 'Come. Come inside. It's months since I've seen you.'

Nathan took a breath and followed him into the lounge. 'Can I offer you a little drinky?'

'Thanks, Pinky, but it's a bit early in the morning for me.'

Not that he'd ever been in one, but Pinky's lounge made Nathan think of a Parisian brothel from the 1930s. Dim behind the deep red drapes, the room was lit with lamps beneath red shades that threw shadows across the red velour wallpaper.

'So, how has life been treating you, darling?' asked Pinky, arranging himself on a thickly upholstered chaise longue.

'Well, thank you, Pinky — until yesterday that is.'

The twin beams of Pinky's gaze homed in on him like searchlights. 'Oh, I'm sorry to hear that. Do tell.'

'You remember Marika Molohan?'

'How could I forget? Lovely woman, so talented, and what a beauty!'

'Well, she's dead,' Nathan said bluntly.

The little man's hands flew to his mouth. 'Surely not. But . . . how?'

Pinky's eyes appeared over the hands covering his face.

Not wishing to go into the details, Nathan merely said that a friend had given him the news. 'I spent all last night thinking about her and wondering where she went after she disappeared from the scene. I mean, she seemed to be here one minute and gone the next. Someone told me she'd taken a job as a private tutor, but I find that hard to believe. She couldn't have needed the money, she was too good a performer for that, she was so much in demand.'

'It's true though, sweetie. She did take up private tutoring. It was after that simply *disastrous* affair she had.'

Trying hard to conceal his shock, Nathan, who knew nothing about any affair, said, 'Oh, but that was ages ago, wasn't it?'

'Well, yes, but that's why she left so suddenly, wasn't it? She rode off into the sunset with her hero, but it turned out to be a pipe dream. Her gallant knight in the proverbial shining armour whisked her away up county somewhere,' Pinky raised an eyebrow, 'but things didn't work out.'

'That so?' Nathan puffed out his cheeks. 'So, what happened to her? Surely, if it all went wrong, she could have just come back?'

'Well, dearie, this is where the plot thickens.' Pinky shifted on the chaise longue, ready to relate his story. 'I don't know what went wrong exactly, but whatever it was, it was a total disaster. Someone she knew from years back gathered her up and took her under his wing, but he turned out to be a tad overprotective, so I'm told. They say he made her give up performing, and more or less made her a prisoner. Then, can you believe it, the bastard started seeing another woman!'

Nathan was starting to feel sick. Pinky's revelations were like a blow to the solar plexus. 'So, why didn't she just leave him and come back to the people who loved and appreciated her?'

'Because, sweetie, by this stage, she had lost all her confidence. The poor woman was ruined. No longer able to face the public, all she could do to earn a crust was private tutoring.'

'Where was she doing this . . . tutoring?' asked Nathan, now wishing he'd accepted the little "drinky".

Pinky spread his hands. 'Darling, I haven't the slightest idea.'

Nathan's heart sank.

Pinky must have seen the expression on Nathan's face. 'However. I do know someone who might help you. The same someone who told me about her abusive lover.' The little eyes took on a malicious glint. 'You were in love with her, weren't you?'

Though he felt his hackles rise, Nathan told himself that in this spiteful little creature lay his best hope of finding out what he needed to know. And what did it matter anyway? He sighed. 'Who wasn't in love with Marika in those days?'

'I always thought you would have made a rather charming couple,' said Pinky, 'even if she was older than you. Pity you never had the balls to do something about it, she might not have run off with that animal in that case.'

Following this sudden vicious barb, rather than feeling angry, Nathan experienced a terrible sense of regret. Why hadn't he done anything about it? For he hadn't been "a little bit in love with her", as he'd put it to Liz, he had idolised Marika. Pinky was right, he hadn't had the balls.

'You said you know someone?' he said mildly.

If Pinky was surprised that his wounding remark had elicited no reaction, he didn't show it. 'Well, I'll just give them a bell, and we can take a little stroll into town so you can meet them.'

Having made the call, Pinky glanced at the ornate ormolu clock that he liked to refer to as his "darling little bit of bronze doré" and stood up. 'Come along, sweet cheeks, we're going visiting.'

* * *

Liz was making up the bed for their guest when she heard the house phone ringing. The agitated voice on the other end of the line wasn't one she recognised.

'I need to speak to Matt Ballard quite urgently, please. My name is Penny Turner.'

Matt had mentioned seeing her, so Liz said, 'He'll be back shortly, Penny. Can I take your number and he'll call you straightaway?'

'Oh, well, only if it's within the next twenty minutes, because my shift starts then. Tell him I have some information for him.'

'Perhaps you can tell me, Penny. I'm Liz Haynes, his partner, we work all our cases together. It wouldn't happen to be about the Bunker, would it?'

After a silence that lasted several seconds, Penny Turner said, 'Yes. Well, indirectly. You see, a boy has gone missing. He spoke to his brother about the Bunker a few days before he disappeared. The family is dead rough, but the two boys are — well, sort of okay. I see Lee sometimes, that's the brother, and he's really worried about Dean. He reckoned that Dean went on this mysterious trip somewhere, and when he came back he seemed sort of . . . changed. Not long after that he disappeared for good. He'd been raving about something he called "Secret Bunker Training", before he vanished.'

'Just like the boy we are looking for,' breathed Liz.

'Look, I need to go. I'd give you the family's address if I thought they'd let you over the doorstep, but there's no chance of that — not that you'd want to set foot in that pit in any case. What I can tell you is that Lee has a part-time job, after school, at the convenience store in Eastly Road. He's a decent kid — God knows how with those parents — and he'll talk to you.'

Liz thanked her, told her she'd pass this on to Matt, and ran downstairs to write the names down before she forgot them.

Telling David about the call, she said, 'I wonder how many kids are getting drawn into this weird set-up.'

'If you ask me, just one is too many,' muttered David. 'I find it frightening.'

'The unknown always is,' Liz said sagely, privately thinking that the reality might turn out to be even more so.

David looked at his watch. 'Jeff should be here in half an hour. I'm looking forward to seeing him. We haven't been able to get together so often since we started at uni. I'm not too far away, being at Peterborough, but Jeff is at Loughborough. It's not that far, but it does involve a bit of travel.'

Liz, too, was looking forward his visit. After David had reminded her about Jeff's handstand on the car park wall, other memories had begun to come back. She had an over-riding impression of Jeff as a kind, sensitive boy. He probably still was. David certainly held him in high esteem.

'I'll call Matt and tell him about Penny Turner, hopefully he'll be on his way back so he can meet Jeff when he arrives.'

Matt sounded dispirited. His visits to the Coopers always left him feeling that way. Penny's call had given him something positive to do. He was just saying that he would stop off at the convenience store on his way home, to have a chat with Lee, when Liz heard David call out, 'Got something!'

She ended the call and went into the incident room, where she found him with a creased sheet of paper in his hand.

He waved it at her. 'At last, a place! Ever heard of Waters End?'

'Vaguely, but I can't pin-point it.'

'Hang on.' David turned to his laptop. 'It's further up from here, and towards the east coast. It looks to me like a tiny village.'

'In what context did Molly mention it?' asked Liz.

'She says here that she is considering buying a little property there. She says she'd been there without telling any-one about it, or that she was thinking of moving out. The cottage was called The Old Post Office.' He grinned happily. 'This is big, Liz. Wherever she was when disaster struck, it couldn't have been too far from this place. As soon as we get Jeff settled, can we go look for it? You never know, the person who was selling that cottage might have known her, or where she was staying.'

'Absolutely. Jeff might like to come with us. We can't do any more about the Bunker until he's met up with Ewan at the Community Centre this evening. Matt also says he'll go and speak to the boy Lee, so we've got plenty of time this afternoon. Well done, kiddo. I knew you'd find a location before long.'

'I'm trying not to get too excited in case it turns out to be a dead end, but you never know, we might have a lead at last.' He stopped, as if struck by a thought. 'Let's take the key that Matt found in Joe's things. It could have been Molly's, not Joe's, and she gave it to him for safe-keeping, like the things she gave to others.'

Though Liz wasn't sure their luck would be that good, she couldn't help being infected with some of David's enthusiasm.

CHAPTER FOURTEEN

Arriving at Kool Annie's, Nathan realised he should have known where Pinky would take him. And who else could Pinky's mysterious informant be but Annie Travis herself, the owner, who knew everything that went on within at least a mile of her bar.

'Now, seeing as it's close to lunch time, you can't say it's too early for that drinky now, can you, petal?' Pinky looked at him expectantly.

'Sorry, Pinky, I'm going to be driving later, and eleven thirty is hardly lunch time. I'll get you one though. What'll you have?'

The order sorted, Pinky asked if they could have a word with Annie, and the bartender ambled off to find her.

'So, is it Annie herself who knows about Marika, or someone she knows?' asked Nathan.

'Well, sweetie, I think it's both. Annie knows more than I do, but I have an idea she'll point you in a different direction — if you're that keen to find out, and don't mind a bit of a drive.'

Nathan didn't mind at all. He'd have driven to Land's End to meet someone who could tell him about Marika. What he did mind was Pinky's reluctance to tell him something he obviously knew. Surely he could have just told him where this "bit of a drive" would take him. He could be halfway there by now.

Annie arrived some five minutes later. On the surface, she looked like a typical East End pub landlady with her powdered face and bright red lips, ample bosom barely covered by a low-cut blouse, and the black hair with a few grey roots showing. However, Annie was sharp as a scalpel and had a business head rivalling that of the CEO of Amazon. She ran a bar because she chose to, besides, it was a family business. Nevertheless, she had fingers in any number of other pies, all supposedly legitimate and all successful.

Indicating a quiet table in the corner, she sat down and fixed her gaze on Nathan. 'Pinky tells me you want to know what happened to Marika Molohan when she moved away.'

'That's right, Annie.'

'Why?'

'Oh, come on, Annie!' Pinky nudged her. 'He was madly in love with the woman, and he let her roll out of his life without doing a thing about it. Now she's dead, the poor fellow feels guilty.'

While Nathan would gladly have throttled Pinky, he had to admit that that was exactly what he'd done. At least he had the small satisfaction of telling Annie something Pinky didn't know. 'She's not just dead, Annie, Marika was murdered. I need to know what happened when she left here, where she went, and who with. Ultimately, I need to find out who killed her.'

'Really? I'd say that was a job for the Fenland Constabulary, wouldn't you?' said Annie dryly. 'Not a *keyboard* player.'

Her words had hit home. Nathan scrambled to his feet. 'Sorry, I'm clearly wasting your time. Forget it. I'll find out for myself.'

'She fell in love — lust, whatever — with a guitarist,' said Annie, with a smile of amusement. 'So get off your high horse and I'll tell you what I heard.'

With a muttered apology, Nathan sat down. A guitarist. Who? 'Please go on.'

'She told me he played like a man possessed, under the spell of some unearthly force. She was drawn, couldn't get enough of it. His name was Karl Harriman, and as far as I could see, nothing but a loser — not to mention being ugly as sin.'

The name meant nothing to Nathan, which was odd. Surely, if this musician had been as good as all that, he would have heard of him.

'I didn't know it was *him* she ran off with,' Pinky said. 'I remember seeing him around years ago, and my dear, he was perfectly repulsive.'

'And she went away with him?' Nathan asked.

'They went up to Newcastle. This Harriman fellow was auditioning players for a new group he was forming. Marika was to be lead vocalist and pianist when one of their numbers called for it.' Annie sat back, getting into her story. 'It was supposed to take music in a new direction, by fusing classical music with hard rock. Whatever that means.'

'Well, there's nothing new about that,' said Nathan with a shrug. 'That kind of thing was around as far back as the sixties.' He wondered what on earth Marika had been thinking of. With the gift she had, why in heaven's name would she want to join some crappy rock band that nobody had even heard of?'

'Did this group record anything, or do any live shows?' he asked.

'Nope,' said Annie. 'What Marika didn't realise until she shacked up with him was that Karly boy was possessed by drugs rather than the music. What's more, he had every intention of dragging her down with him.'

Nathan was speechless.

Annie sighed. 'Even after she found this out she was so besotted with him that she couldn't bring herself to walk away. I don't know if she ever did hit the drugs — somehow, I don't think she did — but she very soon discovered that all he was after, apart from sex and money, was her voice, her virtuosity.'

'That can't be true,' Nathan cried. 'Marika wasn't like that. I can't believe that a woman so highly educated, with such ... class, could fall for some no-account junkie rock musician.'

'Love makes fools of us all, dearie,' said Pinky quietly.

How true that was.

'I think I should get you a drink,' Annie said, 'because there's worse to come.'

Nathan nodded dumbly. A drink was exactly what he needed.

Annie ordered three whiskies and continued her story. 'Well, finally she reached the end of her tether, and rang an old friend of hers from down this way. She told this friend that Harriman had drained her bank accounts and she was at rock bottom. This friend — Clarice, I think her name was — told her she knew someone who would be prepared to drive up to Newcastle, pick Marika up and take her back to his home, out of the clutches of Harriman, who was likely to try and force her to stay.'

The whiskies arrived and Nathan gulped his thirstily, thankful for the alcohol that burned his throat and for a second or two, eased the pain of what he was hearing.

'Marika leaped at the offer, and left Harriman that evening.' Annie shook her head. 'But she'd jumped out of the frying pan and straight into the fire. Her supposed saviour had been an ardent fan of hers for years, and at first, he treated her like royalty, asking only that she give piano lessons to his nephew.' She looked at Nathan. 'You know what's coming next, don't you? This man became possessive, then controlling. Gradually, as Marika started to recover from her experience with Harriman, he put the pressure on, and the downward spiral began again. When she hit an all-time low, he grew tired of her and started seeing another woman. It ended when he threw Marika out.'

'Who was he?' Nathan managed to say.

'His name was Bolter, Frederick Bolter, but he liked to be called Rick. And don't bother looking for him, he's dead.'

Nathan swallowed the last of his whisky. He was starting to feel like a punch bag. 'Dead?'

'Killed in a car crash,' Annie said. 'The car was being driven by the woman he left Marika for. Nice piece of irony that.'

'And Marika? What happened to her?' asked Nathan.

'At this point the story gets a bit sketchy.' Annie gave him a look of uncharacteristic sympathy. 'All I can tell you is that she managed to find lodgings somewhere, and began giving private lessons. Eventually she found a permanent position as a sort of music tutor-cum-governess, if such a thing exists these days.'

'Where was this?' Nathan asked, thinking that this must be the drive Pinky had mentioned.

'I can't say,' Annie said. 'Could have been anywhere. But I'll give you the name of a man and the village he lives in. It's my belief that he was Marika's closest friend at that time.' Annie yelled to the bartender, asking him to bring her a pen and paper.

She scribbled on the slip of paper and handed it to Nathan. 'Here you are, and the best of luck to you. I mean that, it was a crying shame what happened to Marika. The world is all the poorer without her playing.'

'And singing,' added Pinky solemnly.

Nathan looked at the words Annie had scrawled on the slip of paper: *George Miles. Oaken Cottage, Beckersby Village.*

As soon as he got home, he searched for the address on the internet. Beckersby was a tiny village, just over half an hour's drive away, not far from the coast. Nathan toyed with the idea of ringing Liz but decided to go there himself first, in case it turned out to be a dead end. He couldn't shake the feeling that what Annie had said was only the start of the story. On top of those terrible disasters, a further one had been added, and this one had culminated in her death.

As ever, he was already beginning to vacillate on his way out of Greenborough. Was he really up to this? Should he even be doing it? After all, he was a musician, not a detective. Maybe he should have called Liz after all . . .

But Nathan did not turn back.

* * *

143

A graphite grey Ford Fiesta pulled up outside Cannon Farm and a young man sprang out. Liz recognised Jeff Jones at once, despite all the time that had passed. It was his boyish smile. Tall and thin as he now was, with what David referred to as a Tik-Tok hairstyle, that had not changed. David was right, too, about Jeff not looking his age. She would have put him at around sixteen.

Jeff hurried over to her and gave her a hug. 'Auntie Liz! It's been ages. You look great!'

He then embraced David, who had followed Liz out of the house.

'Welcome to Cannon Farm,' said Liz. 'Matt's on the phone, he won't be long. Come on in.'

Jeff took two large bags from the boot of his car. 'Don't worry, I'm not moving in. One is my football kit and a few other things I thought might be useful.'

After David had taken Jeff to his room and showed him around, Matt emerged from the incident room, looking somewhat anxious.

'I'm very pleased to meet you, sir,' Jeff said upon being introduced, 'and I am keen to help, if I possibly can.'

Liz noticed an unusual look come over Matt's face, one she couldn't quite decipher.

'The name's Matt, lad, forget the sir, it makes me feel ancient.'

It wasn't long before the conversation turned to the video clip David had shown them. 'It's hard to believe anyone can pull off a stunt like that,' Matt said, 'I mean, jumping from one building to another? Well . . .' He peered at Jeff. 'Do you have a death wish or something, lad?'

'Far from it,' laughed Jeff. 'I find it exhilarating and — if that's not too pretentious — life affirming.'

'It must take an incredible amount of training and hard work, I should think,' added Liz.

'It's a discipline,' said Jeff, 'like many others. It's a case of developing your physical and mental strength by means of challenges, then repeating these until you find the best way of overcoming them. Basically, I'm pushing the boundaries of getting from A to B in the least amount of time and using only what the environment provides in order to do it.' His smile widened. 'I'll shut up about it now, before I bore you to death.'

'It's fascinating,' said Liz. 'I've never forgiven you for that scare you gave me when you were a youngster. Don't think I've forgotten that, Jeff Jones! Anyway, on to our cases. We have a lot to explain, and not a lot of time.'

Soon, they were on to the Bunker, at which point Jeff's expression was anything but boyish. 'And now you say another boy has gone missing. That's terrible. But can that sort of thing really go on, taking impressionable kids and turning them into career criminals? It seems hardly credible.'

'No worse than giving kids rifles and turning them into child soldiers,' Matt said.

Liz noticed Jeff's expression. 'Sadly, Jeff, if you'd come up against some of the things Matt and I have faced in our time, you'd have no trouble believing it. There are some evil people around, even here in the misty Fens.'

'I know,' said Jeff. 'I see it all the time in kids coming out of dysfunctional families. It's just that I work with like-minded people who care about kids, and try to help them move forward into a better life.'

'Two different aspects of the same thing, I guess,' Liz said. 'As coppers, we mainly got lumbered with people for whom it was too late, the criminals that is. Even so, we are all striving for good, and that's why we must stop this consortium, or whatever it is, that is aiming to turn kids who do have some hope into hardened criminals.'

'I'm with you on that,' said Jeff. 'Just tell me what you want me to do.'

'Play football to start with,' said David. 'They'll be training tonight, at the Community Centre. Dazzle them with your skills, and then make friends with their star player. Get him to talk to you if you can. He's the only person we know who has actually been to this Bunker and returned.'

'And the aim is to discover where it's located, is it?' asked Jeff.

'Initially, although . . .' replied David, looking from Liz to Matt.

'Yes,' said Matt. 'We'll take this one step at a time. However, if you felt able to, well . . . If at some future point there was a chance you might get inside the place, and only if you could do so safely . . .'

'I understand,' said Jeff calmly. 'A thing like that cannot be allowed to continue unimpeded. We'll start with football and I'll see how the land lies.'

David was smiling at Matt, his eyes shining in gratitude and relief. Liz wondered how Matt's sudden change of heart had come about. Maybe it was his latest visit to Liam's parents, following shortly upon the video David had shown them, that had galvanised him into a need to act.

That decided, they set about planning the rest of the day.

'One thing I must do is talk to the lad Penny told you about, Liz,' said Matt. 'I'll wait for him outside the shop after school. I'm not sure what I can do until then.'

Before she could answer, Liz's mobile rang. It was Hazel Webber.

'That was fun,' she said, 'not too arduous. Now, would you like me to read the results out now, or do you want to collect the book?'

'You're something else, Hazel!' exclaimed Liz delightedly. 'That's amazing. And so fast.'

'Well, to be honest, I did sit up half the night on it. Some of the words were lifted as they are, as in the word *grave*, for instance, others she built up from single letters, as in *anvil* and *scales*. Those took a bit of time.'

'Can you tell us what she says, Hazel? We'll call by later and pick up the book,' said Liz. This deserved an exceptional houseplant. She switched to loudspeaker and found a notepad and pen. 'Ready when you are.'

'Well, your young man told me that Molly was fond of cryptic clues, and I fear this is more of the same. It's a list of places, or areas within a particular place. You will need to know where she's talking about to get any sense out of it.'

Liz wrote down the message. Hazel had not been wrong, this was a treasure hunt with clues that made no sense.

'. . . *Beneath the anvil. By the third silver birch. In Rupert's grave. Close to William Arbuthnot. Under the scales.*' Hazel made a tutting noise. 'And I have a nasty feeling that these places might contain yet more clues. Anyway, if you need further assistance, it seems my brain has not yet atrophied, so throw it my way. Oh, and tell David not to forget that bottle!'

Liz remained staring at her phone for several seconds. 'Well, guys, I reckon this makes our trip to Waters End even more necessary. How about a cup of something and then we'll hit the road?'

While David explained to Jeff where they were going and why, Matt followed Liz into the kitchen. 'Why don't you come with us, Matt?' she said. 'Nothing much is going to happen till later.'

'I think I'll stay here, sweetheart, and get in touch with a few of my old contacts. I'll also see if there's any news of Smokey. There's that bank card I found in his things — you know, the one in the name of Johan de Vries. I might even ring our reluctant liaison officer and see if he's turned up anything exciting.'

'Fat bloody chance,' muttered Liz. 'I had hoped that we could infuse a bit of enthusiasm into that lad, but I've a feeling he could be a lost cause.'

'Let's give him a chance,' said Matt. 'But if he falls short, I won't be covering for him, that's for sure.'

'And then Charley Anders will hit him where it hurts, and that could be a career-changer, couldn't it?'

'I just hope it doesn't backfire on her,' said Matt grimly. 'Chief Superintendent Edwin Norton does not like Charley one bit.'

'The feeling is mutual, I believe,' added Liz. 'But she has some powerful allies, and a crap detective is no good to anyone. If the shit hits the fan, I'm backing Charley.' She finished making the tea, glanced at the door and lowered her voice to a whisper. 'Jeff is quite different to most lads of his age, isn't he? He has a kind of . . . how can I put it? Almost as if he's older and wiser than us. Or does that sound ridiculous?'

'No, and I'm beginning to understand why our David feels the way he does about his friend. I believe we could trust him to help us, Liz. I never thought I'd be saying this but I really think he would act wisely, and not be tempted into taking any stupid risks.'

Liz could have cheered. She had feared that Matt would dig his heels in. David, of course, would be over the moon.

They went back to the lounge carrying the tea.

'Ever been to Waters End, Matt?' Liz asked.

'I think I've passed through it on a couple of occasions. It had a lovely little Norman church as I recall, with a pub next door that had a funny name which has escaped me.'

'That's more than I know,' said Liz. 'I just hope we'll be able to find The Old Post Office, that's all.'

'And a link to Molly,' added David.

Liz wasn't sure why, but she had a positive feeling about this nondescript little hamlet.

CHAPTER FIFTEEN

Just as Liz, David and Jeff set out, Nathan Venner was arriving at Beckersby Village.

He wasn't impressed.

'What a shit-hole,' he muttered under his breath, turning his gaze from sad little cottage to miserable looking house. There wasn't even anyone around to ask the way to Oaken Cottage. The one street was deserted, like the setting for some creepy old movie. Either all the inhabitants had been spirited away by some evil force or a shootout was about to take place.

'Can I 'elp you?'

Nathan jumped. An odd little figure was peering in through the partially open passenger window.

The man was very short, but that was probably down to the severe curvature of his spine, and he had a wizened, impish face. He smiled toothlessly at Nathan.

'Oh, er, yes. I'm looking for Oaken Cottage, sir. Have you heard of it?'

It took him a while to realise that the man's loud guffaw of laughter was because Nathan had called him "sir", which he evidently found terribly funny.

'Oh, I knows it all right. Looking to buy, is yer?'

'Er, no. I'm looking for an old friend. Do you happen to know George Miles?'

'Oh 'e's long gone.'

'Sorry?'

'George. He upped and moved out, a good few years back. S'far as I can tell, no one knows where 'e is now.'

Nathan's heart sank. 'So, is the house empty?'

'Nah. The folks that bought it from George come into some brod, so they's moving up the ladder. Our little village ain't good 'nuff anymore.' He screwed up his face in distaste.

At least there was someone to talk to. These people might know where George went. 'Could you direct me there, please?'

The old man gestured vaguely in the direction of a handful of cottages that straggled down a fen lane and out of the village. 'Last one before the fields start. Gotta stump of an old oak in the garden. Storm backend o' 1987 took it. Saw it go, I did. Turrible night, just turrible.'

Before the man could embark on a long story about that terrible night, Nathan thanked him and drove on.

Unlike the rest of Beckersby, Oaken Cottage was rather pretty. It had obviously been cared for over the years, the residents had even taken the trouble to carve the giant stump of the devastated oak tree into the shape of an owl.

He went up to the door and pressed the bell, hearing a tinny tune echo throughout the house, and which brought a smiling woman to the door.

'Oh! I thought you were Amazon Prime.' She gave him a puzzled smile. 'Sorry, but what do you want?'

Deciding there was no point in fabricating an explanation, Nathan told her that George Miles was the only person left who might know something about a dear friend's disappearance.

The woman surveyed him for a few moments, and then opened the door wider. 'Come in. I can't promise, but we might have something about him in our household files. We've stacks of paperwork about the place at present, as we've put it on the market.'

He followed her into a delightful country kitchen. Glancing around appreciatively, he said, 'I'm surprised you want to leave here, it's so lovely. Where are you moving to? Somewhere nearby, or are you going out of the area?'

'It's a pity, I know, but we need to be closer to the town. We have a small business which is expanding, and trying to run it from out here is not working out. We love the cottage itself but, well, the village is a difficult place to live if you are an incomer. The locals stick together, and you are never made to feel part of it. Also, it's lonely for the kids, they need more children to mix with and have fun. I reckon the average age of the population is seventy-five.' She gave a rather bitter laugh.

'I met one, although I think it's some years since he saw seventy-five,' said Nathan, rolling his eyes.

'Little gnome with no teeth?'

'That's him.'

'Then he probably told you we'd won the lottery or something.' The woman shook her head. 'That's Crazy Len as the kids call him, and they aren't far wrong. Batty as they come, that one.' She gave a wry smile. 'My name is Kirsty, by the way, Kirsty Holmes. Far from what Len says, we are almost bankrupting ourselves to move closer to town and into a house with enough space for a proper office.'

She was so open and friendly that Nathan found himself confiding in her. He told her about Marika's death and how he regretted losing contact with her. 'George Miles really is my last hope of discovering what happened to her.'

Kirsty Holmes took a large box file from a shelf and opened it out. 'I'm sorry. I hope I can be of some help.' She began to leaf through the papers and documents. 'My husband knew George from before we came here. They were both volunteers at the dog rescue centre over at Poultenby Marsh. According to Mick — that's my husband — George was a really nice man back then, but he changed. By the time I met him — when we were buying this cottage — he was a wreck. Mick thought he'd had some sort of breakdown, after which he went all secretive. He seemed to think everyone he met was a threat and meant to harm him, so he avoided them. Very sad.'

Things were taking a sinister turn. Nathan wondered what could have happened to make George, a nice man who loved dogs, suddenly become a furtive, cowering recluse? The parallels with Marika's life were plain to see. She, too, had hidden herself away, believing that she was being threatened. And Marika had been right.

Meanwhile, Kirsty was still turning over papers. When she reached the bottom of the box she said, 'Looks like the best I can do is give you the name of the conveyancer who handled the purchase of Oaken Cottage. I'm so sorry, I hoped we might at least have had a telephone number for George.' She found a pen and paper, and wrote down the name "Rivers and Connaught Solicitors, conveyancer Lucy Simmonds". 'Apparently, George purchased another cottage, even more remote than this. Mick says it's miles from the nearest village. He felt sorry for George and would have liked to visit him, but he couldn't be found. It upset my Mick — he's a big softy.' Kirsty handed him the memo. 'I'm sorry I can't be of more help.'

Nathan thanked her, folded the sheet and put it into his pocket. 'It's another step closer. Now I must let you get on. I appreciate your help and wish you all the best with the move.'

He drove away, disappointed that he hadn't found George Miles. Still, he told himself, it wasn't a complete dead end — unlike the village of Beckersby.

* * *

Mid-morning and work at the station was in full swing. DC Darren Norton sat at his desk, wondering what he should do. He was beset with conflicting emotions. He was still furious at having been assigned to a bunch of private detectives. People like that belonged in crappy old paperbacks, lurking in their raincoats under gas lamps. He deserved better than

152

that. Them and their "investigation room", and their white-board they were so proud of. And one of them wasn't even a detective, just some student they'd got in. How dare that little shite tell *him* how to follow leads. What a fucking cheek!

On the other hand, his own enquiries hadn't been exactly fruitful while theirs were sodding well racing ahead. He hated to admit it, but he'd been shocked at how much they had achieved in so short a time. And the victim! What he'd thought to be some dead old bag lady had turned out to be that woman in the photograph, a beautiful lady seated at a concert grand piano. What was he to make of that?

He fiddled with his pen, tapping out a rhythm. He had assumed that at least it would be an easy task — allow these guys to piddle around and get what results they could and simply lift their findings and word his reports as if they were his own. Now he was not so sure. Having seen what they'd come up with, it looked like he'd have to abandon his plan and make some kind of input. Though it went against the grain, he might even have to pull his finger out and do what they had asked of him. With the sullen expression of a child in detention, he checked his electronic pocket notebook and read: *Nathan Venner, friend of Marika . . . check whereabouts of MM after leaving Greenborough.* Venner had called back — eventually — but he had little to tell him about where the woman had disappeared to after she fell off the face of the earth. Venner had given Darren a bit of information about her background — basically, she was wasted as a piano teacher. Well, he'd see what the police database came up with, there was an outside chance she'd committed some driving offence, in which case he'd have an address for her.

The next item on his list was *Liam Cooper and the Bunker.* There, he had the upper hand and wasn't about to share what he knew. He would check out the missing kid's name, and that was that. Anything he knew or supposed about the Bunker was staying with him.

Norton felt a thrill of anticipation. As far as he knew — and he had kept his ear to the ground — no one else in the station had a clue about the place. If the rumours were true and it was what he suspected, this could be his big career move, his ticket out. The Bunker would be his moment of glory. Those private detectives might have the edge with Molly, he'd give them that, but he was ahead of them regarding the Bunker. And ahead it would stay.

* * *

'So, where's the village?' asked David.

'We're in it,' said Liz. 'This is it. Yet another tiny village reduced to a few cottages scattered along the road that passes through. Oh, look. There's that church Matt mentioned, and the pub with the funny name — it's the Saucy Squirrel.' She pointed to a tower rising between some tall old trees, and an old building with a pub sign hanging drunkenly above the door. 'Let's park up and walk around, see if we can find someone to talk to.'

She had been expecting more of the place than this collection of dilapidated buildings, but at least with so few of them, The Old Post Office should be easy to find. In fact, they found it almost at once.

'It's over here,' called out Jeff, pointing to a rather run-down little house whose front door opened on to the street. 'And it's inhabited. There's a cat curled up on the windowsill.'

'You make the enquiries, Liz,' said David. 'If whoever opens the door sees all three of us, they might think we're Jehovah's Witnesses or something.'

So, David and Jeff wandered over towards the church, while Liz rang the doorbell.

An elderly man answered and peered short-sightedly at her. 'Yes?'

Mustering her best smile, Liz explained.

It took a while, but the old man finally relented. 'I know who you mean. It was me trying to sell this place back then.' He glanced a little sadly at the peeling paintwork. 'It looked a lot better when that lady came to look at it, believe you me. Then, when it fell through, I gave up on my dream of a little retirement cottage and decided to see out the rest of my days here.'

'Why did it fall through, sir?' asked Liz.

'Dunno really. She said she was keen, and then, well, nothing. I'm told she just disappeared.' His face creased in a frown. 'I know fear when I sees it, me duck, and that lady was frightened. She was a looker, but her face was all washed out — worry, you know. I fretted over her for quite a while. It didn't seem right for a beautiful lady like that to be so scared.'

Liz nodded. It wasn't right. 'I suppose you didn't keep her address, did you? Or the name of the estate agent?'

'I forget the name, lass. I threw all them papers out long back. Sorry.'

Her heart sank even lower.

'But I do know, roundabout-like, from Elsie the postie, that the lady was staying somewhere in Marshdyke-St-Mary.'

Liz could have hugged the old guy. She knew that village. Many years ago, a key witness in a case she'd been working lived in that very place. It was a "proper" village, considerably larger than this, around fifteen miles from here. She thanked him profusely and raced across the road to catch up with the lads.

'We have a lead! Back to the car, gentlemen. Next destination, Marshdyke-St-Mary. I've a strong suspicion that that is the place Molly ran away from.'

* * *

'Well, wonders will never cease!' What had prompted Matt's utterance was a call from Darren Norton.

'Mr Ballard?'

Noting the emphasis on the "Mister", he said, 'It's Matt, lad. Just Matt.'

Ignoring this, Norton said, 'Well, I thought you should know that the body of another vagrant has been found, and you can be pretty sure that you won't be talking to your mate Smokey Joe again. Fits the description.'

He had been expecting it, but still, it came as a blow. Another link to Molly's past had been broken. The smug and dismissive way Norton had spoken rankled, so Matt said coldly, 'Where was he found, and has he been officially identified yet?' he asked.

'In an old barn, somewhere between here and Fenchester. I haven't got the full details yet,' said Norton. 'The farm worker who found him just said it was a tramp. The crew that attended didn't know Smokey, but the age is about right and the overall description, so it's going to be him, isn't it?'

Wishing the detective would lose his habit of making hasty assumptions, Matt said, 'Surely someone at the station knows him? He's been passing in and out of Fenfleet for donkey's years. Is Swifty on duty? He knows him well enough to identify the body.'

There was a pause. Norton obviously hadn't bothered to follow this up. Matt said, 'If it comes down to it, both Liz and I know Smokey. One of us could identify him.'

'Okay, I'll pass that on to the officer in charge.'

'Do you know the manner of death?' asked Matt. Was he going to have to wring every single drop of basic information out of this man?

'Er . . .'

Matt heard the rustle of papers.

'Nothing obvious, apparently. No indication of any violence.'

'So, if the cause of death is unknown or unclear, they are looking at an unexplained death.' Matt was racing through the procedures, some of which might well have changed since he left the force. Red tape grew like bindweed around the law, and new pieces of legislation took root almost daily. Whatever, it would be referred to the coroner for investigation, and there would be a post-mortem to determine the cause of death. 'Look, I've an appointment in a couple of hours' time, meanwhile, I can go to the mortuary myself. At least we'll know one way or the other.'

Norton didn't put it in so many words but his meaning was clear. If Matt wanted to waste his time, he was welcome. He was quick to reject Matt's offer to meet him there. 'No, I, er, I've got a report to tie up by this afternoon, and I need to chase up a couple of contacts regarding Marika.'

Matt very much doubted that he was doing anything of the sort. More likely was that Norton wished to avoid having to come up against Rory Wilkinson again. He could count on the fingers of one hand the number of people Rory actively disliked, but when he did, he took no prisoners. A few choice phrases could reduce the pompous, the unsympathetic, to abject silence. 'Okay, but perhaps you'd let them know to expect me?'

Norton agreed rather reluctantly, and Matt ended the call. He looked at his watch. He would have to shelve his search into Johan de Vries for the time being. He would have liked to have waited for Liz to get back, but he'd already had a call telling him they were on their way to Marshdyke-St-Mary, where, Liz hoped, Molly had lived and taught music. Matt silently wished them luck. Having lost Smokey Joe, this was their last hope of finding out what had happened to Marika. He left a note for Liz and set off for the morgue, making a quick call to Rory en route.

He had only asked Norton to ring in advance because he wanted to appear to be following correct procedure. He had no wish for the young detective to know the true relationship between them and the pathologist.

'I'm hoping that a quick peek into my cold storage facility will be sufficient,' said Rory. 'Only we're frantic here today, and I haven't had time to make him look presentable. He only arrived half an hour ago, poor old guy.'

'That's all I need, my friend. I *have* to know if our main link to Molly is now gone, dead as she is.'

'The one difference, and this is just a guess, as I only had a cursory look when our John Doe arrived, was that he was not murdered. I strongly suspect a fatal heart attack, but don't quote me on that. It's only a hunch, going by his outward appearance.'

'How ironic,' Matt said. 'Our main lead to Molly's past simply ups and dies.'

'It'd be far worse if someone killed him,' said Rory. 'Anyway, sorry to rush you, but as I have a queue of cadavers, all begging for my ministrations, let's go the cold storage.'

Rory hadn't been joking. The entire morgue was packed with people, trolleys, along with the sinister-looking metal boxes used to transport bodies from the hospital wards to the mortuary.

A few moments later they stood in front of the bank of cold cabinets. 'Okay, my friend. The moment of truth.' Rory placed his free hand on the handle of a drawer. 'I never had the pleasure of meeting your Smokey Joe, so he's a stranger to me. Ready?'

Matt nodded, preparing himself to say goodbye to another long-time local character.

Rory opened the drawer.

'I see from your expression that this particular person is a stranger to you too,' said Rory.

'Absolutely. I've never seen this man before in my life.' Part of him was relieved, as it meant that there was a chance that Joe might still be alive, just in hiding. Another part felt sorry for this sad stranger. 'I'm not even sure that he's a vagrant. He's got shabby clothes, and he's not exactly well-cared for, but,' he stepped forward, 'he doesn't look like a street dweller to me.'

Rory looked closer. 'I think you could be right, Matt Ballard. Very observant. Maybe I'll reorganise my schedule and move this gentleman up the list for his PM. This is interesting.'

'Will you let me know — unofficially of course?' asked Matt, keeping his voice down.

'I certainly will.' A lab technician was beckoning frantically from the door. 'Sorry, Matt, I'm needed. Oh, the price of fame! What it is to be in *constant* demand.'

Matt didn't hang around. He had all he needed. Despite himself, he had to admit to looking forward to informing a certain young detective that his assumptions were yet again incorrect. Yes, it was a relief that it wasn't Joe, but the question remained as to where the hell he was.

He sent a text to Liz, telling her of his mission to the mortuary. Then, clearing his mind of all thoughts of Molly Molohan, he turned his attention to the Bunker. School was out. Time to pay a visit to young Lee at the shop in Eastly Street.

CHAPTER SIXTEEN

Approaching the outskirts of Marshdyke-St-Mary, Liz felt a tingle of excitement along her spine.

Jeff glanced at her. 'You have a feeling about this place, Liz?'

'Yes.'

Apparently, that was enough for Jeff, who didn't ask her why.

They drove slowly into the village, while Liz told them what little she remembered from her previous visits. She did recall thinking that although it was a well-kept, if somewhat straggly village, it had had a strange atmosphere.

'It was nothing I could put my finger on,' she said. 'Just an odd feeling of, well, unease.' She frowned, remembering. 'However, I was investigating a disappearance, a complex and rather sinister case that affected the residents badly, including my key witness, so I put down my disquiet to that.'

'But you feel it now, today?' said Jeff.

'Funnily enough, I started to feel it on the road in. It's probably just those old memories coming back.'

Jeff didn't answer.

'Anyway, forget my fancies, and let me tell you what I know about the place. It has no public transport service and no amenities, not even a post office. It has a small community centre where they hold coffee mornings, parties, and meetings of groups like the Ladies Circle, and the Gardening Club. There is a very pretty church too. I was told it has some remarkably fine and ornate architecture and even attracts the occasional visitor who appreciates that sort of thing. I got the impression that it was kept going by a handful of the locals, who hold fundraising events and raffles.'

'That's often the way in small communities,' said David, gazing out of the window. 'Hey! That's impressive!'

He was pointing at a fantastical structure rising high in the air from an open driveway. Liz smiled. 'Scrap metal art. Brilliant, isn't it?'

She slowed to a crawl so they could take a proper look. The metalwork sculpture represented a dragon-like creature made entirely of old pieces of farm equipment — nuts, bolts and various bits of discarded metal. 'That place used to be a forge. Nowadays they do ironwork, making gates and railings and stuff like that. Wrought iron is very popular around here.'

'So, where do we start?' asked David.

Liz pulled into the side of the road. 'If I remember rightly, there was a rambling old farmhouse off a lane by the village post box. My witness lived next door. The owners were two sisters who ran a sort of rescue centre for injured birds. They even had a "bird hospital" in some dilapidated stables. They were very sociable, always up for a chat. We could start with them. They had lived in the village all their lives, and what they didn't know about the place wasn't worth knowing.'

'Perfecto!' said David, with a grin. 'Sweet old ladies, my favourite source of information. What are we waiting for, let's go charm them.'

'Maybe we should decide on a cover story first,' interjected Jeff. 'They might wonder why we've appeared out of nowhere and are asking a barrage of questions.'

'I suggest we tell them the truth — up to a point,' said Liz. 'We are private investigators, and our client has asked us to find out what happened to his loved one, Marika Molohan, who suddenly disappeared. We have reason to believe she became a private tutor in this area.'

'Don't I look a bit young to be a detective?' Jeff said.

Liz laughed. 'Well . . . I know. We can say you're much older than you look — which happens to be true — and that you are assisting us with interviewing younger people.'

Jeff smiled broadly. 'Nice one! Jeff Jones, Junior PI. I can live with that.'

They had no problem finding Caster House Farm, which was just as Liz remembered it, though somewhat more chaotic. She noticed several sheds, runs and outdoor aviaries, none of which looked too professionally built. Maybe the sisters had turned their hands to carpentry in order to house ever more birds.

They got out of the car and went up to the gate, where a sign told visitors to ring the bell and wait. The bell in question was a large iron affair like a giant cowbell, with a rope hanging from the clapper and an ornate cast iron bird on top. David gave it a hearty yank and jumped. 'Blimey, that'd wake the dead.'

As the sound of the bell died down, an elderly woman came hurrying up to the gate. She was tall and thin and wore an ancient wax jacket, faded jeans and Wellington boots. 'Okay, what have you got? Not another injured pigeon, I hope. We've got a shedful of 'em already.' Then, when none of them proffered an ailing bird, she said, 'Well?'

'We wondered if you could help us with a bit of local knowledge,' said Liz with a bright smile. 'Aaron Callaway told me that you and your sister have lived here all your lives.'

'Aaron you say? Goodness me, he moved away two years ago. Do you know him then?'

Liz told her about the case she had investigated and that she had interviewed him.

'I remember you! You were here about that young woman who disappeared, weren't you?' She unlatched the gate. 'Come in. I'll just fetch Alice and we'll see if we can help.'

She led them towards the house, and the open doors of a sunroom. Not quite a conservatory, it nevertheless housed a couple of large over-stuffed old sofas, a battered coffee table and several bookcases, overflowing with books in no apparent order. A couple of droopy plants cried out for water on the windowsill. The wall adjoining the house was covered from ceiling to floor with framed pictures of birds.

'Sit down and make yourselves comfortable. I'll call Alice, I think she's changing Tinky-Winky's bandages.'

'Tinky-Winky?' Jeff said.

'A cygnet, dear. He's a sweetie, but he's not keen on having his bandages changed. He's suffering from something called Angel Wing that causes the flight feathers to stick out from the body at odd angles. After they've been bandaged flat to the body every day for ten days he should be flying just like normal. Alice is very good with swans, you know. She's very fond of the larger birds, whereas I like the little ones. Oh, I'm Emily Targett by the way.' She hurried off with a, 'Won't be a tick.'

'I'm not sure I'd like to get too close to a swan. Can't they break your arm? That's what I've heard,' David said.

'Only when they're breeding, feel threatened or are protecting something. I understand they have great memories, and they'll remember whether you've been kind to them or not,' said Jeff. 'I know an old guy who lives on the river near our place. He has one that follows him around like a dog. When he gives it a treat, it dips its head, as if it's saying thank you.'

While the lads were chatting, Liz had been looking around and had spotted an upright piano inside the house. If one, or both sisters played, perhaps they'd actually met Molly.

When Emily returned with Alice, Liz was struck by how different the two sisters looked. Whereas Emily was a beanpole, Alice was short and round in both face and body. Only the ancient wax jackets and the muddy Wellington boots were identical.

They stopped at the door and dragged off their boots using an old cast iron boot remover. Emily perched on the arm of one of the sofas and smiled at them. 'Did you ever find that missing girl you were looking for when you were here last?'

'We did,' said Liz. 'She'd got herself involved with some seriously bad people. Luckily we found her before she came to any harm.'

'Oh, that's good,' said Emily. 'We never did hear what happened, and we feared the worst. You hear such terrible things these days. Still, that's by the by. How can we help you? You said you needed some local knowledge.'

Liz told them about Marika, and that she may have been teaching music in this very village.

Neither sister spoke for some considerable time. There was an inexplicable air of tension in the room, quite unlike the warmth with which they'd been welcomed. When Alice wanted to know who was asking for this information, she sounded almost unfriendly.

'I'm sorry but I can't say. Our client wishes to remain anonymous. But you do know who I'm talking about, don't you?' Liz said.

'No. No idea at all,' Alice said abruptly.

'Why would anyone think this person came here to teach?' Emily added. 'Who in Marshdyke would even want to learn? It's a farming area, hardly a breeding ground for professional concert pianists, is it?'

They know her, thought Liz. It was far from what she'd hoped to hear from these two women, but it clarified one major point. They were in the right place. Molly had come here. They just needed to find someone who would admit it.

Having learned during her years in the force that it was no use flogging a dead horse, Liz smiled brightly. 'Not to worry, we must have been given wrong information. I'd love to hear more about your rescue birds though.'

Luckily, both David and Jeff caught on, and they too plied the women with questions about bird care and rehabilitation.

They left some twenty minutes later, having been ushered out with friendly smiles. Their first interview had taught them an interesting lesson about Marshdyke-St-Mary. They would have to approach the place more carefully, and from a different angle, but they were on the right track, which was a great step forward.

* * *

Johan de Vries was no stranger to fear. He had been barely out of his teens when he enlisted in the army and in the years that followed had experienced the worst of humanity and what it could do. After fourteen years in the armed forces, he retired out, and having been in signals, took a job in civilian communications. He hated it. He needed to do something to redeem evil-doers, turn them away from warfare and show them that there was good in the world. It was totally by accident that he chanced upon the Outward Bound movement. A friend of his, an instructor, had been on his way to an open day when his car broke down. Johan had offered to drive him to Dorset, where the event was being held, and he had spent the day watching and listening. By the time his friend was ready to leave, Johan had signed up for a course as an instructor.

He sailed through the leadership training programme, and the years that followed were the best of his life. Until his dream job ended in nightmare. To ease his pain, he turned to his memories of Molly . . .

'Sing for me?'

She laughed, with a shake of her head. 'Oh, all right. What's it to be this time, Joe? Are you in the mood for something classical, how about a piece by Verdi? Or would you rather something gritty and modern?'

'Something moving. You know what I mean. Something with those minor chords that bring tears to my eyes, that gets me right here.' And he thumped his chest with his fist. 'Well, Molly-girl?'

So she had sung for him. And all those years later, sitting on the ground behind a deserted barn, he heard her voice soar above the marsh. How was it possible, he wondered, that a series of sounds could be so indelibly engraved in his memory, on his heart. While he had a breath in his body, that voice would never die, even though the singer was gone.

Joe felt like the loneliest man in the world. In his years on the road, he had travelled widely but he had always gravitated back to Molly. Now his guide star was gone. More than that, her killer was coming for him too, and he didn't know why. He had never found out what had scared her so much that she had taken to the streets in order to hide. She wouldn't say. And because she hadn't told him, he didn't know why they were looking for him.

He leaned back against the wooden slats of the barn and dug the heel of his old boot into a tuft of the couch grass that had colonised the abandoned yard. Maybe he did know something without being aware that he knew. Maybe Molly had told him something, inadvertently, that was important enough to set the hounds of hell on his tail. He'd avoided them once, but how long could he keep running? To get them off his back, he had ditched his precious bike, his bucket of coals and his bag of belongings. He had been too recognisable, too much of a "character". He had to lose Smokey Joe and become someone else. That old bike had been his grandmother's, and it hurt him to toss it into a ditch where it would doubtless be consumed in the mouth of some dredger. His possessions, on the other hand, were a joke. He'd even left a bank card with them, just to make sure they knew the things were his. What he hadn't meant to leave was his key, but he didn't think about that until he was ten miles away. Too late to bother about it now. It was probably at the bottom of a refuse bin, along with his wardrobe. And then there was his bucket, his talisman.

Only Molly had understood why he had needed that bucket of hot coals. Without it, life was certainly harder. If only he had someone to talk to.

Joe frowned. There was someone, but he would need to find him, and that wouldn't be easy. He would be another target, another link to Molly that needed to be eliminated because of what he might know. A man who didn't want to be found. Joe grunted. If anyone knew how to go under the radar, it was him, so perhaps he should apply some of his own strategies and start hunting. What did he have to lose?

He felt in the lining of his pocket and found a second bank card. Smokey Joe was no more. Welcome to the world, Johan de Vries.

Joe got to his feet. First, he had to find clothes and a damn good wash. He must look presentable if he was to mingle with the public. The local Outreach centre or drop-in hubs were out of the question, he would be recognised. That left one option, and for that he needed money. He reckoned he must be around forty minutes' walk from the nearest village with a post office and a cash machine.

He set off towards the lane that would take him away from the marsh, Molly's voice still singing in his ears.

* * *

Three men sat at a wooden trestle table in a dimly-lit, cavernous space with bare concrete walls and no windows. One had a notepad in front of him, the other two, tablets. There was a door behind them, and a wider one opposite, at the far end of the room. The place smelt musty, as if from long disuse.

The man in charge, known only as Cash, was shorter and stockier than the two men that flanked him, who were both heavily-muscled and athletic.

Cash wrote something on his pad, and then glanced at his two associates. 'Are we ready?'

'Ready,' they echoed.

Cash spoke into an intercom. 'Bring them in.'

The main door swung open. A figure, clad in black, his hands secured behind his back and a sack over his head, was roughly bundled inside and pushed on to one of three hard stools lined up in front of the trestle table. Two more figures followed and were seated, a guard behind each.

Cash looked at them and nodded to the guards, who yanked off the hoods.

The flare of a bright light forced all three figures to lower their heads and blink.

The guards left and the lights dimmed. Cash studied the young faces lined up in front of him. 'Ah, the final three.' His deep voice sounded oddly hollow in the enclosed room. 'You will be pleased to know that you have passed the second level in the training programme. Gentlemen — and lady — welcome to the Bunker.'

CHAPTER SEVENTEEN

Luckily, Lee was early for his shift. Matt recognised him at once from Penny Turner's description, and stepped forward, smiling. 'Hi, Lee. I'm a friend of Penny Turner's. She told me Dean is missing, and I want to help.'

Lee looked startled. 'Why? You a cop?'

Matt shook his head. 'I'm a private detective, lad. Your brother isn't the only one who's gone missing. I'm looking for another lad whose parents have asked for my help.'

Lee bit on his bottom lip. 'I can't pay you, I don't have the cash. Whatever I get from this lot,' he jerked his thumb back towards the store, 'goes to feed me and my bro, and to put clothes on our backs.'

'I don't want money, Lee. Not from you. I want to know about the Bunker. I want to get the kids out and see the place shut down.'

'In your dreams!' In a voice that trembled slightly, Lee said, 'Look, Mister, I dunno what Dean's got himself tied up in but it's gonna take a lot more than you to stop it.'

'Surely *some* help is better than none,' said Matt. 'Tell me what you know, and what you suspect, and I'll try to find your brother. No strings, and no payment either. Oh, and it isn't just me, I have others helping. If that place is what we believe it to be, we have to stop it, and fast.'

Lee said nothing for a while, visibly struggling to come to a decision. Then he looked at Matt and nodded. 'Okay. Hold on. It isn't busy today, so I'll see if Mr Patel can give me a bit of leeway before I have to start.'

He hurried into the shop and out again. He beckoned to Matt, who followed him into an alley that ran alongside the store. Outside the back door there was a bench and a couple of ancient plastic patio chairs. Lee pointed to the bench, having decided the chairs probably wouldn't take Matt's weight, and flopped on to a chair. 'I got ten minutes, so what do you want to know?'

'What did Dean tell you about the Bunker?' Matt asked.

'To start with, he said it was really cool. You could let off steam, get fit and have fun, all for free.' Lee puffed out his cheeks, 'As soon as I heard that bit, about it being free, I thought, yeah, right. Like anyone gives kids like us anything for free.' He shook his head sadly, 'Trouble is, Dean ain't street-wise. He acts the big man but he's just a know-nothing kid.' He stared at Matt. 'Do you really think you can find him?'

'Yes,' said Matt, suddenly certain of it. 'We just need to find a way in. I've been told that the kids are picked up in a sort of van. That right?'

'Yeah, but someone has to talk to them first, to sound 'em out like.'

'Any particular place that happens?'

'Dunno if it's a regular place, but Dean used to hang out with some kids on that bit of waste ground at the back of the DIY store on Hammond Street. That's where this guy collared him. He told Dean about this new adventure park for kids that was like special and secret, crap like that.' Lee rolled his eyes. 'Shit, you'd have thought Dean had won the lottery the way he talked about it. Like he was the Chosen One or something. Sodding victim more like.'

'How many times did he go?' Matt asked.

'Three times. After the third trip he never came back.'

'Did you see him being picked up by any chance?' Matt sat forward. 'Come on, Lee. Did you see the vehicle that collected him?'

Lee stared at the ground. 'Yeah. I hid and watched. I thought I'd get the reg number, just in case like. Covered in mud, wasn't it? All I can tell you is that it was like one of them mini-bus things that carries the pickers around to the fields. Grey, and filthy, no writing on it, oh, and darkened windows.'

So, they had more than one vehicle. Matt recalled the boy from Ewan's football team saying he'd been bundled into a closed sided van. 'Were there other kids in this vehicle?'

'I think so. When the door opened, I thought I caught sight of at least one other boy.'

Matt was aware of the time passing and didn't want to get the lad into trouble. 'Lee, what do you think the Bunker is?'

'I dunno, but whatever it is, they're taking kids whose parents either don't give a shit about them, or ones that look like they are heading off the tracks and using them for something bad. I can think of a whole lot of uses for a teenage boy, and none of them are nice.'

So could Matt. 'Give me your mobile number, Lee, and I'll get in touch if we have news of Dean. I promise we'll do our very best to get him back for you.'

Lee stared at the ground. 'Ain't got no phone, Mister. Mine got nicked just after Dean disappeared, and I can't afford another one.'

Matt exhaled. 'Okay, I'll go and get you a cheap one. I'll bring it straight back. Meanwhile, here's my card. I'm Matt. You can trust me, I promise, and you can trust my colleagues too — that's Liz, David and Jeff. Got that? And the phone is yours, lad, so don't say no one ever gives kids like you anything for free.'

Not long afterwards, he went into the convenience store and handed Lee a box with a new phone and charger, along with a top-up card for twenty pounds. 'Let me know if you hear even the slightest hint of something that might lead us to the Bunker, okay?'

Lee nodded. For the first time, he looked Matt in the eye. 'Find my brother, Matt. He's an arsehole, but he's all I've got.'

People like Lee and the Coopers, the ones who are left behind, are just as much victims as the kids who have disappeared, he thought sadly.

* * *

Supper at Cannon Farm was a chaotic affair, what with trying to cobble together a hot meal from what could be found in the fridge, discuss their respective findings and decide on Jeff's best course of action in the coming evening.

'All I can say, Jeff, is that we don't have the luxury of time on our side,' said Matt, busy straining rice and thinking about what Dean had said. 'However you choose to charm that lad it can't be done slowly. With every hour that passes I fear more young lives could be in jeopardy.'

'I'm very much aware of that, Matt,' said Jeff seriously. 'But I'll have to be careful not to scare him off. He's valuable, and we can't afford for him to clam up because I've come on too strong.'

'I suggest you get him onside with your footie skills,' suggested David, stirring the chilli con carne, while Liz clattered plates and cutlery.

'I agree,' said Liz. 'And if you want to make a real impact, do something spectacular. Awe the pants off them with one of your parkour moves.'

'It's not really meant to be used like that,' Jeff said doubtfully. 'It's a discipline, not a party trick — but I hear what you say. And it does have the effect of making people take notice. I'll play it by ear. And I understand the need to get this information as quickly as possible.'

The meal finally on the table, they discussed the forthcoming evening. They would debrief Jeff on his return, no matter how late. David was to go along as chauffeur. The two of them would meet up with Spike prior to going to the Community Centre and take it from there.

By ten past six, Matt and Liz were alone.

'As we're not going out again tonight, do you fancy a coffee and a cognac?' asked Matt.

'I do. I have all these thoughts racing around in my head — old ladies and injured swans, along with that old boy's anxious expression when he told me how frightened Molly was when she viewed his cottage. I could do with something to calm me down before steam begins to rise.'

Matt's mind, too, was whizzing, only his thoughts centred around missing teenagers and anxious relatives. Then there was tonight's meeting at the football club.

He brought the bottle of cognac into the kitchen, and they sat at the table trying to unwind. Matt sipped his drink and sighed. 'I wish we had a better liaison officer. If this Bunker thing is as big as I fear it is, we'll be handing the whole thing over to the police before long, and if it's Norton who'll be dealing with it, who knows how it will turn out.'

Liz nodded grimly. 'I know what you mean. Until now we've always had the good fortune to work with dedicated detectives. I hate to say it, but I'm not sure I even trust him.' She raised an eyebrow. 'Or am I being unkind? Or worse?'

'No, babe. I feel the same.' He stared into his glass. 'Lazy detectives are inclined to be devious. The fellow's no fool, and he'll know that Charley is watching him like a hawk. It's my guess he'll feed whatever we give him into his own reports.'

'What? Pretend our findings are his? My goodness, I hadn't thought he'd go quite that far, but you could be right. Who knows? One thing he doesn't know is that you and Charley are also in contact, so if he tries to pull a stunt like that, she'll know.'

'In which case, he'll cook his own goose without any assistance from us. I wonder . . .'

'Go on, Matt, what were you going to say?' asked Liz.

'I guess I'm wondering if there's something we don't know about Darren Norton. It can't be easy being the grandson of a high-ranking officer who is not exactly revered for his excellent record. It's a well-known fact that Grandad Norton rose through the ranks thanks to the "old pals act". Maybe the kid took a lot of stick because of it.'

'Then why not prove to everyone that you're not tarred with the same brush? If I were in his shoes I'd do everything in my power to show them I can be a good detective in my own right,' said Liz.

'I want to give him a chance, but he doesn't make it easy.' Matt shook his head. 'You should have heard him today, absolutely certain that because they had a dead body, and it seemed to resemble Smokey Joe, therefore it was him. Talk about making assumptions.'

Liz grinned. 'I *assume* you put him right though.'

'Well, yes, but it was water off a duck's back.'

'Even so, I bet he was smarting,' said Liz with some satisfaction.

They fell silent for a while, until Liz said, 'So, if the body wasn't Smokey, there's a chance he's still around somewhere.'

'Rory texted me earlier to say that the body is thought to be that of a local man, a bit of a loner, and unpleasant with it, who lives, or lived rather, in a rundown old cottage about three miles from where the body was found. Oh, and his death was from natural causes.'

Liz took a sip of her cognac. 'So, seeing as how the boys won't be back for a while, why don't you and I do a bit of ferreting into this Johan de Vries?'

Matt winked at her. 'If you ask me, I can think of something better to do while the children are out.'

'Matt Ballard,' said Liz. 'And there was you saying we didn't have a lot of time.'

'Well, you did say you wanted something to relax you.'

'This cognac is doing the trick nicely, thank you.'

They looked at each other and laughed.

'Okay, Smokey Joe it is. Pity, though . . .'

* * *

The time passed quickly for David as he watched his friend work his magic on what had initially been quite a rowdy group of youngsters. They watched in awe as he demonstrated skills they had only ever seen at work in professional teams on TV.

Within the space of half an hour or so, Jeff had artlessly won over the entire group, particularly two girls who had instantly fallen in love with him. David paid especial attention to Toby and noticed that when Jeff moved on to holding individual sessions, the boy hung back and watched from the sidelines.

David went across and sat down next to him. 'You needn't be shy of asking him questions, he'll be pleased to help you with anything you want to know. He's a great guy and he loves coaching.'

Toby nodded, his eyes on Jeff, who was explaining a particular piece of footwork to one of the girls. 'He's different, isn't he?'

'He sure is,' said David. *More than you can imagine.* 'He's a gymnast as well, you know.'

'He seems very . . .' Stuck for words, the boy spread his hands.

'I know what you mean,' David said. 'I've known him all my life. I grew up with him, and even when we were little, I already knew he was special.'

'Why are you here?'

Coming out of the blue, the question threw David, who struggled to find a plausible answer. 'I, er, that is, we . . . Me and him are staying with my auntie, and since Jeff does the same sort of coaching as Ewan, we thought it'd be good if he came and helped out.'

Toby looked at him steadily for several seconds before turning his gaze back to Jeff, and then to Ewan, who now had the group in pairs practising passing.

They watched in silence for a while. Then, without looking at David, Toby said, 'The thing is . . .'

David held his breath and waited, not daring to look at Toby.

'I know why you're here. It's because of Ewan, isn't it? What he said.

Ewan cares about me — he's the only one who ever has. I don't have a family, my dad's a drunk and I don't remember my mum. Then I started training with Ewan. He's a good guy.' Gazing fixedly at the kids now clustered around Jeff, he said, 'You see, I made a big mistake, and I owe it to Ewan to put it right. Ewan reckons I can make it professionally if I really commit to it. Not like your mate there, he's in a different league. But I'm good, and I could be great one day, I know it.'

David glanced sideways at the boy, wondering where this was going.

'Something happened. Me, I got myself out of it, but there's other kids involved, and I keep thinking about them. I told Ewan some of it but I was too scared to tell him the whole thing just in case — well, you know,' he ended a little lamely.

'And that is the mistake? This thing that happened to you?' said David.

'Yeah. You've heard about kids round here disappearing, haven't you? That's why you're here.' He nodded towards Jeff. 'You had the idea of using him to get to me. We're like dazzled by his skills, then he gets us to tell him about all sorts, stuff the grown-ups don't know.'

David smiled. The kid was bright. 'That's really clever, to have worked it out so quick. You're right. The reason we're here is that my aunt and her partner run a private investigation agency and they're trying to find a missing boy who we think might have ended up in this place called the Bunker.'

Toby swallowed.

'Will you talk to Jeff after the session?' David asked.

'Yes. Thinking about it has been driving me crazy. I almost went and told the cops but you don't do that round here. Then I thought of getting Ewan to tell them for me but I wasn't sure if I should. Any case, I've got to tell someone, and Jeff might be the best person.' He gave David a lopsided grin. 'But before that, there's this move I'm not sure of . . .'

'Go for it. And we can give you a lift home if you like, all right?'

'Cool. We can talk in the car.'

David watched Toby stroll back to the others with a sigh of relief. The kid was onside.

* * *

'It's cold. Why isn't it warm in here? Kitchen's supposed to be warm.'

His father sighed. 'It's all right, son, we don't have to have it warm if we don't want to.'

'I want it warm. Mum said it has to be warm.'

He groaned inwardly. He had just begun to feel comfortable in his own home, and now this. 'Okay, son, you know where the thermostat is.'

He watched his son shamble across to it and twist the dial. He smiled. 'Warm now. Like Mum said it should be.'

How little had changed since his wife's death. If anything, things were worse. The cool kitchen had been one of the few compensations, and now that was gone.

'I'm going to skin the rabbits,' Jamie announced. 'I want rabbit pie for dinner tomorrow.'

More work! He knew better than to argue however. Occasionally he was able to cajole or bribe the boy into doing as he wanted, making it appear that the suggestion had come from his son rather than him. Not when he was in one of his present moods. At times like these it was better to go along with him in the hope that the task would put him in a better frame of mind. Skinning rabbits was one of Jamie's favourite jobs. Incongruously, given his bulk and general clumsiness, he could be almost delicate when wielding a knife. He recalled teaching the boy to fillet a fish, the trepidation with which he had handed him the sharp blade, but to his surprise and awe Jamie had copied his every movement with the careful precision of a master chef or a surgeon.

Over the years that followed, the boy's skill with a knife had come in handy on more than one occasion. As soon as the boy left the kitchen, he turned down the thermostat. He'd have to put it back up again later, he couldn't afford to cross Jamie. Ever.

* * *

'I'm sorry I didn't call you earlier, Liz, but I've only just got in. Have you got a couple of minutes?'

The call came from Nathan Venner. He sounded either very tired or slightly drunk. It was half past nine and David had just rung to say they were on their way home. From his excited tone, it sounded like the evening had been a success. Now Nathan was contacting her as well.

'Sure. It's not late. Are you okay?'

'Just totally knackered.' He gave a short laugh. 'I've been driving round the Fens all bloody day in an attempt to track Marika's movements.'

'Did you find anything?' she asked.

'Kind of, though I think I should stick to music, it's a lot less stressful. I'm obviously not cut out to be a detective, half the time I haven't the faintest idea what I'm supposed to be doing.'

Liz would have laughed if he hadn't sounded so dejected. 'Go on.'

'It started really well,' said Nathan, 'I was so determined to get to the bottom of it all, but then I hit a dead end.'

'Nathan, you wouldn't believe how many blind alleys I've been down in my time. It's all part of the job, I'm afraid. Now, tell me what you did find.'

Nathan related Annie's story of Molly's tragic affair with the rock musician who turned out to be a drug addict, and her rescue by a man who proved to be even worse. 'Hell, Liz, what she went through.'

His last words were a cry from the heart. 'But, Nathan, you've done amazingly well to discover all that. We could never have done it so quickly.'

178

'But then the trail petered out. I was told about this man who could help me, he knew the whole story, apparently. His name is George Miles, and he lived in a village called Beckersby.'

'Don't tell me. You got there and found he'd moved on.'

'Yep. And no one seems to have the faintest idea of where he went. Even the solicitors couldn't — or wouldn't — give me any help. He went off the radar, and I've come to a grinding halt. I'm sorry to say I'll have to let you take it from here.'

Liz assured him that if he could send her a detailed account of what he'd unearthed, with names and dates and locations, they would certainly move it forward if they could. 'Beckersby, you say?' Suddenly she realised that it was only a few miles from where they had been that day, Beckersby Village was next to Marshdyke-St-Mary.

'Yes, that's right. That's where this friend of Marika's lived, and where my investigation ended. I was so sure I'd cracked it. Here I was, Marika's knight in shining armour, riding in to uncover the truth so she could finally rest in peace. Some knight I turned out to be.'

'Hey, you!' Liz said. 'Listen up. Forget all this failure crap. With what you've just given me, along with what we've discovered ourselves, we are getting close. I can't say for certain yet, but there's a very good chance we've found the place where everything went wrong for her, and it's less than two miles from Beckersby Village. So you've just confirmed what we suspected — and that's bloody brilliant.'

Nathan, now sounding much happier, promised to email everything he'd heard from Annie, Pinky, and the helpful owner of Oaken Cottage, first thing the following morning.

'That sounded interesting,' said Matt, looking up from his screen.

'We're tightening the net. We now know the place where disaster struck our Molly. Now comes the tricky bit — finding someone willing to talk to us. If they all clam up like the two bird sisters, we are stuck. We need someone on our side, and Nathan Venner might just have given us his name — if we can find him, that is. Someone called George Miles. He'll be our next port of call.'

The sound of an engine was heard outside. 'Ah,' said Matt, standing up. 'David and Jeff are back. Let's see how they got on.'

As soon as she set eyes on them, Liz could see that the evening had been a great success. They looked positively high.

She listened to their story, relieved that the end of this case was in sight. 'He told us the lot, Auntie Liz,' David began 'And we didn't have to coax it out of him. And once he was in the car with us, the floodgates opened.'

'The kid has a conscience,' said Jeff. 'He's afraid for the kids that get sucked in and wants to help stop the racket. But here's the best bit — he knows all the places where the scouts pick up the kids. He's also going to spread a few rumours about a new kid in town who's a really badass tearaway.' Jeff beamed. 'Me!'

'It's practically an invitation,' added David excitedly. 'We've even got a date for Jeff to meet with the scouts — the day after tomorrow.'

'Where?' asked Matt. 'Only I've been given a venue too, the patch of waste ground on Hammond Street.'

'That's one of the places Toby mentioned, but Jeff has to show up at the old cemetery next to the church in Fenfleet Low Road. Kids gather there to smoke weed and drink lager.' David grinned. 'Should be right up Jeff's street.'

Jeff punched him lightly on the arm.

Liz felt a shiver of concern. She knew that nothing would happen on that first trip, it never did. It would be all fun and excitement. But what if he decided to take the next step and go deeper into the organisation? He was without doubt a consummate athlete, but could he act? Could he fool the criminals running the show into thinking he was an off-the-rails kid? The seriousness of what he was about to undertake struck her with the force of a runaway train. 'Look,

Jeff. You don't have to do this, you know. Maybe you should have a think about it.'

'But I *do* have to. And I want to. I'm not being vain but I have a better chance than anyone of getting the proof you need in order to send in the police and close the place down. Those people cannot be allowed to get away with what they're doing to kids who know no better. If we don't act, if I don't go in, I have a terrible feeling that some of those kids will never be seen again — including the boy you're looking for. I couldn't live with that.'

Liz raised her hands. 'I agree with what you say, but it won't stop me worrying.'

* * *

Joe had had a long day, having begun it as one person and ended it as someone else entirely. Smokey was now Johan. He lay in his anonymous hotel room and took stock of his transformation.

He had begun the day by walking to the nearest village where he found a cash machine and withdrew £240, the maximum amount the machine would allow. That was the easy part. Now he had to make himself presentable while avoiding Smokey Joe's usual haunts. Another mile further on, towards Fenfleet, there was a small caravan site, set in a field adjoining a small wood. It was rarely busy at any time of the year, having little in the way of amenities, but a few fishermen stayed there occasionally. Joe knew the place well, it was one of his stopovers on his meandering passage across the Fens. The wife of the farmer who owned it was a kind woman who turned a blind eye when he used the shower block while the site was empty, and let him sleep in one of their old barns. She often brought him a mug of tea before she went off to bed, and sometimes cakes or biscuits. Like the good soldier that he was, Joe had a contingency plan in the event of a sudden change in his circumstances. He had been keeping his eye on one of the caravans, which sat a little apart from the others, partially concealed by trees. This caravan belonged to a man who came a couple of times a month to fish in the nearby lake. He was important to Joe as, apart from being of a similar build to himself, his visits followed an unvarying schedule. Fred always came alone. He would arrive and leave at exactly the same time on each visit. Once there, he spent his days according to a long-established routine. Joe often wondered whether the man simply liked order in his life or had limited time off from business so used his time wisely.

When Joe didn't see a car parked next to the caravan, he knew he could be certain of having it to himself until at least the following day. He made short work of picking the lock and, safely inside, let out a sigh of relief. His man, to whom he had given the name of Fred had, as expected, left the place in perfect order.

He had no intention of upsetting Fred any more than was necessary, but there were certain things he needed to do, upon which his life depended.

He got to work immediately. It was a nice little van — two-berth, in what they called an "End Washroom" layout, meaning a small, neat shower, toilet and washbasin at the rear, and a kitchen to one side. Though the water boiler had been filled, Joe did not wish to drain it, so a shower was out. But that wasn't why he was here. In the compact wardrobe, he found exactly what he wanted — a pair of jeans, a khaki shirt and a thick, navy sweater. In a drawer at the base of the wardrobe, he found socks and a cheap pair of rambler boots. He was relieved to see that all the clothes had been purchased from Matalan, so he had a good idea of what they cost. Now for the next step.

Secure in his "hotel" room, Joe was finding trying to sleep in a proper bed more difficult than he had expected. What he'd thought would be heaven, just felt wrong. It was too soft for a start. He sank down, feeling his spine curve unnaturally, only to struggle with the all-enveloping bed-clothes. After a while he got up, made a cup of tea, and laid himself down on the small, hard sofa. Comfortable at last, his thoughts returned to the day he became another man.

Still in the caravan, he came across an unexpected bonus in the shape of a pack of disposable razors, assorted toiletries, and — praise be — battery-powered hair clippers and a pair of nail scissors. It had taken him almost an hour to complete the transformation. He stared in wonder at the amount of hair that had fallen to the floor. Looking in the mirror, he was shocked to see the face of someone he didn't know. Old Smokey Joe had shed years along with his hair and beard. Staring at his reflection, he was glad that he'd looked after his teeth as best he could, because right now he even thought he could discern the soldier he once had been. Satisfied, he cleared up the hair and left everything as he had found it. He had even had the foresight to bring with him an envelope he had found in a litter bin outside the post office. On this, he wrote a note to Fred, apologising for his intrusion, and for taking his clothes, which he had valued at around £100 at Matalan prices. He put £150 in cash in the envelope to cover the cost. He wasn't yet dressed in his new clothes, since he still had to wash, which he did shortly, the shower block being empty.

Then, Johan de Vries hit the road, looking presentable enough to get a lift into town from a passing farmer. The only thing that Fred had been unable to supply was a jacket so, on arriving in Fenfleet, Johan made for a charity shop, where he picked up a very adequate waterproof.

Finally, an exhausted Johan de Vries found a Premier Inn and booked a room for the night.

It felt strange being inside after so many years on the road. Odd not to be cold. He settled back on the sofa and tried as best he could to sleep. Tomorrow he would embark on his search for the man who might tell him what happened to Molly, and why he was being hounded by people who wanted him dead. George Miles was his last hope.

CHAPTER EIGHTEEN

Amid the clatter of plates and pans, Matt and Liz were chatting while they prepared breakfast for the four of them.

'David is still on a high,' remarked Liz, taking a packet of bacon from the fridge, 'while Jeff seems much calmer. I think he's getting himself mentally prepared for his undertaking.'

Matt said nothing. Despite having agreed to allow the young man to enter the unknown world of the Bunker, he still wasn't entirely convinced that he'd done the right thing. After all, they had no idea of what he could be walking into. It could turn out to be a nest of vipers, and suppose something went wrong?

'We have a whole day to get through before Jeff goes into action,' Liz was saying. 'Have you any plans? For my part, I must get to grips with finding out more about Marshdyke-St-Mary and its inhabitants. No way can we go back there without knowing a whole lot more about the place. Those wacky sisters proved that, I should never have been so candid with them. The moment I mentioned Molly, it was like the shutters came down.' She passed Matt a bowl of eggs. 'Plus, I've got a few calls to make, and a Tesco delivery at nine fifteen. Meanwhile, David can do what he does best, pulling everything he can from the Net. Once I've done here, we can head into town. I want to talk to Chris Lamont in the library. I seem to recall that he used to cover the area around Marshdyke when he was a copper, so he might be able to tell us more about the place. Oh, and I'd like a quick catch- up with Clem, if we can hunt him down.'

'In which case,' Matt said, 'I might take Jeff on a guided tour of Fenfleet and the surrounding area. We can also take a look at those places Toby mentioned — you know, where the kids get together and the scouts watch for suitable candidates.'

Liz nodded. 'Absolutely. It would give Jeff a good idea of the type of behaviour they're looking out for — as long as no one sees him with an ex-copper.'

'Don't worry, I'll make sure I'm not seen.' Matt added tomatoes to the bacon sizzling under the grill. 'I suddenly realised halfway through the night that we haven't yet worked out what we're going to do after Jeff is dropped off after his visit. I have no idea if they keep tabs on the kids when they get back, so we can't just wade in and pick him up.'

Liz pursed her lips, thinking. 'I know. He could walk in the direction of one of the rougher areas of town, as if he was heading back home. As soon as he thinks he's in the clear and isn't being followed, he can call us and we'll come and get him.'

'Good idea, and maybe we should get David to pick him up, rather than one of us,' Matt said.

'In that case,' added Liz, 'you really must do that recce today.'

Their two guests joined them for breakfast, and an hour later, he and Jeff were ready to leave. They were just about to go out through the door when Liz said, 'Why don't we meet for lunch at the Anglers Arms? It'll save us driving all the way back here, and we can discuss our progress before we carry on with our day.'

Matt agreed at once. The Anglers Arms was beside the river, just outside town, a quiet pub that did decent bar food. It was also the sort of place where they wouldn't be likely to run into any of the people Jeff was supposed to be mingling with. 'How about midday? We'll be through by then, but does that give you enough time?'

'We can continue after lunch if we need to, so midday is fine,' Liz said.

That sorted, Matt and Jeff embarked on their tour of the misty Fens and the darker side of Fenfleet.

* * *

While Liz made calls and dealt with groceries, David switched on his laptop and Matt's computer in readiness for his own tour, that of the wider world of the Web. First, he printed out four copies — one for each of them — of the clues Molly had hidden in the text of her book on Chopin:

"Beneath the anvil. By the third silver birch. In Rupert's grave. Close to William Arbuthnot. In the vegetable store."

Where to start? The words *"beneath"*, *"under"*, and *"grave"* suggested that the answers were all buried. He pictured tins or jars, containing messages, just waiting for him to dig them up. *"Beneath the anvil"* made him think of the metal sculpture they'd seen in what had formerly been a forge. He entered *"Metal Works Marshdyke-St-Mary"* into his search engine and found a website consisting mainly of images of the ornate gates and fences on sale, though he did find a paragraph on the welding process itself. The craft had come a long way from the days of anvils, but it was certainly worth a visit.

Next, he typed in *"William Arbuthnot"*. Amid the hundreds of William Arbuthnots listed, not one was even remotely connected to the Fens. Realising he'd get little from a search of the names listed in Chopin, he turned his attention to the village itself.

He had no luck there either. This wasn't proving as easy as he'd thought, and it came as a relief when Liz came in and told him she was ready to set off.

* * *

The three "graduates", now dressed in fatigues and looking a lot less scared, were seated — on chairs rather than stools — in what looked like a military operations room. This time Cash was alone with them. It was the first of three interviews, although the kids didn't know this. Each of his team leaders would question them on how they would react to, or deal with certain situations, and evaluate their responses and their overall performance, following which Cash would make his final decision. Over the past four months over fifty kids, varying in age from thirteen to nineteen, had passed through their hands. They were rigorous in their selection, with over seventy per cent of candidates deemed unsuitable for purpose and sent home. Around ten per cent had been invited back for further assessment. If they failed this part of the procedure, they too were sent away and excluded from further visits. That left a small core of fit and optimistic youngsters who, with the right training, should go far. Out of fifty boys, two had fallen well short, and should never have been selected in the first place. Because these two couldn't be trusted to remain silent, they couldn't just be sent back, and had therefore been dealt with according to the rules of the Bunker. According to the regulations, such failures were to be removed from the area and consigned to the ever-growing host of missing persons, under threat of instant death should they ever return to the Fens. Luckily, kids like that were rare. Key to the success of the Bunker system was the fact that the kids they chose had all been dismissed by society as no-hopers. Cash deliberately selected these delinquent adolescents precisely because they had no future. These he would mould into hardened individuals who could expect great things from a life of crime.

He was especially pleased with this little trio. From what he had seen of them, they were the *crème de la creme*. Now for the final test. 'Last time you were here, we asked you a question. We wanted to know whether you would be prepared to walk away from your home, leave family and friends and make a new life for yourself. You all answered yes. Now I'm asking you to take that one step further. More than just walk away, would you this time sever all ties with family, friends and home, and never go back or see any of them again?' He watched for their reactions. 'Think about it over the next few hours. Here's what we're offering, and listen carefully. If your answer is yes, you will be asked to pledge allegiance, following which you will join us and be trained for your new life. Apart from your code names, which you already have, you will be given new identities — names, birth certificates and any other documentation you might require. In other words, you will become different people. In return, we undertake to invest whatever resources we have in your education and training. You will become part of an elite group of people. We can enable you to achieve everything you ever dreamed of, but we can only do that if you commit fully to the organisation. That means fully — body and soul.' Cash stopped speaking and watched them closely for their reactions as they took in his words. 'You may be asking yourselves what will happen if the terms are too harsh. Well, if that's the case, it won't be held against you. You will be perfectly free to leave here — but,' he held up his hand, 'you will not be allowed to return to your family. You'll be taken somewhere far away from here, and you will be assisted in making a new life for yourself. You must never speak of this place to anyone. If you do so, there will be repercussions, and they will not be pleasant. You will be safe, and so will everyone close to you, but only as long as you never breathe a word about the Bunker. The choice is yours.' He sat back in his chair and smiled — though the smile didn't reach his eyes, which remained watchful. 'Right. Now we've got that out of the way, we can proceed with your interviews.'

* * *

'Oh, I remember Marshdyke,' Chris Lamont said. 'You're right, it was on my patch. And you think it might be where it all started for Molly? Well, that is a coincidence.'

Liz wondered whether it was such a coincidence. Molly could have left her bag of secrets in any one of a thousand places, but she had chosen the library, and had made sure Chris would find it. Molly might well have known of Chris's connection to Marshdyke, which was why she chose him to find the bag, along with the book in which she'd hidden her cryptic messages.

Liz told Chris about their visit to the village, and the strange way the Targett sisters had received her question about Molly.

'God, yes, the sisters. I remember them. Mad as a box of frogs, both of them, but they saved a lot of birds.'

So, thought Liz, if Chris remembered the sisters, he might recall others as well. 'I suppose you wouldn't have a bit of spare time, Chris? We could really do with some advice about other residents we might speak to, since we didn't have much luck with the sisters.'

'Sure,' he said. 'I'd love to help if I can.'

Liz suddenly recalled that Chris, who for many years had been a uniformed officer, had lost his wife to cancer when she was relatively young. He left the force not long after her death and did a lot of voluntary work in the Fenfleet area. 'That would be great. I did wonder if I'd shot myself in the foot by talking to the sisters about Molly. I've an awful feeling they might warn others off talking to us.'

'They are a bit of an odd bunch, but there are some sensible people there too. Mind you, some might have moved or passed away since my day, but I'll give it a bit of thought. Suppose I make a list and ring you later. Or . . . Tell you what, I could come with you if you like.'

Just what they needed. Liz took him up on the offer immediately.

As they were leaving, Chris said, 'Do you remember a PC who was retired out on health grounds after a druggie stuck a needle in her? Her name was Anna Pickford.'

Liz recalled the incident, but not the officer involved.

'The thing is, I did a bit of counselling with Anna and her grandmother, who had brought her up. The old lady lived in Beckersby, a dead and alive hole a mile or two away from Marshdyke. Anna had always hated the place, but after she got hurt, she went back to live with her gran. She'd be a great person to talk to. Tilly — the grandmother — was born there, and you know what these small rural communities are like — they all know the ins and outs of the duck's backside.'

'That's just what we need,' said Liz, smiling at the expression. 'How are you fixed for tomorrow morning?'

'No problem. I can easily get someone to cover for me here. I'd be happy to assist in whatever way I can to find Molly's killer. It's almost like I owe her. Where shall I meet you?'

'We'll come to your house and collect you if that suits? You are between Tanners Fen and the road to Marshdyke, aren't you?'

He gave them the address and they arranged to pick him up at around nine.

Leaving the library, they made for Paws Awhile, the pet shop where Clem often spent time. If he wasn't there, either Billie or Andy Nettles might know where he might be found. Liz had been feeling anxious about the old guy. He'd taken the loss of Molly's precious letter to heart, feeling that he'd let her down by his carelessness. It was hardly his fault — who would even think of stealing a grubby sleeping bag?

Passing the lane leading up to St Benedict's church, they heard people shouting. Curious to know what the commotion was all about, they made their way up the lane.

The shouting grew louder as they approached the churchyard. Inside, a small crowd had gathered, milling around between the gravestones and pointing at something on the ground, some calling for help.

Liz automatically slipped back into police mode and pushed her way to the front, David close behind, to be confronted by a sight that made her gasp. A man was lying in a heap on the ground. Over him, teeth bared, lunging at whoever dared come near, stood a large dog.

'Get the brute off him!' screamed a woman. 'That dog's gonna kill him!'

Liz could see at once what was happening. 'Quiet, all of you! And get back! Can't you see what's happening? He's protecting his master. You're making everything ten times worse, so back off.'

'Dog's soddin' dangerous, lady,' called out one man. 'He'll have you as soon as look at you. We've called for someone to deal with it.'

Anger flooded through Liz. 'If you want to call someone, call an ambulance for Clem! And please, just give him some space.'

David began herding the still shouting crowd back towards the church. 'It's all right. We know this man, so let my aunt help him. She knows what she's doing.'

The crowd fell to muttering, watching fearfully as Liz took a few steps towards the man and his dog. Gunner kept his eyes on her, lips still curled but quieter now. Liz saw that he was trembling. The poor animal was terrified. 'Gunner, old boy, it's me, Liz. It's all right. Good boy, Gunner, let me see if I can help Clem, eh?' She moved a little closer, talking calmly to the dog, assuring him that no one was going to hurt his master. 'Good boy. Lie down now and let's take a look at him, shall we? Lie down, Gunner, good boy.'

It was as much of a shock to her as it was to the watching crowd of people when, with a whimper, the dog laid down at his master's side.

'Good boy, Gunner. Good boy.' Liz beckoned to David. 'Talk to the dog, Davey, slowly and gently, and I'll try to assess Clem. No sudden movements, just keep it slow and easy, okay?'

Not a sound could be heard in the churchyard. Even the birds seemed to be holding their breaths.

As David approached, Gunner moved his tail slightly. There was no doubt that he remembered these two people. They had been kind to his master, and his master had liked them. Now Liz could take a proper look at Clem. She did not like what she saw. There was blood slowly seeping into the grass from an injury at the back of his head. Whether he had been attacked, or had simply fallen and hit his head, she had no way of knowing. Not that it mattered right now, it was a serious injury and Clem needed professional help, fast. She felt the side of his neck and found a pulse, but so weak it was barely there.

Trying not to raise her voice and scare Gunner, she turned to the watching crowd. 'Has someone called for an ambulance?'

'On its way,' a man called back.

Realising how cold he was, Liz took off her jacket and wrapped it around the fallen man. Seeming to sense what was needed, Gunner pressed himself into his master's side. 'Good boy, Gunner, you got it, fella, let's do what we can for him.' She held Clem's hand and told him help was on its way.

When at last the sound of the two tones was heard, she felt Clem's hand move in hers. His eyes flickered for a moment, and . . . had he whispered something? Did he really say 'Molly?' Or had she imagined it?

Now for the next part. She had no idea how Gunner would react to the paramedics. Would he allow them to work on Clem? And how would they react to this big, ferocious beast?

The paramedics threaded their way through the graves towards them and Liz heaved a sigh of relief. Two women, and she knew one of them. Not only that, Emmie, as the paramedic was called, actually owned a rescue dog. Liz instructed them to approach slowly, while reassuring the now stiffening Gunner that these people were here to help.

To her amazement, Gunner backed away and went to David, leaning heavily against his leg and watching the paramedics' every move.

On seeing that, Liz briefly told the ambulance crew the little that she knew, then retreated and stood on the other side of Gunner. The three of them watched as the professionals began to work on her old friend.

'He knows, doesn't he?' whispered David. 'Gunner knows they're not hurting Clem.'

Liz reached down and fondled the dog's ears. Gunner was still trembling, his gaze fixed on his master. 'You're right, he does. I'm just a little concerned about what he'll do when they take the old boy to the ambulance.' As she spoke, she saw a familiar face pushing his way through the crowd still gathered by the church. It was Jack Fleet, shocked and surprised at seeing her there.

Gunner stiffened and growled softly as Swifty moved towards them.

'Slowly, Jack,' she said. 'He's okay, just frightened.' She looked down at the dog. 'He's Gunner, I know him. He's okay.'

The dog didn't look totally convinced but stopped growling.

'Is this a crime scene, Liz?' asked Jack.

She shrugged. 'I haven't the faintest idea.'

'But Clem was Molly's friend, wasn't he? So it could well be.'

'Auntie Liz? There's blood around Gunner's jaw. He's not hurt anywhere that I can see, and he would never hurt Clem, so . . .'

'Oh, shit,' murmured Liz. 'That could put a second person on the scene.'

'One with bite marks on him,' said Jack. 'Which answers my question. I need to call this in.' He stared at Gunner. 'And we need to take a swab of that blood but, well, to be perfectly frank, I'm not sure I've got the balls to do it.'

Seeing the expression on Swifty's face as he looked at the dog, Liz almost laughed. 'Got an evidence bag in your pocket, Jack?'

'Sure, but — Liz, you can't,' Jack said. 'You might think he's frightened, but that doesn't mean he won't bite.'

Liz reached for her jacket and took a clean tissue from the pocket, along with a packet of dog treats she had brought with her in case they found Clem. She opened the pack, and with treats in one hand and the tissue in the other, knelt down by Gunner. 'Here you go, lad, your favourite treats, and let's clean that mess off your face, shall we?'

While David continued to stroke his head, Gunner sniffed Liz's hand, and then tentatively took a treat. On the third treat, she carefully wiped some of the blood from his chin, noting as she did so that it was still red and fresh. This had happened very recently. She dropped the tissue into the open bag, which Jack then sealed up.

Getting to her feet, Liz saw Gunner's lead lying in the grass where Clem had fallen. She picked it up and gently slipped it over Gunner's head while he finished off the snacks. At once, Gunner laid down and rested his head on his paws.

Jack Fleet let out his breath. 'Nice one, Liz. Hats off to you for that. I'll see if I can organise some assistance. We need to see if any of that rabble back there actually saw anything, and get a proper crime scene set up. If he was attacked, they're going to have to get the SOCOs in. This is not what I was expecting when I popped out for a sarnie and a bun! We'll interview you whenever you can make it into the station, if that's okay.' He pointed to the dog. 'Oh, and what are you going to do with him?'

David looked at her, eyebrows raised.

'We'll come to the station this afternoon — I just have to speak to Matt. And as to the dog, we'll take him home, of course. Someone needs to care for him until we know about Clem.'

David breathed a sigh of relief. Now all she had to do was break the news to Matt that they were about to welcome a third guest.

It took a while, but Clem was finally ready to go. To Liz's surprise, Gunner didn't even attempt to move. He watched his master, strapped to a trolley, being carried back past the church, then looked mournfully up at David.

'Come on, lad, you're off for a bit of a holiday.'

CHAPTER NINETEEN

Oblivious to the drama unfolding in the churchyard, Matt and Jeff were waiting at the Anglers Arms wondering where the others had got to, when Liz drew up beside them. She told them about finding Clem, and of the possibility that he'd been attacked.

While he listened, Matt glanced absently back at her car. Then he looked again. 'And what's that?'

'Well, we could hardly leave him there, could we? Bless his heart, he was terrified.'

Matt stepped over to the car window and peered in at the huge beast occupying the entire back seat. 'Will he be okay in there? He's not going to eat the car, is he?'

'That remains to be seen,' said Liz. 'I'm not sure he's ever been in a car before. We can only hope.'

They went into the pub and found a table by the window so they could keep a watchful eye on Liz's Toyota.

As they waited for their food, David told them the story of what had happened in the churchyard, and Liz's heroic response.

Matt squeezed her hand. 'What are his chances? Did the paramedics say?'

'Not good, it depends on what they find after they've done a scan of the head injury. I was thinking that one of us should go to the hospital. The poor old guy has no one, and if he regains consciousness, he'll immediately ask about Gunner. I'd hate him to think the worst has happened.'

'You guys are busy,' Jeff said, 'so if you want to drop me there, I'd be happy to sit and wait for news. Even though he doesn't know me, I can at least explain the situation and allay his fears about his dog, if he wakes.'

'David and I have to go to the station and make a statement,' added Liz. 'That could take a while.'

'Jeff and I can both go,' said Matt. 'Then if the police are there, I can make sure we get to hear what he has to say — if he regains consciousness.' He looked at Liz. 'Gut feeling?'

Liz said nothing for a moment. 'I really couldn't say. Though I think he did regain consciousness for a moment, just as the paramedics arrived. I might be wrong, but I could swear I heard him say Molly's name.'

'Maybe in his confusion he thought you were Molly,' suggested Jeff.

'That could be it,' she said. 'It sounded a bit like a question, you know, like, "*Is that you?*"'

'Let's hope so,' Jeff added. 'Otherwise, it might mean he really was seeing her, and that she was sent to guide him home.'

David said, 'What? Like a spirit you mean?'

'Many people believe that the loved ones of the dying return to guide them to the other side.' Jeff shrugged. 'But let's just hope it was a case of mistaken identity, huh?'

This was unknown territory for the down-to-earth Matt, and all a bit "airy-fairy", as far as he was concerned.

Luckily, he was prevented from voicing his opinion of this kind of stuff by the arrival of their meals.

Anyway, he had a more pressing concern right now. 'I hate to ask, but what are your plans for that giant beast out there — who, by the way, is probably dismantling your back seat as we speak?'

'I think he's asleep,' said David, who'd been watching through the window. 'He's upset and worried. He saw what happened to his master, and it looks like he did his best to defend him. Dogs know stuff. They have an amazing ability to understand what's going on around them.'

Matt knew a lost cause when he saw one. 'Okay, but not in the house. He's used to being outside, so he can sleep in the garage, or maybe the porch, and we'll have another think when we know how Clem is.'

David and Liz shared a look.

As they ate, they talked about the place Matt and Jeff had selected to launch Jeff's new role as a bad boy.

'We've also picked out the route Jeff can follow when they drop him off after his visit. When he reaches a certain spot you, David, will steam in and fetch him home.'

'No problem,' David said. 'Is there anything you need, mate? Clothes, or something?'

'I've brought some clothes with me,' said Jeff. 'And I've worked with enough tough kids to be able to put on the attitude. I've also got myself a background story and a tag name.'

'And that is?' asked Liz.

'Amo. A M O. It's actually a French word, meaning "Little Eagle". But hopefully the people I meet will connect it with "Ammo", as in ammunition.'

How apt, thought Matt, though to him "Amo" suggested love, which was a far cry from the activities of the Bunker.

The meal finished, they made their way outside. To their relief, Liz's car was still intact, though it did emit a strong odour of dog when she opened the door.

David made a big fuss of the dog, then slipped on the lead and walked him around the car park, so he could pee. Back in the car, Gunner laid down quietly again.

'Well,' said Matt, 'pretty good for a street dog, I must say.'

'You should have seen him in that churchyard,' said Liz. 'He'd have taken on the world to protect Clem.' She kissed Matt. 'We'd better go and give our statements. Will you ring us if there is any news about Clem?'

He watched her drive away, the biggest nodding dog in the world looking out of the rear window.

* * *

The three youngsters sat in a small windowless anteroom on two battered sofas, the girl on one while the two boys shared the other, facing her. The gruelling interviews were over, now they were awaiting the verdict. They were a disparate bunch of kids, but they all shared a deep mistrust of humanity. Take the eldest boy, a thin seventeen-year-old with hair so blond it was almost white and eyes of two different colours — one blue, one green. His alcoholic father had been using him as a punchbag, taking out his frustrations on the boy from his first tottering steps. The other boy had almost black curly hair. At fifteen, he was short and muscular for his age, and had been abused by both his mother and her junkie boyfriend. The girl . . . well, she was an enigma. She wore her long fair hair scraped back in a ponytail, which accentuated her hard, thin features. Her lips, too, were thin, tight and unsmiling. She refused to say what had happened to her, although her team leader had a strong suspicion that she had been "shared" among different members of her own family. They had been given the code names of Kurt, Bruno and Leah.

Though wary of each other, they had formed a kind of bond as the selection process proceeded. A mutual respect developed as their fellow "competitors" fell away one by one, finally leaving the three of them, victorious.

Conscious that the room was likely bugged, they kept their voices low.

'Far as I can see,' said Kurt, 'it's win-win all the way. I want to join this lot so bad I'd kill for it, but if I don't make it, I still get to go out of this stinking county, and away from my fucking dad.'

'If what they say is true,' said Leah stonily.

'I hope we all make it through,' said Bruno. 'The three of us, we could make a good team. We could go far.'

The other two remained silent. Kurt agreed with Bruno, though he didn't say so, fearing a cutting riposte from Leah, of whom he was very much in awe.

Leah didn't care whether Kurt and Bruno made it or not. All that mattered to her was that she should make it through. She probably liked the two boys more than anyone else but that didn't mean she'd be shedding any tears if they failed to pass the test. It was a long time since Leah had cried for anyone, even herself.

'I heard a scream last night,' said Bruno suddenly.

'Nightmare, I expect,' said Kurt. He too had heard the blood-curdling sound but he wasn't about to say so.

'Huh. I don't have nightmares when I'm asleep,' said Bruno. 'Mine happen when I'm awake.'

It was a statement neither Kurt nor Leah could dispute.

'Maybe it was whoever screamed was having the nightmare,' said Leah. 'One of them kids who hasn't a chance of making it through.'

'So they go back to their miserable lives,' said Bruno. 'Shame really. This is a chance of a lifetime.'

'Maybe they don't go back to their miserable lives at all.' Leah's voice was so low they could barely hear her.

'True,' Bruno said. 'Cash says they get taken somewhere miles away and dumped. After that they go on the streets, I guess. Still a shame though.'

'That's not what I meant,' said Leah.

The boys stared at her.

'Oh, come on, you two. Work it out. They're not gonna leave all these kids floating around flapping their lips to whoever will listen, are they? Still, if you want to believe in fairytales, be my guest.'

Neither Kurt nor Bruno spoke as they digested what Leah had said.

After some time had passed, Leah gave a dry, humourless laugh. 'Come on, boys, you must have made the connection by now. Not nice, is it?'

It wasn't, because it had never occurred to the boys that they would be lied to about the price of failure, and if that was the fate of some, it could well be the fate of all who failed.

Kurt looked paler than ever, while Bruno appeared to be in shock.

Leah just laughed. 'Sorry, boys, but it's not quite as win-win as you thought, is it?'

CHAPTER TWENTY

Joe was taking his second shower of the day, attempting to rid himself of the stink of the streets that clung to him — the last vestige of what remained of Smokey Joe. In the morning he had ventured out to visit the hole in the wall, and taken the cash to the nearest barber where he submitted himself to a proper haircut and a shave. He felt exposed without the thick beard, the hair shielding his eyes, almost naked. And without his bucket of coals he was doubly vulnerable. Having scrubbed himself almost raw, he stood in front of the mirror and surveyed his handiwork. No one would possibly recognise him now.

He dressed in Fred's clothes and prepared for his next foray. He would need a change of clothes before he was finally ready to set out on the hunt for George. An hour later he was queuing at the supermarket checkout with a trolleyful of clothing, anxious that his bank would question the sudden number of withdrawals on his card. The transaction went through smoothly, and he hurried from the store carrying his new wardrobe in a couple of re-usable bags. Next, was the problem of transport. Without a driving licence he couldn't just hire a car, so it would be back to the road, only this time he would be using public transport. Unless . . . Pondering an idea, he returned to the hotel to sort out his new possessions and check out.

Back in his room, Johan sat heavily on the bed. Already he was missing his life on the road. His new self felt stiff, alien, but there was no going back. Along the winding lanes, beneath that big sky, a stranger was waiting, and that stranger wanted him dead.

After all, he hadn't always been Smokey Joe. Once he had been a soldier, a good one too. The strength and resilience he had acquired during his years in the army had sustained him through the tough days on the road, and they would sustain him now, while he sought justice for Molly.

He closed his eyes. 'Sing for me?'

And she did. Her voice, strong and powerful, filled the dreary hotel room. It would accompany him on the journey to come, right to the end.

He was ready.

Within half an hour, he was knocking on the door of a rundown cottage in a poor area on the edge of town. Joe knew it well.

The man who answered the door looked at him suspiciously. 'What do you want?'

'Derek?'

'Who wants to know?'

'The squaddie who pulled you out of a burning truck somewhere in the Iraqi desert, that's who. Don't you recognise me?'

The man peered at him, then his eyes flew open. 'Joe? Is that really you? Fucking hell! Come on in, man.'

Limping, the man led the way into a dim, cluttered sitting room.

'Siddown, siddown. Jeez, what happened? Last time I saw you, you looked like some old scarecrow that had been dragged in off the fields. And where's your bike? Don't tell me you've lost your soddin' bucket as well.'

Joe shrugged. 'Long story, pal. I don't have time for it now. I came to ask for your help.'

'Anything, man.'

'Do you still have your motorbike?'

Derek nodded. 'Yeah. Can't bring myself to part with it. Stupid, really. I'll never ride it again. I keep it running as a kind of hobby. Passes the time, I suppose. And I've even got myself another one. Don't ask me why, given this.' He slapped the twisted leg that was his legacy from his days in the desert. 'Anyway, bloke I know was just letting it rot in his garage so I gave him a few quid for it and did it up. I'm quite proud of the thing, it's turned out a real diamond. Wanna look?'

After the messy jumble of the sitting room, the garage was something of a revelation. Clean and orderly, tools on hooks and carefully labelled, this was obviously where Derek spent his real life. In pride of place stood two gleaming bikes, along with the skeleton of an old Zundapp 125 surrounded by assorted parts.

'My latest project.' Derek indicated the Zundapp. 'Owner was just about to dump it in a skip. Sacrilege! Bloke didn't know what he'd got. I almost kissed him when gave it me for free.'

Joe smiled but his attention was on the smaller of the two glossy bikes. 'I know it's a big ask, but could I borrow one? Just for a few weeks, then I'll return it.'

Derek beamed at the man who had saved his life. 'Be my guest. They're both taxed, and they need riding. Which one d'you fancy? My old girl, or the baby? They both run smooth as silk. Light to handle too.'

'Much as I love your old BMW, I reckon the Royal Enfield Meteor would be perfect for what I want. She's a 350, right?' Joe's first bike had been an Enfield, and he would often let it idle, just to hear that distinctive "thump" as the engine ticked over.

'Then she's yours, for as long as you want,' said Derek.

'You might not say that when I tell you the next bit,' said Joe. 'The problem is, my licence expired years ago, and what I want the bike for has to be done now. You see, a life could depend on it — mine.'

'Shit, man. What have you got yourself into? Okay, come back inside and tell me what's going on.'

Joe followed his friend back inside, where they resumed their seats in the shabby sitting room.

'Come on then, spill. You know it won't go any further than these four walls,' Derek said.

'It's complicated,' Joe began. 'Someone is after me and I have no idea why. Whoever it is seems to think I know something. The trouble is I don't know what that thing is. The only thing I do know is that a close friend of mine was terrified of something, so scared that she couldn't even tell me, and then she was murdered.'

'Murdered!' Derek said. 'Jesus, that's bad. Who was she, this friend?'

'She called herself Molly but her real name was Marika. Marika Molohan. She sang like an angel, and was a virtuoso pianist who often gave performances. Then something happened, I don't know what, but it was so traumatic that she ended up on the streets. That's where I met her again, when I, too, became a vagrant.'

'Molly, you said? Is that the Molly you were always going on about while we were dodging Iraqi bullets? She was your childhood sweetheart, wasn't she?'

Joe nodded unhappily.

'So how can I help? Do you want to hide out? You'd be safe here, no one gives a shit in this part of town.'

Good old Derek. Joe shook his head. 'Thank you for your offer, but there are things I need to do. I want to find another friend of Molly's, someone who may well be in danger too, but I have to have wheels to do it. That's why I asked about the bike.'

'You said about a licence. So take mine — I'm never going to drive again. The bike is ready to go, and you can have my old leathers and a helmet. If you're stopped, don't take off your helmet, they'll never know the difference.'

'That's really good of you, Derek, but what if it backfires? Then you'd be in shit too. I suppose if anything went wrong, you could just say you forgot to lock your garage and it was nicked along with the bike. But are you really sure? This is my mess, Derek, not yours.'

'Look, just take the licence and give yourself a fighting chance. After all, what can they do to me? Ban me from driving?' Derek slapped his leg again. 'Let them.'

This was more than he had hoped for. 'Jesus, man, I can't tell you how grateful I am. You've just saved my life.'

'Then we're quits, aren't we?' Derek said, and grinned. 'But you do owe me a good few beers.'

'You're on,' Joe said. 'As many as you can drink.'

Soon Joe was seated comfortably on the Meteor. Dressed in leather from head to toe, crowned with a full-face helmet, he looked like any one of the hundreds of anonymous bikers who pass in a rumble and a glare of the headlight and are forgotten before the noise dies away.

Now that he was mobile, Joe's spirits lifted. He'd achieved a lot in a matter of days but only now was he really beginning. Leaving Smokey in a ditch, along with bike and bucket, Johan rode forth on the hunt for the man who might save him.

He opened the throttle. The sound was like the purr of a giant cat. What better partner to go hunting with?

* * *

Liz and David were driving back from giving their statements when David said, 'So, who is this George Miles guy? You said your musician friend had given you a name but when it came to locating him he'd hit a blank.'

'He's an old friend of Molly's apparently, and is said to have lived in Beckersby, the next village to Marshdyke. It seems he dropped off the map after he moved, and Nathan tells me that before he left he became very strange and seemed to think he was being threatened.'

'He probably was,' said David. 'I get goosebumps just trying to imagine what could be so bad that someone would be willing to commit murder just to keep it secret.'

After years on the force, Liz could imagine any number of bad things, but she kept these to herself. 'We'll find out soon, I'm sure. Anyway, locating this George is our priority now.'

And it was, but no matter how hard she tried, she couldn't stop seeing the prone figure of Clem in that churchyard, and wondering if he had survived. This fear turned to anxiety for Jeff, who was about to walk blind into what could be a very dangerous set-up indeed.

'You look very pensive,' said David, reaching back and giving Gunner a pat.

'I can't help wondering if we haven't bitten off more than we can chew in taking on both Molly's murder and this Bunker business. They both seem to be getting deeper and more complicated by the day, and I fear they may be beyond our capabilities.'

'Surely we're not giving up on them, are we?' asked David. 'Not now we've come this far.'

She glanced at David, and seeing his anxious expression, laughed. 'No, we're not giving up, but we do need to recognise there will come a point where we hand them over to the official channels. In the case of the Bunker, a lot will rest on Jeff's initial impression tomorrow. We are prepared to let him make an initial exploratory visit but, depending on what he encounters, it might be his last.'

David opened his mouth to respond when her mobile rang. Matt. 'We are going home, Liz. There's nothing we can do here, I'm afraid. They've put Clem into an induced coma. He's very poorly, and the doctors say this is his best chance for recovery.'

'He's a tough old sod,' said David when the call ended. 'I reckon he'll pull through.'

Liz hoped he was right. 'In that case, we'll need to stop off and get dog food, and some biscuits, and poo bags and, um, a water bowl, and a food bowl. It looks like our new guest may be staying a while. We'll try Poundstretcher they should have all we need.'

Soon they were walking up and down the pet aisle in the big store. 'I'm not sure he'll be too impressed by that squeaky pink cow with the rope legs,' said David, looking askance at the dog toy Liz was adding to their trolley. 'He'll never have seen one of those before, you can be sure of that.'

'I just thought that if he needed something to chew on, this would be preferable to my cushions,' she replied, 'or the carpet.'

'Are we really going to leave him in the garage, Auntie Liz? Don't you think he'll fret without Clem?' David dropped in a packet of training treats.

'I'm sure he will, and that's why he's going to sleep wherever he wants. I've got some old travel blankets in a trunk on the landing, I'll get a few of them out for him to lie on. At least Clem has always looked after him. Gunner's in good condition, and okay, he doesn't smell of violets, but he doesn't stink either.' She flashed a sideways look at David. 'Don't worry, I'll handle Matt. He's as soft as we are underneath it all. Now, let's go and pay for this lot, and by the looks of it, I'm going to need my credit card.'

As soon as they were back on the road, her phone rang again. This time it was Jack Fleet.

'Liz? Sorry, weak signal, but I just wanted you to know that we got that bloody tissue to Forensics. Apparently, the prof nearly bit our officer's hand off for it. He's well invested in finding Molly's killer, isn't he?'

'Talking of which, have you seen DC Norton recently?' Liz said.

'Conspicuous by his absence, I'm afraid.'

She wasn't surprised. 'We just heard from Matt. He says Clem is hanging on in there, so I guess that's the best we can hope for right now.'

'Can you pass on to Matt that Sergeant Johnson said there have been no sightings at all of Smokey Joe since his bike was found in the dyke. And no admissions to hospital, or to the morgue, for that matter. If you ask me, I reckon he's gone to ground, and considering what seems to have happened to Clem, it's probably not a bad move on his part.'

'I totally agree, Jack. But, hell, I'd really love to talk to him. Oh, and while I've got you on the line, does the name George Miles mean anything to you?'

Amid a sudden crackle of static, Jack said, 'George Miles? I can't think of anyone off the top of my head but I'll check him out if you like.'

'I'd be grateful. There's a damned good chance that he's on the hit list too — apparently he was a friend of Molly's.'

Jack whistled. 'Blimey, she's a proper little typhoid Mary, isn't she? Get friendly with her and you're under a death sentence.'

Then the static got worse, Jack gave up and signed off.

'He's not wrong, is he?' murmured David. 'Seems like any friend of hers is in danger.'

Liz turned into the lane leading to Cannon Farm, 'It sounds like someone is systematically removing anyone Molly might have confided in. The stupid thing is that since she was too scared to share what she knew with anyone, this killing spree isn't even necessary.' As she swung into the farmhouse entrance, she wondered if this was true of George Miles. Maybe Miles was the one this faceless killer was really looking for, the one person who knew Molly's secret.

Liz parked and turned off the engine. 'Right. Show our new guest to his room, then I need you to get on that laptop and find me something on George Miles. I believe he's in grave danger.'

* * *

Matt marched into the kitchen, stopped, stared, and shook his head in despair. Lying next to the Aga on several thick blankets was the Dog.

'I thought I said—'

'Come on, Matt. Are you really going to turn him out knowing what happened to Clem, and how that dog obviously did his utmost to save him? Just look at the fellow.'

Matt turned to David, glanced at Jeff, and held up his hands in surrender. To tell the truth, as soon as he'd seen the hound lying there cuddled into a weird pink cow, looking up at him with mournful eyes, he knew he didn't stand a chance. Poor little sod. He and Clem had been joined at the hip, now he probably didn't know which way was up. 'Has he been fed?' he asked meekly.

Liz beamed at him. 'Oh yes, and traumatised or not, he's certainly not off his food. I guess street dogs know to grab every morsel of food that comes their way just in case it's the last they see for a while.'

'Mmm,' said Matt cautiously. 'In which case, I'd be very careful to keep all our food well out of reach. Be warned, we may have a counter-surfer in our midst.'

'Good point,' said Liz. 'Talking of food, who's for an early supper? There's a chicken casserole in the crock pot, we can eat, and then discuss how Jeff is going to play it tomorrow.'

Matt opened a bottle of wine. 'I, for one, am starving. I'm also very anxious that we give Jeff all the advice we can.' He felt a stab of apprehension, the lad looked so very young. 'If it wasn't so absolutely necessary, I wouldn't let you go within half a mile of that Bunker.'

Jeff nodded. 'I understand, Matt, but given what's at stake, I'm willing to take the risk, and believe me, I won't let down my guard for a moment.'

They ate their meal and took their drinks into the incident room. As soon as they were all seated around the old dining table, Matt continued to advise caution. 'You are a rather special young man, Jeff. You have the right ideals, excellent morals and a good heart, but the people you will be dealing with are the antithesis of all that. Whatever they may say, don't forget that they are criminals, whose aim is to turn vulnerable kids into criminals too. Given how hard it has been to find anything out about that place, it is obvious that they will stop at nothing to keep what is going on there secret. And I mean nothing.'

'Don't worry, I won't be taken in. But I'm wondering what to do about my phone. I can't take it with me, it's full of contacts that would give me away immediately if they got hold of it. Likewise, if I carried a burner phone, they'd be suspicious of that, too, wouldn't they?'

Matt raised an eyebrow. 'I wondered if you'd think of that, well, I've devised a way around it. I'm going to give you a mini-GPS tracker that you can easily hide on your person. With that in place we'll be able to track your every move, which means you'll be leading us directly to the Bunker. We won't even need to tail you, we can do it from miles away.'

'Cool. But how will I let David know when I'm ready to be picked up?'

'The tracker will show you moving back towards town. When we see that, David will drive towards the pre-arranged meeting point. When you arrive, keep walking in the direction I showed you this morning, then stop. If you remain still for over two minutes, we'll know it's safe to pick you up. How does that sound?'

'Fine. A lot better than having to carry a phone.'

'I think I might have hit a stumbling block,' said Liz. 'That is great, but didn't someone say that the kids get contacted for their second visit by phone? If Jeff doesn't have one, how can they get in touch with him?'

'He's going to have to say he's lost his phone, or thinks someone has nicked it,' said Matt. 'If they think he has potential, they'll probably just give him a time and place there and then. So it's up to you, Jeff, to come up with a convincing story.'

'I can do that easily. After all, I might not get that far, there's always the chance they'll pick some other kid, but at least you'll know where it is.'

'I think they'll choose you,' said Liz. 'Even as a sullen, moody teenager, you have something about you. If they are on the lookout for special kids, they'll be interested, I'm certain of it.'

'I think so too,' said Matt. 'And, yes, the location is paramount, but if you do get there, anything you can find out about what they are up to would be a massive help.' Matt looked at him sternly. 'But, I know I'm harping on about it, but do keep it low key, don't do anything to attract attention to yourself — other than being a suitable candidate for further visits of course.'

'How are you going to act, then?' asked David curiously. 'Do you have a particular kind of kid in mind?'

'Yes,' said Jeff, 'a boy from my football team called Jason. I spent a lot of time with him. I could tell he desperately wanted to play, but he thought being in a football team wouldn't look cool so he always kept to the sidelines and made disparaging remarks about the others. He was unpredictable too, could go from morose to stroppy in an instant — it was quite impressive.'

Liz laughed. 'I can't see you as either of those things.'

'Oh, I have hidden talents,' Jeff said with a grin.

Matt was silent, having finally exhausted his words of advice. From now on it was down to Jeff. Toby had told him to get to the old cemetery by half past ten in the morning, as the man from the Bunker usually made an appearance at around ten forty-five. This was the first hurdle. Once that had been surmounted they would have their location.

David turned to Liz. 'So, what's next for us? George Miles, I guess.'

'You got it. Off on the trail of our possible next victim.'

'No pressure then. We just have to make sure we get to him before they do — whoever "they" are.'

Jeff decided to get an early night. Liz, too, announced that she was out on her feet. That left David and Matt.

'Shall I take Gunner for a walk? It might help settle him.'

'I'll come with you,' said Matt. 'And by the way, David, you're on night shift tonight. Sleep with one eye open in case he starts eating the table or something.'

'That's fine with me,' said David happily. 'I've always wanted a dog.'

'Then goodnight everyone, and fingers crossed for tomorrow,' said Liz.

* * *

Fenfleet. In the dead of night, a scrawny figure in a black bomber jacket paused in the shadow and then, judging the coast to be clear, darted into one of the cobbled backstreets. Glancing this way and that, he disappeared through a wooden door into a dilapidated building to his right. Closing the door behind him, he ran, two steps at a time, up a dingy staircase until he came to a landing with three doors leading off it, one of which was open a crack. He gave it two short raps and, without waiting for an answer, slipped inside.

The room was ill-lit, the single lamp on a battered office desk threw shadows across the walls and hid the face of the man sitting behind it. It was hard to tell exactly what the building had originally been used for, although the big open rooms on the ground floor indicated that it had probably been a warehouse, with offices on the floor above. The building was now derelict, awaiting demolition. Which suited the man at the desk perfectly.

'You're late. I was just about to leave,' the seated man said, his voice harsh and raspy.

'Bullshit,' said the other. 'You'd have waited all evening for the fifty quid I have here.' He patted his pocket. 'So, what you got for me then?'

'A time and a place, and it's worth a deal more than fifty quid, I'll have you know.'

'I'll be the judge of that,' said the visitor.

'I'm telling you, what I've got is worth at least a monkey.'

'What? Five hundred fucking quid? You gotta be joking.' With a shrug, he turned and made for the door.

'All right! Okay. A ton then.'

Darren Norton stopped at the door. He had been expecting to pay a hundred, and if the information panned out — well, he'd be quids in.

He retraced his steps. 'Where and when?'

'Tomorrow morning, around ten thirty to eleven. A white Renault Master minibus. He'll park in the lay-by outside the old churchyard in Fenfleet Low Road. The driver doesn't hang around. Soon as he's seen what he wants, he's off.'

This was it. He'd been chasing this for weeks, that all-important pick-up point. This was *his* collar, no one else's. And Matt-bloody-Ballard wasn't getting a look-in.

Without a word, he handed over the money and turned on his heel.

* * *

Anxiously, the man watched the kitchen clock. Jamie was late home. Jamie was never late. Jamie was a child of routine, any variation in the order of his days gave rise to a state of extreme agitation. By now, he should be having his late supper of a milky drink and one of his favourite biscuits. His task for the day had been an easy one — just an old man and some mangy dog. Now he was over two hours later than expected.

He considered going to look for the boy, but daren't risk having the boy come home to an empty house. He would panic, with disastrous consequences. Then, at last, he heard the back door open and Jamie came in.

He was hunched over, looking around him as if he didn't quite know where he was.

Now what? He spoke to the boy in a soft voice. 'I'm so glad you're back, son. I was getting worried. Are you all right?'

Jamie almost fell into one of the kitchen chairs, and sat holding his arms out in front of him. 'Make it better.'

The man gasped. The sleeves of Jamie's jacket were covered in blood.

'Oh, Jamie. What have you done?'

'Make it better. Now!'

He stepped closer to his son and carefully peeled back the cuffs of his jacket a few inches, watching for the boy's reaction. He swallowed. This was not good. 'We'll have to get your jacket off, son, and clean you up. I need to see what has happened to you.'

'It tried to eat me. That's what happened. Put a plaster on. Mum always puts a plaster on.'

He'd been in plenty of tight spots with Jamie but this one was very tight indeed. He kept his voice level. 'Maybe we should get your brother. He can fix it much better than I can.'

'No!'

He thought for a second. 'Okay, but do you remember when you hurt your foot in that trap left by the rabbit poachers? Remember what your mum said? She said some things are too big for a plaster, and then we call your brother, and he will make it better. Do you remember that, Jamie?'

The boy pouted. 'Jamie remembers.'

'Good boy. So this is like that, too big for a plaster, and I need someone to help me clean you up.' He smiled gently and ruffled his son's hair. 'If you're good, you can have extra biscuits with your milk, how's that?'

'The chocolate ones?'

'The chocolate ones, son.'

An hour later, Jamie was in his bed, arms bandaged, slurping his warm milk and munching his extra biscuits.

Downstairs, things were not so calm. 'What the fuck happened this time?' His elder son was furious. 'No, don't tell me, I'd rather not know. I'll come back tomorrow and change the dressings and check for infection, then you're on your own. And this is the last time. I'm not coming again.'

The door slammed, a car roared into life and sped away.

Jamie should have been hospitalised, but that was out of the question. If only his wife was here to share the burden. He sank on to a chair, exhausted, every ounce of energy spent. It *was* a burden, and it was becoming too heavy to bear. But what were the alternatives?

With tears in his eyes, he began to consider them.

CHAPTER TWENTY-ONE

George Miles stood at his door and watched the pale light that announced the coming of dawn. His mood was as desolate as his weed-choked garden, as grey as the sky. Fen mornings, how he hated them. Ever since he had discovered Molly's body lying in the marshes by the sea bank, he had wished himself far from this place. He longed for hills, thickly wooded slopes, a view for God's sake. Anything but these dreary flatlands. How was it possible that he had ever loved it?

His gaze ran over the low hedge at the bottom of his garden, to where a derelict mill was now discernible in the early light. Barn owls nested here. He would follow their silent ghostly passage as they hunted the ditches and dykes. Some nights, he would hear the pair calling to each other. His only neighbours, thank God.

A soft whine roused him from his reverie. Alfie, his Springer spaniel, was looking up at him expectantly. George sighed. 'Okay, boy, breakfast it is.'

At the mention of that magic word, the dog turned and raced back to the house, straight into the kitchen.

As George prepared his meal, he discussed their situation with his dog. 'We can't go on like this, Alf. It's no life, is it, hardly even an existence. But what do we do?'

He sat and watched his dog eat. It didn't take long. In moments, the bowl, now licked clean, was being nosed around the floor, until, with a determined flourish, Alfie brought his paw down on the edge of it and turned it upside down. Alfie had finished. George smiled and shook his head, grateful to his small companion. Without Alfie by his side, he would have long ago lost his sanity.

George had gone to extraordinary lengths to make himself disappear while not actually dying. No one knew where he'd gone after he left Oaken Cottage. He hadn't even used a removal company to shift his belongings, but had carried them piecemeal, taking months over the task. He made sure not to give his real name to anyone, referring to himself as Steve. He even shopped in farm shops and roadside stalls rather than the local supermarket. He liked those places where you took what you required, usually eggs, and put money into an honesty box. He purchased cleaning materials and other household goods from a small convenience store attached to the post office in a village that was not his own. He didn't possess a credit card and used his debit card once a month to withdraw cash and pay his bills.

George dried the bowl and put it back on Alfie's shelf with his vitamins and his treat tin, while continuing his deliberations. He was left with one remaining link to his past, which could turn out to be his Achilles heel, but that he refused to sever. Luckily, the person concerned lived and worked in a village miles away from Beckersby. Maintaining that one contact was worth the risk. The cottage he lived in was almost impossible if you didn't know where it was. No satnav ever recognised it, and the lanes that wandered aimlessly over this part of the fen never seemed to lead in his direction. It had always been referred to as the Old Deerbrook place, having once belonged to a man called Albert Deerbrook. George glanced out of the kitchen window at the unkempt garden. George loved gardening and was good at it. In idle moments, he had worked out exactly how to make his wilderness a delight. But leaving it like this was all part of the deception. Until Molly's murderer was locked up for life, nothing would change.

Nothing would change. Was his life going to remain this way forever? When he first met Molly, his life had been good, full of laughter and the companionship of friends. He had had his beloved garden, a house he invested care and effort in. The Molly he met had been terribly damaged by life but her spirit shone through. Molly was . . . how to describe her? "Special" didn't come near it. Then she chanced upon something that undid her, tore her life to shreds, and she had chosen him to confide in. She had never intended it but she had condemned him to suffer as she had.

George felt a wet nose push itself into his hand. He looked down. Smiled. 'Time for your walk?'

The dog ran around him in circles, finishing up with a sneeze of delight.

George pulled on his jacket and picked up the lead. At least there was still walking, something he could enjoy. 'It's the field pad today, lad, right across the big field and back along the lane, it's a good hour, so that should do you till later.'

It was sad that they wouldn't be going to the sea bank again. It had been their favourite walk. But no more. Not after last time.

* * *

Liz was busy in the kitchen when Jeff slouched in to have his breakfast. She did a double take and almost dropped the toast. Gone was the self-assured young man with the straight back and the loose stride of an athlete. This new Jeff had sloping shoulders and the bored air of a disgruntled teenager.

'Bloody hell,' remarked David, coming in a minute or so later. 'Where did you get those clothes? You look like a street kid.'

Jeff grinned broadly. 'I borrowed them from one of my young football team members. The only things of mine are the trainers. I kept them because that's what the kids wear, the more expensive the better.' He looked at his feet. 'And they have special flexible soles and they grip brilliantly if I need to use any of my parkour skills.'

Liz had seen kids in designer trainers that probably cost more than her first car. She finished dishing up the breakfasts, her thoughts turning to her own plans for the day. Jeff was ready to go, the mini-GPS tracker safely hidden away in a tiny zipped cash pocket in the waistband of his jeans.

They ate in comparative silence, each of them contemplating the day ahead. Liz and David would be heading off to pick up Chris Lamont and the three of them would drive to Marshdyke.

Liz wondered what they should do with Gunner. They couldn't leave him alone in the farmhouse all day. She had decided not to tell Matt that when she had gone in to wake David that morning, she had found Gunner in his bed, snuggled against his back. Luckily it was she who discovered them, and not Matt.

'He was crying,' David said sheepishly. 'Then I thought he probably spent his nights lying up close to Clem. I mean . . . What could I do, Auntie Liz? I didn't feel like lying on the kitchen floor all night.'

When they called, the hospital had said that Clem was likely to remain in an induced coma for several days. So Gunner would have to go with them. At least he was good in the car. Liz was anxious for Jeff but there was nothing to be done now but hope he would be safe and that everything would go according to plan.

Chris was waiting at his gate when they arrived.

'Hop in the front, Chris,' she said. 'We have an extra passenger, a friend of David's, so they'll be in the back.'

Chris climbed in, glanced over his shoulder and exclaimed, 'That's old Clem's dog, isn't it? I was going to ask if you'd found him — oh dear.' He looked enquiringly at Liz.

She told him what had happened the previous day.

'Poor old Clem,' Chris said. 'So you're looking after his dog for him. I'm glad he's safe.'

'Okay, what are our plans? Where to first?' Liz asked before they could get into the minutiae of dog care and behaviour.

'I thought we'd start with Anna,' Chris said. 'I rang her last night, and she's happy for us to call in to see her and her gran. So head for Beckersby, and I'll tell you all about my days on the beat in Marshdyke-St-Mary.'

* * *

Joe had to find out where George had gone after he moved. This gave him no option but to go back into dangerous waters. His ace card was his new persona, along with the shiny motorbike. He thought that if he could manage to at least smooth the corners off his Lincolnshire accent, he might well fool even those people who had known Smokey Joe well.

He took one of the long, straight droves towards the area where Molly had once lived. As he cruised along, he tried to remember everything he knew about George Miles. He had met him once or twice many years ago, but his real knowledge about George had been gained during his long midnight talks with Molly, while they sat by his burning bucket of coals and shared its warmth. He wished she'd shared more.

What she had told him was that George was a bit of an enigma, a quiet man, a loner and rather fragile. He had a job in accountancy or bookkeeping and was clever with figures, but his greatest love was dogs. According to Molly, he spent a lot of his spare time working as a volunteer at a dog sanctuary, which was how she first met him. He had found a runaway dog that had escaped from the house where she was giving piano lessons, had brought it back, and the two of them struck up a friendship. Molly said that she found George sympathetic and easy to talk to. He was fond of classical music, and even had a piano in his cottage. He liked nothing better than to sit by the fire with a dog on his lap, listening to Molly play. Over time, she had confided in him the story of her two tragic affairs, and he had encouraged her to go back to her previous life as a musician. In a cruel twist of fate, she had been on the brink of taking his advice when events took a turn for the worse.

By now, Joe was entering what he thought of as enemy territory. The last time he'd been here, an attempt had been made on his life. He had only escaped thanks to his military training and the sharpened wits that came from living on the streets. There were, however, three people he thought he could trust to help him, and who would keep silent about his new persona. He also had a safe place there that Molly had told him about. This was where he was heading now.

The road ahead stretched before him, and his thoughts returned to Molly. He recalled the night when he told her the story of what had happened to send him out on the road with his gran's bike and a bucket of eternally burning coals. It was raining steadily, and they had taken shelter underneath a bridge.

When he had finished, she was silent, tears in her eyes. 'Dear Joe. I so wish I could reciprocate, and tell you my story too, but I can't. It could mean a sentence that I'm not prepared to have you serve. It is my deepest regret that I ever told George Miles. Because of that, he hides away, in fear for his life. I cannot do that to you. After all, you were my first love, I loved you when I was still little more than a child, and I would have stayed with you, I'm sure, if your life hadn't sent you into the army and me into a very different world. I will not make things worse for you than they already are.'

He told her his life was worth nothing anyway, and he would willingly risk what little there was left of it if he could only help her. But she had been adamant. It was an affirmation that she still loved him, and he would always treasure that.

Above the thumping beat of the Enfield, Molly's voice rang in his ears, drawing him to Marshdyke-St-Mary and the man who might at last reveal her secret.

* * *

Matt dropped Jeff off in the car park of one of the big stores on the outskirts of town. Jeff made his way through the shop, out the other side, and down towards the Low Road. Leaving the old Jeff in the car, he now dragged his feet, scuffing his trainers, darting occasional sideways glances from beneath his hoodie. He had always cursed the fact that he looked five years younger than his age. Now it was a blessing.

It didn't take long to find the place. Both church and cemetery were no longer in use, the church up for sale and the future of those who lay buried beside it uncertain. The cemetery was extensive, stretching all the way to a side road that led out into acres of farmland. The grounds were overgrown and uncared for. Toby had told him where the kids hung out, and he made his way through the weeds and brambles to the collection of moss-covered tombs and fallen statues where he could see some kids lounging in twos and threes. They eyed him suspiciously as he drew near and sat down on the edge of a grave.

'You're new here, ain't yer. Not seen you around before,' said a boy with a black eye and a weal on his cheek.

Jeff shrugged. 'I'm staying with a relly, bored out of my skull.'

'Where you from then?' asked another.

Jeff waved a hand. 'Over Peterborough way. Got into a bit of trouble so the folks wanted me out of the way. Now I'm here with my uncle, pissing my time away in this fucking dump.'

No one seemed keen to rise to the defence of their hometown.

'I met this boy at that place where you can skateboard? You know, crappy bit of waste ground behind the station. Anyway, he said if I hung around here, there's this cool place kids can go for training, some kind of boot camp or something.'

The boys looked at him askance, before one said, 'We're not supposed to talk about it.'

'Well, how would I know that?' Jeff retorted. 'Kid never said.'

No one answered.

'So, it's here then, is it?' Jeff asked.

The boy with the black eye nodded. 'Hang on a bit and a van will pull in at that lay-by over there. Mind, you might not get lucky, the geezer only picks some of us. Sometimes he don't take anyone.' He scratched at his crotch. 'What they call you anyway?'

'What they call you?' countered Jeff.

The boy's eyes narrowed. 'Bez.'

'All right,' Jeff said. 'Amo.'

The other two boys told him their names, and they sat and waited. Bez was watching the entrance gate. 'Cal and Dino are late. They'll miss out if they don't shift their arses.'

He had just finished speaking when two more boys could be seen dodging between the graves in their direction. As they arrived, the sound of an engine could be heard drawing closer.

Jeff felt a jolt of anticipation. This was it.

* * *

Matt was on his third take-away coffee of the day, this one purchased from the drive-thru Starbucks where he had parked up. He stared at the screen of his laptop. The tracker was working perfectly, and he could see that Jeff had been stationery in the churchyard for over ten minutes, obviously waiting for the Bunker operative to arrive. Would he get chosen, and if he didn't, what then?

The tracker moved. Bingo! It was moving not back the way he had come, but out towards the farmlands and the marsh. The lad had done it! He was on his way to the Bunker.

CHAPTER TWENTY-TWO

En route to Marshdyke, Liz received a call from Cardiff, who told her that the blood found on Gunner's jaw was indeed human, but that there was no match on the system.

Chris, who had been listening in, raised an eyebrow. 'Interesting. It's rather unusual for a private investigator to have access to forensics, isn't it? Especially not the forensics from a murder case. How did you swing that one?'

'Don't ask,' laughed Liz. 'Let's just say that our CID liaison officer is being spectacularly unimpressive, and the pathologist is keen to have this victim given the attention and professional care that she deserves so, well, he is being kind enough to keep us informed. Oh, and he also happens to be an old friend.'

'I'm impressed. It doesn't do to be too rule-bound in cases like this.' He pointed. 'Take the next lane on the left, follow it around the village until you get to a small cul-de-sac called Victory Close. Anna and her grandmother live at number seventeen, the last bungalow along. It has a red front door.'

The tiny road consisted of bungalows dating from the 1930s. Over the years their occupants had renovated them, adding their own personal touch, so that each one was slightly different from the rest. As far as Liz could see, number seventeen was unaltered, but it was well cared for — the windows were clean and the paintwork fresh.

They were greeted by a chubby, smiling woman who introduced herself as Tilly Pickford. 'My Anna's in t'garden. I'll gier a call.'

They were hustled into a cosy sitting room and told to sit, while Tilly scuttled off to find her granddaughter.

'Check that. It's the original tiled fireplace, isn't it?' remarked David. He looked around the room. 'Neat. It looks newly-built but in an old-fashioned style.'

'Anna and her gran really do look after it,' said Chris. He was about to continue when a slender woman walked in. Chris smiled at her. 'Hi, Anna, thank you so much for agreeing to talk to us. These are the friends I told you about, Liz and David.'

Despite her pallor, Anna's smile was as warm as her grandmother's but when she greeted them her local accent was far less pronounced. Liz was familiar with the dialect but sometimes struggled with the real old Yellowbellies, and Tilly was a true Yellowbelly, born and bred in this little village.

'Tilly's got the kettle on,' she said, shaking back her fair hair. 'Tea or coffee?'

Once the drinks had arrived, Chris explained the reason for their visit.

'Liz will tell you all the ins and outs of it but, basically, we are after some local knowledge. Do you recall a woman who was a piano teacher here? She may have lived with her employer, possibly as a sort of governess. It would have been over Marshdyke way, around ten years ago.'

Tilly looked up from her tea. 'Oah, rum lot they are in that place. But ah reckon that'll be Molly, our George's friend.' She gave a throaty laugh. 'Bechatted 'e were, o'er that 'un.'

Anna smiled. 'Sometimes Gran needs an interpreter. She's saying he was bewitched by her. I remember her myself, although I didn't know her well, and I seem to recall that she was very beautiful, and that George Miles, who lived here in Beckersby, was a great friend of hers.'

Liz was amazed. They hadn't been here five minutes and already they were speaking with people who had actually known both Molly and George. 'What can you tell us about Molly? Where did she teach or — more to the point — who?'

Anna looked to her grandmother, who said, ''E nivver said, just that she taught the nobs childer ter play.'

'There were two or three big posh houses in Marshdyke back then, privately owned. I imagine it was one of those.' Anna was staring at Liz. 'I know you, don't I? Weren't you a DS?'

Liz nodded, embarrassed not to have recognised a fellow police officer. 'I was. Now I'm a private detective. But, I'm sorry, I can't quite place . . .'

'Oh, we never met or worked together,' Anna said, 'but you were the arresting officer on a case I had been involved in and was following closely. I remember being really impressed with the way you handled it. I was a real fan of yours for a time. I aimed to be just like you,' she blushed at this admission, 'then some druggie stuck their needle in me and I finished up with chronic hepatitis B. That was the end of my career. Then I heard what happened to you and, well, I stopped feeling sorry for myself. I mean, it was nothing compared to what you went through. And now here you are, a detective again. You really are an inspiration.'

'She is, isn't she?' said David.

Liz, who was growing more and more uncomfortable with all these expressions of admiration, turned her attention to the grandmother. 'You said they were a rum lot in Marshdyke, Tilly. What exactly did you mean?'

Tilly shrugged. 'Just that, me duck. Rum 'ens, all'v 'em.'

Anna explained. 'It's just that the people in Beckersby are a tight-knit bunch, not too fond of in-comers. They call them "furriners" here, meaning anyone who wasn't born right here in the village. Nonetheless, they are good people on the whole. Like old farming people everywhere, they look after each other. Now the folk from Marshdyke-St-Mary, well, Gran's right, they are odd, and downright unfriendly to outsiders.' She looked at Chris. 'You worked this patch, you know they're not like the rest of us round here.'

'They're not the easiest people to deal with,' he said. 'I never liked getting a call out to Marshdyke, though we didn't have to go there too often.'

'That's cos they sorts they own problems in they own way,' said Tilly. 'Mardy-faced lot, a law unto theselves they is.' She paused and cocked an ear, as if she were listening out for something. 'Lawks! The dilly cart's comin' shortly. Better go an' see 'im round.'

'Dilly cart?' David looked bemused, but then he'd looked that way all morning.

'The lavender wagon.' Chris chuckled. 'They aren't on mains drainage here, David, so the dilly cart comes round to drain the septic tank.'

'I clearly have a lot to learn about Fen culture,' said David with a grin. 'But what did Tilly mean about sorting things their own way. It sounds a bit feudal to me.'

'You're not that far wrong,' Chris said. 'Some of the old rural hamlets are still stuck in medieval times — complete with widow inheritance and incest. And then there's the boggart, of course. You wouldn't want to meet him, he's a creature that lives in the dykes, all green and slimy with long hairy arms.'

Clearly suspecting that his leg was being pulled, David looked to Anna.

'He's not far wrong,' she said. 'Although nowadays communities like that are few and far between. Marshdyke isn't one of them, after all there are well-off people living there, a number of big, old properties and several small businesses. There's the metalworks at the old forge, for example, and a smallholding growing local vegetables, a stables, and the Targett sisters' bird sanctuary of course. It's got no access to public transport but it's not a backwater by any means. The church even brings in visitors because of its distinctive architecture. It's just that they are all kind of insular, they don't want outsiders there at all. It's like they have, well, secrets.'

Liz perked up. 'Secrets?'

'Yes, that's how it seems,' Anna said. 'Secrets. Although I have no idea what they might be. It's probably just my overactive imagination. Anyway, what's this about? Why the interest in the music teacher?'

Liz explained.

'Molly a bag lady? Dead? It can't be!' Anna exclaimed.

'Hard to believe, but it's true. She was murdered, and everything we have learned about the case points to Marshdyke. We are eager to find George Miles because we believe he's in danger too. Moreover, he seems to be the only person who knows what happened, and why Molly ended up on the streets. We need to find him fast.'

'So that's why George disappeared. He sold his lovely cottage and just upped and left. We all wondered why. We loved George and his dogs, and you should have seen his garden, it was a picture. Then, well, all we could think was that he'd had a nervous breakdown. He suddenly went all strange, and very sort of — well, private. He suddenly started avoiding people, which wasn't like him. Then he was gone.' She gazed at Liz, concerned and uncomprehending. 'What the hell was going on in Marshdyke?'

Not was, thought Liz — is. 'I wish I knew.'

'If there's anything I can do to help,' offered Anna. 'I'm on the doorstep, and Gran knows a lot of people around here. Perhaps I can make a few discreet enquiries for you?'

Liz drained her tea. 'We'd appreciate that, but keep it low-key. We don't want people knowing we are still interested in that village. We've already made one almighty blunder by questioning the Targett sisters.'

'Not the weird sisters. Ouch! You'd only get those two to help if you had feathers!'

Chris took a sheet of paper from his pocket. 'I've written the names of a few people who lived there when I was around and whom I think would be safe to talk to. Would you have a look at it and tell me what you think?'

Anna took the paper from him and ran her eyes down the names he'd listed in his small neat handwriting. 'Well, Tim Blake died early this year, he had a heart condition and some virus finished him off. Mr and Mrs Greene moved to the West Country to be closer to their married daughter, but the other two, yes, I'd say they might be approached. Neither of them live right in the village, so that's helpful. I'd start with Callum Stokes, who has the smallholding on the Marsh Road. I get quite a lot of fresh produce from him.'

'I know,' Chris said, looking from Liz to Anna. 'Supposing Anna and I go and talk to Callum, just in case the Targett sisters have put the word out about you? He'd be more willing to talk to one of his regular customers, wouldn't he?'

'And I've got the perfect excuse,' Anna said, 'Just before you arrived, Gran asked me if I'd get her some tates, broccoli and carrots. It's only ten minutes' drive away, Chris could come with me.' She turned to Liz. 'I've had another idea. While we're in Marshdyke, you can go and talk to a friend of mine who's here in Beckersby. Her name is Kirsty Holmes, and it was her who bought George's Oaken Cottage.'

'Perfect,' said Liz. And indeed, having *two* retired police officers on the job was about as perfect as it could get.

So, a short while later, she and David were standing on the doorstep of Oaken Cottage, having stopped to admire the tree-stump carving of the owl in the front garden.

When Liz explained that they had come to ask her what she knew about George, Kirsty's eyes widened. 'That's two people who've come asking about George in the last couple of days.'

'That would have been Nathan Venner,' said Liz. 'He's a friend of mine.'

Kirsty beckoned them inside. 'Bit o' luck you picked now, as Mick, my husband, is at home today, and he knew George quite well. Come on into the kitchen.'

Once more, Liz explained the reason for their visit. Mick smiled reminiscently. 'Ah, George. I really liked that man. You couldn't have met two completely different characters, yet we got on really well. There was George, all quiet and reserved, and me . . . Life and soul I am. Talk to anyone.'

'At great length,' added his wife.

'Anyway, the main thing we had in common was our love of dogs. That's how I met him. We were both volunteers at the rescue centre out in Poultenby Marsh.'

Only then did Liz notice the old collie dog under the table, lying across Mick's feet with his head resting on his knees.

After about twenty minutes, they took their leave, having learned little more about George Miles than Nathan had already told them. On their way out, Mick said, 'I'll tell you one thing. Wherever he is, George'll have a dog with him. He told me once that he couldn't imagine life without a dog. He had three when he lived here, one died and another was very old. I reckon it'd be worth your while going out to Poultenby Marsh and having a word with Deana Pascoe, the woman who runs the rescue place. Tell her Mick sent you. I still help there when I can, but with our new business just taking off, I don't have so much free time these days. If George kept in touch with anyone from back here, it could be Deana.'

* * *

Joe coasted to a standstill and let out an oath. Now what? The day that had started so well was rapidly turning into a disaster. His "safe" place had too many people around, so he had gone to see an acquaintance he believed could be trusted. They had been out. Now he was metres from George's old cottage and once again stymied. This time the obstacle was a Toyota C-HR parked in the driveway of Oaken Cottage.

Having exhausted all his other options, he decided that the only thing he could do was wait for the blasted vehicle to leave. The man who now owned Oaken Cottage, a fellow called Mick, had once been kind to "Smokey" and he was banking on him helping him now. There aren't many people willing to go out of their way to help an old tramp with a puncture. Not only that, but he'd also given Joe his packed lunch. You don't forget that sort of kindness. And then to find that he lived in George's old cottage was one of those coincidences that rarely occur in real life.

Joe parked the Enfield in a field beneath the shade of a stand of trees and prepared to sit it out, while his fears for George were growing by the hour.

* * *

If Jeff had not known what lay behind it, he'd have been very impressed with the Bunker. The chosen five were ushered into the minibus by a tall, amiable man in a black T-shirt and khaki cargo pants. Upon their arrival, this man took them to a small, corrugated iron Nissen hut. Jeff had seen them in the fields, remnants of the Second World War now used to store farm equipment or as workshops. Inside, were rows of seats and a trestle table laid out with cold drinks and an assortment of energy snacks. Eight or nine other youngsters were already helping themselves to the refreshments, so Jeff assumed there was more than one collection point.

The man, who introduced himself as Henderson, gave them a short talk on the background to the "centre". According to Henderson, the land was owned by an ex-army officer whose aim was to give deserving street kids and adolescents from dysfunctional homes a healthy, fun day out. No strings, no payment. They would shortly be taken to a changing room where they would find sports kit — polo shirts and jog pants — for each of them. Their own clothes would be hung in lockers until it was time for them to leave.

As Jeff already knew from Toby, access would be limited to two visits —three if they were lucky — to give as many kids as possible a chance to take part. The aim, he said, was to encourage them to go on to keep fit so as not to fall into bad habits, drugs, or a life of crime. It all sounded so plausible.

Henderson went on to caution them about the need for secrecy. They must tell no one about this place, or it would close. People "out there" wouldn't believe that anyone would be giving these courses for free, and would be suspicious of their motives. Ridiculous, of course, but that's how it was. If they wanted to come again, they must never tell anyone where they'd been. Not much to ask, was it? He warned them that the owner of the Bunker would be "very disappointed" in them, and that there could be serious repercussions for anyone indulging in careless talk. Henderson then moved on to the virtues of team-building.

Henderson finished his talk by asking each of them to come and speak to him individually for a minute or two. Meanwhile, they were all invited to help themselves to drinks and snacks.

It might not have been apparent to the others, but as they were listening to Henderson's little talk, two or more men and a woman had been observing them through a partially open door at the back of the room.

Henderson called out his name.

A chill ran through him. This was his first real test. Whatever happened, he must maintain his act, and be careful not to drop his guard. This man was not as he appeared.

* * *

Matt was staring at the signal from Jeff's tracker, his mouth slightly open. This was not what he had expected. For a moment he wondered if he wasn't doing the very thing for which he'd criticised Darren Norton and making assumptions. But no, this was too much of a coincidence, and Matt didn't believe in coincidences.

He took out his phone and called Liz.

Liz began telling him about their meeting with Anna and her grandmother, and then she paused. 'Are you okay, Matt? You're very quiet.'

'I'm worried. I have no idea what to make of my latest bit of news, so I called to ask you what you thought. As you know from my text, Jeff managed to get himself selected, well, I now know where he is.'

'And?'

'Just tell me if I'm being paranoid, but what would you say if I told you he is on a large tract of privately owned land on the outskirts of Marshdyke-St-Mary?'

CHAPTER TWENTY-THREE

Liz blinked. 'No, it's not possible. There can't be a connection between the two cases, surely. They're two totally different things. But it is bloody creepy that they're both leading us to the same area. I'm not sure how I feel about this. I mean, we could really snooker each other, couldn't we, snooping around after answers to one case and setting up warning bells in the other.'

'You're right. This could be a sodding disaster,' said Matt. 'But what if they are connected? What if Molly discovered something that—'

'Whoa! Don't forget Molly got the frighteners years before this Bunker thing materialised. Even your underworld mates like Bernie are only just getting to hear about it, and the police know nothing. No, it's unfortunate, but they are two separate issues.'

'Yes, I realise the Bunker setup is recent,' Matt said, 'but who's to say the owner of that piece of land wasn't using it for something illegal before then? There *could* be a connection. I'm not saying there is for sure, but we can't dismiss it.'

'Well, okay, but I still think it's pretty implausible. I tell you what. Before he goes to collect Jeff, David can do a search into who owns the land. I don't think you or I should attempt it either, because it could be traced back to us. David can make sure he doesn't leave any "footprints", whereas we haven't the skills to be able to do it.'

Matt, who had been on the verge of doing that very thing, said, 'Okay, I'll leave it to David, and, please, Liz, I know you're in the area but don't be tempted to go and take a look, you might put Jeff in danger. Who knows what kind of security they have.'

'I get you,' she said. 'David is just taking Gunner for a little walk and then we'll be going back to Anna Pickford's place. I'll call if anything important turns up.'

The four of them arrived within minutes of each other. As they got out of the car, Chris and Anna were smiling. Back in the lounge, they couldn't wait to tell the other two what they had found.

'Nice bloke, Callum,' Chris began. 'Helpful too. We only asked him about George, but he brought up the subject of Molly himself, didn't he, Anna?'

Anna smiled. 'I think the whole village must have had their eyes on those two. And maybe they were right. She did come here a lot to see him. Anyway, according to Callum, when the village kids saw Molly arrive, they hung around outside George's cottage, and as soon as they heard her playing the piano, they would run off and tell the adults. Practically the whole village would gather outside and listen.'

This reminded Liz of the time she had heard the Night Singer. It seemed that through her music, Molly had drawn people to her throughout her life. Whoever had silenced her had done a terrible thing.

'Callum also said that Molly didn't stay with the families whose children she taught. She lived in a tiny cottage close to the rectory. And, moreover, she taught not one but *three* children.'

'And did he tell you which families these were?' Liz asked.

'Oh yes.' Chris wore the satisfied air of a cat presenting her with its kill. 'What's more, all three of them, or at least some of their members, still live in Marshdyke.'

Liz almost clapped. This was real headway. 'This is fantastic news, guys, you've done brilliantly, but George must remain our focus. Molly has gone, there's nothing we can do about her, but he is still in danger.'

Chris held up a finger. 'Ah, but we haven't finished. Get this next bit: Callum has a cousin he goes fishing with a couple of times a month, down past Fenfleet way. While he's there, he always pops in to see an old friend of his who also runs a farm shop there, a much bigger concern than Callum's, more of a proper shop.'

Anna took up the story. 'Callum happened to be at the store one day, visiting his friend, when he noticed an old Land Rover outside, with a Springer spaniel sitting in the back. He recognised George's vehicle immediately, and even thought he knew the dog. He was just about to go out to greet him when he saw him climb in and drive off.'

'Callum reckoned he looked awful,' added Chris, 'quite haggard, and he'd lost weight. His friend told him that he came to the shop every two or three weeks and made a quantity of purchases, as if he was stocking up.'

That was exactly what George was doing, Liz realised at once, avoiding the supermarkets in case he met anyone he knew, instead using smaller establishments like the farm shop that were off the beaten track. But more importantly, it placed him within a specific area. She felt suddenly elated. If they could narrow it down, they might just find him.

Now it was the turn of her and David to tell Chris and Anna what Mick Holmes had said, and the conversation turned to dogs.

'If the dog Callum saw him with is one of the original three, he must be getting on a bit by now. What's the betting he rescues another?' David said.

'And he's likely to get one from the centre where he worked,' Liz added. 'Chris, can you spare the time to go there now?

Chris said that was fine, so they said their goodbyes to Anna and her grandmother. But before they left, David took from his pocket the list of odd place names from the book on Chopin and handed it to Anna. 'Do any of these mean anything to you, or maybe your gran?'

Anna read them through. 'Not off the top of my head. Can I keep this? I'll have a think, and I'll certainly ask Gran.'

'Sure. My mobile number's on the back in case you come up with anything.'

'If there's anything else I can do, just ask,' Anna said. 'I'm here all day, and though I'd never tell Gran, I need something more in my life. Even Kirsty's moving away, and when she does, I'll be on my own in a village full of old folk, who make me feel like I should be sitting in my rocking chair knitting shawls. I'm only twenty-seven for goodness' sake.'

'We might hold you to that,' said Liz. 'Having someone out here could be very useful indeed, so ditch the knitting, and have a good look at David's list. It's a hidden message from Molly. She left it with Chris not long before she died, so it must be important.'

Anna's eyes lit up. 'I will indeed. I'll do my best to get you some answers.'

'Just tread warily. Someone out there, someone who's possibly in Marshdyke, is getting rid of anyone connected with Molly. Be careful, Anna. You know what they say — trust no one.'

* * *

Jeff had spent a gruelling fifteen minutes talking to Henderson. Keeping up his performance was exhausting, and he had the rest of the day to get through before he was safely away from this place.

He told Henderson of a dreadful home life, and his use of exercise as a means to control his violent rages. 'If I don't look after myself, no one else is going to, are they? No one gives a flying fuck about me.' Words borrowed from one of the lads he himself worked with, and which had had a profound effect on him.

The interview out of the way, a man called Simon was now showing him the correct way to use the equipment. Jeff had decided to make use of some of his skills but in such a way as to make them seem like those of a fit and enthusiastic teenager. He told Simon that he was good at gym, it was something he could do by himself, rather than in a team where he might expose himself to ridicule.

Privately, Jeff had to admit that the assault course was impressive and cleverly designed. It consisted of around twenty different obstacles designed for people with varying abilities. Like the real thing, it had nets, water jumps and ropes to be scaled, but there was also a massive, covered area with inflatables to play in. There was even a battle beam and foam pit to knock about with. The clever combination of exercise and fun was just the thing to draw kids, who would probably agree to anything just to get another shot at this fabulous playground. It seemed like a lot of money to throw at turning kids into criminals. He kept glancing at the closed doors of a big, windowless barn that stood at the very end of the obstacle course like the entrance to hell. He would have to wait for a second, or even third visit to discover the purpose of that menacing edifice.

For now, he concentrated on running, jumping, climbing, scaling walls, while trying to tone down his usual way of tackling these. Despite having to hold back, he was beginning to enjoy himself. At the same time he was aware that he was under constant scrutiny. Two men and one woman, most likely the ones he had glimpsed during Henderson's welcoming address, were observing his and his companions' every move. If they were looking for the fittest, he was pretty sure he'd pass, even though he was keeping his true abilities concealed.

Only once did he come near letting down his guard. He and another boy were instructed to stand facing each other in the centre of a pair of raised, inflated discs. Each was handed a large rubber "sabre" and told to knock his opponent out of his "ring of safety", the winner being the first to do so. The intention being to use your weapon to dislodge your rival without falling over in the process. Using his martial arts training, and the sense of balance this conferred, Jeff made a single lightning-fast move, catching his opponent off guard and sending him flying out of the ring. Realising that he'd given himself away, Jeff put it down to beginner's luck, and thenceforward wobbled around as clumsily as the other boy.

After an hour, a break was announced and they trooped back into the Nissen hut for refreshments. Henderson gave them another talk, about taking care to keep rehydrated, stretching before doing any kind of exercise, and generally looking after their bodies.

Henderson's manner was relaxed. Now he joked with some of the more outgoing boys and girls. There was friendly chaffing, a bit of back-slapping. Watching him, Jeff wondered again about what lay behind this strange set-up. It was just so elaborate. Why not just drag a handful of street kids into a van, take them somewhere quiet and make them an offer they couldn't refuse? Money. Designer clothes. The chance to get back at the society that had treated them so unfairly. There was no need to go to all these extraordinary lengths just to turn out a few criminals. No, there had to be more to this than even Matt and Liz suspected, and it would be down to him to discover what it was.

Refreshments over, they were told they could go out for another hour. As everyone made for the door, Jeff noticed a man he hadn't seen before hurry in, scowling. He went over and spoke to Henderson.

Jeff bent down and took off one of his trainers, shaking it as if to get rid of a stone or some other piece of debris. He was too far away to hear what was being said, but the man definitely sounded angry, and Henderson's face became hard. As he followed the others through the door, Henderson's eyes fell on him briefly. The look in them was decidedly unfriendly.

* * *

Henderson beckoned to his two colleagues. 'Race has just given me a piece of disturbing news. He thinks the driver of the minivan who went to the cemetery pick-up was tailed.'

Gordon and Smith swore. 'What? All the way here?' asked Smith.

'No, but only because of a stupid accident. A tractor shed its load on a roundabout. Our driver got through but the traffic behind him was held up. Nevertheless, someone knows about that pick-up point. Race thinks it's not the first time he's seen that vehicle either. We need to call a meeting with Cash. This is serious.'

'You're right. I'll ring him now,' said Gordon, heading towards the door at the far end of the hut.

'What do we know about this car?' asked Smith.

'Black VW T-Cross. Race is sending the reg across to HQ. They'll be able to find the owner. Meanwhile, you and I need to check a couple of other things, like why now, after months of everything running like clockwork. Either some kid we thought we could trust has squealed, or,' he frowned, 'one of the kids from the cemetery pick-up is a plant.'

'There were five from there, weren't there? Three new kids, and two second visits? My money would be on a second visit kid,' said Smith. 'Got over-excited about this place and blabbed to the wrong people.'

'I'm not so sure,' said Henderson slowly.

'What are you thinking?'

'I've a feeling about those new kids. We should keep a close eye on them. I could be wrong and it's someone who has been watching us for a while but still . . . Anyway, we'd better go and see if Gordon has managed to contact Cash. Simon is watching the kids, so they're okay for now, although I reckon we should close down earlier than usual. We'll give them another hour or so, then get them back to town. One thing is certain, we need to act fast to shut this VW driver down before he fucks the whole thing up.'

'Well, we're nearly there,' Smith said. 'Only a couple of weeks and then we'll have cracked it and all this will be gone. And no interfering bastard is going to get in our way.'

* * *

The Poultenby Marsh Dog Sanctuary was proving difficult to find. Liz finally spotted a cluster of buildings half-hidden behind a stand of tall trees along a winding fen lane that led down to the marsh.

'Well, the barking won't be bothering any neighbours, will it?' said David, casting his eyes around the endless expanse of fields and the vast bowl of the sky. 'There *are* no neighbours.' He ran a hand through Gunner's thick fur. 'Don't bother about what those notices say, we're not leaving you here.'

They pulled into a large concrete parking area beside a well-kept grassed exercise run. Stepping out of the car, Liz noticed dog agility equipment, along with bales of hay and piles of logs that evidently served as places with interesting smells for the dogs to sniff at. 'This is really well organised,' she said to Chris. 'Have you ever been here before?'

'Never. And I agree with you about the set-up. It's all very clean, and there's no noise. I've been to a few rescue places where its bedlam.'

'Auntie Liz, I'll stay in the car with Gunner if you don't mind,' David said. 'Poor fellow's picked up on where we are, he's shivering.'

'No problem, David,' Liz said. 'We won't be long.'

Inside the reception, they were greeted by a young woman and an older man. Both wore sweatshirts with a logo featuring a black dog and the initials PMDS.

Liz asked to speak to Deana Pascoe. 'Tell her Mick sent us.'

The two volunteers smiled at the mention of Mick's name. While the young woman went to find Deana, Liz asked the man if he happened to know George Miles.

'Good old George. Haven't seen him since Bono died,' the man said. 'That was his boxer dog. I thought he'd be back for a new friend for Alfie, now he's on his own, but he hasn't.'

The girl reappeared. 'Deana's over at the enclosure. Will you come with me?'

She took them out of a back door and down a long, covered way that led to the kennels themselves. Like the rest of the place, these were spotless.

Deana turned out to be a tall, willowy woman, with short-cropped dark hair, wearing heavy-rimmed glasses. 'Friends of Mick's, are you? Wanting to join my merry band of canine carers?' She grinned. 'Unpaid, of course.'

'Not this time, I'm afraid.' And Liz explained the reason for their visit, while the smile faded from Deana's face.

'Oh my God! We've been wondering where he was. I rang him any number of times, until I received a reply to say the number was no longer in use.' She shook her head. 'He's such a lovely, gentle man. Who on earth could wish him harm?'

'That's what we are trying to find out,' said Liz. 'But it looks like you can't help us either.'

'No, I'm sorry. Feel free to ask the others, but I'm sure they would have told me if they'd seen him. He was one of our staunchest supporters, and a good friend to boot. We all miss him.'

Liz felt deflated. She had been so certain they would find a lead here.

She was about to leave when Deana said, 'There's one thing that might help. It's a bit of a long shot, mind. You see, we dog-lovers are funny about certain things, vets being one of them.' Deana raised an eyebrow. 'When you find a veterinarian you trust, you stick with them, and don't go any-where else. George has taken Alfie to the same vet ever since he got him. His other dogs, Bono and Flinders, were with the same woman, who's the one we use as well. Come back to the reception and I'll get her details for you. Her name is Sue Harrison and her clinic is in Summerdyke.'

Having given Liz the vet's number, Deana accompanied them to the car. 'If you find George, please tell him to come back and see me. He has friends here, people who care about him. Please find him, and do all you can for him. He has a good heart, and whatever has happened, it won't have been through any fault of his.'

'We'll do all we can. And you've been very helpful, thank you.'

As she spoke, Deana caught sight of Gunner. 'Hello, that's a big chap you've got there. He's a fine fellow, to be sure. How long have you had him?'

'Er, twenty-four hours or so,' said David. 'We are kind of doggy-sitting for a sick friend.'

'Well, he's certainly fond of you,' said Deana. She stood back as Liz started the engine. 'And good luck finding our George.'

Liz sped away, the scenery passing in a blur, until Chris said, 'It's okay, Liz, you can slow down a bit. We have plenty of time before I need to get back to the library. Anyway, I'm not passing up an opportunity to meet someone who just might have his address.'

With a laugh, Liz took her foot off the accelerator. 'Thanks, Chris. It would have been a bit tight getting you home, then back out to Summerdyke before David has to collect Jeff.'

It was not nearly as easy to get to see Sue Harrison as it had been Deana Pascoe. Finally, one of the veterinary nurses took them into a small consulting room and asked them to wait.

Sue hurried in, looking a little flustered. 'It's manic here today. I'm sorry, but I really don't have long.'

Liz again explained that they were looking for George Miles and why.

Sue's half-apologetic smile vanished and she eyed them suspiciously. 'Sorry, but I don't know either of you from Adam, and I certainly don't just hand out my clients' details to whoever happens to ask.'

Liz was taken aback. 'We are terribly worried about him, Ms Harrison. As I explained, this is connected to a recent murder, and I believe Mr Miles is in grave danger. If you know anything about where we might find him, I'd be grateful for your help.'

'Then why aren't the police here?' Sue responded. 'That card means nothing. Anyone can go and get a card made.'

She knows exactly where George is. Liz decided on another approach. 'Deana Pascoe believes what we say. That's why we are here, she gave us your name and address. You have made it abundantly clear that you know where George and Alfie are. I respect your loyalty and I'll not press you further. The police can do that if necessary. Just do one thing for me, if you would. If you are in contact with him, just give him my number. It's on that card, both my home and mobile numbers are there. It could mean the difference between life and death for George. I hate to lay that kind of responsibility on you, Sue, but it's that serious. Finally, you can ring DCI Charlotte Anders at Fenfleet police station, and she will confirm that the Haynes and Ballard Detective Agency are officially liaising with them in this investigation.' With that, she thanked the vet and turned to go.

'He told me people might ask about him, people who wish him harm. George is terrified of something. He said he was risking his life coming to me, but he would do so for Alfie's sake.' Sue Harrison looked at the floor. 'I was hoping it wouldn't come to this. Part of me believed he had suffered some kind of breakdown, and it was all in his mind. I have no idea what happened and I don't think I want to, but I like and trust George. He's a good man. I won't give you his details, but I will give him your number. He can decide whether or not to talk to you.'

'That's all I ask,' said Liz gratefully. 'And I do appreciate it.'

It was something, she supposed. Now it was down to George, and failing that, an official visit from DC Darren Norton, God help them. All she could hope was that George Miles would see sense and ring her.

CHAPTER TWENTY-FOUR

At precisely two thirty, the youngsters were taken to a shower block, where they took off their kit, showered, and put their street clothes back on. Jeff was on edge. It was plain to him that something unexpected had happened. The two who had been watching them during the first session were missing, as were Henderson and the other instructors and they were left in the hands of a man called Simon, plus a new man, Kit, who was introduced as a medic. For the first time, Jeff missed his mobile phone. He needed to tell Matt and Liz of his suspicions but he had no way of communicating with them. Recalling the look Henderson had given him as he left the Nissen hut, he realised that from now on, he would have to be careful not to drop his guard for a second.

'Everyone back to the main hut, please!' Simon called out. 'One last word from Henderson and you'll be taken back to town.'

Back in the Nissen hut, Jeff could sense the tension radiating from Henderson.

'One more quick word with each of you, then make your way to the vehicle that brought you — except for the group from the churchyard. You will be going back in a Land

Rover. We won't be dropping you there, but it will be close by. Me and the team hope you've had a good time today.'

Jeff watched Henderson speak to the other boys. As far as he could tell, he was asking them for their mobile numbers. Would he be able to return if he didn't have one to give him? And why the change of vehicle and a different dropping off point for their group alone?

Henderson was now calling his name out. Taking care to look bored, Jeff made his slope-shouldered way over to the waiting figure.

'Simon tells me you handle the equipment pretty well, Amo.'

Jeff shrugged. 'Fat lot of good that'll do me down at the Job Centre.'

Henderson stared at him thoughtfully. 'Don't knock it, Amo. There's plenty of jobs that call for someone who's agile and strong. And if you were prepared to develop your other skills as well, you might go far. Now, if you'd just give me your cell number, you might get a call to say you can come back for a second time, if you want to. Well, what is it?'

'Ain't got one, have I? Some bastard nicked it.'

Henderson shook his head. 'You teenagers. You're the third kid whose phone has been lost, damaged or stolen. Well, if you want to come back again, be at the car park at Aldi the day after tomorrow at ten thirty sharp. And don't be late, he won't hang around.'

Jeff nodded. 'All right. And, er, thanks. This is a pretty cool place.'

'Just don't shoot your mouth off about it. And I mean that.'

Jeff scuffed the toe of his trainer on the ground. 'No chance of that. Who've I got to talk to in that dump? No one.'

He went out to the waiting Land Rover Discovery, wondering if he'd got away with it. Something serious appeared to have happened back there, and from the look that Henderson gave him, he knew he could be under suspicion.

As they drove away, Jeff was relieved to be out of there. For a while, he had wondered if the only way he'd get out was over the high, mesh fence.

* * *

At least Joe now knew that he no longer needed to fear being recognised. The look of amazement on Mick Holmes's face when Joe revealed himself as the old tramp he had once helped on the road was almost comical. Mick was only convinced that he was who he said he was when he described what was in the packed lunch Mick had given him that day.

Joe rode away no wiser as to that elusive address but knowing that he wasn't alone in his search for George Miles. Some private detectives were trying to find him too. From what Mick had said, they were working alongside the police to solve the case of Molly's murder. He was surprised to learn that the police were even mildly interested in the death of a vagrant and wondered what this might mean.

Joe was now heading back the way he had come. He had decided against going into Marshdyke itself, instead trying one more time to find his "safe place". If there was no joy there, he would contact the number Mick Holmes had given him for the detective agency that was looking for George.

* * *

Anna and Tilly sat in the kitchen, the list of places and names David had left with them on the table in front of them. None of them meant a thing to Anna, but Tilly wasn't so sure.

'Me 'ead's all mizzy-mazzy raight now,' she muttered, 'but summat seems to be a tuggin' at the old memry.'

'What's that, Gran?' Anna asked.

The old lady frowned. 'Rupert.'

Anna got up to put the kettle on. 'Other than the bear in those children's stories, I can't say it rings any bells with me.' She badly wanted to help Liz, for whom she felt the deepest admiration. This had only grown when she understood what it must have cost her to get her life back on track after the life-changing injuries she had suffered.

'Madge! That's it! Madge Kettleworth,' exclaimed Tilly.

Anna looked round. 'Who's she?'

'Dead 'n' buried now, duck, but she were in service at the Whistlers' house. Yah know, the big 'ouse behind t'church? The old Vicarage.'

Anna knew which house she meant, and what's more, Whistler was one of the three families Callum had told them of, whose children Molly had taught. 'So what's the connection to Rupert, Gran?' she asked.

'Madge's cat. Damned great thing, it were. Can see it nah, big tab-cat called Rupert.'

And if Madge were "dead 'n' buried", Rupert would be too, and that might mean a grave. *In Rupert's grave.* 'I don't suppose you know if she buried it, do you, Gran?'

'Oh yes!' Tilly nodded furiously. 'Old man Whistler let 'er 'ave a quiet spot in back o' the garden. She give it a nice little service 'n all. Piping 'er eyes summit awful she were.'

Tea forgotten, Anna exhaled. This could mean that one of the riddles was solved — if they could only locate this grave after God-knows how many years. 'Gran, you said she cried her eyes out when she buried Rupert. Were you actually with her then, or did she tell you about it?'

'Oh, I were with 'er, me duck! Yer granddad dug the hole hisself. He were gardener to old man Whistler.'

'I don't suppose you could find that grave again, could you, Gran?'

The old lady's face crinkled. 'Well, I knows where it *was,*' she said doubtfully, 'but they's made a lot o' changes to that garden since them days. Not a patch on when my Albert tended it mind. Young Ted does 'is best, but . . .'

Anna tried to think herself back into police mode. Now they had found the answer to one of the clues, what then? How could they gain access to the Whistler family's garden? And if they did, they could hardly start digging up some dead cat's grave. She would need to think about this. Meanwhile, since Gran had solved one riddle, maybe she could do it again. She turned back to the kettle and made the tea.

'Right, Gran, one cup of tea coming up, and you can get that mizzy-mazzy brain of yours working again. You've solved one riddle, so how about the other four?'

'I reckons a chocolate biscuit would 'elp, don't you, me duck?'

Smiling fondly at her gran, Anna reached for the biscuit tin.

* * *

Matt breathed a sigh of relief. The little red dot of Jeff's tracker was moving in the direction of Fenfleet. He rang Liz and told her to get David ready to collect their "agent".

'I'm in the car park of the DIY store in West Street. David knows where it is. He can go and pick up Jeff as soon as the tracker stops moving. The minute we know he's happy that he's not being followed, the three of us will head back home.' He exhaled. 'I'm telling you, Liz, this little escapade has taken a year off my life. I've spent the whole day worried sick about that lad.'

Twenty minutes later, David's car drew up behind him, and David hopped in. 'Hi, Matt, everything all right?'

'I'm not sure. Look here.' Matt pointed to the tracker. 'The vehicle bringing him home just went right past the old cemetery. It's still moving.'

'Perhaps they do that sometimes, to throw anyone watching off the scent. Although Toby was dropped off where he'd been picked up.'

They followed the course of the tracker until finally it stopped.

'I know where he is,' Matt said. 'That's a quiet side road about a quarter of a mile from the old cemetery. I hope Jeff remembers which direction he is supposed to be heading in.'

'Don't worry about Jeff, Matt. He won't get lost,' said David. 'So, shall I head off there now?'

'Yes, but take it slowly. I'll call you when he stops and give you his exact location, okay?'

'Got it. Just call me Uber. I'll ring you when we set off for home.'

Once more, Matt was left alone to worry. One thing was for sure, no way was he going through this again. The warning bells were sounding like klaxons in his head. They now knew where the Bunker was, and that was enough. No matter what Jeff told them, he was not going to be persuaded to allow him to go back in.

The tracker stopped. There was a short delay, then it started moving again, only much slower, this time in the direction of the rougher neighbourhoods of Fenfleet.

Good lad. Matt's heart rate having returned to something approaching normal, he rang David.

'He's on his toes to the rendezvous point. Be ready to move towards.'

'I suppose that's police-speak.' David sounded amused.

'Sorry, lad, old habits die hard.'

'It's okay, I get the picture, though I refuse to say "Wilco." Anyway, I'm ready and waiting.'

Twenty minutes later, they were all on their way back to Tanners Fen, Matt's anxiety having turned into impatience. What had Jeff met with out there, on the marshland by Marshdyke-St-Mary?

They were almost home when his phone rang. The call came from an unknown number. 'Is that Matthew Ballard?' a man's voice said, 'of the detective agency?'

'Yes. How can I help you?'

'My name is Johan de Vries, and I believe we are both looking for the same man. George Miles.'

Matt was momentarily stunned. Johan? Could this be Joe?

'It's all right, Mr Ballard, I thought you might be surprised. Yes, I'm the man you knew as "Smokey".'

The man was silent for a moment, then he said, 'It's about Molly, Mr Ballard, Marika Molohan. Can I meet you somewhere?'

'Do you know Tanners Fen, Joe?'

There was a soft laugh. 'I know every inch of this part of the Fens, Mr Ballard. I travelled every road here for more years than I can count.'

'Then go to Cannon Farm, near the sea bank. I'm heading there now. Do you have transport?' Matt recalled the weed-draped bike that had been dragged from the ditch.

'Oh yes. I've upgraded. I can be there in thirty minutes.'

'Then we'll see you soon. And, Joe?' Matt chuckled. 'You have no idea how pleased I am to hear your voice.'

CHAPTER TWENTY-FIVE

'Something's not right.'

Bruno and Kurt stared blankly at Leah.

'What d'yer mean?' asked Kurt.

'Think about it, dumbass. This place runs like clockwork. You know what I mean, everything happens at a set time, like they've got a timetable or something. Cash was supposed to give us our final pep talk half an hour ago, so where is he? I don't like it.'

The two boys glanced at each other. Apart from the fact that it didn't pay to argue with Leah, she had the nose of an animal for trouble and could sniff it out from a mile away. In their room at the back of the barn, they were cut off from the wider Bunker, and Leah's words made them uneasy.

'It might be one of Cash's tactics,' Kurt said. 'You know, keep us waiting, seeing how we cope.'

Leah shook her head. 'It's not that kind of wrong.'

Suddenly, Smith burst into the room. 'Get your things together! All your kit, don't leave anything behind.' He flung three large grab bags in their direction. 'Come on. Move.'

Bruno picked up one of the empty bags. 'What's up, Smith?'

'You're being shipped out. No more questions, pack your stuff. Now!'

With a shrug, Kurt grabbed one of the bags and made his way to his bunk.

Leah was already in her cubicle, stripping the tiny wardrobe and drawers of her meagre possessions.

Satisfied that they were all doing as they were told, Smith left.

'You were right,' Kurt said to Leah.

'Yeah,' she said, 'but shipped out *where?*'

They had been told, Kurt recalled, that those of them who made the grade would be moved on for further training, otherwise they'd be shipped off to some far-flung city and left to make a new life for themselves. But he also remembered Leah's words of the day before and wondered if there was another, more sinister, fate in store.

His bag at his feet, he stood waiting nervously for someone to collect them. A young boy, frightened and terribly alone.

* * *

An hour later, two vehicles crossed paths at the gates to the Bunker, a black 4x4 going out, and a white unmarked Transit van coming in.

The van reversed into a covered area next to the barn, where Smith stood waiting to receive it. 'Load still intact, is it?'

'Yeah,' said the driver, 'or it was when I set off anyway.'

'All right. Keep it locked and wait for me to come back. I won't be a minute.' Smith hurried off to get Gordon. This was one particular cargo he wouldn't be able to handle on his own.

* * *

Matt burst into the kitchen and announced the imminent arrival of a very special visitor.

Liz gasped. 'Smokey! Oh, thank God he's alive. Is he really on his way here? I can hardly believe it.'

Matt's unexpected news caused quite a flurry. 'He sounded different,' he said. 'Sort of, well, perky. And when I asked if he needed a lift, or had he got himself a new bike, he said he'd "upgraded", whatever that means.'

Jeff was the only one of them who seemed less than excited. 'If it's okay with you guys, I'll go and get changed. Then I really do have to talk to you about today, things happened that you need to hear about.'

'Off you go then,' Liz said, and looked at Matt. 'It's a pity Smokey Joe chose now to turn up. We really need to hear what Jeff has to say about the Bunker, but Smokey could be pivotal to Molly's case.'

'I suppose there's not much we can do about it,' said Matt. 'Smokey's on his way here — and by the way, he called himself Johan de Vries, so maybe we should drop the "Smokey".'

'I'll try to remember,' said Liz, 'though I've known him as "Smokey" for so long it'll be odd calling him — what did you say the name was?'

When the gleaming motorcycle thundered to a halt outside, Matt wondered what the delivery could be.

David looked out of the kitchen window. 'Hey! I've seen that guy before. I recognise the bike. I met him when I was walking Gunner while you were at Mick Holmes's cottage in Beckersby. He was parked up at the side of the lane, and he said hello to Gunner.'

So, it had been Mick who had brought them together. Matt joined David at the window and the two of them watched him put the bike on its stand and pull off the full-face helmet. So it was a courier after all, thought Matt.

'Er, don't you think someone should let him in,' said Liz, 'instead of gawping at him through the window.'

David hurried to the door and admitted a thin man of medium height, with short, wavy grey hair. Despite the weather-beaten features, this new Joe revealed himself to be quite a few years younger than Matt, and bore not the slightest resemblance to the "old" tramp with the bicycle and the bucket of hot coals.

'Joe?' Matt asked hesitantly.

Joe made a little bow. 'The same, Mr Ballard. My circumstances have changed, you might say, and I realised that if I wanted to stay alive, I'd have to change along with them.'

'Well, you've done a bloody good job. I'd never have recognised you in a million years.'

'That's very good to hear,' said Joe, meaning it. 'It should give me a bit of an advantage if it comes to the crunch.'

Matt shook his head. 'Hell, man, we all thought you were dead. And look at you now! Well, all I can say is thank heavens you had your wits about you. I assume it was you dumped the bike?'

Joe nodded. 'I had to buy myself some time.'

'Perhaps we could all go into the lounge and sit down,' Liz said. 'We clearly have a lot to talk about, and if Joe will excuse us, we really need to listen to what Jeff has to say.'

Jeff was hovering anxiously in the background.

'I can wait outside, if you like,' offered Joe.

Matt shook his head. 'No need. It's a different case, Joe, but knowing this area as well as you do, you might be able to help.'

Once they were settled in the lounge and Matt had given Joe a rundown on the missing teenagers and the Bunker, Jeff then gave them an account of his day. He described the layout, the people in charge and the way they drew the kids in.

'It's bloody clever,' he said. 'They assess the kids' abilities and interests, then tailor a programme to fit each individual. I didn't know it until I chatted to a boy on the journey home but apparently, they even have computer games consoles in one section for anyone who isn't comfortable with the assault course.' Jeff paused. 'I couldn't see any sign of an actual bunker, just the assault course, a Nissan hut and a large barn, but from the top of one of the climbing nets, I noticed another structure at the back of the barn. It looked like a big, low, concrete block, half overgrown with brambles and grass, so I guess that must be it.'

'Where is this place?' Joe asked.

'An area of land between Marshdyke-St-Mary and the marshes,' said Matt.

An odd look passed across Joe's face.

'Joe?' Matt asked.

Joe didn't answer immediately. 'It's the old Bruton place.'

Liz gasped. 'Bruton is one of the names given to us by Anna's friend, Callum Stokes. It's one of the three families whose children Molly was teaching.'

'That's right,' said Joe tightly. 'She did teach one of the Bruton boys — Benjamin was his name.'

'Yes!' exclaimed David. 'She mentions Benjamin a lot in her notes.'

'Whoa, folks!' Matt held up a hand. 'I know it's important, but can we keep to the Bunker for now? We mustn't lose sight of our missing boy, Liam Cooper, and for heaven's sake, let Jeff finish. Now, lad, what happened to make you so uneasy?'

Jeff told them of the man who'd rushed in and said something to Henderson that he obviously found extremely disturbing, after which the people who'd been watching them suddenly disappeared, leaving one instructor and a medic to supervise the kids. 'That wasn't the only thing that got me worried,' said Jeff, 'it was the way Henderson looked at me. He was definitely suspicious. When we were on our way out, a number of other vehicles were coming in, and they weren't hanging around. I got the feeling it was some kind of red alert.'

Matt and Liz glanced anxiously at each other. The only thing that could cause such a reaction was a security breach. 'But he let you leave, Jeff. If he was so suspicious, I wonder why he didn't try to keep you there.'

'Well, he had a last chat with each of us before we left, and when it came to my turn, I sensed that they had identified the problem, and it wasn't anything to do with me. He accepted my explanation for not having a cell phone number, and what's more, invited me to come back the day after tomorrow, so I'm guessing I'm in the clear.'

'Did they say why they were using a different vehicle and dropping you beyond the pick-up point?' asked Liz.

'No,' Jeff said. 'I can only assume that they thought the cemetery and the van were being watched.'

'Exactly,' replied Matt thoughtfully. 'But who by? We were miles away, and according to Norton and Swifty, the police know nothing about the Bunker, so it can't be them.'

'Someone else is interested then,' said Liz. 'And they're not doing a very good job of observing.'

'This all makes me very edgy,' said Matt. 'I can't help thinking about Bernie's reaction when we asked him about it. He looked downright scared, and if a hard nut like Bernie is frightened of them, they must be seriously bad news. He called them a new breed of criminal, heartless and with no sense of honour. If that's the case, and if they were able to identify the problem so easily — in the time it took for our Jeff to swing on a rope and scale a net or two — they've probably sorted it by now. And like they say, "by any means necessary".'

The others were silent as they considered the implications of this.

'What I don't understand is why the police aren't all over it,' said Joe.

'Because there is no evidence, and one missing habitual runaway doesn't warrant a major inquiry,' said Matt. 'And,' he turned to Jeff, 'if they raided it today, what would they find? A group of do-gooders, an altruistic landowner and a handful of stalwart volunteers all helping improve the lives of underprivileged kids. Isn't that right, Jeff?'

'Absolutely.' Jeff said. 'And a bunch of happy smiling teenagers. If I hadn't known what was behind it, I'd have had nothing but praise for what I found.'

Matt turned to Joe. 'Okay, Joe, you said you know who owns this place. Any more you can tell us?'

'Well,' Joe said, 'there's a big house on the far side of Marshdyke called Bruton Manor. In its day, it was a magnificent spread, with well-kept gardens and a swathe of surrounding land. The Bruton family were filthy rich, they owned huge farms both here and in Warwickshire. In the years up to and during the Second World War, they had a run of bad luck — mainly due to bad investments — and they sold off most of their farms, but they retained all the land around Marshdyke, including a stretch of grazing land along the marsh. That big barn belongs to the Brutons, along with the concrete bunker behind it. It was a World War Two relic that old Francis Bruton had converted into a bunker at the time of the Cold War.'

'Are there still Brutons living there now?' asked Liz.

'Yes, I believe so, although I haven't been that way for a few years. Molly told me to steer well clear of Marshdyke, and I took her advice — until today.' Joe looked apprehensive. 'I got as far as Beckersby, and now I'm here.' He looked directly at Matt. 'What I will say is that the surviving members of the Bruton family are more likely to have rented that barn and the surrounding land out, rather than set anything up themselves. They are far from altruistic, believe me. They always were a bunch of money-grabbers and I can't see that having changed in the last few years. I know — they wouldn't even spare a crust or a drink of water for a homeless person.'

Matt received this information in silence. So Molly had been in the very place their other inquiry had taken them to. How was it that their two cases were converging like this?

The sound of the landline ringing jolted him from his thoughts.

Liz answered. 'Hi, Anna. Yes, have you got something for us?' She grabbed a notepad and pen and started scribbling, while her caller continued to speak. Call ended, she turned to the others, her face alight. 'Anna and old Tilly Pickford have been going through the list of riddles from the book on Chopin. Tilly has worked out two of them, and Anna just rang Chris Lamont at the library, and they think they've solved a third.'

'Cool! What are they? Where are they? Which ones were they?' David gabbled.

'Guys! Have a thought for Joe. He hasn't the faintest idea what you're talking about. Why don't you explain before we go any further. Meanwhile, I'll contact Charley Anders and update her on the Bunker. I'm beginning to think we're approaching the time when we need the police to take over.'

Charley sounded fraught. 'I hope you're calling to ask for your old job back, because I'm telling you, if I have one more day like today, you can have it.'

Matt smiled. He remembered days like that, when any career would have seemed preferable to the one he had chosen.

She sighed. 'And now you are going to add to my worries. I can feel it coming.'

'Sorry, Charley, but, well, yes.' He went on to tell her about the Bunker and what they suspected was going on. When he told her where it was situated, Charley sighed. Loudly. 'Shit, Matt. I'll need a bloody good reason to enter that place without a warrant. It's private property, no crime has been reported, and funnily enough, the JP doesn't hand out warrants based on Chinese whispers.'

'I know, I know. I'm just making you aware of what we suspect. Then, if it boils over into something you can act on, you'll be able to do so immediately. I promised I'd keep you updated, and that's what I'm doing. I'm not asking for a helicopter and an ARV, just that you be aware of the situation.'

Charley grunted. 'I'm sorry, Matt. It's been a crap day. Of course, I trust your judgement completely, but we are stretched to capacity, and I'm telling you now, if all hell breaks out at your Bunker, I'll be hard-pressed to find a sodding squad car, let alone a helicopter!'

So that was that. He had been going to ask for a bit more support than they were getting from Norton, but that obviously wasn't going to happen. Things must have got overwhelming since they'd last spoken with Charley. 'Then I won't trouble you further, Charley. Just one last thing — can you get DC Norton to ring me asap? And you did allocate some uniformed assistance should he need it. As far as I know he's never asked anyone for support, or made any inquiries of his own regarding our Molly. We are streaks ahead of him, and he's contributing very little, so gee him up for us, if you would.'

'Hold on, Matt.' There was a long pause, during which he could hear Charley talking to someone. 'He's not at his desk. One of the others said he went out following some lead or other, but he didn't tell them where he was going. That was hours ago.' She heaved a sigh. 'I despair of that young man, really I do. But I'll do what I can, and I'll have a word with uniform about letting you use Swifty Fleet as a kind of official contact.'

'Thanks, Charley, and I'm sorry things are so stressful at present.'

'That's life in the force, Matt, as you well know. I'm sorry you caught me at one of those manic moments. But listen. Don't take on more than you should, and don't get into danger, okay? I'd never forgive myself if either of you got hurt, especially Liz. If the shit hits the fan, I'll be there for you. I'll find the resources from somewhere. And if you can find some concrete proof of a crime having been committed, I'll be on it like a ton of bricks, okay?'

'Received and understood, and good luck with all you have on at present.'

Very slowly, Matt put the receiver back in its cradle. Now what should he do? Since he was not prepared to let Jeff go back to the Bunker, how would he ever get Charley the evidence she needed? Which meant that two young boys — Liam Cooper and young Lee's brother, Dean — were condemned to join the ranks of the missing. He doubted they were still in the Bunker. If they had been deemed good criminal material, they would have been moved on, if not, who knew? They could be dead and buried, lost forever out in the marshland.

He sank down on to a chair and put his head in his hands. He sat like this for a while before rousing himself. He was all Mr and Mrs Cooper had to pin their hopes on. Even if the worst had happened to Liam, they needed to know. He couldn't let those poor people down, or young Lee, a boy with only his little brother to love. No. They had started this investigation and they'd bloody well finish it.

Matt stood up and marched determinedly back to the lounge. They would work out a proper plan of action. Two cases to solve — one involving a huge operation, and another that was smaller but equally important. Not quite the retirement he had expected, but at least life wasn't boring.

CHAPTER TWENTY-SIX

Liz contemplated the disparate group ranged around her living room. These were the people who were to help her solve two challenging and very serious crimes. A university student, a soldier turned vagrant, a young Parkour practitioner and, finally, Liz herself, a retired, semi-disabled detective. Their supporting cast consisted of a librarian, a former police officer, a keyboard player, an elderly woman code-breaker, and — she glanced at Gunner — one very large dog.

She watched, as if from a great distance, David, telling an astonished Joe about Molly's bag of scribbled notes and the clues buried within them.

'That's Molly all over,' Joe said. 'If only she had told me what happened in Marshdyke all those years ago, I'd have helped her. I would have laid down my life to keep that woman from harm. But, generous as ever, she kept silent for my sake.'

He had been in love with her, Liz realised. As had Nathan, George Miles, and who knew how many others. All bewitched by the music of the magical Night Singer.

'So, tell us about these riddles your friends found the answers to.'

Liz blinked. Joe was addressing her. 'Well, starting with "Rupert", old Tilly knew that there had been a cat of that name whose owner buried it in the grounds of a house belonging to a family called Whistler. So, we know where Rupert's grave is. Next was "Beneath the Anvil".' She glanced at David. 'Nothing to do with the forge, I'm afraid, it actually refers to a cloud formation known as the Anvil cloud. It seems there was once a small school in Marshdyke that catered for the local children until the advent of school buses closed it down, and the foyer is decorated with murals on the theme of the weather. A section of this mural depicts the various cloud formations. One of them is an anvil cloud, or *cumulonimbus incus*, a flat-topped cloud that heralds the advent of a bad thunderstorm. Tilly is certain that this is the anvil Molly was pointing to.'

'Awesome!' exclaimed David. 'We'd never have worked that one out.'

'The last one, solved by Chris and Anna, is that it has something to do with an old house called — wait for it, David — Cedar Leigh, but which was originally called "Silver Birches".'

'At last,' David said, 'there's my elusive Cedar Leigh.'

'What's more, it has a gravel drive lined with silver birches. So we now have three places to start looking.'

Joe, however, looked unimpressed. 'I love treasure hunts as much as the next person, but, forgive my saying this, George Miles knows exactly what happened. Maybe we should be looking for him rather than digging holes in and around Marshdyke? What's more, George's life is in danger. I know this because I too was attacked. I only survived because of my army training but George was an accountant, for heaven's sake. What chance does he have?'

He was right, of course. Their excitement over the riddles seemed childish when a man's life was at stake. So, what now? Should they abandon their hunt for those clues?

'How's it going?' Matt had just entered the room and his voice interrupted her thoughts.

'We've been telling Joe about the situation to date, and he's just reminded us of the urgency of finding George Miles. As far as we are aware, George is the only person who knows what happened to Molly, and someone wants him — and

Joe — dead. So, we have to focus on that rather than the clues Molly left.'

Matt paced up and down the room while he digested her words. 'Okay. This is what I suggest. Charley has just told me we can't expect any help from the police, so I think our only course is to gather everyone who has assisted us in either of the two cases and hold a meeting. We've reached a point where we can't continue on our own, so as far as I see it, our only hope is to delegate some aspects of the work to those trusted individuals.'

'You mean like Chris Lamont?' said Liz.

'Yes, and Anna, if she's well enough,' said Matt. 'They are both former police officers, so they won't need their hands holding. Anna, in particular, could be very useful since she lives in the Marshdyke area.' He turned to Joe. 'And you'll help too?'

'That's why I'm here. I need to find George, so any way I can help you to do that, count me in.'

'Excellent, Joe, and you're right, Matt,' Liz said. 'It's the only way forward. Why don't we ring them now, so we know who we're talking about, and then we can work out a plan. What do you think?'

'I think let's do it,' said Matt with a smile. 'You get on the landline to Chris and Anna, and maybe your friend, Nathan. I'm going to update Swifty and put him in the picture, then try to get hold of Darren Norton. He's our weak link but we need to keep CID informed of what we are up to, so he has to be involved.'

* * *

The man tore savagely on the side of his thumbnail. His son was poorly, more than that, Jamie had a fever and was practically raving. Even his hard-hearted brother, who had come to change his dressings, had expressed shock at the state he was in.

'He belongs in hospital. It looks to me like he's developed a serious infection, sepsis most likely. His temperature is off the scale, and he's even more confused than he usually is — if that's possible. This time, Father, you don't have a choice. You either call an ambulance or he dies. And if you still won't do it, I will.'

For the first time in years, he had faced up to his eldest son and pointed out one or two home truths to him. He had left, white-faced, but without having called the emergency services. As the door banged shut behind him, the man knew that he would never see his son again. His eldest boy, the one with the brains, had never understood about the bloodlines, while Jamie, the dunce, had understood only too well. It was all so unfair.

If Jamie didn't survive, he was on his own. Without Jamie, it would be down to him to sort what remained of this terrible mess and put an end to what had been started so many years ago. So be it. Shaking the blood from his gnawed finger, he went to the fridge and took out the milk. He set it on the stove to warm for Jamie's night-time drink. It was far too early, but in the state he was in, Jamie wouldn't know. He placed a couple of chocolate biscuits on the tray. The lad would be unable to eat them, but he'd expect them to be there, as always. He then crushed a handful of tablets into a powder, added them to the steaming mug and stirred.

It didn't take long. He held his son to him, telling the boy he loved him, and watched as the drink went down. Even in the throes of a raging fever, Jamie followed the time-honoured ritual and drank his goodnight drink to the dregs. 'Good boy. Now go to sleep,' he whispered.

'Jamie done good?'

'Yes, son, Jamie done good.'

Ten minutes later, he was outside Jamie's room and locking the door. The windows had already been sealed, so there was no way out.

* * *

Matt swore under his breath. Norton was still not picking up. He decided to ring Swifty instead, but before he could dial the number, Swifty himself was on the line.

'DCI Anders told me to ring you. Your detective seems to have gone off the radar. He's been out of touch since late this morning and we're beginning to get a bit concerned. According to our CCTV cameras, he took his car and flew out of the gates like a rocket. The traffic cameras picked him up moving east through the town, then nothing. He must have taken to the side roads. Since then, there's been no sightings, though he did ring in just before lunch. Apparently, he told one of the detectives that he was off to check out one more lead and would be back after that, but he omitted to say where he was. Then, well, nothing.'

Digesting this piece of news, Matt recalled the odd, fleeting expression on Norton's face when he'd mentioned the Bunker. He remembered, too, the apparent red alert that Jeff had told them about. No. Surely that idiot detective hadn't . . . it wasn't possible. Or was it?

'Hello? Are you still there, Matt?'

'Yeah, sorry.' Matt had forgotten that Swifty was still on the line. 'We haven't heard anything from him, Jack. Could you let me know if he turns up?'

'Of course, Matt. And don't forget, I can assist if you need me, the skipper has told me to be on hand.'

'That's good news, mate, and don't worry, I'll be calling. We've quite a lot to deal with our end.'

'Before you go, Matt, tell Liz I'm just about to check out someone she wanted to know about — er, George Miles? The name rings a bell but for the life of me I can't think why.'

'I'll tell her, and thanks, Swifty. It's good to know you're there for us.'

'My pleasure, sir.'

Matt ended the call and looked at the clock on his phone. It was a quarter past five. He hurried back to the lounge, his mind on the vanished DC Norton. Could that cocky young detective really be so stupid?

'They're all in, Matt, all three of them are on their w—' Liz stopped. 'What's the matter?'

He told Liz of Norton's unexplained disappearance.

'I wondered at the time if he knew something about that place,' said Liz. 'I thought I might have been imagining it but he definitely reacted to the name.'

'What a plank,' muttered David.

'It fits, doesn't it?' added Jeff. 'We wondered if they'd clocked someone watching the pick-up point. It must have been Norton.'

'Which leads us to suspect that his sudden disappearance is courtesy of Henderson and his crew,' said Matt.

'Meaning that if our devious detective isn't dead in a ditch, he's now inside that Bunker that he was so sodding interested in,' Liz said.

'What car does he drive?' asked Jeff.

Liz closed her eyes for a second, trying to recall the vehicle she'd seen drawing up outside Cannon Farm. 'I know — a black VW T-Cross.'

Jeff exhaled. 'Then I'm pretty sure they've got him. You know I said there were vehicles approaching the enclosure when I was being driven out in the Land Rover. Well, one was a white Ford van, another a big 4x4, a Toyota, I think, and a smaller black car driven by the man who delivered the bad news. I'm sure it was a black VW.'

'It's enough for me, lad, but to get the police involved we'd have to be certain it was Norton's,' said Matt. 'Damn it! Every time I get the priorities lined up in my head, someone moves the goalposts. Now we have two men in danger — George, and that idiot Norton.' This was not good at all. 'When are the others arriving?'

'Within the hour,' Liz said, just as her phone began to ring.

'Liz,' Swifty said. 'I knew that name meant something to me. He was the guy who found Molly's body. I've got his address right here.'

Joe almost catapulted out of his chair before sinking back down again. 'It was George who discovered her? Oh no, that poor man.'

'Hold on, Swifty. Let me grab a pen.' David handed one to her and she wrote it down. 'Got it. I can't thank you enough, Swifty, that's fantastic.'

'I'd go out there myself,' said Swifty, 'but I'm afraid he might do a runner if he sees a police car. He was in a right state. Oh, and apparently, his place is a bugger to find, it doesn't even have a number on it, so best of luck.'

Liz thanked him and ended the call. 'Okay, Matt, how do we deal with this?'

'He knows you, doesn't he?' Matt said to Joe.

'I've changed a lot since we last met years ago, but I do know how to reassure him that we're both old friends of Molly's. And I really do want to go, Matt. He's the reason I'm here.'

'Why don't I go too?' suggested David, 'and take Gunner. We know that George is a dog person, so he'll be more likely to trust someone with a dog. And I'm not exactly intimidating, am I?'

'That sounds good to me,' said Joe. 'We'll take the car and park nearby, then walk the dog to George's house.' He looked at Matt. 'Is that okay with you?'

It was the best they could do, so he agreed. 'What's the address, Liz?'

She read it out. 'It's about half an hour from here, right out in the wilds.'

Joe smiled. 'I know that lane. There aren't many houses, in fact there's only three along there. Forget the satnav, I've got this.'

'Then get away now, and take care, both of you,' Matt said. 'Don't forget, you aren't the only people looking for George Miles. You too, Gunner. Look after these two for me, and that's an order.'

Gunner stood up and walked across to David. Matt felt a whole lot easier knowing Gunner was at David's his side.

* * *

Henderson slammed his fist down on his desk. A copper. That was the last thing they needed. Why the hell hadn't HQ told them that when they gave them the licence number and the address? Now they had a fucking detective trussed up in a storeroom.

Smith marched in. 'What the hell do we do now?' he demanded. 'This could screw the whole operation.'

'Tell me something I don't know,' barked Henderson. 'One thing is for sure, we don't get paid enough to kill policemen.'

'Yeah, that's not in my job description either. But it can be arranged. Not everyone cares about who they top.' Smith flung himself into a chair and glowered at Henderson. 'We can't keep him here, that's for sure.'

'Then we arrange an accident, don't we?' Henderson said. 'We've got his car, we've got him, and there are some pretty dangerous marsh lanes out there. Well?'

Smith shrugged. 'I suppose that's a possibility, as long as it happens fast. Just the thought of him being here gives me the screamers. And I can't believe he's acting on his own. Any moment now we could have blue lights and sirens coming at us across the soddin' fen.'

'I get what you're saying, Smith, but just cool it, would you? There's no point us shouting at each other. This is not our cock-up, it's HQ's, we're agreed on that, but we still need to sort it before we start getting unwelcome attention. Like you said, in a week or two this place will be history. We have what we need and we can move on. Meanwhile, we still have the perfect cover, it's just this one little problem, and that can be dealt with.'

'I suppose you're right. And thinking about it, if that detective hadn't been on his own, we'd have had visitors by now. Maybe he was just being nosey, or was following up a lead off his own bat,' Smith said. 'So, what's the plan then?'

'I think we should run it past Gordon. He'll know who the best person is to arrange something like this. The most dangerous time of day for driving on these fen lanes is just after twilight, when visibility is at its worst. That gives us roughly three and half hours, and as we can't have it happen right on our doorstep, we need to act fast.' Henderson stood up. 'Come on, let's get this sorted.'

* * *

George Miles sat at the kitchen table and stared again at the message his vet had sent. Was this an honest offer of help, or a trap? Stacked at his elbow were six boxes of paracetamol. More than enough to end this miserable existence.

He looked down at the dog lying at his feet. He could no more take that dog's life than fly to the moon, but he couldn't abandon him either. Having been abused and then left for dead, Alfie didn't deserve the same thing to happen again.

George fondled the spaniel's ears. If only he could ring that number and rid himself of all these years of anguish, but he didn't dare.

'There is one other option, old lad,' he said. 'How do you feel about a long holiday walking the north Yorkshire moors? We could pack a bag and just head off. How does that sound?'

Alfie wagged his tail. Alfie always wagged his tail. Anything George suggested was fine with him.

George stood up. 'Right. That's decided then. I'll pack a bag and some food to tide us over, and we'll hit the road.'

It took George thirty minutes to pack up everything that constituted his life in this cottage. One bag for him and a heap of necessities for his dog — towels, leads, bowls, food, flasks of water, treats.

Finally, he made the house secure, fastening windows and switching off the water.

He was just about to depart when a loud knock on the door made him freeze in his tracks.

No one called here. No postman, no delivery van . . . then he remembered that he'd left the door open while he took what he needed out to the Land Rover.

'You're a hard man to find, George Miles.'

The voice was a familiar, friendly, but he couldn't quite make out the speaker, who was standing in the doorway with the light behind him. He approached, warily.

'Good Lord! What on earth are you doing here? And how did you find me?'

'Patience and perseverance, George. Can I come in? This won't take a minute, I can see you're about to go out, but I've got some news for you.'

Wishing he'd left ten minutes earlier, George stood aside for his visitor to enter.

CHAPTER TWENTY-SEVEN

'How do you manage to find your way around in this remote place?' said David, as they followed the twists and turns of a nameless lane that seemed to lead nowhere but endless stretches of ploughed fields.

'I wasn't going anywhere in particular, so to pass the time I started to try and make a map of the area in my head.' Joe gazed across the vista before them. Not a single human figure could be seen. 'After a while, I came to love it.'

'How come you took to the road, Joe?' David asked. 'And why that bucket of hot coals? Tell me to mind my own business if you think I'm prying.'

Joe smiled. 'Oh, I don't mind you asking, it's just something I never talk about.' He glanced at David who was just then easing the car around a tight bend, frowning in concentration. He liked this young man. 'This will probably sound weird, but I did it from a sense of guilt. Someone lost their life, and I felt I was to blame. It happened many years ago, but I probably relive it at some point every day of my life.'

'Then, please, don't go over it again for my sake. I'm such a nosey arsehole, I ought never to have asked.'

Joe directed him to take the next right and continue along beside a broad watercourse. 'Maybe it's time I did tell someone about it, otherwise I'll never move on. We have plenty of time before we get to George's lair.'

David turned on to the long straight drove Joe had indicated. 'Well, if you're sure it won't be too painful for you.'

'After I left the army I kind of drifted for a bit, doing various assorted jobs. Then I became an outward-bound instructor. I'm a strong swimmer and my favourite activities were those that involved going out on the water — canoeing, kayaking, white-water rafting, the lot. I was probably the most experienced of all the instructors when it came to water sports. On the day it happened, I had four boy scouts with me, a great bunch. I was using the experience of white-water rafting to develop life skills like team-building and confidence. We were negotiating a very tricky stretch of the river, full of rocks and rapids, when out of the blue, one of the boys stood up and just keeled over, off the side of the raft and into the water. I had three others to consider while at the same time getting the fallen boy to safety. So, I guided the raft into a shallow, secured it and took to the water, leaving the others on the raft. It was a nightmare, negotiating pounding rapids in a steep, fast river. I did dive after dive, expecting at any moment to hit my head on a rock or for my energy to give out. I found him, but by the time I managed to get us both out of the water, he was dead.' Joe's words caught in his throat for a moment. 'He was freezing. I did everything I could to revive him, but nothing worked. I ended up just holding him tightly. It was over half an hour before help arrived and I've never in my life been so bitterly, deadly cold.'

'I cannot imagine what you must have been through, Joe. And thank you for sharing it with me,' David said quietly.

'Anyway, the post-mortem results showed that he'd been dead before he even fell from the raft. He suffered from undiagnosed and untreated Sudden Death Syndrome, an inherited heart condition which nobody knew about because he was adopted. I was exonerated of all blame, but in my eyes, a boy had died in my care, and I couldn't live with that.' He stopped talking, drained. He hadn't mentioned the bucket, but David could work out for himself why he carried those hot coals. If he could possibly help it, no one was ever going to be cold the way that boy had been.

Joe cleared his throat. 'Anyway, enough of me. Right now, we have a good man's life to consider. We're half a mile from George's place, so turn up that lane you can see on your left.'

A minute or two later, a house came into view, set back off the road behind a stand of stunted trees that had been planted as a windbreak against the relentless east winds.

'That has to be it,' murmured Joe. 'Slow right down, David — hang on. Didn't you say George still has his old Land Rover? So what's that old Ford doing parked at the side of the barn?' Joe's antenna was picking up warning signals. 'Park up and stay with the car. Have your phone at the ready, and if you see any trouble, get out of here fast and dial 999. Got that?'

'I'm coming with you,' David said at once, unfastening his seatbelt.

'No! No arguments. I need you here. Watch and wait. Something in that house is not right.'

'Then for God's sake, take Gunner,' hissed David.

Without giving Joe time to object, David jumped out of the car and opened the back door. 'Go with Joe, there's a lad. Look after him.' He waited a few seconds to make sure the dog had obeyed, then climbed reluctantly back into the driver's seat.

With Gunner by his side, Joe made his way gingerly towards the house, through a tangle of undergrowth. The garden was a mess. Joe guessed the reasoning behind it — simple deception. George Miles would never have a garden like this, therefore, George Miles didn't live here.

Gunner following, Joe went around the side of the house and crept along beside the wall until he could see the front door, which stood slightly ajar. He stopped to listen. From within came the sound of someone shouting.

He stood up, took a stealthy look through a small window and gasped in horror.

George Miles was sitting, looking dazed and frightened, in a high-backed kitchen chair. His wrists had been tied to the wooden arms and there was blood running down the side of his face from a wound on his temple.

The source of the shouting was a largish man standing over George with a shotgun and making threatening gestures. From the fragments that drifted out through the window, it seemed that the man was demanding to know something. George, cowering beneath this onslaught, kept shaking his head.

There was another noise too, a high-pitched keening that didn't seem to be coming from George. Joe weighed up his options. Given that the man had a weapon, all he had on his side was the element of surprise.

Joe took a deep breath and launched himself through the door with a fierce battle cry.

* * *

Liz was beginning to wonder if she should open Cannon Farm up as a guest house. Her kitchen was full of people all talking excitedly and, as she watched them it suddenly came to her that every single one of them, except Jeff, was damaged in some way. Matt, all but destroyed by a terrible case that haunted him still; and that same case had almost cost Liz her life. Anna's beloved job had been stolen from her by a drug addict. The untimely death of Chris's wife had shattered his life and ended his career. David's childhood illness had brought his dream of becoming a police officer to a sudden end. Joe — who knew what he had suffered to send him out on the road to spend his days as a vagrant? Even Nathan was living with the guilt of failing to come to the aid of Marika, the only woman he had loved.

Meanwhile, Matt was opening the meeting. With a scraping of chairs, they gathered around the old kitchen table and fell silent.

'We are very grateful to you all for giving up your time to come to our aid. You all know why you are here, basically, we have two cases which have become too much for us to handle on our own, and the police say their hands are tied until we can come up with some solid evidence that they can act on.' He concluded by saying that Joe and David had gone to George Miles' address to persuade him to accompany them to Cannon Farm where he would be safe from the nameless threat hanging over him. 'If David and Joe bring him back with them, we will finally have the answer to who and what lay behind Molly's death.'

'Since there is no guarantee that they will succeed,' added Liz, 'we have three of Molly's clues to follow-up on, and which may lead us to at least some of the answers.' She turned to Anna and Chris. 'Would you two be willing to try and find where she hid them?'

'I suggest the Anvil first,' said Anna promptly. 'I know exactly where that tile painting is in the old school, and I also happen to know that the flooring beneath it is woodblock, so it'll be easy to take up.'

'Thank you,' Liz said. 'If you can do that, we'll know the kind of thing we can expect to find at the other sites Molly listed. How do you propose getting into the school, Anna?'

'There'll be a weak point somewhere,' said Chris, producing with a flourish, a Swiss knife from his pocket. 'This has been a great help in days gone by. We'll get in.'

'How soon can you go?' Liz asked.

'The minute we finish here,' said Anna with a glance at Chris.

'The sooner the better,' he said. 'That old school has a back entrance to the playground. It's not overlooked and the grounds are a mess. There's next to no chance of us getting spotted.'

'We'll see what we can find and ring you immediately,' said Anna.

Matt nodded. 'Then why don't you two go now? We can let you know of any new developments that arise. Just remember, you don't have warrant cards anymore, none of us do, so don't take any chances.'

Liz noticed the smile pass between them. They'd do whatever it took, sod the absence of a warrant card.

As soon as they had left, Nathan asked how he could help.

'How are you with technology?' asked Matt. 'When David gets back, I'm going to ask him to do a search on the three Marshdyke families Molly worked for. Maybe you could help with that?'

'Right up my street,' said Nathan enthusiastically. 'I do mixing all the time, and produce videos.' With a smile, he produced a flat bag that had been sitting on the floor at his feet. 'I even brought my laptop along.'

Matt stood up. 'Then it's time we introduced you to our incident room. This way, sir.'

Jeff had remained silent during the meeting, so Liz asked him what he was thinking.

'I have an idea, but I don't think Matt will like it.'

'Will *I* like it?' she asked.

He grinned. 'Probably not, but it's still a bloody good idea.'

'Come on then, spill.'

'We all agree that the thing with the Bunker is getting too big for us to handle but the police have no justification for raiding it, right?'

'Uh-huh.'

'Well, I know how we can alter that.'

'What do you mean?' Liz asked.

'Well, earlier this afternoon I saw what I believe to be DC Norton's car being driven towards the Bunker by one of the guys who picks up the kids.'

'If it really was Norton's car. We have no proof of that,' Liz said.

'True,' said Jeff. 'But Norton is missing. His car is missing. You and Matt both suspect that he knows something about the Bunker, and you know Norton's not a team player. *I* know that something happened out at the Bunker at the very time Norton set off for an unknown destination and hasn't been seen or heard of since.' His eyes narrowed. 'So what's the odds they have him?'

'I'm with you, Jeff but I'm playing devil's advocate here. I suppose you want us to bring in the law, so how are we going to do that? I know what the police will say — that their hands are tied. We've been through that before, it's why we called on the others to help. Now, where is this heading?'

'*We* don't bring them in, I do.'

Liz heaved a sigh. 'You were right. Matt will not like this, though I still don't understand.'

'Listen.' Jeff leaned forward, elbows on the table. 'I can get into that place, Liz. I've identified no less than four entry points that would present no challenge for someone like me. What I'm suggesting is that I get inside, locate Norton's VW, photograph it, send it to you and your DCI and get out fast. The police will then have the proof they need to search the place for a missing officer. A police drone could do it but they're too noisy. My way could be the only chance of finding Darren Norton before something happens to him, or, if he's dead already, getting his body back and arresting whoever was responsible.'

On the brink of agreeing with him, Liz brought herself up short. It was undoubtedly a good idea, but Jeff was their responsibility, and if anything went wrong . . . these were hardened criminals and not to be taken lightly. 'Jeff,' she said, 'you can't do that. You were lucky to get out of there once already — you thought Henderson was suspicious of you, didn't you? That place must be riddled with cameras, and one is bound to pick you up. Then you'll be dead meat.'

But Jeff remained unfazed. 'I checked for cameras, and there are fewer than you might expect. Most of them are focused on the assault course and the concrete bunker itself. The car won't be in either of those places. I expect it'll be behind the Nissen hut where I saw several vehicles parked up. I don't even have to get close, Liz. My phone camera has a great zoom lens. I can do it, I know I can.'

Liz wanted to say yes. She had seen his video. Getting in would present no problem whatsoever, but as she knew well, things didn't always go to plan. People were not where they were supposed to be, timings changed, something unforeseen occurred. What's more, she had always had back-up, whereas Jeff would be alone. No, she could not allow it.

While she was mulling it over, Swifty called.

'Just a quick update. Norton still hasn't turned up, or his vehicle. Because of his connections, the big guns upstairs have censored all media coverage for the time being — they're not sure how to play it — but it will hit the headlines tomorrow. You can't keep something like this under wraps for long.' He chuckled. 'DCI Anders is dusting the ceiling and shows no sign of coming down. I've never seen her so angry.'

Just as she ended the call, Matt reappeared. She told him what Swifty had said. 'And, er, Jeff has a suggestion.'

Matt listened to every word, and called it a brilliant idea. Then, as they had both expected, he said no.

'Okay,' said Jeff, clearly not ready to give up yet. 'What if I took someone to cover my back? If I can't go alone, what if two of us went in?'

'Like who?' Liz said. 'My days of scaling walls are well behind me, Matt would never make it, and we all know about Davey's limitations.'

'I'm not thinking of you guys, but what about Joe? He was in the army, wasn't he? Who better to watch my back? If we can prove that the missing officer's car is in there, the police can carry out their raid.' He gazed at Matt. 'If Darren Norton isn't enough of an incentive, please consider those boys you're looking for. One more thing goes wrong in that place and they'll pull the plug on the whole operation. Then you'll never get them back. We have a chance to put an end to this, but we have to act now. Let me go in. One photo is all it will take.'

Instead of digging his heels in, Matt sat down and passed the back of his hand across his forehead. 'We'll talk to Joe when he gets back. What you are suggesting goes completely against the grain, but there seems to be no alternative. As you said, lives could be at stake.'

CHAPTER TWENTY-EIGHT

Joe's rescue mission didn't go quite as planned, mainly due to the intervention of his over-enthusiastic guard dog.

On hearing Joe's battle cry, the man threatening George swung around to face him. Fortunately, the shotgun was a heavy old double-barrel, and he was unable to bring it up to a firing position before Joe got to him. Joe had him disarmed when they were both knocked off their feet by a forty-kilo canine projectile. By the time Joe had got his breath back and was on his feet, the man had staggered out through the door, slamming it on the dog that was hot on his heels. Joe glanced at George, who was white and bleeding profusely, and gave up the chase.

Joe untied him and began to clean the wound, while Gunner began scratching furiously at the door to the pantry.

'For heaven's sake, Gunner. Back off, would you.' Joe dropped the cloth he was using, went to the pantry door and opened it. Out flew a distraught black and white spaniel who ran straight to George and stared up at him, whining.

'Alfie,' George murmured groggily. 'It's all right, lad, I'm okay.' He reached down and laid a hand on the dog's head.

Seeing the violently trembling hand, Joe was pretty sure that George Miles was very much not okay. He knew from the army that blows to the temple were not good. George needed professional care.

Joe looked around for a phone, but couldn't see one and he had never possessed a mobile.

'George, mate, have you got a phone? You need an ambulance.'

George muttered something unintelligible.

Alfie, meanwhile, was whining and Gunner was endeavouring to escape by digging under the front door, clearly hopeful that his prey might yet be caught. Joe swore.

'George, listen. I'm just going to get my friend to ring for an ambulance. I'll be right back.'

Joe ran to the car and told David to call an ambulance — George was probably suffering from concussion, and he had a deep wound on the side of his head.

'Who was the guy in the car, Joe?' asked David as he pulled his phone from his pocket. 'He went off like a bat out of hell.'

'Fuck knows. George must have known him though, or he wouldn't have let him in. Oh, and can you put the Incredible Hulk back in the car? I've a feeling my so-called guard dog might have bust one of my ribs.' He turned to go, and then stopped. 'And ring Cannon Farm, they need to know what's happened. I'll stay with George until the ambulance turns up. I just hope they can find us.'

Back inside, Joe found George slumped sideways in the chair. The hand resting on the dog's head was now still.

'George! Come on, mate. You can't go to sleep on me, you have to tell me who the hell that was. Who was that guy who hurt you?' He closed his eyes for a moment, willing George to come round. 'Think of Molly, George!'

George gave a sound somewhere between a groan and a whimper, and his head fell forward.

Joe was gripped with a terrible panic. 'Oh please, no! Not again. Please. I couldn't bear it if someone else died on my watch.'

Just as despair threatened to overwhelm him, he suddenly experienced an odd sense of calm. It was as if someone had placed a reassuring hand on his shoulder. It would be all right. George would not die.

Joe took a deep breath. He raced up the stairs to the bedroom and returned carrying a duvet, which he wrapped around George, telling him that Molly was with him, asking him to give them a name so that her death could be avenged. 'It's up to you now, George Miles. Only you can give Molly the rest she deserves.'

For one fleeting moment, Joe was certain there were three of them in that little kitchen, and he wasn't counting Alfie.

* * *

Chris smiled with satisfaction as the old sash window slid up. He put his trusty knife back in his pocket and whispered, 'I'll go in and undo the back door.'

'It's all right, I can get through here,' said Anna.

Inside, she got her bearings and led the way to the main foyer.

The old school had the damp smell of disuse, and had a strange eerie feel to it. You could almost hear the echo of children's voices along the empty corridors.

Both Chris and Anna still had their pocket Maglites, standard issue for all police officers. It was still early but some of the windows had been boarded up, and the place was dark.

'Here we are,' said Anna, her voice hushed. 'The weather pictures.' She ran the beam of her torch across them. 'And this is the one we are looking for.'

She had alighted on a painting about two feet square, that depicted a strange, flat-topped cloud formation called *Cumulonimbus incus*. This was the anvil cloud, the bringer of storms.

They shone their torch-beams on to the floor below and swept them across the worn wooden block flooring.

Chris knelt down and felt around, searching for a loose one. Finding what he was looking for, he took his knife out and began to prise it away.

It was tightly wedged, and dig as he might, he couldn't lift it. 'Shit. It feels like the underfloor is solid.' He stood up and closed the penknife. 'This will never budge, and I'm sure it's been in place since the floor was laid.'

'What now?' Anna said. 'Gran can't think of anywhere else that has an anvil. This is so disappointing.'

As she spoke, her torchlight wavered across the floor. Chris absently followed it with his eyes, until something caught his attention. 'Hang on! Look there.' He shone his own light on to the skirting-board joining the floor with the wall. Over the years, some of the plaster had crumbled, leaving a gap between it and the wall. It looked like something had been wedged there.

Chris opened his knife and dug out a piece of cardboard. It was discoloured with age, but the writing — an elegant cursive — was perfectly legible. A single name, "Fiona McEwan".

'That it? But that tells us nothing.' Anna sounded quite indignant.

'Ah, don't be so sure,' Chris said. 'Let's get out of this place and call Matt and Liz. You never know, this name could be the key to the whole investigation.'

'I suppose since we're so close to home, we could call in and ask Gran if she remembers this person,' said Anna, still less than optimistic. 'She knows people in this village going back generations.'

Chris stood up with a shiver. 'I'll be glad to get out of here, it's too spooky for me.'

Anna laughed. 'You great wuss!'

* * *

Since they were at home, Anna thought they might as well have a cup of tea. Chris sat with the old lady, willing her to remember who this Fiona McEwan might be. That piece of cardboard couldn't have been stuck there so close to the anvil by anyone but Molly. It had to be connected to whatever had frightened her so badly. She had gone to extraordinary lengths to reveal her secret, which surely must have been terrible indeed.

'Ah, that'll be the one.' Tilly beamed at him. 'Fiona. Fiona Mac, they called 'er. Lovely girl, hair the colour of shiny copper.'

'Who was she?' asked Anna, mugs in hand.

'Private secretary, or so she called 'erself. We all thought she were a bit more'n that, if you catch my drift.'

'Who did she work for, Gran?' asked Anna, placing a mug of tea in front of Tilly.

'Edward Bruton's eldest son, Reginald. One o' them bigwigs in the village. Liked to call hisself a company director as I recall.' There was a disdainful edge to her voice. 'Though what he was director of, no one could say. Money-grabbin' lot, them Brutons was.'

Chris and Anna looked at each other. Bruton again. The name kept cropping up during the investigation.

'What happened to her, Gran?' asked Anna.

'Well, one night she just upped and left. Norra word to a soul.' Tilly shook her head. 'There were a right old to do about it. Reginald were beside 'isself, and o' course, there was all these rumours about 'im and 'er flyin' about the place.'

This set off a number of speculations in Chris's head. Had this Fiona chanced upon whatever had terrified Molly? If Fiona was such a "woman of the world" as Tilly had suggested, had her sense of self-preservation been much stronger than Molly's? Had she run for her life? 'You know what,' he said. 'I think Molly was trying to tell us to find Fiona McEwan and ask her what happened back then.' He took out his phone and called Matt.

* * *

Matt's head was spinning. He had taken three calls in quick succession and was starting to feel as though he was manning a news desk just as a major story was breaking.

'Okay' he said to Liz, 'the upshot of all that is, first, that the swelling on Clem's brain is beginning to recede, and if all continues to go well, they'll be bringing him round tomorrow morning. Then David called to say that the ambulance had arrived at George Miles's place, and they were preparing to take him to hospital. They think he is badly concussed and will have to have a scan. He'll be kept in overnight for observation.'

'That's good news about Clem,' said Liz, 'George too, just so he doesn't finish up like Clem. And the other call?'

'Chris says Tilly remembered Fiona McEwan who, guess what, worked for one of the Brutons. One thing's for sure, we'll be looking into that family very closely as soon as we get going again.'

'Especially as the Bunker is on their land,' Liz added.

'Speaking of the Bunker . . .'

Jeff had just walked into the room. 'Sorry to butt in, but if I don't get down there soon, it'll be dark, and then I'll never be able to get a picture of that car. It's going to be tight even if I leave now. And I can't wait till tomorrow, they could have cleared out by then.' He stared at Matt. 'You must let me go alone. We cannot have deaths on our hands when we have a chance of stopping them.'

'Get yourself ready. I'll go with you,' Matt said.

'No!' Liz almost shouted. 'David said the ambulance was taking George to hospital. Joe knows the back roads, so they can meet up with Jeff somewhere near Marshdyke, then Joe can still go with Jeff.'

There was no time to argue. 'Ring David now. Tell him exactly where Joe should meet Jeff.'

Liz made the call. 'They're just leaving. And you, Matt, have work to do. That was a serious assault, a police matter. They'll want to interview Joe and David and forensics will want that shotgun, so you need to buy Joe some time.'

'Okay, I'll ring Swifty.' Matt turned to Jeff. 'Go! And for God's sake, keep yourselves safe.'

* * *

While all this was unfolding, Nathan proceeded quietly with his search.

Bruton. Whistler. Conway. Three old Fen families who, between them, owned the biggest, most prestigious properties in Marshdyke. Bruton, the proprietor of Bruton Manor along with much of the surrounding farmland, was stinking rich. As far as Nathan could see, there was no pie in which he did not have his fingers.

Whistler owned the Old Vicarage, its garden a fine example of Victorian landscaping, complete with orangery, greenhouse and herb garden laid out like the face of a clock.

Compared to these two heavyweights, the Conways were a relatively modest family. Theirs was a lovely old manor house simply called Cedar Leigh. Nathan could find little about them other than that the oldest surviving Conway — Richard Cardew Conway — was a businessman connected in some way to the police. Nathan had found several photographs showing Conway, glass in hand, hobnobbing with the higher echelons of the force.

All three residences were clustered at the very edge of the village, separated from the rest of the dwellings by about a quarter of a mile. They were certainly keeping the plebs at arm's length.

'How's it going, Nathan? I've got another name for you.' Liz handed him a sheet of paper. 'See what you can find on this lady — Fiona McEwan, secretary by trade, employed by Reginald Bruton. Rented lodgings in or around Marshdyke ten years ago. Last heard of high-tailing it out of the village at dead of night.'

He smiled. 'Okay. It makes a change from the landed gentry. I'm doing my best but I think David would do a whole lot better.'

'He's well tied up, I'm afraid. He's taking Joe out to the Bunker so he can provide back-up for Jeff. He's going in again.'

Nathan glanced up at her and saw how terrified she was.

He gave her a reassuring smile. 'Try not to worry, Liz. I'm sure they'll be all right. I had a look at that video of Jeff, and I was blown away. I've never seen anything like it. If anyone can carry it off, it's him.'

'I know, but, well, I've been in any number of dangerous situations in my time and I've seen how the most carefully planned operations can go tits-up in the blink of an eye. I won't be happy until I see them walk back in through that door.'

'I know what you mean,' Nathan said, and he meant it. Nathan was no stranger to anxiety.

Half an hour later, he burst into the adjoining room. 'I think you need to have a word with your police contact. Fiona McEwan was registered as a missing person ten years ago.'

* * *

Jeff and Joe were about to penetrate enemy territory. Jeff had already worked out the best way to get in, and the spot from which Joe could keep a lookout for any unexpected developments. Joe's warning signal would be a low whistle, like the call of a marsh nightbird.

'One whistle for take care, twice for get the hell out of there.'

They left David with the cars in a small lay-by around five minutes' walk from the Bunker. From the top of the higher climbing frames on the assault course, Jeff had seen a row of trees running along one side of the compound. At one point these trees encroached right up to the wire fence that marked the perimeter. The six-foot-high fence, comprised of the standard small grid, high tensile mesh, was a walk in the park for Jeff. The spot he had chosen to take his picture from was to the side of the barn, as close as he could get to the parked vehicles. What he liked about it was the absence of cameras, and if there were no Bunker staff around either, he should be in and out in minutes.

'How are you on climbing?' he whispered to Joe, indicating the wire mesh of the barrier.

'Don't you worry, I've scaled any number of those in my time on the road. It'll be a doddle.'

Jeff had originally planned to leave Joe outside the fence, but it would certainly be safer to have him close by. 'Okay, then we both go. It's getting da—'

They heard the sound of an engine drawing near.

'Shit. I thought they'd have been finished by now,' Joe muttered.

They crept along the perimeter fence until the trees petered out. In front of them lay open farmland and the marshes, and beyond that, the main gates. The mini-van that was used to collect the kids was approaching at speed.

'I don't like the look of this,' whispered Jeff, pointing to a small group of people gathered by the gates. 'And there's another car just about to leave. We have no time to waste, let's get this over with.'

They crept back to their original spot and scaled the fence, dropping to the ground and remaining there for a moment, crouched down and listening. Then they began to inch their way along the side of the barn.

Inside, people were moving about. They could hear the occasional shout of someone issuing an order.

The light was beginning to fail, shadows were gathering. It had become almost impossible to make out any one vehicle. Jeff knew he must act fast.

'Watch the main barn doors and that side door to the Nissan hut, Joe. I'm going into where the cars are parked. If it's there, I'll photograph the licence plate and we'll be gone. Use your warning call if you absolutely need to and keep well out of sight.'

'Understood,' said Joe. 'Be careful.'

Keeping close to the side of the barn, Jeff worked his way around to where the cars were parked. On reaching them, he hunkered down and took stock. At least he was alone in here. He counted four vehicles. He recognised the two at the front from his earlier visit, but there were two more parked further back. One was the black VW.

It was too dark in there to get a clear picture without using a flash. Jeff decided to risk it. He had just lined up the shot when he heard the cry of a night bird. One whistle. Then a second.

Jeff sank to the ground, his phone in his hand, listening to the tramp of feet just outside. He prayed they hadn't come for one of the cars, because if they started moving them out, he'd have nowhere to hide. Jeff listened intently, trying to gather what was going on.

'We move them out in fifteen. Smith will look after the boys, and Gordon will go with the copper.' The speaker was Henderson.

A woman answered, but she was too far away for him to hear what she said.

'Oh, don't worry about him, he'll be here in a minute or two. He'll sedate them for the trip,' said Henderson.

Then they were gone, back into the Nissen hut. Jeff moved quickly. This really was his last chance to save the detective and whoever else was about to be ferried out. Swiftly, he took the shot he needed and crept out of the garage.

It took him no time at all, but it felt like hours before he finally reached Joe.

'They're clearing out,' he hissed. 'I have to send this image immediately, then we are out of here, okay?'

'Quick as you can, son. I've a seriously bad feeling about this place.'

Jeff sent the image to Liz and Matt, and to DCI Charlotte Anders. He had a message ready to attach, giving the location along with the words: *Immediate action required to save DC Norton's life.*

Then they were over the wire fence and into the trees, and haring back to the cars.

'I'm too old for this,' panted Joe as they neared the cars, 'but it still goes against the grain to leave people behind and not try to rescue them.'

'I know, but we wouldn't have stood a chance against that lot back there,' said Jeff. 'And we need to be well away from here before they start moving out. You go with David and I'll follow.'

The heavens were in their favour that night, for as the two cars drove away, clouds began to roll across the marsh, obscuring the rising moon. They had done what they could. Now it was down to the police. He only hoped they would be in time.

CHAPTER TWENTY-NINE

'They've done it!' called out Matt. 'They're on their way home, and what's more, Charley has acted. There are several units heading towards Marshdyke right now.'

'Yay!' Liz punched the air. Thank goodness the DCI had so much faith in Matt. Any other senior officer would still have been weighing up the pros and cons. Even now, it would be tight, but Charley's prompt action gave them a good chance of succeeding.

'If this works, Liz,' Matt was saying, 'that's the end of our involvement with the Bunker. I just need to know that Darren Norton and those teenagers are safe and then we'll have done with it.'

'Thanks to Jeff and Joe,' added Liz with feeling, and hugged Matt tightly. 'Thank you for taking a chance with Jeff. I know you hate to put anyone in danger, but he was right about the bigger picture, and he's probably saved several lives, including that idiot detective.'

'I'm a stubborn old git, aren't I? I suppose I didn't want the responsibility of sending a lovely kid like him into a potentially life-threatening situation.'

'But you did the right thing in the end,' said Liz. 'Now we can give all our attention to the other murky goings-on in Marshdyke.'

'Yes,' he said, 'and I'm starting to believe they are very murky indeed. My worry now is that they really are still going on. Someone has attempted to kill both Clem and George — Joe too, only he was too canny for them. Anyone who was close to Molly is still in danger.'

'Are you saying that ten years on, it's still ongoing?'

'It could be,' Matt said. 'Whatever it was, they are right now getting rid of people who know about it. They wouldn't be doing that if it was all in the past.'

'Hmm. Ten years isn't much in the context of a long-term activity. Think of the drugs trade. I think the biggest discovery so far is that card with the name on it. We need to find the other clues as quickly as possible, and if, like Fiona McEwan, they all turn out to be names of missing people, then you're right, it is murky.'

'So, let's hold an early morning meeting and decide how we are to search for the rest of Molly's clues. And just think — we have a bigger team now than we had when we were back in CID.'

Liz laughed. 'We do. And two police dogs to boot.'

'Two? *Two* dogs?'

'Well, David and Jeff could hardly leave George's Spaniel alone in an empty house, could they?' Liz assumed an innocent expression. 'And Gunner has a new best friend.'

Matt rolled his eyes. 'Saints preserve us! We're turning into an animal sanctuary.'

'I could think of worse things to be. And it's only short-term in Alfie's case.'

'Alfie's case?' Matt eyed her suspiciously. 'And what about Gunner?'

'He's a bit different, isn't he? I mean he doesn't trust many people, but he does trust us, especially David. Until we know what kind of recovery Clem is going to make, I guess he's a, well, a more long-term house guest.'

'When you say long-term—'

'Dear me, look at the time,' Liz interposed quickly. 'Poor Nathan is still at the computer. I'd better take him a coffee and see if he can come back tomorrow. Want a drink, Matt?'

'I certainly do,' he said. 'A large one.'

Liz went to the kitchen and was busy making the drinks when Matt's mobile rang. He walked in, having put the call on loudspeaker.

'Yes, Swifty, I understand. They can come to the station to give their statement tomorrow.'

'It's just that every spare officer is legging it around the marshes tonight, so there's a good chance there'd be no one available to take their statement,' Jack Swift said.

'Any news yet, Swifty?' asked Matt tentatively.

'No. It sounds like bedlam over the radio but I can let you know when I hear something. Could be late though.'

'Doesn't matter,' Matt said. 'I doubt we'll be able to sleep in any case, not until we know whether you've got DC Norton back safely, and those kids.'

Jack promised to let them know and ended the call.

It was going to be a long night.

* * *

Evenings in Marshdyke were usually undisturbed and une-ventful. However, on this particular evening the lights came on, curtains were pulled back, doors were opened and the inhabitants peered into the gloom, wondering what had hap-pened to disrupt their peaceful repose. Neighbour called to neighbour, all anxious to know the reason for the sudden onslaught of police cars, blue lights and screaming sirens.

'It's something out on the marsh!' called one man. 'They're heading out that way.'

'It must be really serious!' yelled another. 'They're com-ing from all directions.'

'Oh my goodness, maybe it's a terrible accident,' said a frightened woman. 'It could be a plane crash.'

'Maybe we should check online, see what the news says.'

Suggestions were batted backwards and forwards, through windows and over fences, but no one chose to go to the marsh to see for themselves. That they would find out soon enough seemed to be the consensus and, as long as it didn't affect them, it was best left to the police to sort out. In Marshdyke, it was always best to turn a blind eye.

This attitude wasn't universal, however. Three Marshdyke families were very concerned indeed. One, in particular, fastened all the locks, doused the lights, kept the curtains tightly closed and prayed that no one would come knocking on their door.

* * *

'Hi, Matt. I thought I should ring you myself to let you know the outcome.' Charley Anders was obviously still wired. 'Jack Fleet will fill you in on the details but thanks to you, we have our detective back, and three teenage boys, including your missing runaway, Liam Cooper, and that lad Dean.'

Matt closed his eyes for a moment, uncharacteristically moved. 'Are they all right? Not . . . hurt, are they?'

'Not physically. They'd all been given a sedative and we'll be taking them to hospital for observation, but the FMO is confident that whatever they were given wasn't too heavy. Psychologically — who knows?'

'And the men who were running this show?'

'Good and bad news. We have five men and a woman in the custody suite right now but two got away. Unfortunately, we believe one of those to have been the ringleader.' Charley sniffed. 'Getting proof of what they were up to isn't going to be easy, but at least we have them for abducting a police officer and unlawful imprisonment of those boys.'

'Have the parents been notified, Charley?' asked Matt, smiling at the thought of the Coopers' amazed faces.

'I thought that where the Cooper family and Dean's brother are concerned, you might like to be the bearer of good tidings. It's late, so a friendly voice rather than a police-man knocking on their doors might be kinder, don't you think?'

He was grateful. He had carried the burden of responsi-bility for young Liam for a long time. 'I'll ring them immedi-ately, Charley, and thank you for acting so promptly.'

Charley Anders burst out laughing. 'I don't know about that. I should be thanking you. I think you and your team may well have made it possible for us to shut down an oper-ation that could prove far bigger than we are even vaguely aware of yet.'

For once, Matt was heartily glad that they could now bow out gracefully leaving the mountain of paperwork to someone else. He thanked her again and ended the call.

He paused at the door and gathered himself. For a long time, he had been certain that they would never see Liam again, and now he was about to tell his parents that their son was safe. This was all thanks to Jeff, and his conviction that the car he had seen belonged to DC Darren Norton, and for obtaining proof of it so that the police could act.

Matt remained standing with his hand on the doorhan-dle. Charley had thanked him, but what had transpired that evening had been nothing to do with him. It could have gone a very different way if he had remained adamant that Jeff should not take that risk.

* * *

While Matt was talking to Liam's parents, Liz took a call from an exuberant Jack Fleet. She put the call on speaker and they all listened to Swifty's description of the high-speed chase along the Fen lanes, and the resulting apprehension of four vehicles.

'They didn't give up easily either. Some of our officers are pretty sure that a couple of the guys they eventually took down were ex-army. One had to be tasered before they could cuff him. Just two vehicles made it away, and the pursuit driver said he saw three young adults in one of them, two boys and a girl, and he said they looked terrified. Apart from failing to nail the boss man, it was not saving those kids that really upset everyone. Whoever drove the vehicle they were in knew the Fen lanes very well, and he drove like a pro.' Swifty yawned. 'Anyway, that's all for now, it's been a long day!'

'But an exciting one,' said Liz, regretting the times when she had been part of those high-speed chases.

'Oh yes, all thanks to the Haynes and Ballard detective agency. You guys are now officially the dog's bollocks, according to the boys and girls in the mess room.'

'As a matter of fact,' laughed Liz, 'that's quite appropriate at present, as Matt thinks I've opened a dog rescue centre in his kitchen.'

After Swifty ended the call, Joe, who had waited around to hear news of the outcome of the raid, said that he'd be off to his hotel but would be back the following morning.

Jeff held out his hand. 'Thank you for going with me this evening. I felt a lot better knowing you'd got my back. It went well, though, didn't it?'

Joe grasped his hand and shook it. 'If you discount the moment I saw those barn doors open and people walk out, knowing you were in there somewhere. Jeez, did I shit myself then.'

'Before you go, Joe,' Liz said. 'You know this area better than anyone. What do you reckon the villagers think about what was going on at the Bunker? They know the land belongs to the Bruton family, but I wonder what they believe is going on there.'

Joe shrugged. 'It's hard to say. They were certainly secretive, and Anna and Chris confirmed that, but Molly made me realise it went much deeper than that. I was thinking earlier of a particular term she used, and it's just come to me — a bad seed. She said there was a bad seed growing there.'

Liz frowned. 'What did you make of that, Joe?'

'Incest,' he said. 'Well, that's what I thought then. I've seen a lot of it over the years in the really isolated rural spots. In the days before people had cars and technology, some people just never got to meet anyone outside their immediate family. Cousins paired up with cousins, and worse sometimes. That was my interpretation anyway. More of a bad gene, I guess.'

'And now?' asked Liz.

Joe picked up his crash helmet and went to the door. 'I really don't know, Liz, but whatever Molly meant, it literally terrified her to death.'

The motorbike roared off into the distance leaving the house quiet again. Matt returned to the kitchen shaking his head. It had been an emotional moment for him.

He flopped down on to a chair. 'At least we can now give our all to Molly. Things could move quickly if we find those other clues, couldn't they?'

'The only thing that might be a problem is that after what happened at the Bunker tonight, the people of Marshdyke will be doubly suspicious and we might never get anything out of them,' Liz said.

'All the more reason to have Chris and Anna with us,' Matt said. 'Anna and her old gran certainly won't present a threat.'

'Absolutely, and I forgot to tell you earlier, Anna thought being seen with Chris might look suspicious, so she's told Gran to let it slip that they're an item.'

'Well, you never know,' said David, 'they might just become that very thing.'

Jeff laughed. 'What? Hadn't you guys noticed? A tenner says that after this is over, they'll still be seen about together.'

'You think so?' David said. 'But she's a lot younger than him, isn't she?'

'So?' Jeff smiled. 'My mum is ten years younger than my dad. Age means nothing, believe you me.'

Liz, being quite a bit younger than Matt, was forced to agree. 'And on that happy note, I suggest we call it a day. David, perhaps you'd let the dogs out for a pee before you go up?' She wondered if there was enough room on David's bed for two dogs.

She was alone in the kitchen when David and the dogs came back in.

'I, er, thought I'd smuggle Alfie up after you'd all settled, being that he's going to miss George.' He looked at her hopefully.

Liz smiled. 'It's all right with me. Just don't let Matt find them. It might be a good idea to have them back downstairs before he gets up. Sweet dreams, nephew!'

* * *

Cash stared at the hollow-eyed trio. 'Welcome to your new home. Go to your allocated rooms, get your kit unpacked and bed down for the night. Tomorrow, I'll tell you what's going to happen next.'

'But the Bunker. It's . . .' Leah stared back at him.

'I just said, I'll tell you tomorrow. We'll be carrying on with your programme, just in a different place. So work hard and enjoy it. Come on, jump to it. I've got more important things to do than babysit you lot.'

When the house was finally quiet, Cash poured himself a large whisky and sank into a chair. Somehow, he had escaped, and with their most valuable commodities in one piece. That dump on the edge of that stinking marsh was history. It, and the people in it, were expendable anyway, while he still had the jewels in the crown.

CHAPTER THIRTY

Joe had spent another restless night. Tonight, it hadn't been the discomfort of the too-soft bed that had kept him awake but the thought that he was on the brink of discovering the secret that had led to the death of the only person he had ever truly loved. Not only that, he had been galvanised by the day's adventure. It had reawakened memories of comradeship and the adrenalin rush of active duty. In other words, he was on a high.

Now, showered and breakfasted, he was his usual cool self. First, before returning to Cannon Farm, he had a couple of things to attend to, one being the purchase of a mobile phone. The other was to call the hospital to find out how George was faring. Though he hardly knew George Miles, he felt they shared a bond through Molly. It was no small thing.

Since he wasn't a relative, the hospital would tell him nothing. Besides, George had been the subject of an assault and it was therefore a police matter. He would have to wait until he got to Matt and Liz's place to find out how he was.

The phone had been a simple matter. A helpful assistant, who looked about twelve, had taken him through the basics and he now knew how to make a call, send a text and take a picture, which was fine for the time being. Not quite kicking and screaming, Johan de Vries had been dragged into the twenty-first century.

* * *

By nine o'clock, Cannon Farm was about as busy as Matt had ever seen it. Cannon Farm had always been his sanctuary, his retreat from the evils of the criminal world. He surprised himself by his reaction to all these people crowding his home. He realised he was energised by it. It felt like the old days, the good ones.

He had been woken by the unmistakeable sound of scratchy claws on the wooden floor of the landing. It seemed David was taking his job of nanny very seriously, to the extent of smuggling his two orphan charges up to his room for the night. On any other day, Matt might have been annoyed by this, but this morning he was only glad not to have been woken in the early hours by the howling of a couple of lonely dogs. David's secret was safe with him . . . for now anyway.

He thanked everyone now gathered in the incident room, and outlined what needed to be done.

'Anna, do you think you could gain access to the Whistler property and locate Rupert's grave?'

'We've already worked out where it is, with Gran's help, so yes, I'm certain I can find it.'

'Chris, would you go with Anna, please? And I hope you can come up with a plausible excuse for tramping through someone else's garden before someone tells you to bugger off.'

'We've been thinking about that,' said Chris, 'we had an idea we'd be landed with that little assignment. We considered a lost dog, or "have you seen my cat?" but we've settled for something rather more subtle.'

'And that is?'

'Bribery.'

'And that's subtle?'

'Probably not, but it is usually effective,' said Chris dryly. 'Anna knows the lad who gardens for the Whistlers,

299

and the poor little sod isn't exactly well paid. We reckon a tenner will see us in and probably get us a lookout too.'

'From what Gran says, the cat's grave is in an overgrown spot in a spinney at the far end of the garden, so it's not over-looked, and it's not far from a rear gate that leads to where young Ted takes all the grass cuttings.' Anna smiled. 'He's a good kid, and he won't rat on us. He hates Charles Whistler, but work is hard to come by in the rural areas and his family is on the breadline.'

Matt took out his wallet and handed her two ten pound notes. 'Give him one, and if he gets you in and out safely, he can have the other. It'll be money well spent.'

Now he turned to David. 'Would you work with Nathan on the computer searches, please? We know so little about the three Marshdyke families Molly worked for. Try and concentrate on the period ten years ago when Molly first discovered the information that got her killed. That okay with you, Nathan?'

'I'll be glad of David's help,' said Nathan. 'I was way out of my depth yesterday.'

'Don't put yourself down,' Matt said. 'You discovered that Fiona McEwan was a missing person, and that was damned important.' Next, Joe. 'This is an odd one, Joe, but you see all this . . .' He pointed to the heaps of paper spread across the big dining table.

'I could hardly miss it,' said Joe.

'If it's not too painful, do you think you could cast your eyes over some of these notes and see if a name or a place means anything to you? You knew Molly better than any-one.' It was a lot to ask of someone who cared for her.

'Sure, anything to help,' said Joe.

'What about me, Matt?' asked Jeff.

'You, lad, will be doing what you do best. Sneaking into places you shouldn't. I did a quick search for Cedar Leigh on Google Earth this morning, and I saw what looks like some old beehives or something, clustered around the third birch on the right. It could be the hiding place for her clue.

Trouble is, the property has a high wall and big wrought iron gates.'

Jeff's eyes lit up. 'I was just thinking I needed a little exercise.'

'Liz will go with you and drop you off somewhere close by. I reckon there was so much coming and going last night that one more unfamiliar vehicle shouldn't attract too much attention.'

'And I'm looking for what exactly?'

'The last clue was a piece of card with a name on it. This one could be the same, or something quite different. In other words, I have no idea.' Matt chuckled. 'I rang Swifty earlier, and he said that no one answered the door at the Conway house last night, so they could be away. Whatever, be very careful. This is a different kind of trespass to yesterday's.'

'No worries,' Jeff said. 'I won't be seen, I promise.' He pulled out his phone. 'I'll just take a look at the place first.'

'So, that leaves me as coordinator,' said Matt. 'I'll be here to field calls and try to help if you need any additional information or anything crops up. I'll also keep in touch with Swifty regarding George's progress. He was going to dig up anything he could find on our missing woman, Fiona McEwan.' He looked around at his new team and smiled. 'Okay, guys, let's get digging.'

* * *

They were halfway to Marshdyke when, suddenly, Anna let out a cry. 'Chris! I think I know where the scales are. Can we do a detour?'

Chris slowed down. 'Before or after we do the Whistlers' garden?'

'Now. Ted will be there all morning and the place I'm thinking of isn't far out of our way. We need to go back to see Callum Stokes. Take the next on the right.' Anna was almost jumping up and down in her seat. 'It's been bugging me ever since we spoke to him that day.'

301

Luckily, Callum was in the shop, busy packing eggs into wicker baskets. 'More veg for your gran, Anna? Or more information? Has it got something to do with last night's car chase?'

'None of that, Callum. I want to know if you still have all those old things in your grandad's shed,' Anna said.

Callum, who'd obviously been longing to discuss the previous night's drama, frowned at her. 'What? Well, yes, most of it. Like I said, I've been meaning to get some of it cleaned up and put it on display but I haven't got around to it yet.'

If Callum was puzzled, Chris was totally in the dark. 'Come on, guys, What shed? What stuff?'

Anna explained. 'Before he had this shop, Callum's grandad used to sell his produce from an old shed on his farm. It was one of those honesty boxes — people helped themselves and left the money for what they'd taken. I used to come here with Gran when I was a little girl.'

'And he had scales to weigh it on,' said Chris. 'I get it.'

'Exactly,' said Callum. 'The set he had was one of those big, heavy old things where you balanced your goods with individual metal weights. I reckon it dated back to the seventeenth century. I thought they'd give a nice authentic touch to the shop.'

'Can we have a look at them, Callum?' asked Anna.

'Sure. I'll get the key.' Callum went into a tiny office behind the counter and returned with an old-fashioned key on a brass fob. 'They're still on the bench where you saw them last. Why the interest, Anna?'

'Fingers crossed, we may find a message from Molly there.'

* * *

'I've got another name for you!' said Matt, bursting into the incident room. 'Anna has solved the scales clue. Like the last one, it was a card with a name on it — Raymond Henshaw. I must say, she's really excelled herself.'

They found the name with no trouble. Henshaw's family were still looking for him. He had disappeared around eleven years ago, and they had never given up hope of finding him. He had worked with his father supplying dried logs in that part of the Fen. When he failed to return home one evening, his father went back over his route, found his Land Rover and the trailer, still loaded with logs, but no sign of Raymond. He had never been seen or heard of since. The Land Rover had been parked a mile from Marshdyke-St-Mary.

'Two missing persons,' said Nathan. 'And Molly knew about them. What on earth can it mean?'

'I'm starting to get the creeps,' said David. 'I keep coming up with these dark imaginings.'

'Not nearly as dark as mine,' muttered Matt.

David glanced up at him. He really looked upset. 'So,' he said quickly, 'I guess that means the other clues will be names too, and probably missing persons. I still can't understand why this could have so traumatised Molly that she didn't dare talk about it, even to her closest friends.'

'You have to remember that Molly had suffered terribly at the hands of two men, both of whom she trusted,' said Nathan. 'She was just beginning to pull herself out of it when she made the discovery.'

'Having finally found peace in a quiet rural village, she was instead thrown into a nest of vipers. Knowing how sensitive she was, the dark secrets she uncovered must finally have broken her,' Matt said.

Joe looked up from his papers. 'You didn't see her towards the end. It was truly heart-breaking. I believe she was torn in two. Part of her was desperate to tell what she knew, hence all this,' he swept a hand over the mass of papers, 'and those clues. The other part was concerned with the daily struggle of survival on the streets.'

David listened in silence, pondering on the evil humankind could do. He was beginning to wonder about his choice of career. If Molly had been so badly damaged by the things she had seen, what might it do to him? He recalled the last case he had helped his aunt and Matt with, during which two young lives had been destroyed. He supposed it came down to a question of justice. Someone had to obtain justice for the victims, for Molly. So, who better than them?

He turned back to his screen.

* * *

Armed with a ready excuse for their presence, Liz parked up and sat in the car. She and Jeff were to be journalists, collecting the residents' impressions of the previous night's drama. On the passenger seat beside her were arrayed the tools of her supposed trade — mobile phone, electronic notepad, and an old-fashioned clipboard.

Jeff, meanwhile, was in his element. He paused beneath the trees and took stock of the wall enclosing Cedar Leigh. The gate would have been the easiest way in, but it was in full view of the road, so instead, he chose a secluded spot not far from the silver birch trees inside the wall that he had to reach.

Having scaled the wall with ease, he now made his way through a line of rhododendrons to one side of the drive. He approached the trees. Had Molly meant the third tree from the gates, or the third tree from the house?

The house was quiet, showing no signs of life. Which wasn't to say that someone wasn't watching him from one of the windows. He had to work fast. Luckily the whole garden was planted over with shrubs and trees, and there was plenty of cover.

Matt had been right about the beehives. They were clustered on a grassy patch around the third tree from the end of the drive and, to Jeff's relief, were long disused. Apparently, he'd got here just in time, as two had been dismantled and were stacked ready for removal.

Cautiously, he approached the tree. As far as he could tell, the clue had to be hidden in or around the nearest hive.

Glancing behind him to make sure he hadn't been seen, he examined the hive. Where was Molly most likely to have concealed her piece of cardboard? The hive was a typical old-fashioned beehive with a gabled roof and three box-like wooden sections that could be pulled out with the honeycombs attached.

Deciding to work from the top down, he removed the already crumbling roof. By the time he got to the bottom shelf, he was beginning to think he'd never find it. Then he struck lucky. Between the two warped pieces of wood of the last shelf was a small plastic envelope with a piece of card inside.

Jeff didn't stop to read it. He pushed it into his pocket, and with a last look around, slipped back into the bushes.

A few minutes later, he was in the passenger seat of Liz's car, presenting her with his trophy.

'You found it. Brilliant!' Liz gave him a quick hug. 'Let's see if we have another name.'

Leaning over to read the card, he saw:

When you have the four names, find my final note in the dragon's wing.

'That's got to be the scrap metal dragon,' he said. 'You pointed it out to us when we were here before.'

'I like the sound of that word, *final*, don't you?' said Liz. She picked up her phone. 'Let's tell Matt, and see if he wants us to go there directly, or whether we should hold back a bit.'

Matt told them that Anna and Chris had located the name of another missing person at the scales. 'That means that if they can find Rupert's grave, we only have William Arbuthnot left — whoever he is. It's driving David mad that he can't find a single mention of him on the internet.' Matt advised them to hold off visiting the metalworks until they knew where the family that owned it stood — would they be friendly or hostile? 'Swifty is going to visit George in hospital, so why don't you meet him there? If he's with you, you'll get a chance to talk to the patient. No one's going to stop you if you're accompanied by a police officer.'

However frustrating it was to have to leave the village without the very last clue, Jeff was beginning to understand that being a private detective was very different to being in the police. They never could go all in, but always had to skirt around their quarry. What was it Matt always said? 'Softly softly catchee monkey.'

CHAPTER THIRTY-ONE

No one among the seven people in the big old kitchen was smiling.

'I swear to you, there is absolutely nothing connecting us or the village to past or current events.' The speaker was finding it hard not to betray the emotion that at any moment threatened to break through his calm demeanour.

'What if the police start digging deeper?' said one man.

'Let them, they'll find nothing. The men running that outfit leased the land and paid their rent bang on time every month. They were using the place as a centre for underprivileged kids, end of story. It was all legal and above-board.'

A woman glared at him accusingly. 'But how are you going to get the police to believe that story? What if one of those men starts to blab? The police have most of them in custody, so what have they to lose?'

'Look,' he said, 'only Cash knows about our involvement, and he's still free. He'll stay that way too. He made plans for what he'd do in the event of something like this happening, and he'll not be found. He was our only connection and that's now been cut off.'

'So, what happens now?' came a voice from the back.

He held up his hands. 'What you would expect to happen, of course. How do people normally react on such an occasion? With righteous indignation, that's how. We cannot believe that something like this could have been going on right under our noses. As far as we knew, it was a laudable initiative for helping children and promoting a healthy lifestyle. Jesus. Just act normally, for heaven's sake. At least my wife's not around to see it. She's in Peterborough, caring for her sister after an emergency operation so I'll be on my own for several weeks.'

There were a few sympathetic murmurs but no offers of help. He didn't expect any. He and these people were bound together by a shared secret, but that didn't mean they were close. Far from it. If anything, their mutual resentment amounted to outright hostility, though the face they presented to the world outside their village was quite different. As far as outsiders were concerned, they were the epitome of what a rural community should be — caring, neighbourly, tight-knit. Well, they were tight knit all right, bound together whether they liked it or not.

'Where's Jamie?' someone asked.

He'd been waiting for this question. 'He was in town until the early hours, still hunting for the letter, so he missed last night's events. He's asleep now, and will probably stay that way till lunch time. I'll be telling him the men on the marsh just disappeared overnight. He'll accept that.' Somehow, he managed to sound matter-of-fact.

'And did he complete his, er, other tasks?'

He cleared his throat, recalling George Miles, the man with the dog and their sudden attack. The bites on Jamie's hands. 'Not quite, but it'll be sorted by tonight.'

Thank God no one questioned him further. They didn't even mention his other son, but why should they? He wasn't part of the village community.

'Look. Just get through the next few days. The police won't be around for long. There may be media attention, perhaps a lot of it for a few days, depending on what the police have said. Soon, Marshdyke will be as it's always been, you'll see.'

To his surprise, someone agreed — one of the women. 'He's right. We must deal with it. After all, deceiving the world is nothing to us, is it? We've been doing it for long enough.'

She sounded bitter.

The meeting broke up and, one by one, the drifted away, back to their "normal" lives as contented inhabitants of a quiet, sleepy little village.

* * *

Young Ted Poole was up a ladder, trimming one of the privet hedges, when Chris and Anna arrived.

'Whistler's out for a bit, so that makes it dead easy,' he said, pocketing his tenner. 'I'll let you in the back gate and show you where to look. Up here, I'll be able to see when he gets back, and I'll keep an eye open in case he comes into the garden. In any case, he never goes down to the spinney. No reason to, it's all overgrown now and he's too tight to get it sorted.'

'Thanks, mate,' said Chris. 'We appreciate it.'

'Me too,' said Ted, slapping his pocket. 'Come on then.'

They tramped after him through the extensive grounds, to an overgrown path between overhanging trees and straggly shrubs.

'This is about where I think that old pet grave was,' said Ted, pointing to a small glade in between the trees. 'It used to be nice here, tidy, like someone took care of it, but now it's just wild.' He shrugged. 'Well, better get back to the hedge. Happy hunting.'

Anna puffed out her cheeks, 'Phew! This is a bit of a jungle, isn't it?'

'Isn't it just. Thank goodness Tilly told us what to look out for,' Chris said.

'It's supposed to be near a silvery-coloured conifer with rhododendrons to the right of it,' Anna said.

They stared around, until Anna spotted a cedar that looked like the one they wanted. Pushing through the undergrowth, Chris could make out indications of the way the garden must have looked in its heyday. Statues, now encased in ivy, and a pergola, weighed down by rampant climbers, marked what had once been carefully landscaped vistas.

'Look! Rhododendrons,' Anna exclaimed. 'This is it, I'm sure. Now we just need to find bloody Rupert.'

They searched through the long grass, pulled nettles and brambles aside. Just as Chris was starting to wish he'd brought a scythe or something with him, Anna let out a cry, and started madly pulling up handfuls of ground elder.

'It's here! Look. A little stone vase, like you see in cemeteries.'

Heads together, they cleared away all the overgrowth to reveal a flat grey stone, a paving slab with the vase crudely cemented on the top and with a small plaque on the side. *Rest in peace, darling Rupert.*

Chris felt slightly embarrassed at being so elated by the discovery of a dead cat. Then he saw the look on Anna's face and smiled.

'Now we need to find the card. Come on, Chris, it's not in the vase, so do you think you can get this slab up?'

Still smiling, he hunkered down and heaved. The result was a couple of broken nails and a pain in his back. 'Bloody thing's stuck fast.' He raised a finger. 'But never fear!'

With great foresight, he had brought along several garden tools, including a short-handled spade with which he levered up the slab.

'It's there!' Anna cried. 'In a plastic bag.' Chris held the stone up for her.

'We've done it!' Anna stared at the bag in her hand. 'Shall I open it?'

'Go on then, let's see if we have the final name,' Chris said, as excited as her.

Anna took out the card. '*Shannon Brown.* Oh my God! Shannon!'

'You know who this is?'

'We were friends. Shannon was Callum's girlfriend. I can't believe this.' Anna gazed, open mouthed, at the piece of card. 'She worked for the Conway family at Cedar Leigh but what she really wanted was to join the police, like me.'

Chris put his arm around her. 'I'm so sorry, Anna. But what happened? Where did she go?'

Anna shook her head. 'We let her down. We thought at the time that something was wrong, but . . . oh!'

Tears were forming in her eyes. 'Come on, Anna,' Chris said. 'Let's get out of here in case Whistler comes home. We'll talk in the car.' Hastily, he pulled the brambles and weeds back over the grave, took her by the arm and led her back to the gate.

In the drama of their discovery, he had nearly forgotten Ted and his second tenner. Leaving Anna to go ahead to the car, Chris went back to find him.

Ted accepted the money gratefully. 'The pay here is crap, now Mum can get the nipper something nice.'

Taking note of the lad's threadbare sweatshirt, Chris took out his wallet. 'Give that to your mum by all means, but treat yourself to something with this.' He pushed a rolled up twenty pound note into the kid's hand. 'And thanks for your help.'

Back in the car, Anna had recovered. 'Sorry about that, but it was such a shock. Shannon was such a lovely girl, and now, if Molly is leading us where I think she is, she's probably dead.'

Privately agreeing with her, Chris said, 'Why do you think she left Marshdyke?'

Anna sighed. 'She had a controlling brother. Her father died in an accident and the brother, who was a good few years older than her, took on the role of head of the household.' Anna frowned. 'And how. The mother, who was weak, mentally and physically, submitted to him as she had his father. Shannon, on the other hand, resented him. She was very bright, and would have made a bloody good detective,

310

but her brother wouldn't have it. She said he even turned up at a party she was attending and, in front of her friends, dragged her out, bundled her into the car and took her home because she'd stayed out after ten o'clock. She was *twenty*, for heaven's sake.'

'What a bastard!' Chris said.

'Eventually Shannon left home and got a job working for the Conways as a data analyst. That's when she met Callum.'

'Was it serious?' asked Chris.

'It was, but she was torn. Anxiety about her mother and what the brother might do next held her back from commit-ting fully.' Anna gave another sigh. 'The brother even came here one day, and there was a terrible row. Anyway, it wasn't a big surprise when Callum and I got texts. She was sorry but she feared for her mother's sanity and she was going to have to give up her job and go home. That was the last we heard of her.'

'Did either of you try to get in touch with her?'

'Oh yes. We called and sent messages but she never answered. The silly thing was, she'd never given us her home address. All we knew was that it was somewhere in the Fenfleet area. And her surname was Brown — well, you can imagine how many of those there are in a town the size of Fenfleet.' As she spoke, Anna was staring straight ahead through the windscreen. 'After a while, Callum told me that since she obvi-ously didn't want to be found, we should respect her wish and stop looking for her. This was at the time when I had to give up policing, and the illness that resulted from the attack gave me little time for anything else. I should have thought like a copper instead of sitting back and letting Shannon disappear from our lives. I mean, the fact that she sent a text instead of speaking to us should have alerted me. Shannon didn't do that sort of thing.'

'Well then,' Chris said. 'Think of this clue as a message from her. She's giving you a chance to put things right.'

Anna reached out her hand and squeezed his shoulder. 'You are good for me, Chris Lamont.'

Chris had a feeling he was smiling like some crazy idiot he was so pleased. She thought he was good for her! And her touch had given him goosebumps. Maybe something good might come of this odd murder hunt.

* * *

As soon as Anna called him with the name of Shannon Brown, Matt was roused to action. David did a search and found nothing on her at all, not even a brief news report after she went missing, so Matt rang Swifty. 'Can you get a check on a Ms Shannon Brown, please, Jack? She is thought to have lived in or around Fenfleet, would probably be around forty years of age now, and was last heard of ten years back. At the time, she had an older brother and a sick mother and was a computer analyst working for the Conway Company.'

Swifty took the details. 'I'm still at the hospital but I'll get that run through for you. By the way, the DCI asked me to let you know that DC Norton is recovering well and would like to talk to you when you have the time. So would she, but as you can imagine, she's run ragged at present.'

'Is Liz still with you?' Matt asked.

'She's sitting with George. Poor fella's not doing too well, so they're hanging on to him until they can get a psychologist to assess him. He does have a concussion, but it's not as serious as they feared.' Jack chuckled. 'Your Liz did more to help him than any of these medics when she said his dog was safe, well fed, and has a new best friend. Now he knows his precious Alfie is being looked after, he's calmed down a lot.'

'Good,' said Matt. 'By the way, did your guys retrieve that shotgun from his house?'

'It's with forensics, Matt, and knowing the prof's interest in your case, I'm guessing we'll get a report back on it in double quick time. And before you ask, yes, I'll let you know if there's anything interesting in it.'

Matt thanked him and hung up. He now had a decision to make. First, they must find William Arbuthnot, and then they would have all the names. The problem lay with that final clue. Anna and Chris were pretty sure that the metalworks was owned and run by a Whistler. Not a member of the immediate family, but a relative nonetheless. Anna, who had never met him in person, thought his name was Clive. That put their dragon right in the heart of "enemy territory". So, should they wait until dark and get their nimble-toed sleuth to slip in unnoticed, or try to think of a plausible reason for visiting the place?

Unable to make up his mind, he decided to bring everyone back for a further meeting. This final clue could be the answer to the mystery, so they should all agree on how to proceed. After all, Molly's life and fate were deeply personal, in some way, to every one of them.

* * *

On their way back to Cannon Farm, Liz stopped off at a shop in Fenfleet and bought sandwiches, crisps and some snack bars. Liz being Liz couldn't possibly have everyone going without lunch.

Matt and David made the tea and coffee and handed out cold drinks, and when everyone had helped themselves to the snacks, they went into the incident room. Liz wondered how long it had been since this elegant dining room had hosted so many guests. She was sorry the occasion didn't warrant fine wine and good dining rather than the convenience store sandwiches the guests were all happily munching, but this was no occasion for laughter and small-talk. They had arrived at the cusp of this mystery, and the tension was palpable.

Matt began the meeting. 'I think we need to decide on the facts of the case and where it is leading us. By that I mean what do we think Molly was trying to tell us about what happened in Marshdyke ten years ago.'

'And resulted in her death,' added Joe.

'Exactly,' said Matt. 'We must first find bloody William Arbuthnot, and then decide how we go about retrieving the last clue from the scrap metal dragon.'

'And decide what we do with that information,' added Liz. 'It's vital that no one else gets hurt. You are all here because you have seen a terrible wrong done to someone you loved and you wish to see that justice is served. However, we must not let ourselves be driven by revenge. We will uncover the secret behind Molly's death but we can't promise to see it through to the end. Once we have evidence that a crime was committed, we will deliver that evidence into the hands of the police.'

'But, please, don't be disappointed. Remember that whatever the outcome, it could not have been attained without you and your commitment,' said Matt.

'Right, before we all burst into tears, let's draw up that list of facts,' Liz said.

Matt went to the whiteboard and pointed to the photograph of Marika Molohan — their Molly. 'Here is the story as we have it: the life of a beautiful and talented musician spirals out of control following two catastrophic affairs. Trying to get back on track, she takes up a job teaching three young pupils in Marshdyke-St-Mary. There, she comes across something so terrible that she dare not speak of it to anyone, instead she sets down her suspicions in written notes and a journal. We assume she had no proof, certainly nothing she could take to the authorities, but with time she becomes fearful for her own life and that of others.' He looked around. 'All right so far?' He turned to Liz. 'I assume George Miles still isn't talking?'

Liz shook her head, recalling his terrified expression, his eyes, darting about the room but always returning to the uniformed officer stationed at his door. 'The only thing I could get him to talk about was Alfie, his dog. He's been traumatised by the attack and he's terrified that they'll send him home and he'll be alone and vulnerable again.'

'I'll make sure that doesn't happen,' said Joe. 'I'll stay with him, or he can stay with me, whatever. I'll not let him be alone.'

'Thank you, Joe. That's good to know,' Matt said. 'Until this is cleared up, he is in grave danger. The police know that, so it could mean he goes into a safe house for a while.'

'Then I'll go with him, if he'll agree to it.'

Matt continued his account. 'Molly's fears came to a head when something awful happened to her or possibly someone close to her. She either discovered something or was in fear for her life from something that so terrified her that she ran away and took to the streets. She lived the life of a homeless person for years, known to everyone as "Molly the Bag Lady". Then the past caught up with her. Once again, she was in danger. Still too scared to go to the police, she started to leave clues for someone to follow. Then she disappeared for a second time. She left her bag containing all the notes she'd made in the local library. She chose that place knowing that Chris worked there, a former police officer and someone who had always been kind to her.'

'We used to joke about never being able to take the copper out of someone who'd once been in the police. She said it amused her to see the way I watched the borrowers, like I was sizing them up for possible criminal intentions,' Chris said.

'She also made sure to point out her favourite book, a study of Chopin,' said David. 'She knew you'd be curious about why it seemed so important to her. If only that arsehole hadn't nicked the sleeping bag she'd given to poor old Clem. The letter she'd hidden inside it might have given us the whole story.'

'Oh, I don't know. I think we aren't doing too badly without that,' said Matt. 'Just think — we now have three names, and possibly the final clue, once we work out how to get at it. I reckon that's pretty impressive.'

Somebody's mobile rang, and there was a general hasty patting of pockets until Anna told them it was her gran calling.

She listened, the smile she habitually wore for old Tilly growing wider by the second. By the time it was ended, her expression was positively jubilant. 'You're never going to believe this, Tilly has just found William Arbuthnot.'

Everyone stared at her, their mouths agape.

'Apparently, there used to be a pub in the village called the Wellington. Well, when it first opened there was a great

315

deal of heated discussion about what it should be called. The Conways, who she thinks had put money into it, wanted to name it after one of their distant forebears, but the richest family in the village, the Brutons, insisted on "The Wellington". The Wellington it was, but the Conways' relative was called — wait for it — William Arbuthnot. According to Tilly, the Conway family had already had a sign painted with that name on it, and that sign still exists.'

'Where?' the others chorused.

'Two of the Conway daughters have horses, which they stable near the house. The old sign is hung in the tack room, and unless they've thrown it out, Tilly thinks it'll still be there.'

'More breaking and entering?' asked Jeff, who seemed to have warmed to his new profession of cat burglar.

'That might not be necessary in this case,' said Anna. 'My next-door neighbour's daughter is horse mad. She spends all her free time there, mucking out the horses and grooming them in exchange for the occasional ride. She'll know if the inn sign is still there.'

'Pity we have to wait until school's finished for the day,' said David.

'You've forgotten it's the school holidays, mate,' said Chris. 'Duh.'

Anna, meanwhile, was back on her phone. 'Better than that, I already have her number. Harriet does the occasional job for me and Gran every now and then. I'll text her now.'

Liz held up her hand. 'Hang on a minute. Are you sure you can trust her?'

'Absolutely,' Anna said. 'She's a lovely kid, and very good to Gran.'

'Well in that case,' Liz said, 'maybe she can go now. You could ask her to see if there's anywhere around it where a small piece of card could be hidden.'

Anna made the call. 'She was going there tomorrow in any case, but she says she can easily go today. And if what we are looking for is — in her words — "A tatty old picture of an ugly old bloke in weird clothes" — then the sign is still there.'

Nearer ever nearer, thought Liz excitedly.

'As long as no one else is there, and there usually isn't, she'll have a look for that card and ring me if she finds it. So you're off the hook this time, Jeff.'

'What a pity,' he said with a grin. 'Mind you, my father would never forgive me if I got myself arrested.'

'So, while we wait for Harriet to call, I suggest we discuss how we're to get to that dragon,' Matt said.

'How about a good old diversion?' said Nathan. 'We used to do that if something went wrong at a gig. Suppose Jeff and I go — no one there knows us — and I make a big fuss about selecting the right wrought iron gates for my garden. I can ask if my son could take a look at the dragon, as he's keen to see how it was put together.'

'And if they say no?' asked Matt.

'Then I'll say what a pity, because they'll be losing out on a big sale. I'm sure that'll make them think again.'

'It might work,' said Matt. 'And it would account for Jeff's close examination of the dragon. Anyone else got any ideas? If not, we'll go with Nathan's suggestion.'

None of the others could think of a better strategy.

'I'll prepare my story,' said Nathan. 'Maybe I could take a photo of your wooden gates, Matt? If I have the measurements, it'll make us look like serious buyers.'

Jeff offered to look at the website.

Everything depended on how well Molly had concealed the message, and how long it took Jeff to find it. It had been there for a decade, and Liz feared that it might have fallen out or been thrown away as litter. Their biggest advantage lay in the fact that no one knew Nathan. Jeff had only been there once, when they visited the Targett sisters, so he too was pretty safe.

'I guess all we can do now is wait,' said David. 'Hell, I hate waiting.'

'We can also do as Matt suggested,' said Joe, 'and share our ideas of what we think happened and who might be behind it.' No one spoke. 'Anyone? Who wants to go first?'

317

CHAPTER THIRTY-TWO

Leah felt as if she had been thrust into an entirely new world. She had never been in the countryside before. To her surprise, she found it suited her perfectly. At first, the absence of buildings in which to shelter had made her uneasy, as did the quiet, the lack of people. Then she found she could breathe. She felt free.

She took to walking alone in the garden, taking in her surroundings and all the new things she was discovering — soft ground, the rich smell of mouldering leaves instead of the bitter stench of dirt and diesel. The house itself was old, full of creaks and interesting corners. Her room was sparsely furnished but comfortable.

She was well aware that this was only an interlude. They had been selected for something, and soon they would be called upon to use their special skills. Meanwhile, she—

What was that? A rabbit had just hopped out from behind the shrubs and was nibbling contentedly on the grass. Leah had never seen anything like this before. A new type of creature. They too were a new breed. And they would go far.

* * *

Cash had planned to take a day or two to relax before moving on to the next stage. Now he was here, he realised this was no longer necessary. Why wait? Everything was in place and he was keen to get well away from that stinking bunker.

That idiot detective had chosen the perfect moment to intervene. The fool had provided him with the perfect pretext for ridding himself of the dross — Henderson and all those other gullible fools. Meanwhile, he had his special ones, the three he had had his eye on since the supposed "boot camp" was first established.

He had been part of a big organisation then, a ruthless conglomerate that had its eye on the long-term future of their criminal enterprise. They would pick young delinquents from the streets and use them mainly for drug trafficking, something like a wider network of county lines. While he scoured the provinces for possible recruits, he began to conceive of a much bigger venture. Bigger but more streamlined, this would consist of himself, a few highly skilled employees and a trio of young misfits with remarkable talents — Leah, Karl and Bruno.

A very profitable future lay ahead for Cash. In a year or so from now, he would launch his protégées into the world. And the world wouldn't know what had hit it.

* * *

Finally, David spoke up. 'I think Matt and Liz should go first. Being "real" detectives, they know the kind of crime that the entire population of a village would possibly be covering up.'

'Okay,' said Liz, 'Then Nathan and Joe, because they knew Marika before she went on to the streets. And you, David, having read her notes and journal entries. If we combine all these different aspects, we can then begin to separate the wheat from the chaff, as it were.'

It took them about half an hour to build up a picture. Matt summed up their contributions:

319

'It seems we all agree that Molly observed various individuals suddenly leaving the village for one reason or another and never being heard from again. Over time, she put two and two together and concluded that they had not left of their own accord. In fact, they probably never left at all.'

'She realised that a very dangerous person was living in their midst, probably a supposed pillar of the community. But she had no proof. Not only that, she had been through so much trauma in her past life that she may have had little trust in her own convictions,' Liz added.

'And there we have it,' said Joe.

'So now everything rests on what I find in the wings of a dragon,' Jeff said.

* * *

While they took a break for tea, Anna, who had been staring at her phone, willing it to tell her a message had come in, finally got a WhatsApp. 'There are people around so she daren't talk, but she says she has found the clue!'

'Another name?' asked David, half out of his chair, ready to run to his laptop.

'Kai Burnett. That's K A I,' Anna said. 'It was stuck on the back of an old map of the county.'

David was off.

'This Kai is going to be another disappearing act, isn't he?' Anna said. 'It's definitely not a name I know.'

Liz was staring into space. 'But I think I do. Let me think . . . Ah yes. A child went missing, close to the marsh. He'd been staying with some relatives. His name was Kai.'

Anna frowned. 'Are you sure? I would have heard about something as serious as that, and I don't remember it at all.'

'No, you probably wouldn't. It was all over in a matter of hours. The child had simply been playing hide and seek with his cousins and was soon found. The police had been notified so the family called to apologise.'

'So, why is Molly naming him then?' asked Anna.

'I wish I knew.' Liz took her phone from her pocket.

'Swifty, old mate, another query for you. A little kid called Kai Burnett apparently went missing while playing near the marsh, way back, maybe nine or ten years ago. An alert was put out, then it was cancelled. Can you run a search for me? I'd like to know where he was staying.'

'I don't need to even check, Liz. It was me who took the call. I remember it to this day. It always turns me up when I get a shout for a missing child. He was staying with a family called Bruton, in that lovely little village of yours — Marshdyke.'

'Can you recall who reported him missing, Jack?'

He was silent for a moment. 'Ah, I remember. It was an anonymous caller, a woman, I think. That's right. She said she feared for a child's life and gave us the name and where he was last seen.'

'And what was the Bruton family's reaction to that?'

'Well, it was a very long time ago,' said Jack. 'Now I think of it, I recall getting the impression that they didn't know a thing about it, they weren't even aware the kid was missing. Then just as a major search operation was about to get under-way, they called to say the boy was home safe, and no harm done.'

It was very clear to both Liz and Anna that it had been Molly who had made that call. The family — the Brutons — had covered it up, which was why she had given them the name of Kai Burnett via one of her hidden cards.

'We'd better tell David,' said Liz. 'He won't be finding much information on that kid. What on earth have we wan-dered into, Anna?'

'Something darker than any of us ever imagined,' Anna said. 'It's beginning to turn into a nightmare, and I'd *really* like to wake up.'

* * *

Armed with the measurements and photos of the Cannon Farm gates, Nathan and Jeff set off for the metalworks.

'I wish I'd paid more attention to that beast when Liz first took us to Marshdyke,' Jeff grumbled. 'I was just amused at how incongruous it looked in the middle of that village.'

'I love the Fens,' said Nathan wistfully, 'and that village is like some horrible canker that's fastened itself to a beautiful tree. It needs cutting out and burning.' They drove on in silence, watching the flat arable fields roll by.

'I hope I don't let everybody down,' Jeff said. 'I know vaguely what I'm looking for, but there are two wings, and I can't for the life of me fathom out where or how Molly managed to secrete a piece of card in one of them.'

'Don't fret, kid,' said Nathan. 'Do your best, that's all anyone is asking of you. Like Liz said, there's a good chance this clue is long gone. It's been out there exposed to the elements for a decade, so if you do find it, it'll be a bloody miracle.'

'It won't be near the top, anyway. Molly would never have reached it. As far as I can recall, one wing was raised and the other down, almost resting on the ground. I guess I should concentrate on the parts of it that are within easy reach of the ground.'

'Molly wasn't very tall but her piano playing gave her enormous dexterity. With her long fingers she could easily have reached into the smallest gap.'

'Well, Dad, here we are,' said Jeff. And there it was. The great dragon looking down at him had a singularly disdainful air.

It took a while to find the person in charge, who wasn't the friendliest of Fenmen. From the work on display, he was clearly an artist. Perhaps he thought trading was beneath him.

'Clive Harborne?' asked Nathan cordially. 'We're looking for some wrought iron gates and you were recommended to us by a friend.'

Scenting a sale, the welder unbent a little. 'Oh yeah, sure. What were you looking for exactly?'

Nathan launched into his spiel, finishing with, 'While I'm making my selection, would my son be able to have a look at that dragon out there? He's keen to have a go at scrap metal art himself.'

'Oh, could I?' Jeff said, managing to sound all of about ten. 'It's so cool.'

'Sure, help yourself,' said Clive. 'Just be careful, there's a lot of pieces of metal lying around in the grass.'

Thanking him profusely, Jeff skipped off to do battle with the dragon.

* * *

David cleared the whiteboard until only the name Marika "Molly" Molohan remained at the top. To this he appended a list of names, bracketed together under the label, "Missing".

'Sadly, I think it's too late for all this.' He indicated the heaps of papers on the table in front of Joe. 'If only she had handed that letter to the proper authorities instead of hiding it in an old sleeping bag.'

'I'm sure she would have, David, if she hadn't been terrified out of her mind. You have no idea what that's like, what it can do to you. A boy like you, you've never known real fear in your life.' Joe saw how his words had hurt David, and apologised. 'You have to agree, though, that you haven't been out on the streets, wondering every night whether you'd make it to morning. Besides, even if she had gone to the authorities, would they have believed her? Some dotty old bag lady? I don't think so.'

'Meanwhile, she was a hero,' said David. 'Despite the threat to herself, she still cared enough for you to try and keep you out of harm's way.'

'She did that,' said Joe. 'She sent me off on some wild goose-chase to keep me out of the way. That's why I disappeared. I thought I was helping her. God, I was so bloody thick. If only I'd refused to go, I might have . . . Well, never mind. It's no good sitting around thinking "if only", is it? It's not going to bring her back.'

'You're helping her now though,' said David.

'We all are,' Joe said.

'Amen to that.' Liz and Matt had just walked into the room.

'This hanging around is doing my head in,' said Matt, flopping into a chair.

'Agony,' said Liz. 'Will Jeff find it, or won't he? Oh, and Jack called. He can find no mention of Shannon Brown, apart from an address, but she and her family had left there years ago. There's no employment or health records for her either. It's like she stepped off the edge of the world.'

'Like the others.' David was staring at the whiteboard.

'Did I hear someone mention Shannon?' Anna, followed by Chris, came into the dining room. 'Any news?' When they told her there was barely any record of her existence, she said, 'I have no idea what to tell Callum about her.'

'Nothing yet,' said Matt. 'We shouldn't talk to anyone about these people until we know a whole lot more about what happened to them. I hate to say it, but it's very much a case of trust no one.'

* * *

Jeff stared up at the beast. Where to start? He'd have to go about it systematically, while making it appear that he was simply fascinated by the sculpture and how it was put together.

The wings were formed of overlapping sheets of thin metal, like scales. The only problem was that there were so many of them. He ran his fingers over the joins, conscious of time passing. How long would Nathan be able to tarry over his choice of design?

He glanced up at the raised wing. Like a bat's wing, it had metal claws made from old dinner knives at each of the points. The lowest of these, almost touching the beast's front leg, looked slightly different to the others. It curved a little less sharply, the two edges of the knife forming a kind of tube. He squinted, peering closely at this claw. Wasn't that something inside it?

Jeff inserted his index finger into the tube and twisted it. With his heart in his mouth, he eased out a plastic bag. Inside it, a thin piece of card. Rust from the metal claw coated the bag, so he put it in his pocket unopened. He had found the final clue.

* * *

Nathan was just beginning to run out of steam when Jeff appeared at his side.

'Wow, that creature is just awesome. Thank you so much for letting me look at it.'

Nathan could tell from his smile that Jeff had found it. 'Thank you for your help. We'll make our final decision and get you to come out and measure up. I just need to check my diary, next week is pretty full on.'

They made their get-away without too much haste. Once they were out in the street, Nathan said, 'I'm assuming we've cracked it.'

'I'd be surprised if we haven't,' said Jeff. 'I didn't dare risk trying to open it in case I damaged it — it's damp and covered in rust, but it's a card, so what else can it be?'

'We'll find out shortly. Well done, lad, you're a hero — again!'

'I almost crapped myself when I saw all those metal sheets on the wings. I thought I'd never find it.'

Nathan smiled. 'Not as much as me, I bet. There's only so much you can say about a bloody gate.'

* * *

Late that afternoon they all gathered around the table to see the card that Jeff had retrieved. Every one of them held their breath as Liz's gloved hands fumbled with the plastic package.

'Hmm. Water has got inside it, part of the card has rotted.'

It took Liz five long minutes to extricate the soggy card.

'Here's hoping it's still legible.' Slowly, gently, she unrolled the piece of card and read it.

At her shocked gasp, everyone craned forward to see. The letters were faint, but the two words were unmistakable: The Bunker.

CHAPTER THIRTY-THREE

After a few moments of stunned silence, everyone began speaking at once. Only Matt was quiet. He saw the whole story played out before him but speeded up, like one of those old silent movies. Right now, he was watching the final scene, and it was terrible to behold.

Liz was watching him anxiously. 'What do we do now?'

He wished he knew. 'Okay, everyone. Let's gather our thoughts and try to work out our next course of action. For once in my life, I have the unenviable task of trying *not* to think like a police officer. This is not an official murder investigation, and it won't be until we have some concrete evidence to hand over to the police. We have a list of people who may or may not be missing persons, and a rotting piece of card, *possibly* written by a disturbed and frightened street dweller.

'So, here's what I'm going to propose. If we all agree with it, we can decide on our next course of action.' He cleared his throat. 'I believe Molly discovered that either the Bruton, the Whistler, or the Conway family — or perhaps all three — were engaged in some evil activity whose purpose we don't yet know. Whatever it is, it has been going on for years, decades even.'

'Joe said that Molly spoke of a "bad seed",' said Liz. 'To my mind that means something going on within a family, perhaps from generation to generation.'

'Absolutely,' said Matt. 'And Molly found out about it when she was teaching that family's children. Here's what I think: Molly gave us names and a place. I believe those missing people are somewhere in that bunker, they are all dead and they have been for years.'

No one spoke. No one disagreed.

'The question is,' concluded Matt, 'who killed them? And why?'

* * *

He had always known this day would come. What he hadn't reckoned on was having to deal with it alone. The plans he had made all involved Jamie — making use of his physical strength, his fearlessness, and his unquestioning obedience.

With or without Jamie, it had to be done. All his bridges had been burnt, and there was no going back.

He sat in his pleasantly cool kitchen, enjoying the silence.

He had genuinely loved his wife but, oh, the noises. The constant clicking of the biro. The clink clink clink of the teaspoon as she stirred her tea. He even knew why those noises put him so much on edge, knew he suffered from *misophonia*. But no one had ever told him how to deal with it.

He looked at his watch. Five more minutes of blessed silence before he must finish the job and leave Marshdyke-St-Mary for ever.

* * *

Liz looked up at the whiteboard with its list of names. What the hell were they to do next?

Matt was right not to hand the investigation over to the police. Liz had known of officers who had worked for two solid years to solve what was apparently a water-tight case, only to find their felon walk free because a small piece of evidence could not be produced. They must not allow that

328

to happen here. So far, their entire case rested on supposition and conjectures that Charley Anders could do nothing with.

Meanwhile, their "team" was looking to them for guidance. Liz resorted to the time-honoured expedient of more tea.

'Okay, heads up, everyone!' Matt announced. 'Fact one . . .'

Liz suppressed a smile. Matt the policeman was coming to the fore.

'The so-called adventure park, along with the barn and the bunker, is already the focus of an ongoing police investigation so, before we do anything else, we have to find out how far they have got.'

Liz picked up her phone. What would they do without Swifty? She put her phone on loudspeaker and made the call.

'Our lads and lassies went through that place from top to bottom,' he said. 'Whoever was running it made a damn good job of clearing up. They left nothing useful behind — no paperwork, no technology, nothing but a load of rubbish. The SOCOs have been out there but it's one of those messy sites where you finish up with a skip full of trace evidence that is totally useless. So far they've dealt with an office, a dormitory and a small room, kind of a cell, in that bunker thing.'

'So, what's the state of play there now, Swifty?' Liz asked.

'They'll be pulled out shortly, if they haven't gone already. I reckon that by this evening it'll be down to one crew stuck in a car full of Mackie Ds.'

Matt nodded. Just what he wanted to hear. 'That's the way it goes these days, I suppose. You mentioned a little room like a cell. What's the story with that?'

'Oh that,' Swifty said. 'As you know, the place was a kind of boot camp, like the ones you see on TV. According to the guys in custody, the final step in their training was a verbal test. You know the sort of thing — you've been captured by the enemy, so what do you do? The room was used for that.'

'I see,' Liz said. 'Sounds like your guys are happy that they've found everything there is to find out there. That right?'

'Oh yes,' said Jack. 'It was pretty well empty, they hadn't even locked up. Our people got precious little in the way of evidence, so now they are widening the search. They're certain it's not a local organisation. They just picked the most isolated spot they could find that was suitable for their needs. It really looked the part too, especially with that old bunker on it.'

Liz ended the call and turned to Matt. 'Just as we expected.'

'Yes. By this evening that area will be all but deserted. We need to do some research.' He turned to David. 'You checked out bunkers, didn't you? Joe said that one of the Brutons had his old Second World War bunker converted into a usable nuclear fall-out shelter during the Cold War. Could you see if those were made to a specific design? Or constructed in a certain way?'

'I don't think they were, Matt,' David said. 'All the spec I saw concerned the thickness of the walls and the best materials to use for maximum protection and so on. The design depended on the depth and the number of people to be accommodated. Some had plant rooms, generators and cold storage rooms. It was quite an eye-opener, I must say.'

'Excuse me,' Chris said. 'Are we assuming that because the bunker is owned by the Bruton family and stands on their land that they are most likely responsible for the disappearances Molly noted?'

'They are obviously in it up to their necks,' Matt said. 'But there is still the possibility of a conspiracy between the families, and the Brutons just happened to have a nice convenient solution on their doorstep.'

'Perhaps I could do some searches on what was said about it in the local press,' offered Nathan. 'Gossip, and odd happenings that leaked into the papers maybe twenty, thirty years ago. I've got a friend who loves digging into all the rumours and conspiracies that get bandied about in the Fens.'

'Go for it,' said Matt. 'We need whatever we can get hold of.'

'I could go back to Gran,' suggested Anna. 'A couple of chocolate biscuits and a pot of tea can often jog her memory. I can't believe that there have been no rumours doing the rounds in Beckersby all these years.' She shrugged. 'I don't know about the bunker, but we might be able to pick up a hint or two about the "bad seed" of Marshdyke.'

'That would be really helpful,' Liz said. Tilly was proving to be a mine of information.

Chris offered to go with her. 'And if young Harriet is around, I wouldn't mind having a quiet word with her about the family. Sometimes people forget about someone who is always there in the background, and who picks up quite a lot from conversations they overhear. Servants used to know all about the people they worked for, didn't they?'

'That's a good point, Chris. We may not have much time before whoever is responsible for whatever is going on reacts in some way. We can't afford any more mishaps,' Matt said.

'Keep in touch,' added Liz, 'and we'll let you know what's occurring at this end. If we decide to make a move, will you be able to come back and join us?'

'Try and stop us!' Anna said. 'We're in for the long haul, aren't we, Chris?'

'Have you got something for Jeff and I to do?' said Joe. 'We feel a bit like spare parts and neither of us does waiting patiently — we need to be doing something.'

Matt gazed at them thoughtfully. 'I'm considering giving you two a job that is right up your street.'

'Oh?' Joe said.

'A little later today, I would like you both to go back to the marsh and see if you can get into that bunker.'

'Cool,' said Jeff, smiling his trademark smile.

'There'll be a patrol car, don't forget that,' warned Matt. 'But if you can get in, I need to know if there is anywhere in that concrete bunker that could be used to conceal bodies.'

Jeff and Joe looked at each other. 'No problem, boss. Leave it to us.'

Liz glanced at her nephew and saw his wistful expression. Poor David. He would have loved to join them but he just wasn't physically capable of scaling fences and climbing walls.

But David had his own kind of strength. Just as Joe and Jeff didn't do idleness, neither did he do self-pity. He turned back to his laptop. 'A lot of the bunkers are German made, and they're pretty awesome ones too. The British ones seem to be either the small bunkers that were used as workplaces rather than shelters to stay in, or big underground ones, like the Cabinet War Rooms. It says here that between six hundred to a thousand camouflaged underground bunkers were built in case of German invasion, and most were supposed to have been destroyed at the end of the war. I can't find any that the Bruton bunker would have been based on, especially as he had it altered into a nuclear shelter. Which is something that doesn't make sense to me. If the Brutons are as mean as everyone says they are, how come they were willing to spend a fortune on something they might not even use? The chances of an all-out nuclear war were fairly remote even in the Cold War era.'

'Good point, Davey,' said Joe. 'And another thing, nuclear shelters were usually in the basement or out in the garden. What's the point of a shelter that's miles from where you live? Four minutes was the approximate length of time it would take from the launch of a Soviet missile to impact in the UK. The whole family would have fried before they got within sight of their safe place.'

'Come to think of it,' added Jeff, 'I didn't see any sign of a ventilation pipe or escape hatch.'

Liz suddenly realised what this meant. 'There never was a nuclear fall-out shelter. Bruton put that rumour about to cover himself if anyone noticed something going on out there. If he did work on that old bunker, it was to make it into a burial chamber, not a refuge from an apocalypse.'

'So, why didn't the police notice this?' asked Nathan.

'Because they didn't know what they were looking for,' Matt said. 'They found a big underground room and assumed that was all there was. If there is a burial chamber, it is probably very well-hidden.'

'Think how long this must have been going on,' said David. 'The Cold War started in the sixties. Have people been disappearing since then?'

'And why,' Jeff said.

'Bad seed,' whispered Liz. 'I know nothing about mental disorders but I guess they can be inherited just like physical ones.'

This was one of those times when Liz yearned to have a warrant card again. With that behind her, she could have dug as deep as she liked into that family. As it was, she was relying on the memories of an elderly lady and snatches of conversation a stable hand might have overheard.

CHAPTER THIRTY-FOUR

Anna and Chris finally called at about six o'clock.

'We think it's the Whistler family that has the dark history, Matt,' said Anna. 'Tilly remembers there being gossip about one of the children, who was "different" in some way. He wasn't the first, either. Many years ago, another boy had been sent away and was never heard of again.'

'That's very possible,' said Matt. 'In the old days, family members deemed insane were shoved out of sight in asylums. There was a lot of stigma attached to mental illness in those days.'

'It goes deeper than that, Matt,' said Anna excitedly. 'It's a bit complicated to explain over the phone, but we're on our way back.'

Liz suggested that while they waited, she and David should go out and get some food for them all.

'Good idea,' said Matt. 'I've a feeling we'll all be here well into the evening. If Jeff and Joe find anything about that bunker that supports our suspicions, I'm going to see to it that Charley Anders brings the entire Fenland constabulary down on that poisonous village.'

Though it seemed a lot longer, in less than an hour, Liz was handing out plates of fish and chips to the hungry team.

'Okay,' said Matt. 'Over to you, Anna and Chris. Tell us what good old Tilly has dug up from her memories.'

'Not just Tilly,' Chris began. 'We spoke to three separate informants, and their stories all correspond.'

'It appears that the families are all interlinked in a web of dubious business ventures along with incestuous relationships,' Anna added. 'Tilly says their money-making schemes are common knowledge, but what is less well known is that the Whistlers, the Brutons, and the Conways are interrelated, and it's been going on for generations She's certain that hundreds of years ago, those three families were the only people inhabiting this remote part of the marsh, hence Molly's "bad seed".'

Matt had seen the results of incestuous marriages before, and knew that the progeny were often quite pitiful. This was slightly different, but he could only think that over generations of "keeping it within the three families", the gene pool would get very murky indeed.

'We were lucky,' said Chris, 'because when we arrived at Anna's, young Harriet had just got back from the stables and was outside her cottage, chatting to Ted, Whistler's gardener. Thanks to the tip he'd been given when we went there to dig for Rupert, he was more than willing to dish the dirt on his employers.'

'The bottom line is,' said Anna, 'besides what my gran told us, both Harriet and Ted have overheard some vitriolic remarks on the part of all three families. On the surface, the Brutons, Whistlers and Conways might be all sweetness and light but underneath they positively hate each other. Putting two and two together, I'd say the present generation are suffering for the sins of their forebears.'

'Meaning they've inherited some seriously bad genes,' said Nathan, 'which they'd love to rid themselves of but can't.'

'It certainly appears that way,' said Chris. 'Worse than that, we've come to the conclusion that there is a dangerously sick individual in one of those families whom they're all protecting, and this is the person Molly found out about. We have no idea who it might be, but from the odds and ends picked up by Harriet, it would seem that the surviving family members will do anything to prevent word of this person's existence spreading beyond the village.'

Matt put down his fork. 'In light of what you've told us, I think it's almost time to step back and hand this over to the police.'

Seeing their disappointed expressions, he said, 'But before I do that, I suggest the lot of us go out to Marshdyke this evening and wait for Jeff and Joe to come back from their visit to the Bunker. I think we all deserve to know what they find there. Then, depending on what they discover, I'll make the call.'

No matter how much they might wish to see this through to the end, the case had now gone way beyond the remit of a group of civilians. They would perform this last service for Molly, and then stand down.

'We've done everything Molly asked of us,' Matt said, 'and when it's finally over, I hope she'll finally have some peace.'

* * *

Jeff and Joe decided not to wait for nightfall. They needed the light, and this time there would be no villains to avoid, just a couple of bored coppers in a police car.

Jeff ducked under a strip of cordoning tape. 'Look at that, the door's not even locked.'

'And the crew in the car are more interested in watching the big barn and the assault course than this heap of concrete,' added Joe.

As described, the room resembled a cell — windowless, with a single door. There was a trestle table and a few chairs, and an electric cable feeding two or three power sockets.

'Well, this isn't right, is it?' grunted Joe.

'No, it certainly isn't,' Jeff said. 'The interior is half the size of the exterior, so what's in between?'

They checked every inch of the walls and floor, but they were flat, the concrete smooth.

'Maybe the outside has more to offer,' said Joe.

Jeff slipped out first and called softly to Joe that the coast was clear. They crept to the rear of the bunker, where they would not be seen from the police car.

As far as Jeff was concerned, the sooner this place disappeared beneath the encroaching vegetation the better. Before long, it would be part of the landscape, as if the Bunker had never existed.

But not quite. Despite the lush overgrowth, there was still a sinister atmosphere hovering about this lump of concrete.

'It looks all wrong, doesn't it?' said Joe, staring at the edifice. 'Even allowing for thick walls, this is big enough to accommodate at least two more rooms. Since there's no access from the inside, I guess we'll have to try the outside.'

They spent the next fifteen minutes crawling around on their knees, ripping up the overgrowth. Slowly, they made their way around the walls, searching for patches of more recent vegetation that might conceal a hidden entrance.

Jeff was beginning to think they'd never find it when Joe gave a quiet laugh.

'Oh, very neat. Here, look at this.'

Kneeling beside him, Jeff saw a rigid panel slotted into the bunker wall, roughly three metres by two, made from plaited willow twigs intertwined with artificial ivy and covered over with branches from an elder.

'Ta-da! We have an entrance,' Joe said.

Beneath the panel was a thick wooden door and, incongruous in the weathered wood, a good old Yale lock.

Joe laughed softly. 'They must have placed a lot of faith in their camouflage panel. A child could pick this.'

'But can an ex-soldier?' asked Jeff with a grin.

Throwing him a disdainful look, Joe took a small flexible pick from his pocket and in the blink of an eye, the door stood open. 'I'll go first,' he said. 'I can't leap off buildings like you, but I do have a little more knowledge of booby traps.'

The passage they entered smelled of nothing but damp earth. Their torch beams, bouncing off bare walls, lit up what they thought was a dead end but which led them into what looked like an office. It had evidently housed a considerable amount of computer hardware. The equipment had gone, but the connections, along with the wires and leads, still lay on the floor.

Closer inspection revealed horizontal ventilation shafts, and a door that led to an alcove with a small generator.

Joe roamed around like a hound trying to pick up a scent. 'All moderately new,' he muttered. 'I'm surprised they had so much of it if all they were doing was recruiting young criminals. Anyway, it doesn't help us find our buried victims.' He took a last look around. 'Okay, Jeff, back outside. I'm afraid we'll have to start digging again.'

Still mindful of the police crew, they felt their way around the rest of the bunker. This time it was Jeff who made the discovery.

'Is that a drain cover?' he said, as they both stared down at the heavy metal hatch.

'Not like any I've ever seen,' said Joe.

'I could be wrong but isn't this over the extra space that we can't account for?' Jeff said.

Joe merely raised an eyebrow.

Jeff knelt and ran his hand over the cold iron. 'How on earth are we supposed to lift it? I can't feel anything to get a hold of.'

Joe was on his knees beside him. 'There are two flanges, one on each side. I'd say a couple of tyre irons or crowbars would lever that up.' He squinted at it. 'It's certainly not been put there recently, so it has nothing to do with our criminal gang . . . This is it, Jeff. We've found what Matt asked us to. I think we should go back, don't you?'

Taking care not to be seen, Joe and Jeff retraced their footsteps to the perimeter wire and climbed back over. As soon as they were on the other side, Jeff rang Matt. 'There *is* something there, Matt. We'll be with you in five minutes.'

* * *

Their three cars were parked on an area of hard-standing on the edge of a farmer's field on the outskirts of Marshdyke village that was used for tractors and farm vehicles to turn. In a nice piece of irony, it was probably Bruton land.

Matt had chosen this spot for the view. From here, it was possible to see across the fields and the marsh all the way to the Wash. He felt he needed a reminder that there was still a world of beauty out there. It seemed right to bring the people who had helped him get to this point. They too needed a reminder of what their efforts had all been for.

Looking out across the miles of Fenland, Matt prepared himself to ring Charley Anders. They had come such a long way to reach this point that it was not easy to relinquish the reins.

'I hope Molly's looking down to see us all here,' said Joe softly, gazing up into the wide Fenland sky.

Chris smiled. 'She certainly led us a merry dance, but soon she'll be vindicated.'

'And that,' Matt jerked back his thumb towards the village, 'is where the canker set in.'

From where they stood, they could see Bruton Manor surrounded by its extensive grounds. A little to the left, the Whistlers' old vicarage. Almost hidden from view lay Cedar Leigh, its tall chimneys the only visible indication of the Conways' elegant residence.

'What a nest of vipers,' breathed Liz. 'It looks so peaceful from here, like one of those idyllic rural landscape paintings that the Victorians loved so much. Smoke rising into the evening sky, sea birds lazily winging their way inland . . .'

Matt sniffed. Smoke rising into the evening sky . . . but there was no smoke coming from the chimneys of Bruton Manor. So where was that smoke coming from? A bonfire?

No, it was closer to the building than that, and it seemed to be coming from more than one place.

'Look! Bruton Manor! It's on fire!'

Nathan pointed. 'So is the Whistler place . . . Jesus Christ! Look!'

'I'll dial 999!' Chris snatched his phone from his pocket.

'Let's get down there, fast!' Matt yelled. 'We are closer than the villagers, and there could be innocent people caught up in it.'

The three cars hurtled down the lane. On reaching the entrance to the Manor, Matt called out to Chris, 'You go on to the Whistlers' place and do what you can.' He waved to Joe and Jeff. 'Go on to Cedar Leigh and warn the Conways!'

'What the hell is going on?' Liz said. 'One fire, sure, it's an accident. But two?'

Matt didn't answer. He knew exactly what was happening.

Liz exhaled. 'It's the end game, isn't it? Someone knows it's over. There's nowhere he can run to now, so he's organised a grand finale.'

Gravel flying from their wheels, they raced down the drive towards the house.

Matt had seen a lot of fires in his time, and knew how fast they could travel. This one, however, was simply terrifying. The entire building was ablaze.

They parked as close as they dared and got out, but it was immediately obvious that there was nothing they could do. Even so, they didn't want to turn away before making sure that no one needed their help. With the heat from the flames burning their faces, they squinted up at the windows but could see no sign of life.

'Not that I know much about it, but am I right in thinking that this wasn't one fire that got out of control, but a whole lot of fires started at the same time?' Nathan said.

'Whoever did this,' said Matt, taking a few steps back as the heat intensified, 'was certainly leaving nothing to chance. Come on, let's get out of here and find the others. Maybe the Whistler place isn't as bad, and I didn't see any smoke coming from the Conways' place. Hopefully, Jeff and Joe have managed to raise the alarm there.'

As they drove away, Matt heard the distant sound of sirens. It was far too late to save Bruton Manor, but the fire service might be able to keep the neighbouring properties from catching alight. For a moment, he had forgotten how evil these people were. Whatever they had done, surely they didn't deserve a fate as terrible as this. He put his foot down.

* * *

Chris was relieved to see Matt's car in the lane outside the Old Vicarage. He was worried about Anna. She insisted on helping him, but he was very aware that she wasn't healthy and might do herself harm.

'We are pretty sure the place is empty,' he called out, 'or as much of it as we could get to. We've been yelling our heads off, but no one has answered.'

'The fire is spreading,' added Anna breathlessly, 'but so far it's confined to the left-hand side of the house and the outbuildings. We shut as many doors as we could find before we had to get out.'

'Thank God you did,' said Liz. 'We could hear the fire service on our way, so they'll be here soon.'

'Any news from Joe and Jeff?' asked Matt.

'No,' said Chris. 'Maybe we should head down there now and see how they're doing?'

'You and Anna go ahead,' Matt said, 'and take David and Nathan with you. What with all the drama, I completely forgot to contact Charley Anders, and I really must do that now. What I have to tell her could turn out to be far, far bigger than this.' He gestured towards the burning house.

The three of them piled into Chris's car and headed back along the lane towards Cedar Leigh.

'Look! Smoke,' said Nathan. 'I thought they might have got away with it, but it looks like they haven't after all.'

Though Cedar Leigh was a more modest property than the other two houses, it was still a fine example of classic

British architecture. Chris experienced a pang of regret that something so irreplaceable was about to be lost.

Taking care to leave the way clear for the emergency vehicles, Jeff parked up and the four of them hurried towards the house.

'Why aren't the villagers here?' panted Anna, struggling to keep pace with the men. 'Something like this usually brings people flocking from miles around to see what's going on.'

She was right. Chris looked over to where the village lay, dark and silent. Where were all the do-gooders, the rubber-neckers, the men striding forward to take charge?

Jeff and Joe appeared at the open front door.

'Where the hell's the fire brigade?' Joe called out. 'We heard the sirens, they should be here by now. They could save this place if they only got a move on.'

'Shall I go back to the entrance and try to flag down a passing car?' offered Nathan. 'At least they can drive down to the village for help. Joe's right, it's too late for the others but this house could be salvaged.' Nathan turned and ran back down the drive.

'What's the situation here, Joe?' Chris said. 'I gather no one is at home.'

'Jeff thought he heard someone upstairs but we can't get to them.' Joe frowned. 'I'm damned if I can find the source of the fire. There's an office area over there, which is definitely alight, and we've done our best to prevent the fire from spreading to the main house.'

Chris looked around. 'Where *is* Jeff?'

'I bet that silly sod is back inside. He's convinced he heard someone in there.' He gripped Chris's arm. 'Stay here with Anna and David, and when that bloody fire engine gets here, show them that office.'

Before Chris could protest, Joe had run back into the house.

'Should we go after him?' David said at his side. 'If the house suddenly catches fire Jeff'll be in danger.'

Chris shook his head. 'No way. Joe won't let any harm come to him, and don't forget, your Spiderman friend could be out of a window and down a drainpipe faster than it'd take us to get through the front door. Joe will fi—'

They heard a dull whump, followed by a loud roar and a cracking noise.

'Shit! That's a propane gas cannister gone up,' groaned Anna. 'There's no mains gas out here, we all use bottled gas. Luckily, it'll be outside the house.'

Growing increasingly anxious himself, Chris was trying to appear calm, for David was almost beside himself with worry about his friend.

Then Nathan was running towards them. 'The police are here! They're going to reroute a tender from the Vicarage.'

Chris sighed with relief. At least help was finally on its way.

'Oh no! I've just thought of something!' In an instant, David was gone from his side, haring across to the side of the house. He was shouting something but his words were lost in the roar of the flames.

'David! Come back!' shouted Chris.

Anna started forward, about to follow David.

Chris caught hold of her arm. 'No, Anna! Stay here. Someone needs to tell the fire service about that office, and about the gas cannister going up. I'll go after him.'

The back of the house was like a battleground. The exploding gas bottle had caused a number of small fires that were beginning to coalesce, and this bigger fire was moving forward, consuming everything in its path. Patio furniture twisted and buckled in the flames, a small wooden toolshed was burning like a bonfire. Chris gave it a wide berth, aware that people kept noxious weedkillers in their garden sheds.

He kept shouting David's name but there was no answering call. Chris knew David had been rejected by the police because of his physical weakness and was afraid for the boy. Suppose he fainted?

To his horror, he saw that part of the house itself — a doorframe and a windowsill — were starting to glow and crackle. A wooden trellis suddenly burst into flames in front of him, forcing him back.

'Chris! Help us!'

He swung round to where the voice was coming from, and saw a pair of French windows flying open. It was Jeff, calling to him.

Chris ran towards him and saw Joe half carrying half dragging someone from the house.

Along with Jeff, he took the slumped figure from a gasping Joe, and they frogmarched her to safety.

'I wonder who she is,' wheezed Chris.

'Who knows,' panted a soot-coated Joe, and pointed to Jeff. 'But this cocky little git was right, there *was* someone in the house. Pity she was up two flights of stairs though. The fireman's lift never was my speciality.'

As they laid the semi-conscious woman down, Anna hurried up to join them. As soon as she saw who it was, she exclaimed, 'Frankie! It's Francesca Conway, the granddaughter. She's—'

The deafening screech of sirens drowned the rest of her words. The police and the fire service had both arrived at the same time. But where was David? 'Jeff, come with me!' Chris said. "David went round the back somewhere and he hasn't come back. He was yelling something but I couldn't make out the words.'

'Oh hell!' Joe struggled to his feet. 'I'll come too.'

'Relax, guys.' Anna was staring back over her shoulder, a wide grin on her face. 'I think you'll find the word he was yelling was "horses".'

Chris spun round, and his mouth fell open.

David, his wet shirt draped over his head and across his mouth, was leading two huge horses and a collie dog on to the front lawn.

'Bloody hell! It's Lawrence of Arabia,' spluttered Joe.

Jeff giggled. 'Just don't tell Matt you've rescued another dog, or you'll be out on your ear.'

They must have made a curious sight, four dishevelled figures rolling around in helpless laughter while a house burned behind them.

* * *

Unaware of the drama being played out at Cedar Leigh, Matt was telling Charley Anders of their suspicions about the Bruton bunker.

'Someone murdered Molly to prevent her revealing what she knew, which means it's still going on. It has to be stopped right now, so as to bring decades of evildoing to an end. And now it appears that someone is trying to cover their traces by setting fires in the houses where it all took place. However, they don't yet know that we've worked out what's hidden in the bunker. Charley, I'm not asking you to launch a major offensive. Just send a couple of trusted men with two crowbars and a camera to take a look under that trapdoor. Then, based on what they find, act as you see fit. That's all.'

He waited for her to come to a decision. 'Okay,' she said slowly. 'In light of the cock-up we made of our own search, I'll get someone back out there faster than the speed of sodding light. Your request is sanctioned, Matt Ballard. I'll be in touch.'

Matt stared at his phone, only dimly aware of the commotion in the background — the familiar two-tone note of sirens, the flashing blue lights.

Liz squeezed his hand.

'I know, darling. We're almost there. But right now our little band of amateur sleuths is out at those burning houses. We'd better make sure they're all safe.'

Matt shook his head to clear it. 'You're right. We'd better go on foot. It looks like a disaster movie over there.' As they were about to set off, he paused for a moment and turned his gaze on her. 'Have we finally succeeded, Liz? Have we done enough, do you think?'

'More than enough,' she said. 'There are a lot of unanswered questions but Charley will fill in the blanks as they go on.' She looked out to the circle of flashing lights where the smoke pooled. 'Where are all the people? Why are these houses empty? And why did the village not turn out in force to help, or at least gawp?'

He had no answer. Had the three families simply cut and run? Or was there something darker at work here? 'I don't know about the three families, but I do have a theory about the villagers. I reckon that after years of being dictated to, they saw the smoke and flames and thought, "At last! Burn in hell."'

'But what about the Brutons, Whistlers and Conways? What's happened to them?'

'As you said, Liz, that's for the police to sort out. Haynes and Ballard hereby announces Case Closed.'

EPILOGUE

22.35 p.m. The Bunker, Marshdyke-St-Mary
Present: DS Bryn Owen and PC Jack 'Swifty' Fleet

Neither man spoke as their torch beams fell on the trapdoor.

Black smoke continued to billow from the three gutted buildings. Caught by the sea winds, it swept across the fields like the dying traces of some terrible battle.

Neither Bryn nor Jack wanted to be here, but they had been especially chosen by the DCI as her most trustworthy officers. Furthermore, they were loyal friends of Matt Ballard. They knew all that, but they still didn't want to be there.

'Okay, Swifty,' said Bryn, grasping one of the two crowbars. 'Let's get it over with. It's gonna be bad, so we don't want to be prolonging the agony.'

Together, they slid their crowbars under the iron cover and heaved.

It came up more easily than they expected, sending them both staggering backwards. They shifted the heavy door to one side and shone their torches into the cavity beneath.

'Steps,' said Jack, pointing his torch beam into the black hole. 'Leading to what, I wonder?'

'Well, there's only one way to find out. Will you go first, or shall I?' Bryn bowed. 'Age before beauty.'

'Ah, but you're the higher-ranking officer.'

But for once, the banter fell flat.

'Okay,' Bryn said. 'Got the lights?'

Jack produced two hand-held halogen lights and switched them on.

Bryn went ahead, with Jack following a few steps behind.

The stairs were concrete, deep and wide enough to take their policemen's boots. They descended in silence.

'There's a door at the bottom,' Bryn said, his voice tight and a little shaky. He stepped down onto a small landing. 'No lock. Just a handle.' He looked back at Jack. 'Ready?'

'As I'll ever be.' Jack placed a hand on his shoulder. 'Let's see what our Molly got killed for.'

It took Bryn a few moments to understand what he was seeing. Instead of the charnel house he had been expecting, they had entered a smallish square storeroom, clean and tidy and basically empty, except for a couple of heavy-duty plastic boxes and several piles of what looked like large sacks of potting compost, or possibly builder's material. There was a trapdoor in the middle of the floor with a brass handle to lift it by.

'That's lime in those sacks,' said Jack flatly.

Bryn surveyed the labels. 'Yeah, it is.'

Jack cleared his throat. 'Isn't that what they used to use in, erm, graves — mass graves that is — to help speed up decomposition?'

'I read an article about the plague once,' added Bryn, 'it said they used it to mask the smell and kill off bacteria to stop the disease spreading.'

'That right?' Jack said. They knew they were delaying the inevitable, but neither of them wanted to lift that hatch.

'DS Owen!'

They both jumped. They heard the heavy tread of footsteps slowly descending.

'It's all right, dear hearts. It's not a boggart, or a Will 'o the Wisp, just a nosey pathologist.' Professor Rory Wilkinson stepped into the room and beamed at them. 'Or in your case, your fairy godmother, come to save you from an unpleasant task. A little bird told me that this could be something that's more up my alley than yours, so here I am, cherubs.'

Bryn could not remember ever being so happy to see someone, especially a pathologist.

Rory took stock. 'There is considerable debate over lime and its effectiveness. What's more, this lot,' he pointed to the sacks, 'is hydrated lime. Tests show that it actually delays decay, and in some cases even preserves tissue. Imagine!' He looked at the trapdoor, then back to his audience. 'Are we of the same opinion here, gentlemen? Some unpleasant individual brought bodies down here, popped them down there,' he jerked a thumb at the trapdoor, 'chucked a load of lime over them and trundled off home for tea.'

Bryn and Jack nodded.

'Well, we'd better check our hypothesis.' Rory grasped the brass handle and pulled.

* * *

Less than a mile from the noise and mayhem at Bruton Manor, the men and women called out to the bunker worked in almost total silence. Professor Wilkinson, who was leading the team, had been obliged to send out a request for specialist help. People were needed here who had experience in the identification of multiple corpses buried in mass graves, usually in the aftermath of a war. He estimated that there were more than nine bodies in that cellar, in various stages of decomposition, that would all have to be retrieved.

The trap, when raised, revealed a chute like the funnel on a combine harvester. As he had suspected, the bodies had been slid down the chute and a sack of lime tipped in after them. With the aid of a camera he examined the cellar and concluded that it should have had a water course passing through it, thus the cellar would have flooded when the tide came in and drained as it receded. Rory could see no such drain here.

Having spent an hour or so in the storeroom, Rory trudged back up the steps and out into the night for a few moments of fresh air. The discovery of a crumpled, bedraggled dead woman had brought them here, to this point. Molly the bag lady had led them here.

He looked up into the blackness. 'Dear lady, your work is almost done. Now you can leave it to science. Forensics will tell us who was responsible, now you can rest.'

Yes, there was evidence aplenty, and he still had the handkerchief that had ended Molly's life. To the untrained eye, the houses were nothing but charred ruins, yet he knew there would be evidence left in little pockets that had escaped the flames. There always was.

He stood up and stretched. 'Get yourself together, Wilkinson. There'll be no beauty sleep for you in the months to come, so you'd better bloody well get used to it.'

* * *

The following day
8.30 a.m. DCI Charley Anders's office.

'I'm sure you are aware that this needs very careful handling, DCI Anders?'

Gripped by a strong desire to punch Chief Superintendent Edwin Norton on his pudgy nose, she said, 'Of course, sir. The correct procedures are already in place, as I'm sure you are aware, and the Serious Crime Unit are on their way from HQ.' She glanced at her watch. 'I'm expecting DCI Morgan Flint and her team to arrive within the next fifteen minutes.'

Was that surprise she saw on Norton's face — and something else?

'Flint? I thought she was a DI with Intelligence,' he said sharply.

'Promoted and transferred across earlier in the year, sir. She's heading up this investigation now.' A happy thought. Morgan Flint took no prisoners. Charley couldn't have wished for a better person to lead them. She would make sure the job was done properly, with no whitewash.

Norton turned towards the door. 'Then carry on. And remember, media silence until we are in full possession of the facts. After which,' he glowered at her, 'I will be present at all media events. Understood?'

As the door closed behind him, Charley gave him a two-finger salute. No wonder Matt hated that man.

Of course, Norton had not been referring to the findings in the Bunker. That was bad enough, but what the Chief Super meant was the bodies the fire service had found in the remains of the three houses at Marshdyke. Three at the Manor, another two at the Old Vicarage, and a further two at Cedar Leigh. The Brutons, the Whistlers and the Conways were no more. With the exception of a lone survivor, rescued by two of Matt's helpers, and who was being guarded like the crown jewels until she was well enough to talk to them. It seemed there were a few other family members who had been absent at the time of the fires and were now missing. Maybe they had fled, but Charley couldn't be sure that more bodies would not turn up at a later date.

That bloody detective agency of Matt Ballard's! All this because of a dogged search for a missing tearaway, and their conviction that a dead vagrant and a bag of wastepaper was worthy of an investigation. Charley began to laugh.

* * *

8.30 a.m. Fenfleet landfill site

The refuse lorry made its way to the top of the ramp, turned and raised the hopper, sending twenty-six tons of waste on to the stinking mass of rotting food and garbage below. Amid the detritus was a blue and red sleeping bag with a letter still sewn into the lining. It had been an important letter, telling of a woman's terror at what was going on in the household in which she worked as a teacher. It told of the hunched form of a disturbed young man pushing a heavy wheelbarrow towards the old bunker and returning with it empty. Nonetheless, the writer would not have been disappointed to see it disappear. The truth had been told, letter or no letter.

* * *

9.45 a.m. Matt Ballard's kitchen

Halfway through doing the dishes, Matt heard his phone. Drying his hands, he said, 'Darren. How are you? Recovering, I hope?'

'Thank you, sir, I'm fine now. Still shaken . . . I guess it will take a while to sort my head out.'

There was a difference in the young man's tone. Gone was the sneer, the supercilious attitude. 'You've been through a lot, lad, don't rush the process. It'll get easier with time, never fear.'

'Well, you should know, sir.' Norton paused. 'I'm, er, about ten minutes from Tanner's Fen. Would you mind if I called in to have a talk with you? If it's not too inconvenient, that is. There are some things I need to say, and . . . oh . . . well . . .'

'I'll get the coffee on. Come right over,' Matt said.

The man who walked through the door was a far cry from the Darren Norton who'd so annoyed him in the early days of the case.

Rather than facing him with a room full of people, Matt had decided to talk to him privately. They now sat in the garden, each with a cup of coffee, while Matt waited for Norton to begin.

After a silence that was beginning to grow uncomfortable, Norton suddenly burst out with, 'I am so sorry! Not to put too fine a point on it, I acted like a real arsehole.' He met Matt's kindly gaze. 'I'm just hoping that I haven't done so much damage that there's no way back. I do want to be a detective, a good one, and I know I can do it, but I'm afraid it

352

might be too late.' He lowered his voice. 'And there are other factors that might see me pushed out of the force. That's why I need to talk to you.'

Matt suddenly realised that this was no ordinary apology for bad behaviour, or a last-ditch attempt to save his job. He sat forward. 'I'm listening.'

'Ever since I was a little kid, my grandfather has always been presented to me as a role model, the person I must emulate if I want to get ahead. And who was I, just a kid, to dispute that? He was high up in the police force, rich, well-connected and powerful.' Norton looked down at his feet. 'And like a mug, I bought it all.'

Matt knew not to interrupt.

'Those men at the Bunker were going to kill me, Matt. If it hadn't been for you and your friends, I wouldn't be sitting here now. It was you who saved me, not my grandfather. More than that, it was him who put me there in the first place.'

'How do you mean?' said Matt quietly.

'I ran a couple of snouts, or I thought I did.' He grunted. 'Actually, it was Grandfather who ran them, and they fed me information that *he* wanted me to have. Chief Superintendent Edwin Norton knew all about that set-up with the adventure park and the kids, and it was him that leaked the rendezvous point so that I would chase out there.'

'What for, lad? Did he want you to get the kudos? A step up the ladder? Or . . .'

'I think it's the "or",' Norton said. 'He knew I had my suspicions about the Bunker, and he didn't want me interfering. I think he arranged for me to disappear — permanently.'

This was a very serious allegation. Matt knew the man was a bastard, but would he go as far as to have his own flesh and blood murdered?

'There's one other thing, Matt,' said Norton. 'Grandfather is related to the Conways of Cedar Leigh in Marshdyke. He's a first cousin, and he's close, if you get my drift.'

Matt thought back to what had been said about that village. He got it, all right.

'I've come to you for advice. I don't know what to do. Can you help me? I trust you, and whatever you suggest, I'll do it, I'll even testify against Chief Superintendent Norton if I have to. I've been making preparations, my money is safe — I have a trust fund, and some money that was left to me by a relative. I've left the family home and am now renting a flat in Fenfleet. I'll cope on my own — and this time without a role model.'

'Good for you, Darren,' Matt said, his head full with thoughts of Edgar Norton, up to his neck in dirty dealings while in the guise of a respected officer. 'And yes, I'll help you. It will be my pleasure.'

* * *

One Month Later
Cannon Farm, Tanners Fen

It had taken her some time to get all of them back together again, but Liz had persevered, and this evening they were gathered at Cannon Farm. The idea had been to use the dining room for its original purpose and have a proper candle-lit supper. However, the whiteboard with the names she hadn't the heart to erase, still dominated the room. So, as the weather was good, they settled for a barbeque, which Liz thought Joe especially would enjoy.

After the food and the general conversation, they turned to the subject that had brought them all together.

Matt and Liz had spent several gruelling weeks being interviewed by the Serious Crime Unit. Matt had also held some private discussions with Morgan Flint regarding a certain chief superintendent, who had suddenly seen fit to announce his retirement. Charley Anders had given them the rest of the story, which she said they had a right to know, as without them, youngsters would still be undergoing training for a life of crime, and people would still be going missing in Marshdyke-St-Mary.

Now, they believed they had all the pieces of the jigsaw in place. There had been any number of questions to answer, but what everyone really wanted to know was who set those fires? Who consigned so many people to the inferno that followed?

'It's a complex case that goes back many generations, so I'm going to simplify it as best I can.' Matt topped up his glass and sat back in his chair. 'First, it was Whistler who decided that it was time to end the whole thing for once and for all. He was entirely responsible for the deaths of all the people burned in the fire. His body was found at his home. He was the last to die, killed by his own hand.'

'But we checked the Vicarage and Cedar Leigh,' said Chris. 'Other than Frankie Conway, there wasn't anyone there, I'm certain.'

'Ah, but you didn't have time to look in every single room, especially the ones that were locked, or in the cupboards,' Matt said. 'All the victims had been sedated, tied up and stashed out of sight prior to their homes being set alight, so they wouldn't have heard you calling.'

'What about Frankie Conway?' asked Anna. 'She wasn't drugged, she was just overcome by smoke.'

'She was never meant to be there,' said Liz, sipping her wine. 'She was out at the stables, mucking out the horses, and tore her shirt, so she went back to change. Whistler had set incendiary devices with timers and she got caught up in it. Thank God you stuck to your guns about hearing someone, Jeff, or she'd be another fatality.'

'It was Joe that got her down all those stairs. I know I couldn't have done it,' Jeff said.

Joe grinned. 'My back hasn't been the same since. But hey, between us, we got her to safety. That's what counts.'

'And thankfully, Francesca has been a mine of information about the three families,' added Matt. 'What with her, the born-again DC Darren Norton and a surprisingly well-informed new witness, the police now have the whole sordid history of lechery, interbreeding and greed. Believe me, those three families took "free love" to a whole new level.'

'Who's this well-informed new witness?' asked Joe, leaning forward.

'One of the men arrested after the raid on the Bunker who has turned King's evidence. He was a doctor there. His name is Christopher Whistler, known as Kit. He knows all about that accursed village.'

'What? The medic?' exclaimed Jeff. 'The one I saw at the Bunker? He's a Whistler?'

'And a qualified doctor. He's Whistler's eldest son. He had a brother called Jamie, a badly damaged child—' Matt looked around at the amazed faces. 'I said it was complex, and it is. This entire horrific outcome is the result of decades of immorality and corruption involving the three families.'

'It's not a case of the lord of the manor chasing the lusty young serving wench,' said Liz. 'This was a powder keg of deception, lies and promiscuity. It's doubtful that any of the present generation have a clue about their true parentage. DCI Morgan Flint has already discovered that a boy named Benjamin Bruton was Jamie and Christopher Whistler's half-brother. Whistler's wife gave birth to three boys, two of whom were born impaired, victims of the family's twisted past. Bruton took Benjamin to bring him up.'

'And is that the big secret? The one that our Molly chanced upon?' Nathan asked. 'The one she was killed for?'

Matt nodded. 'You remember Tilly told us about rumours of a boy who was sent to an asylum many years before?' said Matt. 'She said he was what the locals called "different".'

They all nodded.

'Serious Crimes have discovered that it happened again. As I said, of Whistler's three boys, two were born with defects, and one was so lacking in emotion that he saw nothing wrong in killing things, or people. That boy was Benjamin Bruton.'

David gasped. 'That can't be right. Molly talks about him, he was one of her pupils. She really cared for the boy, and she said she feared for him.'

'According to Kit Whistler, his half-brother Benjamin had a sort of Jekyll and Hyde character. He was intelligent

356

and keen to learn but they daren't send him to school with other children in case he harmed one of them. He was clever enough not to let her see that side of his nature. And anyway, our Molly was a kind soul who saw the best in people, even when they treated her badly.'

'I can vouch for that,' said Nathan earnestly.

'She saw the bright little boy, not the monster. Although,' Matt paused, 'I suspect that when she said she feared for him, maybe she saw something in him she didn't understand.'

Joe was looking puzzled. 'You said two damaged children, and one was a boy called Jamie. Was he a killer too?'

'I hardly know how to answer that,' sighed Matt. 'I can only tell you what we know. Frankie Conway described Jamie as "a hulking beast, with the innocence of a child, and the strength of an ox". Kit said his brother should have been institutionalised as a small child. Jamie had severe learning disabilities and his only wish was to please his beloved father. He took everything anyone said quite literally, even a humorous remark or passing comment. Kit believed this led to the death of his mother. Apparently, she had the annoying habit of clicking her biro, and one day his father happened to mutter, "if she doesn't stop that, I'll throttle her". Jamie overheard him, and when his mother next clicked her pen in that way, he strangled her.'

'Jesus,' said Joe. 'The Whistlers must have lived on a knife edge.'

'I wouldn't feel too sorry for them,' said Matt. 'The three families had a far bigger problem with Benjamin and his homicidal tendencies. Anyway, as soon as they realised what Jamie was capable of, the wicked bastards made use of him to do their dirty work for them. He was their fixer, the one they sent to clean up. He killed Benjamin because his father told him that his half-brother deserved to die.'

'And he disposed of him down the chute at the Bunker?' asked Jeff, looking rather pale.

'Yes, he did. With his strength, he was easily able to carry a body and take it to the bunker in a wheelbarrow.' Matt grimaced. 'However, the rot had set in years before Jamie and Benjamin were born. People had died during what Kit suspects to have been various acts of depravity. Bruton had the idea of converting his bunker as a handy repository for their bodies.'

'One last thing,' said Liz. 'Rory Wilkinson reported finding another body in a room in the Old Vicarage that had somehow escaped the flames. It was Jamie Whistler. He had been killed a day or so before the others, and would probably have died anyway, from sepsis after having been bitten by a dog.'

David sighed. 'They sent him to kill Clem, didn't they?' He reached down and fondled the dog that lay at his feet — the dog that seemed to have found a home at Cannon Farm. His original owner, Clem, had been discharged from hospital and was now living in a nice little flat in a warden-controlled block in Fenfleet, where pets were not allowed. Gunner visited often, but unless the "no pets" order was lifted, Cannon Farm was where he would stay. Alfie was safely home with a much-recovered George and two new rescue dogs from the Poultney Marsh Dog Sanctuary, where he now worked full-time.

Matt noticed Nathan's glance at Joe, and Matt knew what the next question would be, so he forestalled him. 'And yes, it was Jamie they sent to kill Molly. The handkerchief in her mouth had belonged to Whistler, and Jamie was in the habit of carrying it about with him when he went "hunting".'

'So much wickedness,' Liz sounded close to tears.

'But it's finally over — forever,' said Chris. 'They've cleared the sites of the fires and there are hoardings going up in Marshdyke.'

Anna smiled. 'I'm told it's going to be a housing estate — a big one. I never thought I'd be pleased to see one of those going up in the village, but it will bring new life to the place. And a future for those who have lived under the shadow of those three evil families for so long.'

'What about the Bunker?' asked Jeff.

Joe grinned at him. 'The bulldozers moved in a few days ago. We'll be doing no more scaling of fences, my friend, at least not in that place. It's gone. The Bunker no longer exists.'

This news lightened the atmosphere considerably. Liz handed around more food and Matt refilled glasses. When he got to Joe, he took a key from his pocket. 'I've been meaning to give this to you. I found it in the cuff of your jacket when I searched your bag after it was found in the ditch. I guessed it might be important.'

Joe's eyes widened. 'Look at that! My reminder that I once had a home. It was the front door key to the cottage where I was born. The cottage is long gone, but I kept the key as a lucky charm when I was travelling.' He swallowed. 'Thank you, Matt, I appreciate you keeping it for me.'

To allow Joe to recover, Matt turned to his friends. 'So, what does the future hold for you all? You start, Jeff.'

'When I finish uni I'm going back to Asia for a while. I learned a lot there, but there's more to discover before I move forward.' He blushed. 'And if all goes well, Frankie Conway is going to come with me. She's a really nice girl, we've been seeing quite a bit of each other. She lost everything in that blaze, although thankfully she has some money. When the lawyers have finished sifting through her family's dodgy finances, she could be very comfortably off one day, but that could take years. Right now, I think travel and getting to know other cultures will help her to leave the past behind.'

Nathan was going back to teaching. He'd had his break and he missed his students, so he'd applied for a full-time post at the music college. David had another year to go at uni, and was still enjoying his course. Then he announced that he had a date the following day.

'And I'd like some advice on the best bottle of wine to take, Auntie Liz.'

Liz asked what sort of wine the young lady might like — red, white, sweet?

'She said anything alcoholic, as long as it's accompanied by a houseplant.' He grinned. 'I think that's the least Hazel Webber deserves for the work she did on Molly's book.'

Joe said that he was on the road again but this time by motorbike. His friend had made him a gift of the Enfield. Joe said he intended to keep in touch with George, but since he was happily occupied with his dogs, he himself would keep moving for a while longer until he felt the need to settle. He wanted somewhere with enough space for his old army buddy Derek, who might need help as he got older, and who better to offer it than one of his brothers-in-arms.

Chris and Anna didn't say much, but maybe they didn't need to. You only had to look at the two of them together to know what would happen — in the fullness of time. What they did say was that if ever Matt and Liz needed some additional help, they only had to call on them. They might be unfit for active duty but they still had their brains.

Liz decided it was a good moment for Nathan to play for them. When she invited him to come, it was on condition that he brought his keyboard, so he was ready.

He played a mix of modern songs and folk tunes, to which they sang along. He followed them with a lilting ballad that drifted like Fen mist through the twilight. When it was over, he looked around at the group of friends. 'Can we raise a toast to Molly?'

Matt stood up and lifted his glass. 'Marika Molohan! Our Molly. You didn't make it easy for us, but we've told your truth at last. Now you can rest in peace. To Molly!'

They all raised their glasses. Then Nathan began to play the most haunting piece of music that Matt had ever heard.

'Marika loved to play this,' said Nathan quietly. 'It was her favourite piece.'

'And she wrote her own words to it,' added Joe with a sigh. 'She would sometimes sing it to me on a cold night while we sat by my bucket of embers.'

Joe raised his voice. The song rang out, clear as a bell, he sang of love, a love that never died, a love that transcended even death.

As he listened, Matt could have sworn that he heard another voice join the song, a woman's voice, sweet and pure, like that of an angel. The wine, of course. Or was it?

THE END

AUTHOR'S NOTE

The character called Smokey Joe is a memory from my early childhood. He really did exist. An old homeless man, who rode an ancient bicycle, and from the handlebars dangled an old galvanized bucket full of burning coals, or whatever he could find to burn. Seventy-plus years on, I can still see him riding down the road, smoke billowing everywhere, and my mum yelling, 'Get inside, girl, and close the door! Heaven knows what he's burning from that awful smell!' I never knew his story, so I've invented one for him. Here's to Smokey Joe!

THE JOFFE BOOKS STORY

We began in 2014 when Jasper agreed to publish his mum's much-rejected romance novel and it became a bestseller.

Since then we've grown into the largest independent publisher in the UK. We're extremely proud to publish some of the very best writers in the world, including Joy Ellis, Faith Martin, Caro Ramsay, Helen Forrester, Simon Brett and Robert Goddard. Everyone at Joffe Books loves reading and we never forget that it all begins with the magic of an author telling a story.

We are proud to publish talented first-time authors, as well as established writers whose books we love introducing to a new generation of readers.

We have been shortlisted for Independent Publisher of the Year at the British Book Awards three times, in 2020, 2021 and 2022, and for the Diversity and Inclusivity Award at the Independent Publishing Awards in 2022.

We built this company with your help, and we love to hear from you, so please email us about absolutely anything bookish at feedback@joffebooks.com

If you want to receive free books every Friday and hear about all our new releases, join our mailing list: www.joffebooks.com/contact

And when you tell your friends about us, just remember: it's pronounced Joffe as in coffee or toffee!

Milton Keynes UK
Ingram Content Group UK Ltd.
UKHW012129011223
433643UK00005B/427